LISA JACKSON

DON'T BE SCARED

Tears of Pride
Devil's Gambit

ZEBRA BOOKS
Kensington Publishers Corp.
www.kensingtonbooks.com

ZEBRA BOOKS are published by

Kensington Publishing Corp.
900 Third Avenue
New York, NY 10022

All Kensington titles, imprints, and distributed lines are available at special quantity discounts for bulk purchases for sales promotion, premiums, fund-raising, and educational or institutional use.

Special book excerpts or customized printings can also be created to fit specific needs. For details, write or phone the office of the Kensington Sales Manager: Kensington Publishing Corp., 900 Third Avenue, New York, NY 10022. Attn. Sales Department. Phone: 1-800-221-2647.

Zebra and the Z logo Reg. U.S. Pat. & TM Off.

First Printing: March 2024

Tears of Pride was previously published in the US by Harlequin in 1984.

Devil's Gambit was previously published in the UK by Severn House in 1985.

ISBN-13: 978-1-4201-5689-8
ISBN-13: 978-1-4201-5690-4 (eBook)

10 9 8 7 6 5 4 3 2 1

Printed in the United States of America

Contents

~~~

TEARS OF PRIDE

Chapter One

He stood alone, and his vibrant blue eyes scanned the horizon, as if he were looking for something . . . or someone. The cold morning fog on the gray waters of Elliott Bay hampered his view, but the lonely, broad-shouldered man didn't seem to notice. Haggard lines were etched across his forehead and an errant lock of dark brown hair was caught in the Pacific breeze. Noah Wilder didn't care. Though dressed only in a business suit, the icy wind blowing across Puget Sound couldn't cool the anger and frustration burning within him.

Realizing that he had wasted too much time staring at the·endlessly lapping water, he began to walk along the waterfront, back to a job he could barely stomach. He gritted his teeth in determination as he continued southward and tried to quiet the anger and fear that were tearing him apart. Just half an hour earlier he had been notified that his son was missing from school. It had happened before. Noah closed his mind to the terrifying thoughts. By now, he was used to the fact that his rebellious son hated school—especially the school into which he had been transferred just two months before. Noah hoped that Sean wasn't in any real trouble or danger.

He paused only once as he walked back to the office and that was to buy a newspaper. Knowing it was a mistake, he opened the paper to the financial section. Although this time the article was buried, Noah managed to find it on the fourth page. After all this time, he had hoped that the interest in the scandal would have faded. He was wrong. "Damn," he muttered to himself as he quickly scanned the story.

It had been four weeks since the fire, but that had been time enough for Noah Wilder to have the opportunity to curse his father too many times to count. Today was no exception. Actually the fire and the scandal surrounding it were only a couple of problems on a long list that seemed to grow daily. The fire and the suspected arson complicated matters for Noah, and until the entire business was resolved, he knew that he would suffer many more long hours in the office and endure countless sleepless nights. It was just his luck that the blaze had started while his father was out of the country. At the thought of Ben Wilder, Noah's frown deepened.

The early morning was still thick with fog, the air thick with the smell of the sea. A few shafts of sunlight pierced the gray clouds and reflected on the water collected on the concrete sidewalk, but Noah was too preoccupied with his own black thoughts to notice the promise of spring in the brisk air.

An angry horn blared, and a passing motorist shouted indignantly at Noah as he stepped onto the street against the traffic. He ignored the oath and continued, without breaking stride, toward the massive concrete and steel structure that housed Wilder Investments, his father's prosperous holding company. Damn his father! This was one helluva time for Ben to be recuperating in Mexico, leaving Noah to clean up all of the problems at the company. If it weren't for his father's recent heart attack, Noah would be back in Portland where he belonged, and perhaps Sean wouldn't be missing from school again. At the thought of his rebellious son, Noah's stomach tightened with concern. The lines deepened on his forehead. and his thoughtful scowl gave him a ragged, anxious appearance. Unfortunately, Noah could blame no one but himself for his son's attitude.

Noah should never have let Ben talk him into taking control of Wilder Investments, not even for a short period of time. It had been a mistake, and Sean was the person who was paying for it. Noah shouldn't have let his emotions dictate the decision to move to Seattle, and Ben's heart attack shouldn't have made any difference in that decision. Noah uttered an oath under his breath and slapped the rolled newspaper against his thigh in frustration. It had been difficult enough trying to raise a son alone in Portland. But now, in Seattle, along with the problems of managing Wilder Investments, it was nearly impossible for Noah to find enough time for his son.

Noah pushed open the wide glass doors of the Wilder Building and strode angrily to the elevator. It was early in the day, and the lobby was nearly empty. Silently the elevator doors parted and Noah stepped inside, grateful that he was alone. This morning he had no use for small talk with the employees of his father's multimillion dollar corporation. Anyone or anything that reminded him of Ben Wilder only served to deepen Noah's simmering anger.

After pushing the button for the thirtieth floor, he glared at the headlines of the financial section of the paper and reread the beginning of the article that had ruined his morning. His stomach knotted, as the headline jumped up at him. "Burned" Wilder Investments Suspected of Insurance Fraud. Noah gritted his teeth and tried to control his anger. The first paragraph was worse than the condemning headline: *Noah Wilder,*

*acting president of Wilder Investments, was unavailable
for comment against the rumor that Wilder Investments
might have intentionally started the blaze at Cascade.
Valley Winery. The fire, which started in the west wing
of the main building, took the life of one man. Oliver
Lindstrom, the deceased, was in partnership with Wilder
Investments at the time of the blaze . . .*

The elevator stopped, and Noah drew his eyes away
from the infuriating article. He'd already read it, and it
only served to make him more frustrated with his
father and his decision to prolong his stay in Mexico.
To top things off, Sean had taken off from school this
morning and couldn't be found. Where the hell could
Sean have gone? Noah bit at his lip as his eyes glinted
in determination. Regardless of anything else, Noah
promised himself that he would find a way to force
Ben to return to Seattle to resume control of Wilder
Investments. This time Sean came first. There was just
no other alternative.

Noah stepped from the elevator and headed for his
father's auspicious office. He paused only slightly at
Maggie's desk to order a terse directive . . . See if you
can get Ben on the phone immediately." He forced a
smile that he didn't feel and entered the spacious,
window-lined office where all the decisions for Wilder
Investments were made. Pitching the bothersome newspaper onto the contemporary oak desk, Noah shrugged
out of his suit jacket and tossed it unceremoniously
over the back of a well-oiled leather couch.

The bank of windows behind the desk overlooked
Pioneer Square, one of Seattle's oldest and most prestigious areas. Brick buildings, set on the sides of the
rolling hills overlooking the sound, boasted turn-of-
the-century architecture contrasting sharply to the
neighboring modern skyscrapers. The area was packed

with an interesting array of antique shops, boutiques and restaurants.

Beyond Pioneer Square were the soothing gray waters of Puget Sound, and in the distance were the proud Olympic Mountains. On a clear day, they stood as a snow-laden barrier to the Pacific Ocean. Today they were merely ghostly shadows hiding in the slate-colored fog.

Noah cast a glance at the calm view over the rooftops of the city before sitting stiffly down in his father's leather chair. It groaned against his weight as he leaned back and ran an impatient hand through his thick, coarse hair. Closing his eyes, he attempted to clear his mind. Where was Sean?

He shook his head and opened his eyes to see the newspaper lying flat on the desk. The picture of the charred winery met his gaze. The last thing he wanted to think about this morning was the fire. One man was dead—arson was suspected—and the Northwest's most prominent winery, Cascade Valley, was inoperable, caught in a lawsuit contesting the payment of the insurance proceeds. How in the world had he been so unlucky as to get trapped in the middle of this mess? The intercom buzzed, interrupting his thoughts.

"I've got your mother on line two," Maggie's voice called to him.

"I wanted to speak with Ben, not my mother," was Noah's clipped, impatient reply.

"I wasn't able to reach him. It was hard enough getting through to Katharine. I swear there must be only one telephone in that godforsaken village."

"It's all right, Maggie," Noah conceded. "I shouldn't have snapped. Of course I'll talk to Katharine." Noah waited, his temper barely in check. Although he was furious with himself and his father, there was no reason to take it out on Maggie. He told himself to calm down and tried to brace himself against the wall of excuses his mother would build for his father. After pushing the correct button on the telephone, he attempted to sound casual and polite—two emotions he didn't feel at the moment. "Hello, Mother. How are you?"

"Fine, Noah," was the cool automatic response. "But your father isn't feeling well at all." Beneath Katharine's soft. feminine voice was a will of iron.

Noah's jaw tightened involuntarily, but he managed to keep his voice pleasant and calm. "I'd like to speak to him."

"I'm sorry, Noah. That's out of the question. He's resting right now." His mother's voice continued to drone in low, unemotional tones, giving Noah an updated prognosis of his father's condition. As he listened, Noah rolled up the sleeves of his shirt and began to pace angrily in front of the desk. He rubbed the back of his neck with his free hand while he clutched the other in a death grip around the telephone receiver. His knuckles whitened in annoyance as Katharine continued to speak tonelessly to him from somewhere in northern Mexico. Noah cast a dark glance out of the window into the rising fog and hoped for a break in the one-sided conversation.

It was obvious that Katharine Wilder was protecting her husband from the demands of his son. Noah could envision the tight, uncompromising line of his mother's small mouth and the coldness in her distant blue eyes as she spoke to him from some three thousand miles distance.

"So you can see, Noah, it looks as if we have no other choice but to stay in Guaymas for at least another two months . . . possibly three."

"I can't wait that long!"

There was a long unyielding sigh from his mother. Her voice sounded a little more faint. The frail telephone connection to Mexico seemed to be failing. "I don't see that you have much of a choice, Noah. The doctors all agree that your father is much too ill to make the exhaustive trip back to Seattle. There's no way he could hope to run the company. You'll just have to hang on a little longer."

"And what about Sean?" Noah demanded hotly. There was no response. Noah's voice quieted slightly. "Just let me talk to Ben."

"You can't be serious! Haven't you heard a word I've said? Your father is resting now-he can't possibly come to the phone!"

"I need to talk to him. This wasn't part of the bargain," Noah warned, not bothering to hide his exasperation.

"Perhaps later . . ."

"Now!" Noah's voice had risen as his impatience began to get the better of him.

"I'm sorry, Noah. I'll talk to you later."

"Don't hang up—"

A click from a small town in Mexico severed the connection.

"Damn!" Noah slammed the receiver down and smashed one fist into an open palm. He uttered a stream of invectives partially aimed at his father, but mainly at himself. How could he have been so gullible as to have agreed to run the investment firm while Ben was recuperating? It had been an emotional decision and a bad one at that. Noah wasn't prone to sentimental decisions, not since the last one he had made, nearly sixteen years before. But this time, because of his father's delicate condition, Noah had let his emotions dictate to him. He shook his head at his own folly. He was a damned fool. "Son of a . . ."

"Pardon me?" Maggie asked as she breezed into the office in her usual efficient manner. Nearly sixty, with flaming red hair and sporting a brightly colored print dress, she was the picture of unflappable competency.

"Nothing," Noah grumbled, but the fire in his bright blue eyes refused to die. He slumped into his father's desk chair and attempted to cool his smoldering rage.

"Good!" Maggie returned with an understanding smile. She placed a stack of correspondence on the corner of the desk.

Noah regarded the letters with a frown. "What are those?"

"Oh, just the usual—except for the letter on the top of the pile. It's from the insurance company. I think you should read it." Maggie's friendly smile began to fade.

Noah slid a disgusted glance at the document in question and then mentally dismissed it as he looked back at the secretary. She noticed his dismissive gesture, and a perturbed expression puckered her lips.

"Would you put in a call to Betty Averill in the Portland office? Tell her I won't be back as soon as I had planned. Have her send anything she or Jack can't handle up here. If she has any questions, she can call me."

Maggie's intense gaze sharpened. "Isn't your father coming back on the first?" she asked. Maggie normally didn't pry, but this time she couldn't help herself. Noah hadn't been himself lately, and Maggie laid most of the blame on his strong-willed son. The kid was sixteen and hell-on-wheels.

"Apparently not," Noah muttered in response.

"Then you'll be staying for a few more months?"

Noah narrowed his eyes. "It's beginning to look that way, isn't it?"

Maggie tried to ignore the rage in Noah's eyes. She tapped a brightly tipped finger on the correspondence. "If you're staying on as head of Wilder Investments—"

"Only temporarily!"

Maggie shrugged. "It doesn't matter, but perhaps you should read this insurance inquiry."

"Is it that important?" Noah asked dubiously.

Maggie frowned as she thought. "It could be. That's your decision."

"All right . . . all right, I'll take a look," Noah reluctantly agreed. Before Maggie could back out of the office, he called to her. "Oh, Maggie, would you do me a favor?" She nodded. "Please keep calling the house, every half an hour if you have to. And if you do happen to get hold of my son, let me know immediately. I want to talk to him!"

Maggie's smile was faintly sad. "Will do." She closed the door softly behind her.

When Maggie was gone, Noah reached for the document that she had indicated. "What the hell is this?" he muttered as his dark brows pulled together in concentration. He scanned the letter from the insurance company quickly and several phrases caught his attention: *non-payment of benefits . . . conflict of interest . . . lawsuit contesting the beneficiary . . . Cascade Valley Winery.*

"Damn!" Noah wadded the letter into a tight ball and tossed it furiously into the wastebasket He pushed down the button on the intercom and waited for Maggie's voice to answer. "Get me the president of PacWest Insurance Company on the phone, *now!*" he barked without waiting for her response.

The last thing he needed was more problems with the insurance proceeds for the winery located in the foothills of the Cascade Mountains. He had hoped that by now the insurance company would have straightened everything out, even with the suspected arson complicating matters. Apparently he had been wrong, very wrong. Maggie's efficient voice interrupted his conjecture.

"Joseph Gallager, president of Pac-West Insurance, is on line one," she announced briskly.

"Good." He raised his hand to connect with Gallager, but paused. Instead he spoke to the secretary. "Do you have the name of the private investigator that my father uses?"

"Mr. Simmons," Maggie supplied.

"That's the one. As soon as I'm off the line with Gallager, I might want to talk to Simmons." An uneasy feeling settled over him at the mention of the wily detective. "Oh, Maggie . . . did you call the house?"

"Yes, sir. No one answered."

Noah's blue eyes darkened. "Thanks. Keep trying," he commanded through tightly clenched teeth. Where was Sean? Noah turned his dark thoughts away from his defiant son and back to the problems in the office. Hopefully, the president of Pac-West Insurance could answer a few questions about the fire at the winery and why the insurance benefits hadn't been paid to Wilder Investments. If not, Noah would be forced to contact Anthony Simmons. Noah's lip curled into an uncompromising frown as he thought about the slick private investigator that Ben insisted upon keeping on the company payroll. Though he hated to rely on the likes of Simmons, Noah didn't have much of a choice. If the insurance company refused to pay because of the suspected arson, maybe Simmons could come up with a culprit for the crime and get rid of any lingering suspicion that Wilder Investments had had something to do with the blaze. Unless, of course, Ben Wilder knew something he wasn't telling his son.

* * *

The law offices of Fielding & Son were sedately conservative. Located on the third floor of a nineteenth-century marble bank building, they were expensively decorated without seeming garish. Thick rust-colored carpet covered the floors, and the walls gleamed with finely polished cherrywood. Verdant Boston ferns and lush philodendrons overflowed the intricately woven baskets suspended from the ceiling. Leather-bound editions of law texts adorned shelves, and polished brass lamps added a warmth to the general atmosphere.

Despite all of the comfortable furnishings, Sheila was tense. She could feel the dampness of her palms, though they were folded on her lap.

Jonas Fielding mopped the sweat from his receding hairline with a silk handkerchief. Although it was only late May, the weather in the valley was unseasonably warm, and the small, delicately framed woman sitting opposite him added to his discomfort. Her large gray eyes were shadowed in pain from the recent loss of her father. There was an innocence about her, though she was dressed in a tailored business suit. Jonas couldn't help but remember Sheila Lindstrom as a little girl.

Jonas had practiced law for nearly forty years. Though he could have retired years ago, he hadn't, and it was times like this that he wished he had left the firm to his younger associates. Looking at Sheila, he felt very old, and the burden of his seventy years seemed great.

He should have become accustomed to grieving relatives long ago, but he hadn't, especially when the deceased had been one of his friends. Working with family members for the estate was a dismal part of his job, one that he would rather sluff off on a young associate.

However, in this case it was impossible. Oliver Lindstrom had been a personal friend of Jonas Fielding. Hence, he had known Oliver's daughter, Sheila, all of her thirty-one years.

Jonas cleared his throat and wondered why the devil the air-conditioning in the building wasn't working properly. The offices seemed uncomfortably confining this afternoon. Perhaps it was his imagination. Perhaps dealing with Sheila was the cause of his irritability. He detested this part of his job. To give himself a little space, he stood up and walked over to the window before addressing her.

"I understand that all of this business about your father's will and the complication with the insurance proceeds is a bit much for you now, because of your father's death." Sheila's small face whitened and she pinched her lower lip between her teeth. "But you have to face facts . . ."

"What facts?" she asked shakily. Her voice was dry with emotions that wouldn't leave her. "Are you trying to tell me something I already know—that everyone in this valley, and for that matter the entire Pacific Northwest, thinks my father committed suicide?" Sheila's hands were shaking. It was difficult but she held onto her poise, holding back the tears that were burning in her throat. "Well, I don't believe it, not one word of it! I won't!" Nervously she ran her fingers through the thick, chestnut strands of her hair. "You were a friend of my dad. You don't think that he actually took his own life, do you?" Round, gray eyes challenged the attorney.

The question Jonas had been avoiding made him squirm against the window ledge. He rubbed his hands on the knees of his suit pants, stalling for time to compose a suitable answer. He wanted to be kind. "I don't know, Sheila. It seems unlikely . . . Oliver had such zest for life. . . . But, sometimes, when his back is up against the wall, a man will do just about anything to preserve what he has worked for all of his life."

Sheila closed her eyes. "Then you do believe it," she whispered, feeling suddenly small and very much alone. "Just like the police and the press. They all think that Dad started the fire himself and got caught in it by mistake . . . or that he took his own life."

"No one suggested—"

"No one had to! Just look at the front page of the paper! It's been four weeks, and the newspapers are still having a field day!"

"Cascade Valley employed a lot of people from around here. Since it's been closed, unemployment in the valley has doubled. There's no two ways about it, Sheila. Cascade Valley is news. *Big news*." Jonas's voice was meant to be soothing, but Sheila refused to be comforted.

"I guess I don't see why everyone seems to think that my father killed himself. Why would he do that—for the money?"

"Who knows?" Jonas shrugged his aging shoulders as he made his way to the desk. "All of the talk—it's only speculation."

"It's slander!" Sheila accused, lifting her regal chin upward defiantly. "My father was a decent, law-abiding citizen, and nothing will change that. He would never . . ." Her voice cracked with the strain of the past month as she remembered the gentle man who had raised her. Since her mother's death five years before, Sheila had become closer to her father. The last time she had seen him alive, just last spring vacation, he had been so robust and healthy that Sheila still found it impossible to believe he was gone. When she had visited him, he had been remote and preoccupied, but Sheila had chalked it up to the problems that the winery was experiencing at

the time. Although her father had seemed distant, Sheila was sure that no problem at Cascade Valley had been serious enough to cause him to take his life. He had been stronger than that.

Sheila managed to compose herself. There was too much pride in her slender body to allow Jonas Fielding to witness the extent of her grief. "Is there any way I can get the winery operating again?"

Jonas. shook his balding head. "I doubt it. The insurance company is balking at paying the settlement because of the possibility of arson."

Sheila sighed wearily, and her shoulders sagged. Jonas hesitated before continuing. "There's more to it than that," he admitted.

Sheila's head snapped up. "What do you mean?"

"The papers that were in your father's safety deposit box—did you read them?"

"No . . . I was too upset at the time. I brought everything here."

"I didn't think so."

"Why?"

"I found the partnership papers among the rest. Did you know that Oliver didn't own the business alone?"

"Yes."

The elderly attorney seemed to relax a little. "Have you ever met his business partner?"

"Years ago—when I was very young. But what does Ben Wilder have to do with anything?" she asked, confused by the twist in the conversation and Jonas's inability to meet her gaze.

"As I understand it, when the business was purchased nearly eighteen years ago, Ben and Oliver were equal partners." Sheila nodded, remembering the day when her father had made the ecstatic announcement that he had purchased the rustic old winery nestled deep in the eastern foothills of the Cascades. "However, during the course of the last few years, Oliver was forced to borrow money from Wilder Investments . . . to cover expenses. He put up his share of the business as collateral."

A tight, uneasy feeling gripped Sheila's stomach. "You didn't know about that?"

Jonas shook his head. "All the legal work was done by Ben Wilder's attorneys. I would have advised Oliver against it.

Sheila suddenly felt guilty as she remembered the course of events over the past five years. "Why exactly did Dad borrow the money?"

Jonas was evasive. He rubbed his palms together. "Several reasons . . . the economy had been rotten . . . and then there was a problem with the tampered bottles in Montana. From what I can see in the ledgers, sales have been down for several years."

"But there's more to it than that, isn't there?" Sheila whispered. Her throat became dry as she began to understand the reasons for her father's debt to Ben Wilder. *It was her fault!* Guilt, in an overpowering rush, settled in her heart.

Jonas dreaded what he had to say. "Your father took out the loan four years ago."

Sheila blanched. Her suspicions were confirmed.

Hesitating only slightly, the old attorney continued. "As I remember, there were several reasons for the loan. The most important thing at the time was that Oliver wanted to help you recover from your divorce from Jeff. Your father thought you should go back to school for your master's degree. He didn't want for you or Emily to be denied anything you might need, just because your marriage had failed."

"Oh, God, *no!*" Sheila sighed. She closed her eyes

against the truth and sank lower into the chair. At the time of the divorce she hadn't wanted to take her father's money, but he hadn't given her much of a choice. She was a single mother without a job or the skill for decent employment. Her father had insisted that she attend a private school in California where the tuition along with the living expenses for herself and Emily were outrageous. Oliver had forced the money upon her, telling her that the California sun would help her forget about Jeff and the unhappy marriage. Begrudgingly she had accepted her father's help, assuring herself that she would pay him back with interest.

That had been over four years ago, and so far, Sheila hadn't managed to pay him a penny in return. *Now her father was dead*. He had never once mentioned that Cascade Valley was in financial trouble. Then again, Sheila had never asked. Guilt took a stranglehold of her throat.

Jonas handed her the partnership papers. She glanced through them and saw that the attorney's assessment of the situation was correct. After perusing the documents, Sheila raised her head and handed the papers back to her father's elderly friend.

"If only your father had come to me," Jonas offered. "I could have avoided this mess."

"Why didn't he?"

"Pride, I'd guess. It's all water under the bridge now."

"There's a letter demanding repayment of the loan to Wilder Investments," Sheila thought aloud.

"I know."

"But it wasn't written by Ben Wilder. The signature is . . ." Sheila's voice failed her, and her brows drew together as she recognized the name.

"Noah Wilder. Ben's son."

Sheila became pensive. She didn't know much about the man; Noah Wilder had always been a mystery to her. Despite her grief for her father, she was intrigued. "Is he in charge now?"

"Only temporarily, until Ben returns from Mexico."

"Have you talked to either Ben or his son and asked them if they might consider extending the loan?" Sheila asked, her tired mind finally taking hold of the situation. Without help from Wilder Investments Cascade Valley Winery was out of business.

"I've had trouble getting through to Noah," Jonas admitted. "He hasn't returned any of my calls. I'm still working on the insurance company."

"Would you like me to call Wilder Investments?" Sheila asked impulsively. Why did she think she could get through to Noah Wilder when Jonas had failed?

"It wouldn't hurt, I suppose. Do you know anything about Wilder Investments or its reputation?"

"I know that it's not the best, if that's what you mean. Dad never mentioned it, but from what I've read, I'd say that the reputation of Wilder Investments is more than slightly tarnished."

"That's right. For the past ten years Wilder Investments has been walking a thin line with the SEC. However, any violations charged against the firm were never proven. And, of course, the Wilder name has been a continued source of news for the scandal sheets."

Sheila's dark eyebrows lifted. "I know."

Jonas tapped his fingers on the desk. "Then you realize that Wilder Investments and the family itself are rather . . ."

"Shady?"

Jonas smiled in spite of himself. "I wouldn't say that, but then I wouldn't trust Ben Wilder as far as I could

throw him." His voice became stern. "And neither should
you. As sole beneficiary to your father's estate, you
could be easy prey for the likes of Ben Wilder."

"I guess I don't understand what you're suggesting."

"Don't you realize how many marginal businesses
have fallen victim to Wilder Investments this year alone?
There was a shipping firm in Seattle, a theater group in
Spokane and a salmon cannery in British Columbia."

"Do you really believe that the Wilder family wants
Cascade Valley?" Sheila asked, unable to hide her
skepticism.

"Why not? Sure, in the last few years Cascade has
had its trouble, but it's still the largest and most prestigious winery in the Northwest. No one, even with the
power and money of Ben Wilder, could find a better
location for a vineyard." Jonas rubbed his upper lip and
pushed aside the moisture that had accumulated on it.
"Your father might not have been much of a businessman, Sheila, but he did know how to bottle and ferment
the best wine in the state."

Sheila leveled her gaze at Jonas's worried face. "Are
you implying that Wilder Investments might be responsible for the fire?"

"Of course not . . . at least I don't think so. But regardless of who started the blaze, the fact stands that
Wilder Investments is the only party who gained from
it. Ben Wilder won't pass up a golden opportunity when
it's offered him."

"And you think the winery is that opportunity."

"You'd better believe it."

"What do you think he'll do?"

Jonas thought for a moment. "Approach you, unless I
miss my guess." He rubbed his chin. I'd venture to say
that Ben will want to buy out what little equity you have
left. You have to realize that between the first and second

mortgages on the property, along with the note to Wilder Investments, you own very little of the winery."

"And you don't think I should sell out?"

"I didn't say that. Just be careful. Make sure you talk to me first. I'd hate to see you fleeced by Ben Wilder, or his son."

Sheila's face became a mask of grim determination. "Don't worry, Jonas. I intend to face Ben Wilder, or his son, and I plan to hang on to Cascade Valley. It's all Emily and I have left."

Chapter Two

The door to Ben's office swung open, and although Noah didn't look up, his frown deepened. He tried to hide his annoyance and pulled his gaze from the thick pile of correspondence he had been studying. It was from a recently acquired shipping firm, and some of the most important documents were missing. "Yes," he called out sharply when he felt, rather than saw, his father's secretary enter the room. He looked up, softening the severity of his gaze with a smile that didn't quite reach his eyes.

"I'm sorry to disturb you, Noah, but there's a call for you on line one," Maggie said. Over the past few months she'd become accustomed to Noah's foul moods, provoked by his father's business decisions.

"I'm busy right now, Maggie. Couldn't you take a message?" He turned his attention back to the stack of paperwork cluttering the desk. Maggie remained in the room.

"I know you're busy," she assured him, "but Miss Lindstrom is the woman waiting to speak with you."

"Lindstrom?" Noah repeated, tossing the vaguely familiar name over in his mind. "Is she supposed to mean something to me?"

"She's Oliver Lindstrom's daughter. He died in that fire a few weeks ago."

The lines of concentration furrowing Noah's brow deepened. He rubbed his hands through the thick, dark brown hair that curled above his ears. "She's the woman who keeps insisting I release some insurance money to her, isn't she?"

Maggie nodded curtly. "The same."

All of Noah's attention was turned to the secretary, and his deep blue eyes narrowed suspiciously. "Lindstrom died in the fire, and according to the reports, arson is suspected. Do you suppose that Lindstrom set the fire and inadvertently got trapped in it?" Without waiting for a response from Maggie, Noah reached for the insurance report on the fire. His eyes skimmed it while he posed another question to the secretary. "Didn't I write to this Lindstrom woman and explain our position?"

"You did."

"And what did I say? Wasn't it a phony excuse to buy time until the insurance investigation is complete?" He rubbed his temple as he concentrated. "Now I remember . . . I told her that everything had to wait until Ben returned."

"That's right." Maggie pursed her lips in impatience. She knew that Noah had complete power over any business decision at Wilder Investments, at least until Ben returned from Mexico.

"Then why is she calling me again?" Noah asked crossly. That fire had already cost him several long nights at the office, and the thought of spending more time on it frustrated him. Until the insurance report was complete, there wasn't much he could do.

Maggie's voice was tiredly patient. She had become familiar with Noah's vehement expressions of disgust with his father's business. The insurance problem at the winery seemed to be of particular irritation to him. "I don't know why she's calling you, Noah, but you might speak to her. This is the fifth time she's called this afternoon."

Guiltily, Noah observed the tidy pile of telephone messages sitting neglected on the corner of his desk. Until this moment he had ignored them, hoping that the tiny pink slips of paper might somehow disappear.

"All right, Maggie," he conceded reluctantly. "You win. I'll talk to—"

"Miss Lindstrom," the retreating secretary provided.

In a voice that disguised all of his irritation, he answered the phone. "This is Noah Wilder. Is there something I can do for you?"

Sheila had been waiting on the phone for over five minutes. She was just about to hang up when Ben Wilder's son finally decided to give her a little portion of his precious time. Repressing the urge to slam the receiver down, she held her temper in tight rein and countered his smooth question with only a hint of sarcasm. "I certainly hope so—if it's not too much to ask. I'd like to make an appointment with you, but your secretary has informed me you're much too busy to see me. Is that correct?"

There was something in the seething agitation crackling through the wires that interested Noah. Since assuming his father's duties temporarily last month, no one had even hinted at disagreeing with him. Not that Noah hadn't had his share of problems with Wilder Investments, but he hadn't clashed with anyone. It was almost as if the power Ben had wielded so mightily had passed to Noah and none of Ben's business associates had breathed a word of opposition to Ben's son. Until now. Noah sensed that Miss Lindstrom was about to change all of that.

"On the contrary, Miss Lindstrom. I'd be glad to meet with you, but we'll have to make it sometime after next week. Unfortunately, Maggie's right. I'm booked solid for the next week and a half."

"I can't wait that long!" Sheila cried, her thin patience snapping.

Her response surprised Noah. "What exactly is the problem? Didn't you get the letter I sent?"

"That's precisely why I'm calling. I really do have to see you. It's important!"

"You're hoping that I'll reverse my decision, I suppose?" Noah guessed, wondering at the woman's tenacity. He thumbed through his phone messages. Maggie was right. Sheila Lindstrom had called every hour on the hour for the past five.

"You've got to! If we hope to rebuild the winery and have it ready for this season's harvest, we've got to get started as soon as possible. Even then, we might not make it—"

Noah interrupted . . . I understand your problem." There was a hint of desperation in her voice that bothered him. "But, there's really nothing I can do. You understand that my father is out of the country and—"

"I don't care if your father is on the moon!" Sheila cut in. "If you're in charge of Wilder Investments, you're the man I have to deal with. Surely you can't be so much of a puppet that you can't make a simple business decision until your father returns."

"You don't understand," Noah began hotly in an attempt to explain, and then mentally cursed himself for letting this unknown woman force him into a defensive position. It really was none of her business.

"You're right, Mr. Wilder. I *don't* understand. I'm a businesswoman, and it seems utterly illogical to me that you would let a growing concern such as Cascade Valley sit in disrepair, when it could be productive."

Noah attempted to keep his voice level, even though

he knew that the woman was purposely goading him. "As I understand it, Miss Lindstrom, Cascade Valley has been running at a loss for nearly four years."

There was a pause on the other end of the line, as if Sheila Lindstrom was studying the weight of his words. Her voice, decidedly less angry, commanded his attention. "I think it's evident from this discussion that you and I have a lot to talk over," Sheila suggested. Though she sounded calm, a knot of tension was twisting her stomach. "If it isn't possible for you to meet with me today, perhaps you could come to the winery this weekend and get a firsthand impression of our mutual problem."

For a moment the soft, coaxing tone of her voice captivated Noah, and he was tempted to take her up on her offer. He would love to leave the problems at Wilder Investments, if only for a weekend, but he couldn't. There were situations in Seattle that he couldn't ignore. It wasn't just the business; there was Sean to consider. A note of genuine regret filled his voice. "I'm sorry, Miss Lindstrom," he apologized, "It's out of the question. Now, if you would like to make an appointment, how about the week after next—say, June eighth?"

"No, thank you," was the curt reply. She was furious when she slammed the receiver back into the cradle of the pay telephone. The city of Seattle, usually a welcome sight to her, held no fascination today. She had come prepared to push her pleas on Noah Wilder, hoping to make him understand her desperate plight. She had failed. After being put off by his secretary, placed on hold forever, and making five fruitless telephone calls, Sheila wondered if it was possible to reason with the man. He was obviously just a figurehead for his father, a temporary replacement who held no authority whatsoever.

Sheila was lost in thought as she walked down the rain-washed sidewalk before wandering into a quiet bistro that had a view of Puget Sound. The cozy interior of the brightly lit cafe didn't warm her spirits, nor did the picturesque view of the shadowy sound. Her eyes followed the flight of graceful seagulls arcing over the water, but her thoughts were distant.

Absently, she stirred a bit of honey into her tea. Though it was past the dinner hour, she wasn't hungry. Thoughts of the winery sitting charred and idle filled her mind. It just didn't make sense, she reasoned with herself. Why would Ben Wilder leave town and let his obviously incapable son run a multimillion dollar investment business? Pensively sipping the tea, Sheila tried to remember what she could about her father's business partner. Tiny, fragmented thoughts clouded her mind. Though her father had been partners with Ben Wilder for over seventeen years, the two men had had little personal contact. Ben's son, Noah, was a mystery. He was the only heir to the Wilder fortune and had been a rebel in his youth.

Sheila ran her fingers through the thick strands of her shoulder-length hair as she tried to remember what it was about Noah Wilder that kept haunting her? Slowly, vague memories surfaced.

Although she hadn't been meant to hear the whispered conversation between her father and mother some sixteen years in the past, Sheila had listened at the closed kitchen door with all the impish secrecy of a normal fifteen-year-old. From what she pieced together, Sheila understood that her father's business partner's son had gotten some girl in trouble. The family disapproved. At the time Sheila had been puzzled by the conversation and then had quickly forgotten it. Although she had always been interested in Noah Wilder, she didn't know him and had dismissed her parents' secretive conversation.

The recent problems of the Wilder family were just as cloudy in her mind. Her father had mentioned that some of the bottles of Cascade Valley Cabernet Sauvignon had been tampered with and discovered in Montana, and Sheila remembered reading about the supposed S.E.C. violations in one of Wilder Investment's takeover bids. However, she had ignored the gossip and scandals concerning her father's business partner. At the time Sheila had not been interested in anything other than the fact that her marriage was breaking apart and that she would have to find some way to support her young daughter. Her father's business concerns hadn't touched her. She had been too wrapped up in her own problems.

Sheila set down her teacup and thoughtfully ran her fingertips around its rim. If only she had known what her father was going through. If only she had taken the time to help him, as he had helped her. As it was, his name was now smeared by the speculation and gossip surrounding the fire.

Thinking about her daughter's welfare and her father's reputation spurred Sheila into action. She pushed her empty teacup aside. Despite the warnings of Jonas Fielding against it, Sheila knew it was imperative that she talk with Ben Wilder. He had been a friend of her father as well as his business partner, and if anyone could see the logic in her solution to the problem at the winery, it would be Ben.

She opened her purse and withdrew a packet of old correspondence she had discovered in her father's private office. Fortunately the papers in the fireproof cabinet hadn't burned, and on an old envelope she found Ben Wilder's personal address. The envelope had yellowed with age, and Sheila realized that her plan was a long shot. Ben Wilder could have moved a dozen times since he had mailed the letter. But how else would she find him? He was a man who prized his privacy.

Despite the odds against locating him, Sheila knew she had to find someone who might be able to get in touch with him. A phone number was all she needed. If she could convince him that it was in his best interest to reopen the winery, Ben would be able to order the reconstruction of Cascade Valley. *Wouldn't his arrogant son be burned!* Sheila smiled to herself and felt a grim sort of pleasure imagining Noah's reaction when he found out about her plans. He would be furious! Sheila grabbed her purse, quickly paid the check and nearly ran out of the restaurant.

When Noah hung up the telephone, he had a disturbing feeling that he hadn't heard the last from Sheila Lindstrom. The authoritative ring in her voice had forced him to reach for the file on the fire. After glancing over the letters from Sheila a second time and thinking seriously about the situation at the winery, Noah felt a twinge of conscience. Perhaps he'd been too harsh with her.

In all fairness, the woman did have an acute problem, and she deserved more than a polite brush-off. Or did she? Anthony Simmons, Ben's private detective, hadn't yet filed his report on the arson. Could Oliver Lindstrom really have been involved? What about Lindstrom's daughter, sole beneficiary to the old man's estate? Noah shifted restlessly in his chair. Perhaps he should have been more straightforward with her and told Sheila about Simmons's investigation into the cause of the fire. Was he getting to be like his father, preferring deceit to the truth?

Noah's jaw tightened. He felt the same restless

feeling steal over him that had seized him countless times in the past. There was something about the way his father did business that soured his stomach. It wasn't anything tangible, but there was just something wrong. If only he could put his finger on it. Wilder Investments put him on edge, just as it had in the past. That was one reason Noah had quit working for his father seven years before. The quarrel between Ben and Noah had been bitter and explosive. If it hadn't been for his father's recent heart attack and the one, large favor Ben still kept hanging over Noah, he would never have agreed to return, not even temporarily. Noah's face darkened with firm resolve. At least now he was even with his father, out of the old man's debt. They were finally square after sixteen unforgiving years.

Maggie knocked on the door before entering the office. "You wanted me to remind you of the probation meeting," she announced with a stiff smile. This was the part of her job she liked least, dealing with her boss on personal matters. In this case it was like rubbing salt into an open wound.

"Is it three o'clock already?" Noah asked, grimacing as his wristwatch confirmed the efficient secretary's time schedule. "I've got to run. If there are any more calls, or people who need to see me, stall them until tomorrow . . . or better yet, till sometime next week. Unless, of course, you hear from Anthony Simmons. I want to speak to him right away. He owes me a report on that fire at Cascade Valley."

Maggie's eyebrows lifted slightly. "Yes, sir," she replied before stepping back into the hallway.

Noah threw his coat over his shoulder and snapped his briefcase closed. He half ran out of the office and down the hallway before stopping. On impulse he turned to accost his father's secretary once again. "Oh, Maggie?"

The plump redhead was a few paces behind him. "Yes?"

"There is one other thing. If Sheila Lindstrom should call again, tell her I'll get back to her as soon as possible. Get a number where she can be reached. I'll check back with you later."

The smug smile on Maggie's round face only served to irritate Noah further. Why did he feel a sudden urge to amend his position with the intriguing woman who had called him earlier in the day? For all he knew, Sheila Lindstrom might be involved with the arson. He didn't know anything about her. It was crazy, but he felt almost compelled to speak to her again. Perhaps it was the mood of the letters she had sent him, or maybe it was her quick temper that had sparked his interest in her. Whatever the reason, Noah knew that it was very important that he talk with her soon. She was the first one of his father's business associates who had shown any ounce of spunk. Or was it more than that?

He shrugged off the unanswered question as he slid behind the wheel of his silver Volvo sedan and headed for the meeting with Sean's probation office. Noah had been dreading this meeting for the better part of the week. Sean was in trouble. Again. When the school administrator had called last week and reported that Sean hadn't shown up for any of his midmorning classes, Noah had been worried. Then, when he finally found out that his son had cut classes with a group of friends and later had been picked up by the police for possession of alcohol, Noah had become unglued. He was angry and disgusted, both at himself and his son.

If Sean was in trouble, Noah had himself to blame. Sixteen years ago he had begged for the privilege and responsibility of caring for his infant son, and he was the one who had insisted on raising the child alone. Unfortunately, he had made a mess of it. If Sean didn't straighten out soon, it could spell disaster.

Although it wasn't quite three thirty, the Friday afternoon traffic heading out of the city was thick, and driving was held to a snail's pace. Even Seattle's intricate freeway system couldn't effectively handle the uneven flow of motorists as they moved away from the business district of the Northern Pacific city.

The high school that Sean attended was near Ben's home, and in the twenty minutes it took to get to the school, Noah found himself hoping that the probation officer would give Sean another chance. Noah knew that he had to find a way to get through to his son.

Noah's car crested a final hill, and he stopped the car in front of a two-story brick building. At the sound of the afternoon bell, he turned all of his attention to the main entrance of the school. Within minutes a swarm of noisy teenagers burst through the doors of the building and began to spill down the steps. Some held books over their heads, others used umbrellas, still others ignored the afternoon drizzle altogether.

Noah's eyes scanned the crowd of teenagers as it dispersed over the school yard. Nowhere did he see his blond, athletic son. The thought that Sean might have stood him up crossed Noah's mind, but he pushed it quickly aside. Surely the kid wouldn't be that stupid! Sean knew the importance of today's meeting with the juvenile officer. He wouldn't blow it. *He couldn't!*

Noah continued to wait. His hands gripped the steering wheel more tightly with each passing minute. There was no sign of his son. The teenagers on the steps thinned as they dashed across the lawn, heads bent against the wind and rain. The roar of car engines and rattling school buses filled the air. Still no Sean. Noah's impatience was beginning to surface, and he raked his fingers through the thick, coarse strands of his near-black hair. *Where the devil was that kid?* The appointment with the juvenile officer was in less than thirty minutes, and Sean was nowhere in sight.

Angrily Noah opened the car door, pulled himself to his full height, slammed the door and pushed his hands deep into his pockets. He leaned against the car, oblivious to the rain that ran down his back. His eyes skimmed the empty school yard. No sign of his son. He checked his watch once, uttered a low oath and continued to lean against the car.

Chapter Three

It was dusk when Sheila found the address listed on the torn envelope, and even though twilight dimmed her vision, she could tell that the house Ben Wilder called home was immense. The three-story structure stood high on a cliff overlooking the banks of Lake Washington, and the grounds surrounding the manor encompassed several acres. The stately stone house was surrounded by a natural growth of sword ferns and ivy. To Sheila, the building seemed strangely cold and uninviting. Even the sweeping branches of the fir trees and the scarlet blossoms of the late-blooming rhododendrons didn't soften the hard, straight lines of the manor.

An uneasy feeling that she was intruding where she didn't belong nagged at Sheila's mind, and she considered retreating into the oncoming night. She chided herself for her case of nerves. What would it hurt to knock on the door and inquire as to the whereabouts of Ben Wilder? Nothing ventured; nothing gained. Wasn't that the phrase?

It was obvious that someone was home. Not only was there smoke rising from one of the chimneys, but also, several windows in the stone mansion glowed brightly from interior lights. Even the porch lanterns were lit. It was almost as if her presence were expected. A cold chill of apprehension skittered up her spine.

Ignoring her mounting misgivings, Sheila parked her car behind the silver Volvo sitting in the long, circular drive. Before she could think twice about the consequences of what she was about to do, she slid out of her car, gathered a deep breath of damp air and walked to the door. A quiet rain had begun to settle over the city, and droplets of moisture clung to Sheila's hair. After hiking the collar of her raincoat more tightly around her throat, she knocked softly on one of the twin double doors. As she nervously waited, she wondered who would answer her knock and what his reaction would be to her inquiry. Would she really be able to procure information as to the whereabouts of Ben Wilder or was this just one more leg in the wild goose chase she had been participating in all afternoon?

The door opened suddenly. Sheila wasn't prepared to meet the forceful man standing in the doorway. In a house the size of a Tudor, she had expected a servant to greet her, but she had been mistaken. The tall, well-built man standing in the light from the hallway presented himself with an arrogance that spoke of power rather than servility. His face was handsome, though not in a classical sense. His features were even, but severe. The angle of his jaw was strong, and dark, ebony brows hooded deep-set delft-blue eyes. The lines of worry on his face intensified his masculinity and the power of his gaze. His eyes sparked with interest as he looked down on Sheila. Involuntarily her pulse quickened and fluttered in the hollow of her throat. Surely he could sense her unease.

"Is there something I can do for you?" he asked with practiced boredom. Sheila instantly recognized his voice. It belonged to Noah Wilder. Of course! Why hadn't she expected him . . . *or had she?* Had her subconscious sought him out? She swallowed with difficulty while her heart clamored in her chest.

"I was looking for Ben Wilder," was her inadequate response.

"Ben?" He cocked a wary black eyebrow before crossing his arms over his chest and leaning on the doorjamb. The light fabric of his shirt strained over his shoulder muscles. A lazy smile softened the severe planes of his face. "You want to see Ben? Who are you?"

There was something disturbing in Noah's deep blue eyes, something that took hold of Sheila and wouldn't let go. With difficulty she drew her eyes away from the alluring depths of his gaze. She drew in a steadying breath and ignored both her racing pulse and the strong desire to run back into the safety of the night. "My name is Sheila Lindstrom. I believe I spoke with you earlier this afternoon."

He didn't seem surprised by her announcement. His smile broadened to show the hint of a dimple. He was interested but cautious. "You're the lady with the urgent problems at Cascade Valley, right?"

"Yes." At least he remembered her. Was he amused? Why the crooked, knowing grin?

"You called the office and Maggie told you where you could reach me?" he guessed, rubbing his chin while his eyes inched slowly up her body. What was it about her that he found so attractive?

Before she could answer his question, his eyes left her face. A car engine whined on a nearby road, and Noah's head snapped upward. His eyes followed the sound, and every muscle in his body tensed as he looked past her toward the sound.

The car drove past the main gates and turned into

another driveway. "No," Sheila said, responding to his question of a few moments before.

"No?" Noah's interest was once again on the conversation. His eyes searched hers.

"I told you I'm looking for your father."

"And I told you he was out of the country." Something in his gaze seemed to harden.

"I was hoping that someone here might be able to give me an address or a telephone number where he might be reached," she admitted, pressing onward despite the chill in Noah's gaze.

His lips tightened into a scowl, and his voice became still colder. "Come in, Miss Lindstrom, and get out of the rain. You were right. Earlier today you indicated that we have a few things to iron out, and I agree with you. Let's get on with it." He moved out of the doorway as if he expected her to enter.

Sheila hesitated for a moment as her resolve faltered. When his eyes had darkened in disdain, she felt her poise crumbling. She was the intruder. "I think it would be better if I talked to your father. If you could just give me the number. . . ."

"I asked you to come inside! I think it's an excellent suggestion, as it's getting dark and the wind is beginning to pick up. I'm not about to stand here and get wet while I argue with you. The choice is yours; either you can come into the house and talk to me or you can stand out on this porch alone. I'm not going to stand out here much longer. You were the one who was so desperate to talk to me this afternoon. Now you have the opportunity. Take it!"

It was a mistake to enter this man's home. Sheila could feel it, but she was cornered. With what little dignity she could piece together, she reluctantly accepted Noah's invitation and quietly strode into the formal entry hall. Antiques and portraits adorned the walls of the expansive foyer. A large crystal chandelier warmed the entrance in a bath of filtered light, which reflected against the polished wood floor and the carved walnut staircase. Expensive Persian carpets, rich in hues of burgundy and navy, seemed to run endlessly along several of the corridors that branched from the central reception area.

Noah closed the door behind her and indicated the direction she should follow. Sheila tried to hide the awe that was flooding through her at the ostentatious display of Wilder wealth. Although the Wilder name was familiar throughout the Northwest, never had Sheila guessed her father's business partner to be so affluent. The size and elegance of the gracious old house overwhelmed her, and she had to remind herself of Ben Wilder's infamous reputation for gaining his wealth. Nothing stood in his way when he wanted something; no amount of money was an obstacle that couldn't be overcome. She slid a glance toward the tall man walking silently at her side. Was he the same as his father?

Without breaking stride Noah touched Sheila's elbow, nudging her into a room near the back of the house. A dying fire and a few table lamps illuminated the room, which appeared to be a library. Hardcover editions rested on an English reading table, and other books were stored behind the leaded glass of the built-in cabinets. A leather recliner sitting near the fireplace was partially extended, and a half-finished drink rested on a side table, indicating that Noah had been in this room just moments before, waiting. But for whom? Certainly not Sheila. He had no idea that she would grace his doorstep this evening. Once again the overwhelming sensation that she was intruding upon him cut her to the bone. Noah Wilder was just as mysterious as she had imagined.

"Sit down, Miss Lindstrom," Noah suggested as he stood near a bar. "May I get you a drink?"

"No . . . thank-you." She sat on the edge of a wing-backed chair and prayed that she looked calmer than she felt.

"Coffee, perhaps?"

She looked up at him and shook her head. She could feel his eyes on her face; they were the bluest eyes she had ever seen, erotic eyes that mystified her. "No . . . nothing, thanks."

Noah shrugged, pulled at his tie and dropped into the oxblood red recliner facing her. In the warm glow from the smoldering embers he studied her face. His stare was so intense that after a moment of returning his direct gaze, she let her eyes fall and pretended interest in the dying fire. But the blackened logs and the quiet flames reminded her of her father and the inferno that had taken his life. Unconsciously she bit at her lower lip and tried to concentrate on anything but the nightmare of the last month.

Noah was disgusted with himself when he realized how fascinated he was becoming with the beguiling woman he had found on his doorstep. Earlier today he had known that she interested him, but never had he expected to become so utterly captivated by her beauty and unconscious vulnerability. Lines of worry etched across her otherwise flawlessly complected forehead, and a deep sadness lingered in her eyes. Still, she was beautiful. The combination of her thick chestnut-colored hair, her delicately structured oval face and her large, nearly luminous gray eyes bewitched him. Noah didn't fall easy prey to beautiful women; most of them bored him to death. But this intriguing woman with her sharp tongue and gorgeous eyes captivated him. It was difficult for him to disguise his interest in her.

Sheila was nervous, though she proudly attempted to shield herself with a thin veil of defiant poise. Her cheeks were flushed from the cold, and tiny droplets of moisture clung to her dark hair, making it shine to the color of burnished copper.

Noah took a swallow from his drink. What bothered him most was the shadow of despair in her eyes. It puzzled and nagged at him, and he wondered if he had inadvertently contributed to that pain. An odd sensation swept over him. *He wanted to protect her*. He felt the urge to reach out and soothe her . . . comfort her . . . make love to her until she forgot everything else in her life other than him.

His final thought struck him savagely. What was he doing, fantasizing over a woman he had barely met, a virtual stranger? He reined in his emotions and blamed his traitorous thoughts on the long, tense day and the worry that was eating at him. What did he know of Sheila Lindstrom? He tried to convince himself that she was just another woman. One that, for all he knew, wanted nothing more from him than a piece of his father's fortune. He drained his drink.

"All right, Miss Lindstrom," Noah said, breaking the heavy silence. "You have my undivided attention. What is it that you want from me?" He folded his hands and leaned back in the recliner.

"I told you that I want to get in touch with your father."

"And I told you that your request was impossible. My father is in Mexico, recuperating from a recent illness. You'll have to deal with me."

"I've tried that," she pointed out.

"You're right. You did try, and I wasn't very accommodating. I apologize for that . . . I had other things on my mind at the time. But right now I'm prepared to listen. I assume that you want to talk about the insurance claim for Cascade Valley Winery?"

Sheila nodded, a little of her confidence returning. "You see, Ben was a personal friend of my father's. I thought that if I could reason with him, I could convince him of the importance of rebuilding the winery before the fall harvest."

"Why do you think Wilder Investments would want to continue operating Cascade Valley?"

Sheila eyed Noah dubiously. "To make money, obviously."

"But the winery wasn't profitable."

"Only in the last few years," she countered. Was he testing her? "It's true that we've had a run of bad luck, but now—"

"We?" he interrupted abruptly. "Do you manage the operation?"

"No," Sheila admitted honestly. Her face clouded in thought. "No . . . I don't. Dad took care of that. . . ." Her voice faded when she thought of her father.

Noah's question was gentle. "Your father was the man who was killed in the fire?"

"Yes."

"And you think that you can take over where he left off?"

Sheila squared her shoulders and smiled sadly. "I know I could," she whispered.

"You worked in the winery?"

"No . . . yes . . . only in the summers." Why couldn't she think straight? It wasn't like her to be tongue-tied, but then Noah Wilder was more intimidating than any man she had ever met. "I helped Dad in the summers, when I was free from school and college. I'm a counselor at a community college." Sheila purposely omitted the five years she had been married to Jeff Coleridge. That was a part of her life she would rather forget. Her daughter, Emily, was the only satisfying result of the sour marriage.

Noah regarded her thoughtfully. He pinched his lower lip with his fingers as he turned her story over in his mind. His eyes never left the soft contours of her face and the determination he saw in her gaze. "So what, exactly, qualifies you to manage the operation—a few summers on the farm?"

She recognized his ploy and smile. "That along with a master's degree in business."

"I see." He sounded as if he didn't.

Noah frowned as he stood and poured himself another drink. The woman was getting to him. Maybe it was all of the worries over his son, or the anxiety that plagued him at the office. It had been a long, hard day, and Sheila Lindstrom was getting under his skin. He found himself wanting to help her, for God's sake. Without asking her preference, he poured a second drink and set it on the table near her chair. After taking a long swallow of his brandy he sat on the edge of the recliner and leaned on his elbows. "What about the vineyards? It takes more than a college education to oversee the harvest and the fermentation."

Sheila knew that he was goading her, and although she was provoked at the thought, she replied in a calm voice that overshadowed his impertinent questions. "The winery employs a viticulturist for the vineyards. Dave Jansen is a respected viticulturist who grew up in the valley. His research has helped develop a stronger variety of grape, hardier for the cold weather. As for the actual fermentation and bottling, we employ an enologist who is more than capable—"

"Then what about the losses?" he demanded impatiently as he frowned into his drink. Why did he care?

"Assuming that your father knew what he was doing, he made one helluva mess of it, according to the latest annual report."

Sheila's throat was hoarse and dry. The pent-up emotions she had kept hidden within her for the last month were about to explode, and she knew that if prodded any further, her restrained temper would be unleashed. She had expected a rough business meeting with a member of the Wilder family, but she was unprepared for this brutal inquisition from Noah and the way his overpowering masculinity was affecting her. She found it impossible to drag her eyes away from his face. "As I stated before . . . we've had a run of bad luck."

"*Bad luck?* Is that what you call it?" Noah asked. He wondered why his words sounded so brittle in the warm den. "The tampered bottles found in Montana, and the expensive recall? The damaged crops last year because of the early snowfall? The ash and debris from the Mount Saint Helens' eruption? And now the fire? From what I understand, the fire was set intentionally. Do you call that bad luck?" His eyes had darkened to the color of midnight as he calculated her reaction.

"What would you call it?" she challenged.

"Mismanagement!"

"Natural disasters!"

"Not the fire."

For a moment there was a restless silence; Sheila felt the muscles in her jaw tightening. She made a vain effort to cool her rising temper. It was impossible. "What are you inferring?' she demanded.

"That your father wasn't exactly the businessman he should have been," Noah snapped. He was angry at himself, at Ben and at Oliver Lindstrom. "I'm not just talking about the fire," he amended when he noticed that the color had drained from her face. "That loan to him from Wilder Investments. What was it used for—improvements in the winery? I doubt it!"

Sheila felt the back of her neck become hot. How much did Noah know about her? Would she have to explain that most of the money her father had borrowed was given to her?

Noah's tirade continued. "I don't see how you can possibly expect to turn the business around, considering your lack of experience." His fingers tightened around his glass.

Sheila's thin patience snapped, and she rose, intending to leave. "Oh, I see," she replied, sarcastically. "Cascade Valley doesn't quite hold up to the sanctimonious standards of Wilder Investments. Is that what you mean?"

His eyes darkened before softening. Despite his foul mood a grim smile tugged at the corners of Noah's mouth. "Touché, Miss Lindstrom," he whispered.

Sheila was still prepared for verbal battle and was perplexed by the change in Noah's attitude. His uncompromising gaze had yielded. When he smiled to display straight, white teeth and the hint of a dimple, the tension in the air disintegrated. Sheila became conscious of the softly pelting rain against the windowpanes and the heady scent of burning pitch. She felt her heart beating wildly in her chest, and she had the disturbing sensation that the enigmatic man watching her wistfully could read her mind. He wanted to touch her . . . breathe the scent of her hair . . . make her forget any other man in her life. He said nothing, but she read it in the power of his gaze. Was she as transparent as he?

Sheila felt an urgency to leave and a compulsion to stay. Why? And why did the needs of Cascade Valley seem so distant and vague? The closeness of the cozy room and the unspoken conversation began to possess her, and though she didn't understand it, she knew that she had to leave. Noah Wilder was too powerful. When he took hold of her with his eyes, Sheila wanted never to be released. She reached for her purse. When she found her voice, it was ragged, torn with emotions she didn't dare name. "Is . . . is it possible to meet with you next week?"

Noah's eyes flicked to her purse, the pulse jumping in the hollow of her throat and finally to her face. "What's wrong with right now?"

"I . . . have to get back . . . really." Who was she trying to convince? "My daughter is waiting for me." She started to turn toward the door in order to break the seductive power of his gaze.

"You have a daughter?" The smile left his face, and his dark brows blunted. "But I thought . . ." He left the sentence unfinished as he got out of the chair.

Sheila managed a thin smile. "You thought I wasn't married? I'm not. The divorce was final over four years ago. I prefer to use my maiden name," she explained stiffly. It was still difficult to talk about the divorce. Though she didn't love Jeff, the divorce still bothered her.

"I didn't mean to pry." His sincerity moved her.

"I know. It's all right."

"I'm sorry if I brought up a sore subject."

"Don't worry about it. It was over long ago."

The sound of tires screaming against wet pavement as a car came to a sudden halt cut off the rest of her explanation. Sheila was grateful for the intrusion; Noah was getting too close to her. The engine continued to grind for a moment and then faded into the distance. Noah was instantly alert. "Excuse me," he muttered as he strode out of the room.

Sheila waited for just a minute and then followed the sound of Noah's footsteps. She had to get out of the house, away from the magnetism of Noah Wilder. As she walked down the hallway, she heard the sound of the front door creaking open.

"Where the hell have you been?" Noah demanded. The worry in his voice thundered through the hallways. At the sound Sheila stopped dead in her tracks. Whoever he had been waiting for had finally arrived. *If only she had managed to leave earlier.* Whey hadn't she listened to her common sense and left Noah Wilder the moment she had met him? The last thing she wanted was to be caught up in a family argument.

There was a muted reply to Noah's demand. Sheila couldn't hear the words over the pounding of her heartbeat. She was trapped. She couldn't intrude into a very personal confrontation. She had to find a way to escape. Noah's voice again echoed through the house. "I don't want to hear any more of your pitiful excuses! Go upstairs and try to sleep it off. I'll talk to you in the morning, and believe you me, there are going to be some changes in your behavior! This is the last time you stumble into this house drunk on your can, Sean!"

Sheila let out a sigh of relief. It was Noah's son who had come home, not his wife. Why did she feel some consolation in that knowledge? Sheila retreated to the library, but Noah's harsh words continued to ring in her ears. Why was Noah so angry with his son, and why did it matter to her? It was better not to know anything more about Noah Wilder and his family. It was too dangerous.

Once back in the den, Sheila fidgeted. She knew that Noah was returning, and the knowledge made her anxious. She didn't want to see him again, not here in this room. It was too cozy and seemed seductively inviting. She needed to meet with him another time, in another place . . . somewhere *safe*.

She rushed through the room and paused at the

French doors. She pushed down on the brass handle and escaped into the night. A sharp twinge of guilt told her she should make some excuse for leaving to Noah, but she didn't know what she would say. It was easier to leave undetected. She couldn't afford to get involved with Noah Wilder or any of his personal problems. Right now she was a business partner of Wilder Investments, nothing more.

Sheila shuddered as a blast of cold air greeted her. She had to squint in the darkness. Soft raindrops fell from the sky to run down her face as she attempted to get her bearings in the moonless night. "Damn," she muttered under her breath when she realized that she hadn't walked out of a back entrance to the house as she had hoped but was standing on a spacious flagstone veranda overlooking the black waters of Lake Washington. She leaned over the railing to view the jagged cliff and saw that there was no way she could hope to scale its rocky surface. She couldn't escape.

"Sheila!" Noah's voice boomed in the night. It startled her, and she slipped on the wet flagstones. To regain her balance, she tightened her grip on the railing. "What the devil do you think you're doing?" In three swift strides he was beside her. He grabbed her shoulders and yanked her away from the edge of the veranda.

Sheila froze in her embarrassment How stupid she must look, trying to flee into the night. It seemed that her poise and common sense had left her when she had met Noah.

"I asked you a question—what were you doing out here?" Noah gave her shoulders a hard shake. His eyes were dark with rage and something else. Was it fear?

Sheila managed to find her voice, though most of her attention remained on the pressure of Noah's fingers against her upper arms. "I was trying to leave," she admitted.

"Why?"

"I didn't want to hear your argument with your son."

The grip on her shoulders relaxed, but his fingers lingered against her arms. "You would have had to have been deaf not to hear that argument. I'm just glad that you weren't considering jumping from the deck."

"What? Of course not. It must be over fifty feet straight down."

"At least."

"And you thought I might jump?" She was incredulous.

"I didn't know what to think," he conceded. "I don't know you and I don't really understand why you came out here or why you were leaning over the railing." He seemed honestly perplexed.

"There's nothing mysterious about it, I just wanted to leave. I was looking for a back exit."

"Why were you in such a hurry?" He examined her more closely. It was hard to tell in the darkness, but he was sure that she was blushing. Why?

"I don't feel comfortable here," she admitted.

"Why not?"

Because of you. You're not what I expected at all. I'm attracted to you and I can't be! "I've invaded your privacy and I apologize for that. It was rude of me to come to your home uninvited."

"But you didn't know it was my home."

"That doesn't matter. I think it would be best if I were to leave. We can meet another time . . . in your office . . . or at the winery, if you prefer." He was close to her. She could see the interest in his cool blue eyes, smell his heady male scent, *feel* an unspoken question hanging dangerously between them.

"I don't know when I'll have the time," he hedged.

"Surely you can find an hour somewhere," she coaxed. The tight feeling in her chest was returning.

"What's wrong with now?"

"I told you . . . I don't want to interfere in your private life."

"I think it might be too late for that."

Sheila swallowed, but the dryness in her throat remained. Noah looked into the farthest reaches of her eyes, as if he were searching for her soul. She felt strangely vulnerable and naked to his knowing gaze, but she didn't shrink away from him. Instead she returned his unwavering stare. His fingers once again found her arms. She didn't pull away, nor did she sway against him. Though she was drawn to his raw masculinity, she forced her body to remain rigid and aloof as his hands slid up her arms to rest at the base of her throat.

Raindrops moistened her cheeks as she lifted her face to meet his. She knew that he was going to kiss her and involuntarily her lips parted. His head lowered, and the pressure of his fingers against her throat moved in slow, seductive circles as his lips touched hers in a bittersweet kiss that asked questions she couldn't hope to answer. She wasn't conscious of accepting what he offered until she felt her arms circle his waist. It had been so long since she had wanted a man. Not since Jeff had she let a man close to her. Never had she felt so unguarded and passionate. Until now, when she stood in the early summer rain, kissing a man she couldn't really trust. She felt a warm, traitorous glow begin to burn within her.

His hands shifted to the small of her back and pulled her against his hard, lean frame. She felt the rigid contours of his body, and the ache in hers began to spread. Lazily he brushed his lips over hers, and softly his tongue probed the warm recess of her mouth. All of her senses began to awaken and come alive. Feeling she had thought dead reappeared.

When he pulled away from her to look into her eyes, her rational thought came thundering back to her. She saw a smoldering passion in the smoky blue depths of his eyes, and she knew that her own eyes were inflamed with a desire that had no bounds.

"I'm sorry," she swiftly apologized, trying to take a step backward. The hands on her waist held her firmly against him.

"For what?"

"Everything, I guess. I didn't mean for things to get so out of hand."

He cocked his head to one side in a pose of disbelief. "You must enjoy running out on me. Is that it? Are you just a tease?" Was he kidding? Couldn't he feel her response?

"I meant that I hadn't planned to become involved with you."

"I know that."

"Do you?"

"Of course. Neither of us planned any of this, but we can't deny that we're attracted to each other. We both felt it earlier in the study, and we're feeling it now." One of his fingers touched her swollen lips, challenging her to contradict him.

Her knees became weak as his head once again lowered and his lips, deliciously warm and sensitive, touched hers. She was drawn to him, but she fought the attraction. She pulled away. Her own lips were trembling and for an unguarded instant, fear lighted her eyes.

Noah was wary. "Is something wrong?"

She wanted to laugh at the absurdity of the situation.

"Is anything wrong?" she echoed. "Are you kidding? How about everything? The winery is in a shambles, so I came to Seattle hoping that you would help me. Instead, I end up here looking for your father because I couldn't get through to you. On top of that I stumble onto your argument with your son, and finally, I fall neatly into your arms."

Noah put a finger to her lips to silence her. "Shhh. All right, so we've got a few problems."

"A *few?*"

"What I'm trying to tell you is that sometimes it's best to get away and escape from those problems. It gives one a better perspective."

"You're sure?"

"What I'm sure of is that I find you incredibly attractive." Noah's voice was soothing, and Sheila felt her body lean more closely to his.

"This won't work, you know," she whispered breathlessly.

"Don't worry about tomorrow."

"Someone has to." Reluctantly she wrenched herself free of his arms and straightened her coat. "I came here to find your father because you refused to see me."

"My mistake," he conceded wryly.

She ignored his insinuation. "That's the only reason I'm here. I didn't intend to overhear your argument with your son, nor did I expect to get this close to you. I hope you understand."

The smile that slid across his face was seductively charming. "I understand perfectly," he responded gently, and Sheila felt herself becoming mesmerized all over again. He was powerful and yet kind, bold without being brash, strong but not unyielding—the kind of man Sheila had thought didn't exist. Her attraction to him was compelling, but her feelings were precarious.

"I have to go."

"Stay."

"I can't."

"Because of your daughter?"

"She's one reason," Sheila lied. "There are others."

His smile broadened, and she saw the flash of his white teeth. "Come on, let's go inside. You're getting soaked."

"At least I'm wearing a coat," she taunted, noticing the way his wet shirt was molding to the muscular contours of his shoulders and chest.

"I didn't expect you to run out into the rain."

"It was a stupid thing to do," she admitted. "It's just that I didn't want to intrude. I didn't think you—"

"Have problems of my own?"

Embarrassment crept up her throat. "I'm sorry."

"Don't worry about it. I should have been a little more discreet when Sean came home. I lost control when I saw him drunk again." Noah wiped the rain from his forehead as if he were erasing an unpleasant thought. He touched her lightly on the elbow and guided her back into the house.

It was difficult for Noah to ignore any part of her; he couldn't help but notice the quiet dignity with which she carried herself, the curve of her calf as she walked, or the shimmer of her chestnut hair, which had darkened into unruly curls in the rain.

"Thank you for seeing me," she said softly. "I don't suppose you would consider telling me how to reach your father?"

"I don't think that would be wise."

Sheila smiled sadly to herself. "Then I'll be going. Thank you for your time."

"You're not really planning to drive back to the valley

tonight?" he asked, studying the tired lines of her face. How far could he trust her? She seemed so open with him, and yet he felt as if she were hiding something, a secret she was afraid to share.

"No. I'll drive back in the morning."

He stood with his back to the fire, warming his palms on the rough stones. "But your daughter. I thought she was expecting you."

"Not tonight. She's probably having the time of her life. That grandmother of hers spoils her rotten."

Noah rubbed his chin and his dark brows raised. "I didn't realize your mother was still alive."

A pensive expression clouded Sheila's even features. "She's not. Emily is staying with my ex-husband's mother. . . . We're still close."

"What about your ex-husband? Are you still close to him, too?" Noah asked, brittlely. Why the devil did he even care? He watched a play of silent emotions darken Sheila's eyes, and without knowing why, Noah Wilder immediately despised the man who had caused Sheila so much pain. He could feel the muscles in his jaw begin to tighten.

"Jeff and I are civil," Sheila replied, hoping to close the unwelcome subject.

"Then you still see him?" Noah persisted

"It can't be avoided . . . because of Emily."

"Is he good with your daughter?"

"Yes . . . I suppose so. Does it matter?" Sheila asked, experiencing a hot flash of indignation. She didn't like discussing her feelings about Jeff with anyone, especially not a man she was beginning to admire.

"Doesn't it matter, I mean?"

"To me, yes. But why do you care?"

His voice lowered at the bitterness in her words. "I didn't mean to bring up a sore subject."

Sheila stiffened, but pushed back the hot retort forming in her throat. It was none of Noah's business. Her divorce from Jeff had been a painful experience, one she would rather not think about or discuss.

"I think I had better leave," she stated evenly. She reached into the front pocket of her purse and fished for her keys. The conversation was getting far too personal.

"You mean you want to run away, don't you?"

"What?"

"Isn't that what you were doing when I found you out on the veranda, leaning over the rail? Weren't you attempting to avoid a confrontation with me?"

"You were arguing with your son! I was only trying to give you some privacy."

His eyes darkened. "There's more to it than that, isn't there?"

"I don't know what you're suggesting."

"Sure you do." He moved from the fireplace to stand only inches from her. "Any time the conversation turns a little too personal, you try to avoid me," he accused. A dangerous glint of blue fire flashed in his eyes.

Sheila stood her ground. "I came here to talk about business. There was nothing personal about it."

"Save that for someone gullible enough to believe it."

She glared at him defiantly but held onto her poise. "Quit beating around the bush and just say what it is that's bothering you."

"You came over here with the intention of contacting Ben. You were sidestepping me. Don't take me for such a fool. I know that you were deliberately trying to avoid me."

"Only because you were being completely unreasonable!" she snapped. He was impossible! When she looked into his intense cobalt eyes, she felt as if she wanted to float dreamily in his gaze forever. The smell of burning logs mingled with the earthy scent of Noah's wet body. Raindrops still ran down the length of his tanned neck.

"I'm not an unreasonable man," he stated calmly. His hand reached up to touch her chin, and Sheila felt a shiver skitter down her spine. His eyes studied her face, noting in detail the regal curve of her jaw, the blush on her creamy skin and the seductive pout on her full lips. "Please stay," he implored.

"Why?" She longed for an excuse, *any* excuse to spend some more precious time with him.

"We could start by talking about the winery and your plans for it."

"Would you change your position on the insurance settlement?"

The corners of his mouth quirked. "I think you could persuade me to do anything." His finger trailed down her chin and throat to rest against the collar of her coat. Her heart fluttered.

She stepped away from him and crossed her arms over her chest. Eyeing him suspiciously, she asked, "What would it take?"

"For what?"

"For you to listen to my side of the story."

He shrugged. "Not much."

"How much?"

Noah's smile spread slowly over his face and his eyes gleamed devilishly. "Why don't we start with dinner? I can't think of anything I'd rather do than listen to you over a glass of Cascade Valley's finest."

He was mocking her again, but there was enough of a dare in his words to tempt Sheila. "All right, Noah. Why not?" she countered impulsively. "But let's set out the ground rules first. I insist that we keep the conversation on business."

"Just come with me," he suggested wickedly. "The conversation . . . and the night will take care of themselves."

Chapter Four

The restaurant Noah selected was located on one of the steep hills near the heart of the city. It was unique, in that the original Victorian structure had been built by one of Seattle's founding fathers. The old apartment building had been remodeled to accommodate patrons of *L'Epicure,* but the structure retained its authentic nineteenth-century charm. White clapboard siding, French gray shutters and an elegant touch of ginger-bread adorned the entrance. Flickering sconces invited Sheila inside.

A formally dressed waiter led them up a narrow flight of stairs to a private room in the second story of the gracious old apartment house. An antique table sat in an alcove of leaded glass, giving the patrons a commanding panorama of the city lights. Raindrops lingered and ran on the windowpanes, softly blurring the view and creating an intimate atmosphere in the private room.

"Very nice," Sheila murmured to herself as she ran her fingers along the windowsill and looked into the night.

Noah helped her into her chair before seating himself on the other side of the small table. Though he attempted to appear calm, Sheila could sense that he was still on edge. The quiet, comfortable silence they had shared in the car had been broken in the shadowy confines of the intimate restaurant.

Before the waiter left, Noah ordered the specialty of the house along with a bottle of Chardonnay by Cascade Valley. Sheila lifted her brows at Noah's request, but the waiter acted as if nothing were out of the ordinary.

"Why would a European restaurant carry a local wine?" she inquired after the waiter had disappeared from the room.

Noah's smile twisted wryly. "Because my father insists upon it."

The waiter returned with the wine and solemnly poured the wine first into Noah's glass, and upon approval, into Sheila's. After he had left once again, Sheila persisted with her questions.

"*L'Epicure* keeps wine for your father?"

"That's one way of putting it. *L'Epicure* is a subsidiary of Wilder Investments," he explained tonelessly.

Sheila's lips tightened. "I see. Just like Cascade Valley."

Noah nodded. "Although the restaurant carries a full cellar of European wines, Ben insists that Cascade Valley be fully represented."

"And your father is used to getting what he wants?"

Noah's blue eyes turned stone cold. "You could say that." Any further comment he would have made was repressed by the appearance of the waiter bearing a tray overloaded with steaming dishes of poached halibut in mushroom sauce, wild rice and steamed vegetables. Sheila waited until the food was served and the waiter had closed the door behind him before continuing the conversation.

"I take it you don't like working for your father?" she guessed as she started the meal.

Noah's dark eyebrows blunted, and the fork he had been holding was placed back on the table. He clasped his hands together and stared at her over his whitened knuckles. "I think we should get something straight: I do *not* work for Ben Wilder!"

"But I thought—"

"I said I do not work for Ben! Nor do I collect a salary from Wilder Investments!" His clipped words were succinct and effectively closed the subject. The angry edge of his words and the tensing of his jawline left little doubt that he preferred not to speak of his father or his business.

"I think you owe me an explanation." Sheila sighed, setting her uneaten food aside. Somehow she had to keep her temper in check. What sort of game was he playing with her? "Why am I sitting here wasting my time, when you just intimated that you have nothing to do with Wilder Investments?"

"Because you wanted to get to know me better."

Sheila found it difficult to deny the truth, and yet she couldn't help but feel betrayed. He had tricked her into coming with him, when all along he couldn't help her in her quest to save the winery and her father's reputation. Was it her fault for being so mystified by him? Ignoring his wish to avoid discussing Wilder Investments, Sheila continued to push her point home. "I'm listening," she said quietly. "I want to know why you led me on—or have you forgotten our ground rules?"

"I didn't lead you on."

"But you just said that you don't work for Wilder Investments."

"I said that I don't work for *my father,* and I'm not on the company payroll."

"That doesn't make a lot of sense," Sheila pointed

out, her exasperation beginning to show. "What is it exactly that you do?"

Noah shrugged, as if resigned to a fate he abhorred. "I do owe you an explanation," he admitted thoughtfully. "I used to work for Ben. From the time I graduated from college I was groomed for the position Ben's only heir would rightfully assume: the presidency of Wilder Investments, whenever Ben decided to retire. I was never very comfortable with the situation as it was, but—" he hesitated, as if wondering how much of his private life he should divulge "—for personal reasons I needed the security my position at Wilder Investments provided."

"Because of your wife and son?" Sheila immediately regretted her thoughtless question.

Noah's eyes darkened. "I've never had a wife!" He bit out the statement savagely, as if the thought alone were repulsive to him.

Sheila flushed with color. "I'm sorry," she apologized hastily. "I didn't know. . . . You have a child. . . ."

Noah's glare narrowed suspiciously. "You didn't know about Marilyn? If that's the truth, you must have been the only person in Seattle who didn't know the circumstances surrounding Sean's birth. The press couldn't leave it alone. All of Ben's money couldn't even shut them up!"

"I've never lived in Seattle," she explained hurriedly, still embarrassed. Surely he would believe her. "And—and I didn't pay any attention to what my father's business partner was doing, much less his son. . . . I was only a teenager and I didn't know anything about you."

Noah's anger subsided slightly as he noticed the stricken look on Sheila's near-perfect face. "Of course not—it happened years ago."

Sheila's hands were trembling as she reached for her

wineglass and let the cool liquid slide down her parched throat. She avoided Noah's probing gaze and pushed the remains of her dinner around on her plate. Although the food was delicious, her hunger had disappeared.

Noah speared a forkful of fish and ate in the thick silence that hung over the table. It was a long moment before he began to speak again. When he did, his voice was calm and toneless, almost dead from the lack of emotion in his words. "There were many reasons why I quit working for my father . . . too many to hope to explain. I didn't like the idea of being treated as 'Ben Wilder's son' by the rest of the staff, and I had never gotten on well with my dad in the first place. Working with him only served to deepen the rift between us." His teeth clenched, and he tossed his napkin onto the table as he remembered the day that he had broken free of the cloying hands of Wilder Investments.

"I stayed on as long as I could, but when one of my father's investments went sour, he ordered me to investigate the reasons. A manufacturing firm in Spokane wasn't making it. Although it wasn't the manager's fault, Ben had the man fired." Noah took a drink of wine, as if to cast off the anger he felt each time he remembered the painful scene in his father's office, the office Noah now reluctantly filled. The image·of a man near fifty, his shoulders bowed by the wrath and punishment of Ben Wilder, still haunted Noah. How many times had he pictured the tortured face of Sam Steele as the man realized Ben was really going to fire him for a mistake he hadn't made? Sam had looked to Noah for support, but even Noah's pleading was useless. Ben Wilder needed a scapegoat and Sam Steele presented the unlikely sacrificial lamb, an example to the rest of the employees of Wilder Investments. It didn't matter that Sam wouldn't be able to find another job at a comparable salary, nor that he had two daughters in college. What mattered to Ben Wilder was his company, his wealth, his *power*. Though it had all happened years ago, Noah felt an uncomfortable wrench in his gut each time he remembered Sam's weathered face after leaving Ben's office. "It doesn't matter, boy," Sam had said fondly to Noah. "You did what you could. I'll make out."

Sheila was staring at Noah expectantly, and he quickly brought his thoughts back to the present. "That incident," he stated hurriedly, "was the final straw. By the end of the afternoon I had quit my job, yanked my kid out of school and moved to Oregon. I told myself I would never come back."

Sheila sat in the encumbering silence for a minute, watching the lines of grief still evident on Noah's masculine face while he reflected upon a part of his life she knew nothing about. She longed to hear more, to understand more fully the enigmatic man sitting across the table from her. Yet she was afraid, unsure of growing any closer to him. Already she was inexplicably drawn to him, and intuitively she realized that what he was about to tell her would only endear him to her further. Those feelings of endearment would surely only cause her suffering. She couldn't trust him. Not yet.

"You don't have to talk about any of this," she finally managed to say. "It's obviously painful for you."

"Only because I was weak."

"I . . . don't understand," she whispered, gripping the edge of the table for support as she lifted her eyes to meet the question in his. "And," she allowed ruefully, "I'm not sure that I want to understand you."

"You're the woman who insisted that I owed her an explanation," he reminded her.

"Not about *all* of your life."

"But I thought you wanted to get to know me."

"No . . . I just want to know how you're connected with Wilder Investments," she lied. She ignored the voice in her mind that was whispering, *Dear God, Noah, I don't understand it, but I want to know everything about you . . . touch your body and soul*. Instead she lowered her eyes. "You are in charge of the company, aren't you?"

"Temporarily, yes."

"And you do make all of the decisions for Wilder Investments."

"Unless the board disapproves. So far they haven't." The mindless members of the board wouldn't dare argue with Ben's son, Noah thought to himself.

Sheila held her breath as the truth hit her in a cold blast of logic. "Then you were lying to me when you said that you couldn't make a decision about the winery until your father got back into the country."

Noah's mouth twitched in amusement. "I prefer to think of it as stalling for time."

"We haven't got time!"

His smile broadened and his eyes lightened over the edge of his wineglass. "Lady, that's where you're wrong. We've got all the time in the world."

His gaze was warm. Though the table separated them, Sheila could feel the heat of his eyes caressing her, undressing her, bringing her body closer to his. Under the visual embrace she felt her skin begin to tremble, as if anticipating his touch. *Don't fall for him,* she warned herself. *Don't think for a minute that he cares for you. You're just a handy convenience that stumbled onto him tonight. Remember Jeff. Remember the promises. Remember the lies. Remember the pain. Don't let it happen again. Don't fall victim to the same mistake. Don't!*

Carefully she pieced together the poise that he could shatter so easily. "Perhaps we should go."

"Don't you even want to know why I'm back at Wilder Investments?" he invited.

"Do you want to tell me?"

"You deserve that much at the very least."

"And at the very most?"

"You deserve more—much more."

She waited, her nervous fingers twirling the stem of her glass. She cocked her head expectantly to one side, unconsciously displaying the curve of her throat. Why did he work for his father in a position he found so disagreeable? "I had assumed that you took command because of your father's heart attack."

"That's part of it," he conceded reluctantly. "But a very small part." She was quiet, and her silence prodded him on. "Actually, when Ben had the first attack and asked me to take over for a couple of weeks, I refused. I didn't need the headache, and I figured he would have half a dozen 'yes men' who could more than adequately fill his shoes while he was recuperating. So I refused."

Sheila's eyebrows drew together as she tried to understand. "What changed your mind?" she asked quietly.

"The second attack. The one that put Ben in the intensive care unit for a week." Noah's fingers drummed restlessly on the table as he thought for a moment. "My father hadn't trusted anyone to run the company other than himself. When I refused to help him, he ignored the advice of his doctor and picked up where he left off."

"That's crazy," she thought aloud.

Noah shook his head. "That's getting his way. The second attack almost took his life, and when my mother pleaded with me to help him out, I agreed, but only until a replacement could be found."

"And your father didn't bother to look for one," Sheila surmised.

"Why would he? He got what he wanted."

"But surely *you* could find someone—"

"I've looked. Anyone I've suggested has been turned down by the powers that be.·

"Ben."

"Exactly."

Sheila was confused. When she thought of her family and all of the love they had shared, she found it hard to imagine the cold detachment between Ben Wilder and his only son. "Surely there must be some way of solving your problem. Can't you talk to your father?"

"It doesn't do any good. Besides, that's only part of the story. I owed my father a favor—a big favor.

The uneasy feeling that had been threatening to overtake Sheila all evening caused her to shudder involuntarily. "And you're repaying him now, aren't you?"

"In my opinion, yes. You see," he continued in a flat, emotionless voice, "when my son, Sean, was born, there were problems I wasn't able to handle alone. I was too young. I was forced to ask and rely upon my father for help. He complied, and the bastard has never let me forget it."

"But what about Sean's mother?" Sheila questioned. "Certainly she could have helped if there were a problem with the child. Sean was her responsibility as well as yours."

"Marilyn?" Noah's face contorted at the irony of the suggestion and the memory of a young girl he had once thought he loved. "You don't seem to understand, Sheila. *Marilyn* was the problem, at least the most evident problem, and it took all of my father's money and power to deal with her effectively."

"I shouldn't have asked—it's none of my business," Sheila stammered, stunned by the look of bitterness and hatred on the angled planes of Noah's proud face.

"It doesn't matter anymore. Maybe it never did. Anyway, it's all a part of the past, dead and buried."

Sheila pushed herself onto unsteady legs beginning to rise from the table. "There's no reason for you to tell me all of this."

His hand reached out and captured her wrist, forcing her to stay near him. "You asked," he reminded her.

"I'm sorry. It was my mistake. Perhaps we should go."

"Before you see all of the skeletons in the Wilder closets?" he mocked.

She felt her spine become rigid. "Before I lose track of the reason I came here with you."

Her dark eyebrows lifted elegantly, and Noah thought her the most intriguingly beautiful woman he had ever met. "Am *I* coercing *you?*" she asked as her eyes dropped to her wrist, still shackled in his uncompromising grip.

"If you are, lady, it's only because I want you to," he rejoined, but the tension ebbed from his face and his hand moved slightly up her forearm, to rub the tender skin of her inner elbow. "Let's go," he suggested, helping her from the chair. His hand never left her arm as he escorted her down the stairs and into the night. He carried her coat and wrapped his arm over her shoulders to protect her from the damp breeze that still held the promise of rain.

The drive back to the Wilder estate was accomplished in silence as Noah and Sheila were individually wrapped in their own black cloaks of thought. Though separated from him in the car, Sheila felt mysteriously bound to the darkly handsome man with the knowing blue eyes. *What's he really like?* her mind teased. In the flash of an instant she had seen him ruthless and bitter, then suddenly gentle and sensitive. She sensed in him a deep, untouched private soul, and she longed to discover the most intimate reaches of his mind. What would it hurt, her taunting mind implored. What were the depths of his kindness, the limits of his nature? He'll hurt you, her bothersome consciousness objected. A man hurt you in the past, when you opened yourself up to him. Are you foolish enough to let it happen again? Just how far do you dare trust Noah Wilder, and how far can you trust yourself?

The Volvo slowed as Noah guided the car past the stone pillars at the entrance of the circular drive. The headlights splashed light on the trunks of the stately fir trees that guarded the mansion. As Ben Wilder's home came into view, Sheila pulled herself from her pensive thoughts and realized that she had accomplished nothing toward furthering her purpose. She had intended to find a way, any way, to get the insurance proceeds to rebuild the winery, and she had failed miserably. She didn't even know if Noah had the power or the desire to help her. Had the insurance company paid off Wilder Investments? The car ground to a halt as Sheila discovered her mistake. Caught in her fascination for a man she had been warned to mistrust, she had lost sight of her purpose for making the trip to Seattle.

"Would you like to come in for a drink?" Noah asked as he flicked off the engine and the silence of the night settled in the interior of the car.

"I don't think so," she whispered, trying to push aside her growing awareness of him.

"We have unfinished business.

"I know that. You've found a way to successfully dodge the subject of the winery all evening. Why?"

Noah smiled to himself. "I didn't realize that I was. Would you like to come inside and finish the discussion?"

Sheila caught her breath. "No."

"I thought you were anxious to get the insurance settlement," he replied, his eyes narrowing as he studied her in the darkness.

"I am. You know that, but I happen to know when I've been conned."

"Conned?" he repeated incredulously. "What are you talking about?"

"It was difficult to get you on the phone and when I finally did, you refused to see me with some ridiculous excuse that any decision about the winery had to be made by your father. Then you agreed to talk about it over dinner, but conveniently avoided the issue all night. Why would I think that anything's going to change? You haven't listened to me at all. . . ."

"That's where you're wrong. I've listened to everything you've said all evening," he interrupted in a low voice.

"Then what's your decision?"

"I'll tell you that, too, if you'll join me for a drink." His hand reached for hers in the car. "Come on, Sheila. We've got the rest of the night to talk about anything you want."

Again she felt herself falling under his spell, her eyes lost in his and her fingers beginning to melt in the soft, warm pressure of his hands. "All right," she whispered, wondering why this man, this *stranger*, seemed to know everything about her. And what he didn't know, she wanted to divulge to him. . . .

The fire in the den had grown cold, and only a few red embers remained to warm the room. Noah quickly poured them each a drink and took a long swallow of his brandy before kneeling at the fire and adding a wedge of cedar to the glowing coals. As he stood, he dusted the knees of his pants with his palms. Sheila sipped her drink and watched him, noticing the way his oxford cloth shirt stretched over his shoulders as he tended the fire and then straightened. In her mind she could picture the ripple of muscles in his back as he worked.

When Noah turned to face her, she couldn't hide the embarrassed burn of her cheeks, as if she expected him to read the wayward thoughts in her eyes.

"Can I get you anything else?" he asked, nodding toward the glass she held tightly in her hands.

"No . . . nothing . . . this is fine," she whispered.

"Good. Then why don't you sit down and tell me what you intend to do with the insurance settlement, should it be awarded you."

Sheila dropped gratefully into a wing-back chair near the fire and looked Noah squarely in the eyes. "I don't expect you to hand me a blank check for a quarter of a million dollars, you know."

"Good, because I have no intention of doing anything of the kind." Sheila felt butterflies in her stomach. Was he playing with her again? His face was unreadable in the firelight.

"What I do expect, however, is that you and I mutually decide how best to rebuild Cascade Valley, hire a contractor, put the funds in escrow and start work immediately." Her gray eyes challenged him to argue with her logic.

"That, of course, is assuming that the insurance company has paid the settlement to Wilder Investments."

"Hasn't that occurred?" Sheila asked, holding her

breath. Certainly by now, over a month since the fire, payment had been made.

"There's a little bit of a hitch as far as Pac-West Insurance Company is concerned."

Sheila felt herself sinking into despair. "The arson?" she guessed.

Shadows of doubt crowded Noah's deep blue eyes. "That's right. Until a culprit is discovered, the insurance company is holding tightly onto its purse strings."

Sheila blanched as the truth struck her. "You think my father had something to do with the fire. . . . You think he deliberately started it, don't you?" she accused in a low voice that threatened to break.

"I didn't say that."

"You *implied* it!"

"Not at all. I'm only pointing out the insurance company's position . . . nothing else."

"Then I'll have to talk to someone at Pac-West," Sheila said. "One of those claims adjusters, or whatever they are."

"I don't think that will do any good."

"Why not?"

His smile didn't touch his eyes. "Because, for one thing, I've already tried that. The insurance company's position is clear."

"Then what can we do?" Sheila asked herself aloud.

Noah hedged for a moment. How much could he tell her? Was she involved in the arson? Had her father been? He rubbed his thumbnail pensively over his lower lip and stared at Sheila. Why did he feel compelled to trust this beguiling woman he didn't know? As he studied the innocent yet sophisticated curve of her cheek, the slender column of her throat, and the copper sheen to her thick, chestnut hair, he decided to take a gamble and trust her just a little. His intense eyes scrutinized her reaction, watching for a flicker of doubt or fear to cross her eyes.

"What we can do is investigate the cause of the fire ourselves," he explained thoughtfully.

Her eyebrows furrowed. "How?"

"Wilder Investments has a private investigator on retainer. I've already asked him to look into it."

"Do you think that's wise? Doesn't the insurance company have investigators on its staff?"

"Of course. But this way we can speed things up a little. Unless you're opposed to the idea."

If she heard a steely edge to his words, she ignored it and dug her fingernails into the soft flesh of her palm. "I'll do anything I can to clear my father's name and get the winery going again."

"It's that important to you?" he asked, slightly skeptical. "Why?"

"Cascade Valley was my father's life, his dream, and I'm not allowing anyone or anything to take away his good name or his dreams."

"You want to carry on the Lindstrom tradition, is that it? Follow in your father's footsteps?"

"It's a matter of pride . . . and tradition; I suppose."

"But your father bought his interest in the winery less than twenty years ago. It's not as if Cascade Valley has been a part of your family's history," he observed, testing her reaction. How much of what she was saying was the truth? All of it? Or was she acting out a well-rehearsed scene? If so, she was one helluva convincing actress.

Sheila was instantly wary. The doubts reflected in Noah's eyes lingered and pierced her soul. "What do you mean?"

He shrugged indifferently. "Running the day-to-day operation at the winery is a hard job. You'll have to be an accountant, manager, personnel director, quality control inspector . . . everything to each of your employees. Why would a woman with a small child want to take on all of that responsibility?"

"For the same reasons a man would, I suppose." Her eyes lighted with defiance.

His voice was deathly quiet as he baited her. "A man might be more practical," he suggested, inviting her question.

"How's that?"

"He might consider the alternatives."

"There are none."

"I wouldn't say that. What about the option of selling out your interest in the winery for enough money to support you and your daughter comfortably?"

Sheila tried to keep her voice steady. "I doubt that anyone would be interested in buying. The economy's slow, and as you so aptly pointed out earlier, Cascade Valley has had more than its share of problems."

Noah set his empty glass on the mantel. "Perhaps I can convince the board of directors at Wilder Investments to buy out your share of the winery."

Jonas Fielding's warning echoed in Sheila's ears. Noah was offering to buy out her interest in Cascade, just as the crafty lawyer had predicted. A small part of Sheila seemed to wither and die. In her heart she had expected and hoped for more from him. In the short time she had known him, she had learned to care for him and she didn't want to let the blossoming feelings inside her twist and blacken with deceit. She couldn't be manipulated, not by Ben Wilder, nor by his son. "No," she whispered nearly inaudibly as she lifted her eyes to meet his piercing gaze. "I won't sell."

Noah saw the painful determination in the rigid set of her jaw and the unmasked despair that shadowed her eyes as she silently accused him of a crime he couldn't possibly understand. She had tensed when he had mentioned the possibility of buying out the winery, but it had only seemed logical to him. What did she expect of him . . . more money? But, he hadn't even named a price. "I can assure you, Sheila, that Wilder Investments would be more than generous in the offer."

Her quiet eyes turned to gray ice. "I don't doubt that, but the point is, I'm not interested in selling."

"You haven't even heard the terms."

"It doesn't matter. I won't sell," she repeated coldly. How much like the father he so vehemently denounced was Noah Wilder?

Noah shrugged before draining his glass and approaching the chair in which she was seated. "It doesn't matter to me what you do with your precious winery," he stated evenly as he bent over the chair and placed his hands on each of the silvery velvet arms, imprisoning her against the soft fabric. "I only wanted you to be aware of your options."

His voice was gentle and concerned. Sheila felt as if she had known him all her life rather than a few short hours, and she wanted to melt into his soft words. "I . . . understand my options," she assured him shakily.

"Do you?" His blue eyes probed deep into hers, further than any man had dared to see. "I wonder." His lips were soft as they pressed gently against her forehead, and Sheila sighed as she closed her eyelids and let her head fall backward into the soft cushions of the chair. A small, nagging voice in her mind argued that she shouldn't give into her passions; she shouldn't let the warmth that he was inviting begin to swell within her. But the sensuous feeling of his lips against her skin, the mysterious blue intensity of his eyes, the awareness in her body that she had presumed to have died in the ashes of her broken marriage, all argued with a twinge of conscience and slowly took over her mind as well as her body.

His hands were strong as they held her chin and tipped her lips to meet his. A sizzling tremor shook her body in response when the kiss began, and she sighed deeply, parting her lips and inviting him quietly to love her. When his passion caught hold of him and he tasted the honeyed warmth of her lips, he gently pushed his tongue against her teeth and entered the moist cavern of her mouth. Her moan of pleasure sent ripples of desire hotly through his blood. His hands slid down the length of her neck and touched the fluttering pulse that was jumping in the feminine hollow of her throat. His thumbs gently outlined the delicate bone structure in slow, swirling circles of sensitivity that gathered and stormed deep within her.

Sheila heard nothing over the resounding beat of her heart fluttering in her chest and thundering in her eardrums. She thought of nothing other than the cascading warmth and desire that were washing over her body in uneven passionate waves. Feelings of longing, yearning, desires that flamed heatedly, flowed through her as Noah kissed her. Involuntarily she reached up and wound her arms around his neck. The groan of satisfaction that rumbled in his throat gave her a deep, primeval pleasure, and when he pulled his lips from hers, she knew a deep disappointment.

He looked longingly into her eyes, asking her silent, unspoken questions that demanded answers she couldn't ignore. How much did he want from her? What could she give—what would he take?

"Sheila, dear Sheila." he murmured against her hair. It was whispered as a plea. She wanted him, ached for him, but remained silent.

His persuasive lips nuzzled against the column of her throat to linger at the inviting feminine bone structure at its base. His tongue drew lazy circles around Sheila's erratic pulse, and Sheila felt as if her very soul were centered beneath his warm insistent touch. Her fingers entwined in the dark, coffee-colored strands of his hair, and she leaned backward, offering more of her neck . . . more of her being. When his wet tongue touched the center of her pulse, quicksilver flames darted through her veins, and she pushed herself more closely against his body.

His fingers found the buttons on her blouse, and cautiously he opened the top button. As he did so his head lowered, letting his lips caress the gaping space between the two pieces of silken cloth. Sheila moaned against him, asking for more of his gentle touch. He unbuttoned the next pearly fastener, and once more his lips dipped lower, touching her soft, warm flesh. Molten fire streamed through Sheila's veins at his expert touch and in anticipation of his next move. His hot lips seared her skin, and she was not disappointed when his fingers unhinged an even lower button, parting the soft, rose-colored fabric and exposing the gentle swell of her breasts straining achingly against the flimsy barrier of her bra. When his mouth touched the edge of her bra, outlining the lace with the moistness of his tongue, she thought the ache within her would explode. His breath fanned heatedly over her sensitive skin, and she felt her breath come in short gasps. There didn't seem to be enough air in the room to keep her senses from swimming in the whirlpool of passion moving her closer to this man she had barely met and yet known a lifetime. She was drowning in his velvet-soft caresses, losing her breath with each passing instant of his arduous lovemaking. *Take me,* a voice within her wanted to scream, but the words never passed her lips.

She felt the wispy fabric of her blouse as he eased it gently past her shoulders, kissing her exposed neck and arms.

"Let me love you . . ." he moaned.

Her eyes, shining with a burning passion, yielded to his demands. But still the words froze in her throat.

Softly he pulled her out of the chair and gently eased her onto the carpet with the weight of his body. She felt the soft pile of the Persian rug against the bare skin of her back, and she knew that if she wanted to turn back, it would have to be soon, before all of the long-buried desire became alive again. His hands fitted warmly against her rib cage, outlining each individual bone with one of his strong, masculine fingers. A trembling sigh of submission broke from her lips.

He plunged his head between her breasts, softly imprinting his lips on the firm, white skin in the hollow. Her fingers traveled up his neck to hold his head protectively against her as one of his hands reached up to lovingly cup a breast. She took a quick intake of breath at the command of his touch. His fingers dipped seductively beneath the lace and her nipple tightened, expecting his touch.

"You're beautiful," he moaned before kissing the soft fabric of her bra and teasing the nipple bound within the gossamer confinement of lace and satin. Sheila felt her breast swell with desire and a flood of foreign, long-lost emotions raced through her blood.

Gently Noah lowered the strap over her shoulder, and her breasts spilled from their imprisonment. He groaned as he massaged first one, and then the other. Sheila thought she would melt into the carpet as he kissed his way over the hill of one of the shapely mounds before taking it firmly in his mouth and gently soothing all of the bittersweet torment from her body.

"Let me make love to you, beautiful lady," Noah whispered, quietly asking her to give in to him. "Let me make you mine," he coaxed.

In response, Sheila felt her body arching upward to meet the weight of him. Whether it was wrong or right, she wanted him as desperately as he wanted her.

"Sheila." His voice was flooded with naked passion. "Come to bed with me." Her only response was to moan softly against him.

Slowly he raised his head to stare into the depths of her desirous gray eyes. The red embers from the fire darkened his masculine features, making them seem harsher, more defined and angular in the bloodred shadows of the dimly lit room. His eyes never left hers, and they smoldered with a blue flame of passion that he was boldly attempting to hold at bay.

"Tell me you want me," he persuaded in a raspy, breathless voice.

Her dark brows pulled together in frustration and confusion. Why was he pulling away from her? Of course she wanted him, needed him, longed to be a part of him. Couldn't he *feel* the desperate intensity of her yearning?

"Tell me!" he again demanded, this time more roughly than before. Her eyes were shadowed; was there a flicker of doubt, a seed of mistrust in their misty gray depths? He had to know.

"What do you want from me?" she asked, trying to control her ragged breathing and erratic heartbeat. Had she misread him? Suddenly she was painfully aware of her partially nude condition, and the fact that he was *asking* rather than *taking* from her.

"I want to know that you feel what I'm feeling!"

"I . . . I don't understand."

His fingers, once gentle, tightened against the soft flesh of her upper arms and held her prisoner against the carpet. As he studied the elegant lines of her face, his eyes narrowed in suspicion. Never had he been so impulsive, so rash, when it came to a woman. Why did this woman bewitch him so? Why did she make him feel more alive than he had in years? Was it the provocative turn of her chin, the light that danced in her eyes, the fresh scent of her hair? Why was he taken in by her beauty, which was in the same instant innocent and seductive? For the last sixteen years of his life he had cautiously avoided any commitment that might recreate the scene that had scattered his life in chaos. He had been careful, never foolhardy enough to fall for a woman again. But now, as he stared into Sheila's wide, silver-colored eyes, he felt himself slipping into the same black abyss that had thrown his life into disorder long ago. Not since Marilyn had he allowed himself the luxury of becoming enraptured by a woman. And if he had been truthful, none he had met had deeply interested him. But tonight was different. Damn it, he was beginning to care for Sheila Lindstrom, though he knew little of her and couldn't begin to understand her motives. How far could he trust such a lovely, bewitching creature as the woman lying desirously in his arms?

Noah's death grip on Sheila relaxed. "I want you," he said simply in a hoarse voice that admitted what he had felt from the first moment she had appeared on his doorstep.

"I know." She sighed. She crossed her arms over her breasts, as if to shield herself from the truth. But her eyes met Noah's unwaveringly. "I want you, too," she conceded huskily.

The silence in the room was their only barrier, and

yet Noah hesitated. "That's not enough," he admitted, wiping the sweat that had begun to bead on his upper lip. "There has to be more."

Sheila shook her head slowly in confusion, and the sweep of her hair captured red-gold highlights from the flames. Try as she would, she couldn't understand him. What was he saying? Was he rejecting her? Why? What had she done?

Noah witnessed the apprehension and agony in Sheila's eyes and regretted that he was a part of her pain. He wanted to comfort her, to explain the reasons for his reservation, but was unable. How could he expect her to understand that he had loved a woman once in the past and that that love had been callously and bitterly sold to the highest bidder? Was it possible for Sheila to see what Marilyn had done to him when the bitch had put a price on her illegitimate son's head when Sean was born? Was it fair for Noah to burden Sheila with the guilt and agony he had suffered because of his love for his child? No! Though he wanted to trust her, he couldn't tell her about the part of his life he had shoved into a dark, locked corner of his mind. Instead, he took an easier, less painful avenue. "I get the feeling that you think I'm rushing things," he whispered as he pressed a soft kiss against her hair.

She smiled wistfully and blushed. "It's not your fault . . . I could have stopped you . . . I didn't want to."

"Don't blame yourself," he murmured quietly.

In the thickening silence, Sheila could sense Noah struggling with an inner battle, resisting the tide of passion that was pushing against him. She reached for her blouse, hoping to pull it back onto her body so she could leave this house . . . this man before he ignited the passions in her blood and she was once again filled with liquid fire. If possible she hoped to leave the quiet room and seductively intense man with whatever shreds of dignity she could muster.

"Wait!" he commanded as he realized she was preparing to leave. His broad hand grabbed her wrist, and the silken blouse once again fell to the floor.

Sheila felt her temper begin to flare, and the tears that had been threatening to spill burned in her throat. She was tired, and it had been a long, fruitless evening. She had accomplished nothing she had intended to do, and now she wasn't sure if she was capable of working with Ben Wilder or his son. Too many emotions had come and gone with the intimate evening, too many secrets divulged. And yet, despite the growing sense of intimacy she felt with Noah, she knew there were deep, abysmal misconceptions that she couldn't possibly bridge. "What, Noah?" she asked in a tense, raw whisper. "What do you want from me? All night long I've been on the receiving end of conflicting emotions." Her breath was coming in short, uneven gasps. Tears threatened to spill. "One minute you want me and the next . . . you don't. Just let me go home, for God's sake!"

"You're wrong!"

"I doubt that!" She pulled her hand free of the gentle manacle of his grip, scooted silently away from him, snatched up the blouse and quickly stretched her arms through the sleeves. Her fingers fumbled with the buttons, so intent was she on getting out of the house as rapidly as possible . . . away from the magnetism of his eyes . . . away from the charm of his dimpled, slightly off-center smile . . . away from the warm persuasion of his hands. . . .

Noah dragged himself into a sitting position before standing up and leaning against the warm stones of the fireplace. He let his forehead fall into the palm of his hand as he tried to think things out rationally. The entire scene was out of character for him. What the devil had he done, seducing this woman he had barely met? Why was she so responsive to his touch? He knew instinctively that she wasn't the type of woman who fell neatly into a stranger's arms at the drop of a hat, and yet she was here, in his home, warm, inviting, yielding to the gentle coaxing of his caresses. His mouth pulled into a grim frown. How did he let himself get mixed up with her . . . whoever she was? And what were her motives? "Don't go," he said unevenly, turning to face her.

She had managed to get dressed and was putting on her raincoat. She paused for only a second before hiking the coat over her shoulders and unsteadily tying the belt. "I think it would be best."

"I want you to stay, here, tonight, with me."

Sheila took in a long, steadying breath. "I can't."

"Why not?"

"I don't know you well enough."

"But if you don't stay, how will you ever . . . 'know me well enough'?" he countered. He stood away from her, not touching her. It was her mind he wanted, as well as her body.

"I need time . . ." she whispered, beginning to waver. She had to get out, away from him. Soon, before it was too late.

He took a step toward her. "We're both adults. It's not as if this would be a first for either of us. You have a daughter and I have a son."

She paused, but only slightly. "That doesn't change things. Look, Noah, you know as well as I that I would like to fall into bed and sleep with you. But . . . I just can't. . . ." She blushed in her confusion. "I can't just hop into bed with any man I find attractive. . . . Oh, this is coming out all wrong." She took a deep breath and lifted her eyes to meet his. They were steady and strong, though tears had begun to pool in their gray-blue depths. "What I'm trying to say," she managed bravely, "is that I don't have casual affairs."

"I know that."

"You don't understand. I've never slept with any man, other . . . other than Jeff."

"Your ex-husband," Noah surmised with a tightening of his jaw.

Sheila nodded.

"It doesn't matter," Noah said with a shrug.

"Of course it does. Don't you see? I almost tumbled into bed with you . . . on the first night I'd met you. That's not like me, not at all . . . I don't even know you."

His scowl lifted, and an amused light danced in his eyes. "I think you know me better than you're willing to admit."

"I'd like to," she conceded.

"But?"

It was her turn to smile. "I'm afraid, I guess."

"That I won't live up to your expectations?"

"Partially."

"What else?"

"That I won't live up to yours."

Chapter Five

Noah took a step toward her, leaving only inches to separate their bodies. "I doubt that you would ever disappoint me," he whispered. His fingers softly traced the line of her jaw and then continued on a downward path past her neck to rest at the top button of her coat. Easily it slipped through the buttonhole.

Sheila sucked in her breath as Noah took each button in turn. When he reached her belt, he worked on the knot with both of his hands. Sheila felt fires of expectation dance within her while his incredibly blue eyes held hers in a passionate embrace.

The coat parted. Noah's hands moved beneath it and found her breasts. A small sigh came unexpectedly from her lips, and Sheila knew that she wanted Noah more desperately than she had ever wanted any man. It had been so long since she had been held in a man's embrace. As Noah's thumbs began drawing delicious circles against the sheer fabric of her blouse, Sheila told herself that he was different from Jeff. He wouldn't hurt her. He *cared*.

The soft coaxing of Noah's fingertips made Sheila weak with longing. She leaned against him, tilted her head and parted her lips in silent invitation. Warm lips claimed hers and Noah's arms encircled her, crushing her against him. His tongue probed into her mouth to find its mate and touch her more intimately. Sheila wanted more of this mysterious man.

When he guided her to the floor, it was her hands that parted his shirt and touched the tense, hard muscles of his chest. It was her lips that kissed his eyes as he undressed her. She felt the warmth of his hands as each article of her clothing was silently removed.

It felt so good to touch him. Her fingers traced the outline of each of his muscles on his back and crept seductively down the length of his spine. When her fingertips touched the waistband of his pants, she hesitated. How much would he expect from her—how much did he want?

"Undress me," he persuaded, his eyes closing and his breath becoming shallow. "Please, Sheila, undress me."

She couldn't resist. He groaned as she unclasped the belt and gently pushed his pants over his hips. She stopped when she encountered his briefs.

"Take them off," he commanded, guiding her hand to the elastic band of his shorts. She paused, and he read the uncertainty in her eyes. He smiled wickedly to himself.

Slowly his hands moved over her breasts, massaging each white globe until the rosy tip hardened with desire. He teased her with the soft, whispering play of his fingers against her skin. "You're exquisite," he whispered as his head bent and his tongue touched the tip of her breast, leaving a moist droplet of dew on the nipple.

Sheila moaned in pleasure as the cold air touched the wet nipple, and she once again craved the sweet pressure of his mouth against her skin. As if to comply, he again lowered his head and ran his tongue over the soft hill of her breasts, lingering only long enough over her nipples to warm and then leave them.

Sheila felt a hot, molten coil begin to unwind within

her and race like liquid fire through her veins. His kisses touched her breasts and then lowered to caress the soft skin of her abdomen. Lazily his tongue rimmed her navel, and Sheila felt her hips shift upward, pressing against his chest, demanding more from him.

"Please," she whispered hoarsely.

Noah was trying to control himself, to give as well as get pleasure. He was vainly fighting a losing battle with his passion. The last thing he wanted to do was come on like some horny college kid. Already, though he couldn't explain it, Sheila was important to him, and he wanted to please her. It had been difficult, but he had restrained himself to the point where he thought he would burst from the aching frustration in his loins.

Sheila's eyes reached for his, begging him to end her torture and take her. He could resist no longer. He slipped out of his shorts and lay beside her. The length of his body was pressed against hers, and his need for her was unhidden.

"I want to love you, Sheila," he whispered into her ear, while his hands cupped and stroked her breast.

"Yes."

"I want to make love to you and never stop. . . ."

She sighed her willingness. She could feel his breath on the back of her neck and the musky smell of brandy mingled with the scent of burning moss. Everything about the night seemed so right. She moved her legs and parted his. A strong, masculine hand pressed against her abdomen and forced her more intimately against him. Her body seemed to mold against his. It was as if she could feel each part of him, and she had to have more.

His hands moved leisurely up and down the length of her body, touching her breasts softly with his fingertips and then pressing a moist palm to her inner thighs with rough, demanding pressure. Involuntarily her legs parted, and she felt the heated moisture of his lips as he kissed each vertebra of her spine. Sharp, heated needles of desire pierced her when at last he gently rolled her onto her back and positioned himself above her.

Beads of sweat moistened his upper lip and forehead. His dark brow was furrowed, as if he were fighting an inner turmoil. The fire's glow gave his skin a burnished tint and his blue eyes had deepened to inky black. In a ragged breath, with more control than he had thought possible, he whispered, "Sheila, are you sure that this is what you want?" He grimaced, as if in pain, against a possible rejection.

She wrapped her arms around his chest and pulled him down upon her. Her breasts flattened with the weight of his torso. "I'm sure," she returned, caught up in the raw passion of the night.

With a growl of satisfaction he parted her legs with his knees and came to her to find that she was as ready as he. Never had he felt so desperate with need of a woman—not just any woman, but *this* woman with the mysterious gray eyes and the softly curving, voluptuous mouth. This woman with the vibrant chestnut hair that caught the reflection of the fire's glow and framed an intelligent, evenly featured face. As he moved with her, attempting to withhold the violent burst of energy within him, he found himself falling more desperately under her bewitching spell. What was happening to him?

Sheila moaned beneath him, and the tension mounting steadily within him threatened to explode. He didn't care who she was, he had to have her. With a sudden rush of heat, he ignited into a flame that consumed the both of them. Sheila's answering shudder told him that she, too, had felt the ultimate consummation.

He lay upon her, continuing to kiss her cheeks while running his fingers through her hair. She looked at him through eyes still shining in afterglow. "Oh, Noah," she sighed contentedly.

"Shh. . . ." He placed his finger to her lips to quiet her and reached behind him to pull a knitted afghan off the couch. Still holding her in his arms, he wrapped the soft blanket over their bodies. "Don't say anything," he whispered quietly.

Sheila wanted to stay with him. It was so warm and comfortable in the shelter of his arms. But as the afterglow faded and the reality of what she had done hit her, she was horrified. A deep crimson flush climbed steadily up her throat. What was she doing lying naked with a man she had only met a few hours earlier? What had happened to her common sense? It was true that Noah had surprised her with his commanding masculinity and seductive blue eyes, but that was no excuse for making love to him. It wasn't that she hadn't enjoyed it—quite the opposite. The passion that had risen in her was wilder than she had ever imagined, and even now she could feel her body stirring with traitorous longings at the nearness of this enigmatic man. She tried to loosen herself from the strength of his embrace.

"What are you doing?" he asked.

"I think I'd better leave."

"Why?"

"This is all wrong," she began, trying to slide away from him. His fingers clamped over her shoulders.

"This could *never* be *wrong.*" The afghan slipped, exposing one swollen breast. He kissed the soft, ripe mound.

Sheila trembled at his touch. "Don't," she pleaded.

"Why not?" His rich voice had taken on a rough tone.

"I've got to go."

"Don't leave."

She pushed her palms against his chest. "Noah . . . please. . . ."

"Please what?"

"Please let me go."

"Later."

"Now!" Her voice quivered, and she felt tears of frustration burning in her throat. She longed to stay with him, feel his weight upon her, fall victim to his love-making. But she couldn't.

"We have the rest of the night."

"No . . . no, we don't," she said waveringly. Her gray eyes lifted to his and begged him to understand.

Slowly he released her and ran his fingers through his unruly hair. "What is this, some latent Victorian morality?"

"Of course not."

"Then I don't understand."

"Neither do I, not really." She pulled the afghan over the exposed breast, feeling a little less vulnerable under the soft covering.

"Sheila." His finger reached out and carefully raised her chin so she could meet his confused gaze. "We're in the nineteen eighties."

"I know."

"But?"

"I just need time, that's all," she blurted out. How could she possibly explain her confused jumble of emotions. He was so close. She had only to stretch her hand and touch him to reignite the fires of desire. She shuddered and reached for her clothes.

"How much time?"

"I don't know . . . I don't understand any of this."

"Don't try."

Sheila closed her eyes and took a deep breath, hoping to clear her mind. "Look, Noah. I don't even know you, and I'm really not sure that I *want* to know you this well."

"Why not?" he persisted.

She struggled into her blouse. "You and I, whether we like it or not, are business partners."

"Don't give me any of that sanctimonious and over-used line about not mixing business and pleasure."

"I don't think of sex as pleasure!"

An interested black eyebrow cocked mockingly. "You're not going to try and convince me that you didn't enjoy yourself."

"No."

"Good, because I wouldn't believe you. Now, what's this all about?"

"When I said that I don't consider sex to be pleasur-able, I meant *merely* pleasurable. Of course I enjoyed making love with you; I'd be a fool to try and deny it. The point is, I don't go in for 'casual sex' for the sake of pleasure . . . or any other reason."

"And you think that I do?"

"I don't know."

"Sure you do," he replied seductively. "I'm willing to bet that you know more about me than you're admitting."

"'That's no excuse for hopping into bed with you."

"You don't need an excuse, Sheila. Just stay with me tonight. Do it because you want to."

"I can't." She had managed to pull on all of her clothes and stand upright. Noah didn't move. He sat before the fire, his chin resting on his knees, but his eyes never let go of hers.

"Do whatever it is that you think you must," he whis-pered.

Sheila swallowed a lump that had been forming in her throat. She pulled on her raincoat and wondered if she was making the biggest mistake of her life.

"Goodbye, Noah," she murmured. "I'll . . . I'll talk to you later. . . ." She ran out of the house before he could answer and before she could change her mind.

Noah waited and listened to the sounds of her leaving. The front door closed, and a car engine coughed before catching and fading into the night. When he realized that Sheila wasn't coming back, he straightened and pulled on his pants. He was more disturbed by his reaction to her than anything else. How could she have so easily gotten under his skin? Had all of the pressures of the office made him such an easy prey to a beautiful woman? There had to be more to it than met the eye. Why had she so easily responded to his touch? What the hell did she want from him—certainly more than a quick one-night stand. Or did she? He had thought that she had been hinting that she wanted out of the partnership with Wilder Investments. But when he had suggested buying her out, she had seemed indignant, as if she had already anticipated his offer and was more than ready to discard it before hearing the exact price.

Noah's clear blue eyes clouded with suspicion. Without thinking, he reached for the brandy bottle and poured himself a drink. He took a long swallow before swirling the amber liquor in the glass and staring into the glowing coals. What was Sheila Lindstrom's game?

Disregarding the fact that it was after two in the morning, Noah walked over to the desk and picked up the telephone. He looked up a number and with only a second's hesitation dialed it. Several moments and nine rings later a groggy voice mumbled an indistinct greeting.

"Simmons?" Noah questioned curtly. "This is Noah Wilder."

There was a weighty pause on the other end of the line. Noah could imagine the look of astonishment crossing the detective's boyish face. "Something I can do for you?" Simmons asked cautiously. He hadn't dealt much with Ben Wilder's son, especially not in the middle of the night. Something was up.

"I want a report on the Cascade Valley Winery fire."

"I'm working on it."

Noah interrupted. "Then it's not complete?" he asked sternly.

"Not quite."

"Why not?"

The wheels in Simmons's mind began to turn. Wilder was agitated and angry. Why? "It's taken a little longer than expected."

"I need it now," Noah rejoined. His words were tainted with mistrust; Anthony Simmons could feel the suspicion that hung on the telephone line.

"I can have a preliminary report on your desk tomorrow afternoon," he suggested smoothly.

"And the final?"

"That will take a little longer."

"How much longer?"

"A week or two I'd guess," Simmons responded evasively.

"I can't wait that long! What's the hang-up?" Noah inquired. He waited for the slick excuses, but they didn't come.

"I'd like some time to check out the winery myself. You know, look for a few skeletons hanging in some locked closets. . . ."

Noah debated. He didn't like the thought of Anthony Simmons being in such close proximity to Sheila. He had never completely trusted his father's private detective. However, he saw no other recourse; Noah needed information—and fast. Anthony Simmons could get it for him. "All right," Noah heard himself saying, "go to the winery and see what you can find out. Tell the manager—her name is Sheila Lindstrom—that you work for Wilder Investments and that you're trying to speed up the arson investigation in order to get the insurance money."

Simmons was hastily scratching notes on a small white pad on the nightstand. It had been some time since he had pocketed expense money from Wilder Investments and the thought of it warmed his blood. "Is there anything special you want on this Lindstrom woman?" he asked routinely. The moment of hesitation in Noah's response caught his attention. He had been trained to read people, be it in person, from a distance or over the phone. The slight hesitation in Noah's response triggered Simmons's suspicious instincts. There was more here than met the eye.

"Yes, of course," Noah said with more determination than he felt. "Anything you might find out about Miss Lindstrom or any of the employees could be useful."

"Right," Simmons agreed, making a special note to himself about the manager of the winery. He hadn't missed the interest in Noah's voice.

"Then I'll expect a full report in a week."

"You'll have it." With his final words Anthony Simmons disconnected the call and smiled wickedly to himself. For the first time in quite a few years he smelled money—lots of money.

When Noah hung up the telephone, he had an uneasy feeling in the pit of his stomach. Simmons had been too accommodating, too confidently obliging, so unlike the Anthony Simmons Noah had dealt with in the past. His hand hesitated over the receiver as he thought fleetingly of redialing Simmons's number and pulling him off the case. Why did he feel that his final directive to Simmons was somehow dangerous?

Noah shook his head, walked away from the desk and finished his drink in one long swallow. He was beginning to get paranoid. Ever since he had laid eyes on Sheila Lindstrom, he had been acting irrationally. Whether she had intended it or not, Sheila Lindstrom was beginning to unbalance him. The corners of Noah's mouth tightened, and after forcing all thoughts of the intimate evening aside, he walked out of the den and began to mount the stairs. There wasn't much of the night left, but he had to try and get some rest; tomorrow promised to be another battle with his son. Also, Anthony Simmons had promised the preliminary report on the fire. For some reason that Noah couldn't quite name, he felt an impending sense of dread.

Sheila drove as if the devil himself were on her tail. She had checked out of the Seattle hotel without really understanding her motives. All she knew was that she had to get away from this city, the city Noah Wilder called home. The feelings he had stirred in her had blossomed so naturally in the warm embrace of his arms. But now, as she drove through the pelting rain, a cold despair began to settle over her. Why had she fallen such an easy victim to Noah's charm? Why did she still taste the lingering flavor of brandy on her lips where he had kissed her? Unconsciously her tongue rimmed her lips, and she could almost feel the power of his impassioned kiss.

Wrapped in her clouded thoughts, Sheila took the next corner too quickly. The tires skidded on the wet pavement and the car swung into the oncoming lane. Severe headlights bore down upon her, and she was forced to swerve back onto her side of the road. By the time the oncoming car had managed to get around her,

Sheila's heart was hammering in her ears. She had never been a careless driver, but tonight she couldn't seem to concentrate on the rain-washed highway winding through the dark mountains. "Dear God," she whispered in prayer as she clutched the steering wheel more tightly and realized that her palms were damp. Was it from the near collision—or the man who had played havoc with her senses?

Why did she feel as if she were walking a thin line with Noah? It was dangerous to become involved with anyone working for Wilder Investments. Jonas Fielding's fatherly voice echoed in her mind, reissuing the warning he had given Sheila in his office: "I wouldn't trust Ben Wilder as far as I could throw him. . . . *I'd hate to see you fleeced by him or that son of his.*" No, she argued with herself, Noah wouldn't cheat me . . . he couldn't! But hadn't he offered to buy out her portion of the winery, just as Jonas Fielding had warned?

The headache that had been threatening all day began to throb at the base of her skull. She attempted to concentrate on the thin white line in the center of the road, and managed to slow the pace of the car to a safer speed. It had been a long, strained day, and Sheila was dog-tired by the time she crossed the Cascades.

Dawn was beginning to cast irregular purple shadows over the valley as Sheila drove down the final hills surrounding the small town of Devin. Located west of Yakima, it was hardly more than a fork in the road. Originally just a general store, the small hamlet had grown slowly and taken on the family name of the owners of the combined hardware, grocery and sporting goods store. That was years in the past, and by the 1980s, several shops lined the two streets that intersected near the original Devin store. Buildings, some eighty years old, complete with false wood facades, stood next to more recent postwar concrete structures. It wasn't a particularly beautiful town, but it was a friendly, comfortable place to live and a welcome sight to Sheila's weary eyes. She had only left Devin yesterday, but it seemed like a lifetime.

The outskirts of the town were beautifully tended farmlands. Softly rolling hills covered in sweet-smelling new hay gave the air a fresh, wholesome scent. Sheila rolled down the window of the car and let the wind stream past her face to revive her. Her dark hair billowed behind her, and despite the weariness of her bones, Sheila was forced to smile. With the rising sun, her problems seemed to shrink and fade.

The compact wagon rounded a final bend in the road before starting the slow, steady climb up the hill to the winery. From the gates the winery looked as proudly welcoming as ever. The main building was the most prominent, and could be seen from the drive. It had been designed with a distinctly European flair. French château architecture, two-storied and elegantly grand, was complete with stucco walls painted a light dove gray. Narrow-paned windows, graced with French blue shutters, were the full two stories in height, and the broad double doors gleamed in the early morning sunshine. With the stately, snow-laden Cascade Mountains as a backdrop, the parklike grounds of the winery gave the impression of wealth and sedate charm.

If only the truth were known, Sheila thought wryly to herself as she unlocked the rear door of the wagon and extricated her suitcase. It was fortunate, for appearance's sake, that the portion of the winery destroyed by the fire wasn't visible from the road. Sheila placed her luggage on the front porch and strolled lazily past the rose garden to the rear of the main buildings. She picked a single peach-colored blossom and held it to her nose. How long ago had her father planted this particular rosebush? One year? Fifteen? She couldn't remember. Each spring he had planted another variety to add to the abundance of the garden.

Sheila looked at the imposing buildings and meticulously tended grounds that supported the winery. All of the years Oliver Lindstrom had put into the operation of Cascade Valley seemed to slowly pass through her thoughts. He had worked so hard to make the Cascade Valley label nationally known and recognized. Sheila rubbed her palm over her forehead, and her shoulders slumped with a renewed sense of grief for her father. The guilt she bore took hold of her as she silently vowed to find a way for Cascade Valley once again to begin producing the finest wines in the Northwest. She couldn't hide from the fact that it was her fault her father had taken out the loans from Ben Wilder in the first place. If she hadn't needed money after her divorce from Jeff, maybe Oliver Lindstrom wouldn't have needed to borrow the money, maybe he wouldn't have felt so trapped, *maybe he would be alive today*.

Don't think that way, she chastised herself. She again smelled the brilliant peach-hued blossom and tried to shake her thoughts back to a viable solution to her problem. It was impossible; her thoughts were too dark and black, and for a fleeting moment she wondered if perhaps her father did start the fire.

She didn't answer the question and hurried to the back of the buildings. The charred west wing of the manor house, a black skeleton of sagging timbers, was still roped off. A garish sign with bold red letters was nailed to one of the surrounding pine trees. It stated, quite unequivocally, that there was no trespassing allowed, by order of the sheriff's department for the county. *Suspected Crime Area* the sign pronounced boldly, and Sheila's heart cringed at the meaning of the words. The sign, an intruder on her father's personal life, increased the fires of determination burning within Sheila's heart. No one, including Noah Wilder, would take away her father's dream; not if she could help it.

At the thought of Noah, Sheila felt suddenly empty and hollow. As crazy as it sounded, she felt she had left part of herself in the warm den of the stone mansion high on the shores of Lake Washington. The vague thought that she might be falling in love with Noah Wilder flitted through her mind, but she resolutely pushed it away. What she felt for the man was sexual attraction, physical chemistry, that was all. Sheila was too much of a realist to consider falling in "love at first sight." The Cinderella story just never came true. The one love she had experienced had turned sour, and her marriage had become a dismal, humiliating sham. That feeling of love she had foolishly convinced herself she shared with Jeff Coleridge had taken months to grow. But, fortunately, not so long to die, she added ironically to herself.

She kicked a small stone on the flagstone path that led from the garden. There was no way she could be falling in love with Noah Wilder. It was ludicrous even to consider another side to the coin. She had met him only hours earlier in particularly seductive surroundings. She knew virtually nothing about him, except that he was perhaps the most magnetically powerful man she had ever laid eyes on. But what was it that made him tick? Yes, he was mysterious and alluring, but to try and call purely sexual attraction love was sheer folly, at least in Sheila's pragmatic estimation. Too many women fell into that vicious trap.

Sheila knew herself well enough to understand her guilt. Because of her uncharacteristic display of passion in the early hours of the morning, her subconscious was trying to soothe her by substituting love for lust. But Sheila wouldn't allow herself that leisure. To consider what had happened in the Wilder mansion an act of love was pure fantasy, and the easy way out merely an appropriate, if false, excuse.

Sheila sighed to herself as she closed the garden gate. The problem was that there was no way she could avoid Noah Wilder or his enigmatic blue eyes. How could she hope to reopen the winery without his help? Unless his father came back to Seattle to take command of Wilder Investments, she was stuck with Noah. Just at the thought of seeing him again, her pulse began to race. Realistically she attempted to find an alternate solution to her problem, but found no way out of the inevitable conclusion: No one would lend her enough money to buy out Ben Wilder's interest in Cascade Valley. And even if she were lucky enough to get another mortgage on the property, Wilder Investments was unlikely to sell.

Before opening the back door to the undamaged portion of the château, she took one final look at the blackened west wing. "There's got to be a way to save it," she muttered to herself before hurrying inside the house and letting the screen door slam behind her.

Chapter Six

The following Tuesday evening Sheila decided once again to attempt to assess the damage to the west wing of the manor building and try and come up with a temporary solution to the disrepair. She had spent the entire weekend and the last two evenings cleaning up that portion of the rubble that was not considered evidence in the ongoing police investigation. And yet, for all her efforts, the entire west wing was in shambles.

The late afternoon sun cast dark shadows on the charred walls of the château that had housed the commercial end of the winery. The living quarters, attached by a covered portico, hadn't been severely damaged. Sheila looked at the building apprehensively. What would it take to save it? Though parts of the grayish stucco walls had blackened, the elegance of the architecture remained. Several panes from the narrow windows had shattered from the intensity of the heat and a couple of the cobalt-blue shutters hung at precarious angles from their original placement adorning the windows. But the walls of the building had remained intact, and even the gently sloping roof hadn't sustained too much damage.

Sheila sighed deeply to herself. Daylight was fading, she had final term papers to grade, and she had to get

Emily into bed. Right now she couldn't spend any more time working on the winery.

"Emily," she called in the direction of the duck pond, "come on, let's get ready for bed."

Emily emerged from a stand of trees near the edge of the pond and reluctantly obeyed her mother. When she was within shouting distance, she began to voice her disapproval. "Already? It's not even nine o'clock."

"I didn't say you had to go to bed; I asked you to get ready," Sheila pointed out.

Emily's large green eyes brightened. "Then I can stay up?"

Sheila smiled. "For a little while. Right now, why don't you take a shower and I'll fix us some popcorn."

"Let's watch the movie," Emily suggested.

"I don't think so—not tonight. You still have school for another week."

"But next week, when school's out, I can stay up and watch the movie?"

"Why not?" Sheila agreed, fondly rumpling Emily's dark auburn curls.

"Great." Emily ran up the steps and flew through the front door leaving Sheila to wish that she had only half the energy of her eight-year-old daughter. From the exhausting work of the past few days, every muscle in Sheila's body rebelled. She hadn't realized what a soft job she had; teaching accounting to college students didn't entail much physical exercise.

Sounds of running water greeted her when she finally got inside the house. She and Emily were "temporarily" camping out in the lower level of the house. It was the least damaged. Sheila wondered how long this temporary condition would continue. She had used some of her small savings to have the electricity reconnected and the plumbing repaired, but as to the rest of the house, she was still waiting for the insurance settlement. Fortunately she did have a few dollars left in the savings account, but she was steadfastly holding on to them. After paying the expenses of Oliver's funeral she had less than a thousand dollars in the bank and hoped to stretch it as far as possible. With the coming of summer, she was out of a job until school started in the fall.

The interior of the château had suffered from the fire. As Sheila walked through what had been the living room toward the kitchen, she tried to ignore the smoke-laden lace draperies and the fragile linen wallpaper that had been water stained. Several of the broken windows were now boarded, and a fine, gritty layer of ash still covered all of the elegant European antiques and the expensive burgundy carpet. No amount of vacuuming seemed to lift the soot from the interior of the manor.

The kitchen was in better shape. Sheila had taken the time to scrub it down with disinfectant before painting all of the walls. Even the countertop had been repaired, as the heat of the blaze had loosened the glue and caused it to buckle. The hot corn was just beginning to pop when Emily hurried into the kitchen. She was still soaked and attempting to put her wet arms and legs through the appropriate holes in her pajamas.

"It's easier if you dry yourself off first," Sheila reminded her daughter.

"Aw . . . Mom . . ." Emily's head poked through the soft flannel material, and her face, still rosy from the warm jets of shower spray, broke into a smile. "It's just about ready, isn't it?" she asked, running over to the popping corn.

"In a minute."

Emily stood on first one foot and then the other, eye-balling the kernels as they exploded in the hot-air popper.

"What were you doing down at the duck pond for so long?" Sheila asked.

"Talking. . . . I think it's done now."

Sheila looked up from the pan of butter on the stove. "Talking? To whom? Did Joey come over?"

"Naw . . . Joey couldn't come over . . . too much homework. Come on; let's put the butter on the popcorn."

Sheila's dark brows came together. "If it wasn't Joey, who were you talking to?"

Emily shrugged. "A man."

"A man? What man? Was it Joey's dad?" Sheila studied her young daughter intently, but Emily didn't seem to notice. She was too engrossed in fixing a bowl of her favorite snack.

"If it was Joey's dad, I would have told you. . . . It was just some guy."

Sheila could feel her face drain of color. "What guy?"

"Don't know his name." Emily replied with all the matter-of-factness of a confident eight-year-old.

Sheila attempted to sound calm, but the thought of a stranger talking to her young daughter made her quiver inside. "Surely it was someone you know . . . maybe someone you met in town. . . ."

Emily shook her dark, wet curls. "Nope." She began to attack the bowl of popcorn without another thought to the stranger.

Sheila didn't want to frighten her daughter. Emily had grown up in a small, Northwest town where there were few strangers and nearly everyone knew each other on a first-name basis. "What did the man want to talk about?" she asked, pretending interest in the dishes.

"Oh, you know, all about the fire . . . the same old thing."

Sheila felt herself relax. "Oh, so a deputy from the

sheriff's department came by. . . . He should have stopped at the house first."

"Wasn't a policeman or a deputy."

Once again Sheila's nerves tightened. She turned from the sink and sat in a chair opposite Emily's. "The man was a complete stranger, right?"

"Um-hum."

"Not a policeman?"

"I told you that already!"

"But maybe he was a detective? They don't always wear uniforms."

Emily sighed, and with a concern greater than her few years, looked at her mother. "Is something wrong?"

"Probably not . . . I just don't like the idea of you talking to strangers. From now on you stick a little closer to the house."

"I don't think he would hurt me . . . if that's what you're afraid of."

"You don't know that."

"But I like to go down to the duck pond."

"I know you do, sweetheart," Sheila said with more confidence than she actually felt, "but from now on I want to go with you."

"You're afraid of something, aren't you?" Emily charged, her innocent green eyes searching her mother's worried face.

"Not really," Sheila lied. It wouldn't help matters to scare Emily, but the child had to learn to be more cautious. "But sometimes . . . it's better not to talk to strangers. You know that, don't you? From now on, if you see anyone you don't know hanging around, you come and tell me, before you talk to them, okay? No one should be on the property while the winery's shut down, so if someone comes, I want to know it immediately. Fair enough?"

"I guess so."

"Then you do understand why I don't want you to wander off too far from the house when you're alone?"

Emily nodded gravely. Sheila's message had gotten through.

"Good!" Sheila said, attempting to display a light-hearted enthusiasm she didn't feel. "We'll go feed the ducks together tomorrow. It will be lots of fun." Somehow she managed a confident smile for her daughter.

Emily continued to nibble at the popcorn while leafing through a math textbook. Sheila got up to clear the dinner dishes and turned on the radio to cover the sudden silence. Nightfall was imminent, and the lengthening shadows made Sheila nervous. She had always loved warm summer nights in the foothills of the Cascades, but tonight was different. She felt alone and vulnerable. The nearest house was over a mile away, and for the first time in her life the remote location of the winery put her on edge. A stranger had been lurking on the property, talking to her child. Why? Who was the man and what did he want from Emily? Information on the fire? Unlikely. Sheila let her gaze wander out the window and she squinted into the dusky twilight. She attempted to tell herself that the man was probably just an interested tourist who wondered why the daily tours of the winery had been suspended. But if that were so, certainly he would have come up to the main building. The entire incident put Sheila's nerves on edge.

That night, before going to her room, Sheila checked the bolts on all of the doors and windows of the house. When she finally got to bed, even though her tired body ached for sleep, it didn't come. Instead she found herself staring at the luminous dial of the clock radio and listening to the soft sounds of the early summer night.

Everything sounded the same. Why then was she so nervous and tense?

Lack of sleep from the previous night made Wednesday unusually tedious. The lengthy hours of teaching distracted students coupled with the forty-five minute drive from the community college seemed more tiresome than it usually was. Thank goodness there were only a few final days of the school year left. Next week was finals week, and after that Sheila could concentrate on the reopening of the winery. By the end of the summer the harvest season would be upon her.

Emily stayed with a friend after school. Since Oliver Lindstrom's death, Sheila hadn't allowed her daughter to stay at home after school because Emily would be alone. In light of the events the day before with the stranger, Sheila was more grateful than ever that she could trust Emily with Carol Dunbar, the mother of Emily's best friend, Joey. Emily was waiting for her when Sheila arrived, and after a quick stop at the market, mother and daughter finally headed home.

Sheila had contemplated calling the police about the trespasser, but had decided against it. No harm had been done, and if the man was still hanging around, Sheila hadn't seen any evidence of him. When he turned up again, then Sheila would alert the authorities, but right now, due to the unsolved arson and the suspicion cast upon her father, the last thing Sheila wanted to do was talk to someone from the local sheriff's department.

An unfamiliar car was sitting in the driveway near the house when Sheila and Emily arrived home. Sheila's thoughts turned back to the stranger and she felt her heart leap to her throat. Trying to appear calmer than she felt, she braked the small wagon to a halt near the garage and tried to pull together a portion of her poise. Who was he?

"That's the man I was talking to yesterday, Mom. You know, down at the duck pond." Emily was openly staring at the individual who was sitting, slump-shouldered, behind the wheel of an old Chevrolet.

The stranger had been waiting. At the sound of the approaching vehicle he had turned in his seat, pushed back the brim of his felt hat and blown out a final stream of smoke from his cigarette. He tossed the hat onto the front seat as he pulled himself out of the car.

"Wait here," Sheila told Emily.

"Why?"

"Just for a minute. Stay in the car." The authoritative ring in Sheila's voice gave Emily no room for argument. Sheila grabbed her purse and hurried from the car, intent on meeting the man out of earshot of her young daughter. Her gray eyes were cool as she focused on the rather average-looking, slightly built visitor.

"Ms. Lindstrom?" the man in the worn suit coat asked. He strode boldly up to her and extended his hand.

Sheila nodded as she accepted the brief handshake. "I'm Sheila Lindstrom."

"Anthony Simmons," he retorted with a shadowy grin. He acted as if the name might mean something to her.

"Is there something I can do for you?" she asked calmly. The man looked trustworthy enough, but still she was jittery. It was his eyes, light brown and deep set over a nose that had obviously once been broken; they didn't quite meet her steady gaze. Instead, he seemed to be studying the angle of her face.

"I hope so," he replied, shifting from one foot to the other. His face broke slowly into a well-practiced and slightly uneven smile. "I work with Noah Wilder."

Sheila couldn't keep her heart from skipping a beat at the sound of Noah's name. This man standing before her was a friend of Noah's? Sheila doubted it.

"Mr. Wilder sent you?" she asked with a dubious and reserved smile.

"That's right. He wants me to look into that fire you had here a while back." Reading the skepticism on Sheila's even features, Simmons reached into his back-pocket, extracted a wallet and withdrew a white card. He offered it to Sheila. Along with his name the card was inscribed with the nationally known logo for Wilder Investments.

Sheila kept the card and began to relax. "What is it exactly you're to do here?"

Simmons shrugged as if his job were entirely routine. "Mr. Wilder is hoping that I can speed up the investigation of the arson, help clear up the whole mess, in order for the insurance company to pay off on the policy. Didn't he tell you that I was coming?"

Sheila hedged. "He did mention that someone might be coming." Anthony Simmons was not what Sheila had expected.

The investigator's smile widened. "Then we're all set."

"For what?"

"Well, first I thought I'd check over the burned wing of the winery. Didn't the fire start in the aging room?"

"According to the fire department."

"I thought so. After I'm through poking around the burned building—"

"Are you sure you should go in there? What about the warnings posted by the sheriff's department?"

"I've taken care of that."

Sheila couldn't help but be dubious. The deputy had been adamant about the restraining orders surrounding the winery. "You have?"

"Sure. Don't worry about it. After I'm done with the building I'd like to take a look at Oliver Lindstrom's books," Simmons replied.

"Wilder Investments has copies of the winery's records. Didn't Mr. Wilder give them to you?" Sheila was puzzled.

Simmons nodded curtly. "I'm not talking about Cascade Valley. I need your father's *personal* records."

"Why?"

Simmons let out an exasperated breath. He hadn't expected any argument from this Lindstrom woman. Usually the crisp white card indicating that he worked for Wilder Investments gained him entrance to the most securely locked doors. But this lady was different. Even her sophisticated looks had surprised Anthony. He tried a different tactic with her. "Look, Ms. Lindstrom, it's no skin off my nose one way or the other. I just thought that your father's books might speed the investigation." He saw a look of doubt cross her gray eyes, and he pressed his point home. "Besides which, those records might possibly clear your dad's name."

"But the police have checked—"

"They might have missed something. It's my *job* to find what the police and the insurance company might have missed."

"I don't know . . ." But Anthony Simmons could tell that she would give him anything he wanted. He had found her weakness; he had read it in her startled eyes when he had mentioned her father's reputation.

"It's up to you," he called over his shoulder as he headed for the fire-damaged wing.

Sheila hurried back to the car and found an impatient child fuming in the front seat. "Well?" Emily queried.

"He's an investigator, sent by Grandpa's business partners."

"Then it's okay if I talk to him?"

Sheila hesitated. Something about Anthony Simmons bothered her. "I guess so, but, try to stay out of his way."

"Why?"

"Because he's busy, honey. He's here to do a job and you might bother him. If he wants to talk to you again, I'm sure that he'll come up to the house."

Partially placated, Emily scrambled out of the car. "Then I can play by the duck pond again?" she asked.

Sheila managed a smile for the eager young face that was cocked upward at her. "Sure you can, dumpling, but not now. Let's wait until after dinner and I'll go down with you."

For the next few days it seemed to Sheila as if Anthony Simmons was forever underfoot. She couldn't turn around without running into him and having to answer questions that seemed to have little to do with his investigation of the fire. She tried to tell herself that he was just doing a thorough job, for which she should be grateful, but she couldn't help but feel that there was more than "leaving no stone unturned" to Anthony Simmons's overly zealous pursuit of the truth. Maybe that was what kept nagging at the back of Sheila's mind; she didn't really believe that Simmons was looking for the truth. He seemed to her to be more interested in finding a scapegoat for the fire. The pointed way he asked the questions, the quickly raised brown eyebrows, and his cynical remarks didn't live up to the professionalism Sheila had expected. The fact that Simmons had been sent by Noah himself bothered Sheila even more than the short man's unprofessional attitude.

Simmons left within the week, and Sheila breathed a long sigh of relief. He hadn't explained what he had pieced together, and Sheila hadn't asked. She would rather hear Simmons's theories from Noah or even Ben Wilder. The less she had to do with a cockroach like Simmons, the better.

She waited to hear from Noah and was disappointed. Another week passed and school was out for the summer. She had turned in the final grades to the school administration and both she and Emily were home, able to spend a few weeks alone together until Emily left to spend four weeks with her father. In the custody arrangement, Jeff was allowed partial custody of his child. If he had wanted to see Emily more frequently, Sheila wouldn't have objected; after all, Emily was his only child. However, the four weeks he took Emily in the summer were generally more than he could stand. Jeff Coleridge wasn't cut out to be a father—or a husband.

Every summer, because of Emily, Sheila was forced to think about her ex-husband and the four years of her marriage. Fortunately, as time had worn on, the pain she had suffered at Jeff's hands diminished, and this year, because of the fire, Sheila had other thoughts to occupy her mind. This year Cascade Valley and its reopening were her main concern.

Sheila saw the situation concerning the winery: the clock was ticking and time was running out. With the passing of each successive day, she became more anxious about the business. Surely Noah had Simmons's report, and certainly the insurance company had come to some sort of settlement. Why hadn't she been notified? If only Sheila knew where she stood with Wilder Investments and the insurance company, she could begin to make plans for the fall harvest. As it was, her hands were tied. The fate of Cascade Valley Winery rested in the palms of Noah Wilder, and he hadn't had the decency to call.

The one time she had tried to reach Noah, she hadn't gotten through, and her stubborn pride forbade her from leaving her name or phone number. Surely Noah must know how desperate she was.

She tried another angle, but the telephone call to Jonas Fielding was a disappointment. Sheila had hoped that the attorney could prevail where she had failed, but it seemed that both the insurance company and Wilder Investments were stalling. Why? What had Anthony Simmons found out?

Despite her hopes otherwise, Sheila began to understand that there was no way Cascade Valley could put its label on this year's harvest. It seemed there was no other option but to sell this year's grapes to a competitive firm. For the first time in the nearly twenty years in which the Lindstrom name had been a part of the winery, Cascade Valley would be unable to bottle or ferment any wine. Not only would the winery's reputation be further tarnished, but also the potential income from the crop would be considerably reduced. It looked as if she would have to renew her contract to teach and counsel at the community college at least for another year, or until the winery was operating again—if ever. Maybe Noah had been right when he suggested that running a winery was too big a job for a woman, she thought idly to herself as she stacked her father's personal records back in the scarred oak desk. Or maybe it was more than that. Perhaps Noah was stalling for time to add just the right incentive, a little more pressure, all the while knowing that she couldn't possibly save the winery without his help. Would he be so callous as to wait her out, backing her into a trap she couldn't possibly avoid?

She slammed the rolltop desk shut with a bang. What was she thinking? Noah would never use her for his own benefit; he couldn't. She walked crisply into the kitchen and tried to ignore her suspicions. What had Jonas said about Wilder Investments and the reputation of Ben Wilder's firm? Something about forcing businesses on the brink of bankruptcy to their knees with the influence of money. Wasn't that how Ben Wilder had amassed his wealth, by purchasing failing businesses and, one way or another, turning them into profitable ventures for Wilder Investments?

Her growing suspicion crawled coldly up her spine. Without thinking, she picked up the telephone receiver and dialed the number for Wilder Investments. It was nearly five, but with any luck, Sheila would be able to catch Noah at the office. The pride that had kept her from calling him seemed small when compared with the grim fact that he might be using each passing day as a means of squeezing her out of ownership of the winery.

"Wilder Investments," answered a pleasant, if bored, voice.

"Yes . . . I would like to speak to Noah Wilder, please," Sheila said boldly.

"I'm sorry, Mr. Wilder is out for the day."

"Do you know where I could reach him? It's very important."

"I'm sorry, miss. As far as I know Mr. Wilder is out of town for the weekend and can't be reached until Monday. If you'll leave your name and ·number, I'll leave a message for him to call you back."

"No, thank you. . . . I'll try next week."

Sheila replaced the receiver and tried to think clearly. Why hadn't he called? All of his questions and interest in the winery seemed to have passed with the one night she had shared with him. A flush rose in her cheeks as she considered the fact that the interest he had shown in the winery was probably little more than polite concern displayed as part of his seduction; a seduction that had trapped her completely. Unfortunately, it looked as if her entire trip to Seattle had been a waste. Not only had she lost precious time in her battle to save the winery, but she had also been played for a fool. Willingly she had begun to give her heart to a man who considered her only a passing interest that had faded with the dawn.

"What's for dinner?" Emily asked as she breezed into the kitchen and grabbed a cookie from the jar.

"Beef stroganoff," Sheila replied.

"That all?"

"No. I'm making a spinach salad, and if you don't demolish them all before dinner, we'll have cookies for dessert."

Emily, who was beginning to reach into the cookie jar again, quickly withdrew her hand. "I can take a hint," she mumbled.

"Good. Dinner will be ready in about half an hour. I'll call you when it's time to come in."

Emily hesitated and rubbed her fingers in distracted circles on the countertop. Sheila had begun to put water on the stove for boiling the noodles, but she stopped, noticing instead the droop in Emily's slim shoulders. "Is something wrong?"

Emily's head snapped up, and she took a deep breath. "I don't want to go to Daddy's place this summer," she announced.

"Oh, sure you do," Sheila said with a smile. "You love being with Daddy."

"No, I don't." Emily's slim arms crossed defiantly over her small chest. "And . . . I bet he doesn't want me to come."

"That's ridiculous. Your father loves you very much."

"Will you come with me?"

Sheila turned from the stove and faced her daughter. "If you want me to, I'll take you to Spokane, but you know that your dad likes to come and get you himself."

"You mean you're not going to stay with me?"

"I can't, honey; you know that."

"But maybe if you call Daddy and tell him you don't want me to go, he might understand."

"Emily, what brought all of this on?" Sheila asked, placing her arm over Emily's shoulders.

The young girl shrugged. "I just don't want to go."

"Why don't you think about it for a couple of weeks? You're still going to be here for a little while longer. Let's see how it goes and then we'll make a decision—okay?"

Emily's downcast eyes lifted to look out the kitchen window. "I think someone's coming."

Sheila turned her attention to the open window and the sound of a car's rapidly approaching engine. "You're right," she agreed, trying to focus on the sporty vehicle winding its way up the long gravel drive. As the silver car crested the final hill, Sheila felt her breath catch in her throat. The car belonged to Noah.

She was both ecstatic and filled with dread. Noah must have come here with his answer about the winery.

Chapter Seven

The lump in Sheila's throat swelled as she watched Noah's car approach.

"Who's that?" Emily asked, squinting into the sunset and straining to get a better view of the silver vehicle as she looked through the window. Noah braked the Volvo to a halt and got out of the car. He looked tired and hot. He was wearing tan corduroy pants and a loosely knit ivory sweater. The sleeves were pushed up over his forearms to display tanned skin and tight muscles. His dark hair was slightly windblown from the drive, and the shadow of his beard was visible against his olive skin. His mouth, set in a firm, hard line, tightened as the other passenger in the car said something that caught his attention. Sheila felt her pulse begin to race at the sight of him. No other man had ever affected her so deeply.

"Mom?" Emily asked, catching Sheila's attention. "Do you know that guy?"

Sheila managed a frail smile for her daughter. "I'm sorry, Em," she replied, realizing that she had ignored Emily's previous question. "Yes, I know him. His name is Noah Wilder, and he's in charge of the company that owns most of the winery."

"A big shot, huh?"

Sheila laughed. "I think his title is 'temporary president,' or something of the sort. Let's not call him a big shot. Okay?"

"If you say so."

"Just keep in mind that he is important. His decision on the winery is critical." Emily's puzzled expression was not lost on Sheila. "I'll explain more about him later. Right now let's go and meet him at the door." Sheila grabbed Emily's hand and hurried to the front entrance, hoping to forestall any more of Emily's questions about Noah.

When she opened the door, Sheila stood face-to-face with the one man who had touched her to the core, and she felt her poise beginning to slip. Noah wasn't alone. With him was a boy; his son, Sheila guessed. The resemblance between the man and teenager was strong. Though Sean's hair was blond, his skin was dark like his father's, and his eyes were the same piercing blue. Those blue eyes regarded Sheila intently with a deep-seated, undisguised hostility.

"I tried the bell, but I didn't hear it ring," Noah explained.

"It hasn't worked since the fire."

Noah seemed a little uncomfortable, but when his eyes found Sheila's, he held her gaze and spoke softly. "Earlier, you invited me to come and see the winery for myself. You asked me to spend a weekend here, and I've decided that there's no time like the present. Does the offer still stand?"

"Now? This weekend?" she asked.

"If it wouldn't inconvenience you. . . ."

Sheila was caught in the power of his gaze, the warmth and invitation in his eyes. She had to force herself to smile and keep her voice cool and professional. "Of course you're welcome. I'm sure if you stay and see the magnitude of the problem, you'll understand why we have to begin rebuilding the winery as soon as we can."

"I'm sure," he agreed, dismissing the subject. "I'd like you to meet my son, Sean."

Sheila's smile spread as she turned her attention to the boy at Noah's side. She had always had a way with kids, especially teenagers. She genuinely liked them, and it showed in the interest in her eyes. "Hi, Sean. How are you?"

"Fine," was the clipped, succinct reply. His expression of hostility didn't diminish.

Sheila didn't press the issue. "This is Emily." She touched Emily's shoulders fondly.

Noah bent his knees so he could talk to Emily at her level. "It's nice to meet you, Emily." He extended his hand, and when Emily took hold of it, he gave the girl a warm handshake. "I bet you're a big help to your mom. aren't you?"

"I guess so," Emily mumbled before retrieving her hand and stepping backward to put some distance between herself and the forceful man.

"We were just about to have dinner," Sheila stated as Noah rose back to his full height. "Could you join us?"

Sean rolled his eyes and looked away. Noah spoke for the two of them. "If it's not too much trouble. I should have called before I left the office, but I was running late, so I just headed out of town." The lie slipped so easily off his tongue that Noah had no trouble smiling disarmingly down at her. His conscience twinged, but he ignored it.

"It's fine," Sheila was saying emphatically. "I always cook as if I'm expecting the army." She moved out of the doorway. "Come in. I still have a few things to do to get dinner on the table. Or, if you would prefer, you can look around the grounds. I'll give you a guided tour later."

"I'll wait. I think I'd prefer a *personal* tour."

Sheila felt the heat climbing up her throat. Somehow she managed to keep her voice level. "What about you, Sean? Dinner won't be ready for half an hour. You're welcome to come into the house; I've got several books and magazines you might be interested in, or you can do whatever you want out here."

"I don't like to read," Sean replied curtly, but after receiving a dark and admonishing glance from his father, he amended his brusque response with a shrug of his shoulders. "I'll stay outside."

Emily followed Sheila and Noah inside. Sheila busied herself with the finishing touches for the meal, and Noah lounged against the counter, watching her as she worked. Emily hovered near Sheila, uncertain about the upcoming evening.

"You out of school for the year?" Noah asked the girl.

"Uh-huh."

Sheila could feel Emily's embarrassment. Ever since Sheila's divorce from Jeff, Emily was shy with men to the point of wariness, especially any man who showed attention to her mother. To ease Emily's discomfort, Sheila changed the subject. "Dinner's going to take a little longer than I thought, Emily. Why don't you take a couple of cookies and—" she paused to inspect the contents of the refrigerator "—some of this pop outside for you and Sean."

Emily's wide brown eyes lit up. "Really? Before dinner?"

"Why not?" Sheila asked with a smile and handed the cans of ginger ale to her daughter. "Tonight's special."

Emily balanced the cans against her chest while she reached into the cookie jar and withdrew a handful of macaroons. "Great," she whispered, hardly believing her luck at receiving goodies before a meal.

When the back door slammed shut and Emily could be heard in the distance, Noah moved from his position against the counter to stand behind Sheila. She could sense his presence behind her, but she tried to maintain her interest in the sauce she was preparing. It was impossible. His hands wrapped around her waist and drew her close to him. She closed her eyes as she felt his breath rustle the hair at the nape of her neck.

"Is it?" he asked.

"What?"

"Is tonight special?" His words caressed the air.

She attempted to misread him. "Of course it is. It's not often Emily and I have guests for dinner."

"That's not what I meant."

Sheila sighed and turned the burner to the lowest setting. She rotated in Noah's arms and tried to step backward. He didn't let go. "I knew what you meant."

"Do you?"

"Of course I do, Noah. I'm not exactly a naive innocent. I think you were the one that pointed it out to me. I assume you came here to talk about the winery . . ."

"And?" His half smile showed just a seductive hint of white, straight teeth, and a gleam of fascination flickered in his blue eyes.

"And you probably expect to take up where we left off." Sheila's heart was pounding so loudly she was sure he could hear it.

"The thought did cross my mind."

"You're wicked," she accused teasingly.

"No, I wouldn't say *that* . . . *captivated* would be a better word."

"Oh, Noah," Sheila murmured. His words had a magical effect upon her, and she felt unable to resist the spell of tenderness he was weaving. Though she attempted to deny it, she still found something enigmatic and intimately alluring in Noah. A crazy feeling of exhilaration climbed steadily up her spine as she realized that he wanted to be with her. Perhaps she had misjudged him. Perhaps despite everything holding them apart, there was a chance that they could find happiness with each other.

"You look great," he said. His eyes caressed her face and dropped to the tempting white column of her throat.

"In jeans and an old blouse?"

"In anything. . . ." The pressure of his hands against her back drew her close to him; so close that she could feel the strength of his legs where they touched hers and the pressure of his chest against her breasts. "As I recall, you look incredible in absolutely nothing as well." His head lowered and his lips captured hers in a warm kiss that evoked passionate memories. In one instant she remembered his embrace in the rain and his touch in the silent afterglow.

Without thinking she entwined her arms around Noah's neck and parted her lips under the soft pressure of his mouth. His tongue rimmed her lips, and all of the doubts of the last weeks fled with the promise of his kiss. "I've missed you," he groaned when he lifted his head and pulled her roughly against him. "God, how I've missed you."

At the sound of his confession, Sheila felt tears begin to pool in her eyes. "I've missed you, too," she murmured into his sweater. Her voice caught, and she felt him stiffen. Slowly he released her.

"Is something wrong?" he asked.

"It's been a long day . . ." she hedged. How could she begin to explain the storm of emotions within her each time he held her closely?

"Is it a bad time for you? I should have called before I came racing over here."

"No . . . everything's fine. *Really.*"

"Is dinner ready yet?" Emily called just as she was entering the room.

Sheila managed to brush her tears aside. "Just about. You can help by setting the table."

"In the dining room?" Emily asked as she reached in the drawer for silverware.

"No. We'll have to eat in here." Sheila withdrew a linen tablecloth and put it on the small kitchen table. Looking skeptically at the makeshift dining arrangements, her mouth pulled into a pouty frown. "It's not exactly elegant, but it will have to do. The dining room is still a mess."

"From the fire?" Noah asked.

"And the water that was used to put out the flames. I'll show you everything after we eat. Maybe then you'll appreciate my position about the winery."

The door opened and shut with a resonate thud. Sean strode into the room wearing cut-off jeans, a sloppy red sweatshirt and a look of bored indifference. His face was shaped similarly to his father's, except that the sharp planes of Noah's face were softer on his son. There was still a hint of boyish naivete in Sean that he obviously tried to hide under a guise of insolence.

"Time to eat?" Sean asked, directing his question to his father.

"I think you can sit down."

"Good." Sean slid into the nearest chair and avoided looking at Sheila. His fingers tapped restlessly on the edge of the table. Emily took a seat next to Sean and began to chatter endlessly about a hike she hoped to take with him. Sean responded with adolescent nonchalance about the prospect of spending more time with the eager eight-year-old, but Sheila's practiced eye saw the interest he was trying to hide. Three years of counseling teenagers had helped her understand both the kids and their motives.

The dinner was eaten under a thin veil of civility. Sheila had hoped that as the meal progressed the strain of the impromptu get-together would fade and a comfortable feeling of familiarity would evolve. She had been wrong. Before the dinner was over, even Emily could feel the tension building between Sean and Sheila.

Sheila attempted to bridge the gap. "Are you out of school for the summer?" she asked Sean.

Silence. Sean continued to wolf down his food.

She tried another ploy. "Would you like anything else to eat? How about a roll?"

Nothing. Noah's anger had been simmering throughout the meal, but he had decided not to discipline his son in front of Sheila and Emily. Sean's rude behavior forced the issue.

"Sheila asked you a question, Sean," he stated sternly.

"Yeah . . . I heard."

"Then could you be polite enough to answer."

Sean bristled. "Sure." His cool blue eyes sought Sheila's. "Naw . . . I don't want another roll." He turned his gaze back to his father. "Satisfied?"

Emily's eyes widened as father and son squared off.

"No, I'm not. I don't expect much from you, son, but I do think you can be civil."

"Why?" Sean demanded.

"Out of respect."

"For what? *Her?*" He cast his disdainful gaze at Sheila.

"Cut it out!" Noah stated tersely.

Sean ignored him. "Look, Dad, I don't need this."

"What you need is to learn about acting with just a modicum of decency and common courtesy." A muscle in Noah's jaw began to tense.

"Back off, Dad. What I don't need is some lady trying to be my mother!"

"Don't worry about that, Sean," Sheila interjected. "I have no intention of trying to become your mother." With that, she turned her attention back to her dinner and finished eating. Sean cast a skeptical glance in her direction, and Noah's dark eyebrows cocked. However, he didn't interfere. When finished with her meal, Sheila again looked at Sean. "No, I'm sure you've done very well without a mother for the past sixteen years, and I, for one, have no intention of changing that." She rained her most disarming smile upon the confused boy. "Now, is there anything else I can get you?"

"No!"

"Good." Sheila placed her napkin on the table. "Then, if we're all finished, you can clear the table while Emily gets the dessert."

Sean's face fell and his blue eyes sought those of his father, entreating Noah to help him. "Good idea," Noah agreed amicably, but the glint of determination in his eyes demanded that his son obey.

Sheila wasn't finished. She began stacking the plates and handing them to Sean. "Just put the dishes on the counter near the sink, and don't worry about washing them, I'll take care of that later. Let's see, the leftovers go in the refrigerator. Use the plastic wrap to cover them. Can you handle that?"

Sean's hot retort was thwarted by his father's stern glare. Rather than press the issue, Sean scowled and nodded curtly.

"All right, now, Emily; it's your turn." Emily fastened

her frightened eyes on her mother. Never had she witnessed such hostility at a meal. Nor had she ever seen her mother so tough with a guest.

Sheila smiled at her daughter, and Emily's anxieties melted a bit. "You can bring the cookies out to the back patio. I'll bring the coffee and Noah will get the milk." If Noah was surprised that he, too, was issued an order, he didn't show it.

Sean's chair scraped insolently against the tiled floor as he rose from the table. His handsome face was clouded in an expression of disdain, but he managed to clear the dishes. Emily was uncommonly silent as she arranged the macaroons on a small plate. The tension that had been building throughout dinner continued to mount. Noah poured two glasses of milk and escaped out the back door. Emily soon followed. Sheila waited for the coffee to perk, while Sean put things away, making as much noise as he possibly could.

Just as Sheila was pouring the hot, black liquid, Sean exploded. "Maybe you can fool my dad, but you can't fool me!"

Sheila was startled and sloshed some of the coffee on her wrist. The scalding brew burned her skin, but she remained calm. As Sean watched her reaction, she set the cup down and put her hand under cold water from the tap. Her voice was even when she addressed him. "I have no intention of trying to fool you, Sean."

"Sure," he sneered.

Sheila turned to face the tall boy, and she leveled her cool gray eyes on his face. "Look, Sean, I'm not trying to deceive anyone, and I expect the same in return. I don't really care if you like me or not. You have the right to your own opinions. just as I have the right to mine. . . ."

"Don't give me any of your psychiatric lines! I know

you're a school counselor, and I'll just bet Dad dragged me up here so you could do a number on me; you know, analyze me—try and straighten me out." He threw up one of his hands in disgust. "I just want you to know that it won't work on me. Save your breath!"

Sheila managed a smile. "Do you really think that I would bother wasting my time or expertise on someone who didn't want it?"

"It's your job."

"No. I'm sorry, Sean, but you're wrong. I'm not going to beat my head against the wall for someone who doesn't want my help, and that includes you. As for what your father expects from me, it has nothing to do with you. We're business partners."

"Sure."

"I think I will take your advice," Sheila agreed. Sean tensed. The last thing he had expected was for this woman to concur with him. "I'm going to save my breath. I would like to try and convince you to relax and enjoy the weekend—"

"Fat chance," Sean interrupted under his breath.

"Pardon me?"

"This isn't my scene," he spat out, and turned to glare out the window.

"That's too bad, because it looks like you're stuck here for the duration of the weekend." Sean rolled his eyes heavenward, and Sheila poured the coffee into the second cup. When she picked up the tray, she cast a final glance in Sean's direction. "Why don't you come out to the patio and join the rest of us? Emily already took out the cookies."

Sean whirled angrily to face Sheila. "I'm here, okay? That's the end of it. I'm not going to sit with the rest of you and eat milk and cookies. That might be all right for Emily, but not for me. I'm not wasting my time baby-sitting your kid!" he shouted.

The screen door slammed shut and Emily came into the room. From the expression on her face it was evident she had heard Sean's final words. Tears sprung to her soft brown eyes as she stared at Sean.

"Damn!" Sean muttered, and slammed his fist onto the counter. His face burned in his embarrassment as he strode angrily from the room.

"Why doesn't he like me?" Emily asked Sheila. The little girl tried vainly to swallow her tears. Sheila set the tray down.

"It's not that he doesn't like you, Em," Sheila replied, hugging her child. "He's just not sure of himself here. He doesn't know you or me, and he's not really sure how to act."

"He's mean!" Emily sniffed.

"He's not trying to be. Maybe he's jealous of you," Sheila whispered into her daughter's thick, dark curls.

"Why?"

"Sean doesn't have a mother."

Emily was puzzled. She pulled out of her mother's embrace and with a childish imitation of adult concern, looked deeply into Sheila's eyes. "I thought everybody had a mommy."

"You're right, sweetheart. Everybody does have a mother, including Sean. But, I think he's unhappy because he doesn't see her very much."

"Why not?" Emily was clearly perplexed, and Sheila wondered if she had broached a topic she couldn't fully explain. After all, what did she know of Sean's mother? If she had interpreted Noah's story correctly, Sean may never have met his mother. No wonder the kid had a chip the size of a boulder on his young shoulders. Sheila felt her heart go out for the stubborn boy with the facade of bravado. Emily was still staring at Sheila, and she knew she had to find a suitable answer for her daughter. "Sean's parents don't live together," she whispered.

Emily's sober expression changed to one of understanding . . . Oh, they're divorced. Like you and Daddy."

Sheila's expression clouded. "Sort of," she replied vaguely. Emily seemed satisfied for the moment, and Sheila changed the subject quickly. "Let's go out on the patio and see Noah before this coffee gets cold."

"He's not there."

"He's not?"

Emily shook her head. "He's just walkin' around."

"Then we'll wait for him." Again Sheila picked up the tray, and with Emily in tow, walked out to the brick patio that was flanked by Oliver's rose garden.

Noah had been familiarizing himself with the layout of the winery. His walk also gave him the excuse to vent some of the frustration and tension that had been boiling within him since he had left Seattle. The trip over the mountains had been strained; Sean had brooded because his weekend plans were canceled by his father's hastily organized trip. Sean had pleaded to be left alone in Seattle, and when Noah had refused, Sean had ridden the entire distance with his head turned away from his father while he pretended interest in the passing countryside. He had responded to Noah's questions with monosyllabic grunts. By the time they reached the winery, Noah's tension was wound tighter than the mainspring on a watch.

Noah had hoped that Sean would loosen up by the time they had come within sight of the winery, but he had been wrong—dead wrong. Sean was more petulant than ever. It was as if he were intent on punishing his father with his abrasive behavior.

Noah's frown twisted into a wry grin as he thought about Sheila's reaction to his strong-willed son. The embarrassment Noah had experienced at the table had faded into admiration for Sheila as he had witnessed the effective manner in which she had handled Sean. Even Sean had been set on his heels by Sheila's indifferent and coolly professional attitude. She had refused to be goaded by anything Sean had done. Noah had to hand it to her: she knew how to handle kids. Her own daughter was proof of that. It occurred to him that perhaps he would never be able to control his son. It was all too evident that Sean needed a mother as well as a father. Noah had been a fool to think that he could raise a son of his own. Ben's warning, issued sixteen years before, rang in his ears. "You want to raise that bastard on your own? You're an even bigger fool than I thought!"

The screen door slammed, breaking into Noah's thoughts. He lifted his eyes to observe Sean racing angrily from the house. There had obviously been another battle and it seemed as if Sean had lost one more round to Sheila. Noah shook his head as he watched his athletic son run across the backyard, hoist himself effortlessly over a pole fence without once breaking stride, and continue at a breakneck pace into the fringe of woods beyond the orchard.

Noah's thoughts returned to Sheila. There was more grit to her than met the eye. Stunningly beautiful, she was also independent and intelligent. Noah raked his fingers impatiently through his hair as he wondered if he had made a grave mistake in seeking her out. She was more intriguing than he had remembered, and seeing her in the setting of the burned winery seemed to add an innocent vulnerability to her large eyes. Noah felt as if he wanted to protect her, when in fact he had come to Cascade Valley expecting to confront her with the knowledge that her father did, in fact, start the fire at the winery. As yet, Noah hadn't found the right opportunity to broach the subject. The more he was with Sheila, the less he wanted to talk about the fire.

Anthony Simmons's report had been short and concise. Though the detective had produced no concrete evidence to name Oliver Lindstrom as the arsonist, the case Simmons had built against Sheila's father had been complete. Noah knew that the insurance company was bound to reach the same conclusion as he had: Based on circumstantial evidence, it was proven that Oliver Lindstrom set fire to Cascade Valley hoping to collect the insurance settlement and pay off a sizable debt to Wilder Investments. Inadvertently Mr. Lindstrom got caught in his own trap, was overcome by fumes of noxious gas and died in the blaze.

Noah's stomach knotted as he wondered how involved Sheila had been in her father's scheme. Had she known about it beforehand? Was she involved? Or was she, as she claimed, looking for a solution to the dilemma? According to Simmons, Sheila had been polite, but hadn't gone out of her way to help with the investigation. It had been like pulling teeth to get her to divulge anything personal about her father . . . or herself. Was she hiding something? Simmons seemed to think so. Noah didn't. Still, it didn't matter; the bottom line was that he had to tell her about her father and then gauge her reaction to the news. It wasn't going to be easy. Either way she lost. If she already knew that her father was a fraud, she would come out of this mess at the very least a liar; at the most an accomplice. If she didn't know that her father had started the fire, her dreams and respect for the dead man would be shattered. No doubt she would blame Noah for digging up the dirt on Oliver Lindstrom.

As Noah walked back to the patio he tried to find a way to help her rather than hurt her.

Chapter Eight

Noah paced back and forth across the red bricks of the patio. The anxieties of the day were etched across his face in long lines of worry. It was nearly ten. The sun had set over an hour before and Sean hadn't returned. He was obviously back to his old tricks of vanishing without a word of explanation.

Emily was already asleep in her bed. Since overhearing Sean's unkind remarks, she had been quiet. The girl hadn't even put up an argument about going to bed, and Sheila's heart broke when Emily reasserted her earlier assessment of the situation. "Sean doesn't like me, and it's not because I've got a mommy. He doesn't like anybody."

"He's just trying to find out who he is," Sheila had responded.

"That's silly. He's Sean. He just doesn't like me."

"Maybe he doesn't like himself."

Emily hadn't been convinced as she snuggled under her comforter. Sheila had attempted to hand the child her favorite furry toy, but Emily pushed it onto the floor. "I don't need Cinnamon," Emily had stated. "Toys are for *little kids.*" Sheila hadn't argued, wisely letting her child cope with the struggle of growing up. Instead she picked up the toy dog with the floppy ears and set him on the nightstand near Emily's bed.

"Just in case you change your mind." After her parting remarks she had kissed Emily lightly on the cheek and left the room.

"Is she all right?" Noah asked.

"I think so."

"What was bothering her?"

"She took offense to Sean's notion that she was a little kid. She thinks she has to grow up all in one evening."

"Sean's the one who has to grow up," Noah argued. "I don't know if he ever will!"

"It will get better," Sheila said quietly.

"How do you know?"

"It has to. Doesn't it?" The gray intelligence in her eyes reached out to him.

"What makes you so certain? How do you know I don't have the makings of a hardened criminal on my hands?"

Sheila smiled, and her face, captured in the moonglow, held a madonna-like quality that was only contradicted by the silver fire of seduction in her eyes. "Sean's not a bad kid," she pointed out. "He's just not certain of himself."

"He could have fooled me."

"That's exactly what he's trying to do."

Noah strode over to the chaise lounge where she was sitting. "How did a beautiful woman like you get so wise?" He sat next to her and his hand touched her thigh as he leaned over her to kiss her forehead.

"Don't you remember what it was like when you were in high school?"

"I try not to."

"Come on, admit it. Didn't you give your parents a few gray hairs?"

"I don't remember ever getting into as much trouble as Sean has."

"Maybe you were smarter and just never got caught," she suggested.

"Now you're beginning to sound cynical."

"Realistic."

"Yeah, so it's all business, is it?" Sean jeered, walking out of the darkness into the circle of light surrounding the patio. Noah, still leaning over Sheila, barely moved, but Sheila could feel all the muscles in his body become rigid. Slowly he turned to face his son.

"It's about time you got back. Where were you?"

Sean shrugged indifferently. "Around."

"I was beginning to worry about you."

"Yeah. I can see that," the boy snorted. His blue eyes sought Sheila's in a condemning gaze. "You told me you were business partners with him, nothing more!"

"I said that we were business partners and that I didn't think your father brought you up here for a counseling session. I should have added that your father and I are friends," Sheila explained calmly.

"Yeah. *Good* friends."

"Sean, that's enough!" Noah shouted, rising to his full height. Sean's defiance wavered under his father's barely controlled rage. "You apologize to Sheila!"

"Why?" Sean asked, managing to pull together one last attempt at asserting his pride.

"You tell me," Noah suggested.

Sean shifted from one foot to the other as he measured his father's anger. Noah didn't take his eyes off of his son. Realizing he had no other choice, Sean mumbled a hasty apology before entering the house.

"I'll show him his room," Sheila offered. "There's a

Hide-A-Bed in my father's office. I just put clean sheets on it yesterday."

Noah objected. *"I'll* take him to the room. He and I have a few things to get straight; I'm not putting up with his cocky attitude any longer." He rubbed the tension from the back of his neck and followed his son into the house.

Pieces of the argument filtered through the thick walls of the château. Sheila began to clear the dishes off the patio and tried not to overhear the heated discussion. Noah's voice, angry and accusatory, didn't drown out Sean's argumentative tones.

The night was sultry and still. The tension from the argument lingered in the air, and Sheila felt beads of moisture beginning to accumulate on the back of her neck. She wound her hair into a loose chignon and clipped it to the top of her head before she carried the dishes into the house.

Noah and Sean were still arguing, but the hot words had become softer. In order to give them more privacy, Sheila turned on the water in the kitchen and rattled the dishes in the sink. It wasn't enough to drown out all of the anger, so she switched on the radio. Familiar strains of a popular tune filtered through the kitchen and Sheila forced herself to hum, hoping to take her mind off the uncomfortable relationship between Noah and his son. Just as Noah couldn't get along with Ben, Sean shunned his father. Why? Her loose thoughts rambled as she began to wash the dishes. She didn't hear the argument subside, didn't notice when Noah entered the room.

He leaned against the doorjamb and watched her as she worked. Her hair was piled loosely on her head, and soft tendrils framed her delicate face. A thin trickle of perspiration ran down her chin and settled below the open neck of her blouse. He could almost visualize it resting between her breasts. Her sleeves were rolled over her elbows, and her forearms were submerged in water so hot it steamed. A vibrant rosy flush from the hot night and the even hotter water colored her skin. She was softly humming to the strains of music from the radio, and though the sound was slightly off-key, it caused Noah to smile. She had to be the most beautiful woman in the world.

"Don't you have a dishwasher?" he asked, not moving from the doorway. He enjoyed his vantage point, where he could watch all of her movements.

She laughed. "Oh, I've got one all right, but it doesn't work."

"Can't it be repaired?"

Sheila turned to face Noah, while still wiping her hands with the dish towel. "I suppose it can."

"But you haven't called a repairman?"

"Not yet."

"Why not?"

"Because I enjoy washing dishes," she snapped sarcastically.

Noah finally understood. "You're waiting for the insurance money, right?"

"Right." Sheila's expression softened. "A dishwasher is the last thing we need right now. Emily and I use very few dishes, so it's not exactly a hardship."

"That kind of thinking will send you back to the nineteenth century," he teased.

"That kind of thinking will keep me out of debt . . . at least for a little while." Sheila's eyes clouded with worry for an instant, but she bravely ignored her problems. The best way to solve them was to apprise Noah of the hopeless condition of the winery. She tossed the dish towel over the back of a chair and boldly reached for Noah's hand. "I promised you a tour of the grounds."

"I can think of better things to do," he suggested huskily.

"Not on your life." She pulled on his hand and attempted to ignore the laconic gleam in his eyes. "Now that I've got you on my territory, you're going to see exactly what I've been talking about." She led him to the front of the house. "Let's start with public relations."

"Public relations? For a winery?"

"Not just any winery, Noah. This is Cascade Valley, the Northwest's finest. My father always ran the winery with the opinion that the public comes first. Anyone who was even the slightest bit interested in Cascade Valley has always been treated as if he were an important dignitary." She led him down an asphalt path that led from the château toward the park grounds of the vast estate. Though the grass was overgrown, Noah could tell that in the past the grounds had been immaculately groomed. Stands of dark pine trees surrounded the long grass and the untrimmed shrubbery. The air was fragrant with the scent of pines and lilacs. A hazy moon gave an iridescent glow to the shadowy night.

"Sounds as if your father spent a lot of time and money humoring tourists."

Sheila refused to be baited. "It paid off, too. Word of mouth was our first form of advertising." Sheila glanced at Noah to interpret his reaction. Though it was dark, she could read the hardening of his gaze, feel the tensing of his hand over hers, sense the clenching of his teeth as his jaw tightened.

"What kind of tours did your father give?" Noah asked, pressing the issue.

"At first they were nothing out of the ordinary. One

of the staff would just show the tourists around. But, as public interest grew, Dad had to hire a woman to pass out literature about the winery and give tours of the buildings every afternoon in the summer." Sheila motioned her hand toward a small lake shimmering in the moonlight. "Dad had the duck pond built about six years ago. Then be added the gravel paths through the woods. Later he installed the picnic tables and the benches."

"I'm surprised he didn't give away bottles of Cabernet Sauvignon, too," Noah muttered caustically.

"You didn't approve of my father, did you?" Sheila accused.

"I didn't know him."

"But you're passing judgment."

"Not on the man," Noah pointed out. He took his hand away from Sheila's and rubbed his chin. How could he explain to her that her father was an arsonist who had only wanted to get money from the insurance company to pay his debts? If Oliver Lindstrom had been a little more daring and a little less clumsy, it might have worked. "I'm only questioning some of his business practices. Public relations is usually sound, but not when it devours all of a company's profits. What's the point? If your father had paid less attention to putting on a show for anyone who happened to wander by and had more concern for his profits, maybe he never would have had to borrow money from Wilder Investments in the first place!"

Sheila felt the hairs on her neck prickle with anger. "The reason he borrowed the money had nothing to do with the tourists or the duck pond, Noah. That nearly paid for itself in the gift shop alone," she argued. Indignation flashed in her eyes as she came to the defense of her father. "Dad took a survey of all the people who came here one summer and it proved him right; nearly seventy percent of the tourists bought more than one bottle of Cascade Valley a month."

"What about the other thirty percent?"

"I don't know."

"Do you think those people, those who bought your product, were swayed because of a duck pond, or picnic tables?"

"No . . . but . . ."

"Of course not! Those people would probably have bought the wine without all of this . . . grandstanding. The money would have been better spent in production or research, even advertising. Sure, these grounds look impressive, but it's the quality of the product that counts! Wouldn't it be wiser to use this acreage for cultivation?"

"I don't know if the soil is right . . ." she hedged.

"So check it out"

Her simmering anger began to boil. "I guess you don't understand, Noah. We're not only selling the best wine on the West Coast, we're creating an image for the consuming public. We're not competing with cheap muscatel. Our opposition is the finest European wine on the market. Every summer we provide samples of our product at a wine-tasting celebration and the public is invited. We introduce the newest varieties, invite a few celebrities and generally promote the image of Cascade Valley wines as sophisticated, yet reasonably priced.

"Sounds expensive."

"It is," she admitted reluctantly. "But, most often, we get national media attention. That kind of advertising we can't afford to lose."

"But you didn't get any national attention for the last few years, did you?"

She shook her heard as if she had expected this question and seemed resigned to a fate she couldn't avoid. "No."

"Why not?" He knew the answer, but he wanted to hear it from her.

Sheila bit her lower lip nervously. Her words rang with honesty and despair. "Dad was afraid. With all of the news coverage on the tampered bottles of chardonnay found in Montana and the problems with the crop because of the early snowfall, Dad thought it would be best for Cascade Valley to keep a low profile." She paused for a moment to study the ribbon of silver moonglow on the pond. "This was the year he had hoped would change all of that."

"How?"

"Because we planned to introduce our reserve bottling of Cabernet Sauvignon."

"Reserve bottling?" Noah repeated. "Something new?"

"For Cascade Valley, yes." She turned to face him, her expression sincere. "It could be the biggest breakthrough we've had."

"Tell me about it." Noah was interested. This was the first hint of good news at the winery.

Sheila shook her head. "Not now. On Monday Dave Jansen will come by. He can tell you all about it. . ." She stopped midsentence, as if she'd assumed far too much about him. "You can stay until Monday, can't you?" Why was it so imperative that he remain for more than just one night? Now that he was here, she desperately wanted him to stay.

"Is it that important?" he asked, his voice as low as

the soft breeze that had begun to whisper through the pines.

"Yes, it's important," she admitted, but lied about the reason. "I think you should see for yourself. . . ."

His fingers lightly touched her shoulders, and through the light cotton fabric they warmed her skin. "What I meant was, is it important that I stay with you?"

Her lips felt desert dry. She had to lick them in order to find the courage for her truthful reply. "I'm glad you came here, Noah." She admitted with only a trace of reluctance. "And I'd like you to stay, not just to witness the damage from the fire, nor just to evaluate the winery. I *want* you to stay here with me, for *me*." Her honesty filtered softly through the warm night air. The words of confession surprised her. After Jeff, she thought she had lost the *need* of a man's embrace. She had never expected to admit how much she wanted a man, because she thought that part of her had died. She had assumed that Jeff had ruined her for a relationship with any man, that the cynical feelings he had created in her would remain forever.

But she had been wrong, hopelessly mistaken. The strong man touching her lightly on the shoulders had changed her mind about many things, one of which was love. Though she couldn't yet admit it to him, Sheila knew that she loved Noah as she had never loved before.

"Then I'll stay," he whispered. His thumbs smoothed the fabric over her collarbones. "I want to stay with you, sweet lady."

Sheila sighed through trembling lips as Noah reached up and unclasped her hair. It billowed down in a chestnut tumble to frame her face in copper-tinged curls. Noah gently kissed her eyelids, and Sheila felt her knees begin to give way. His arms came protectively around her waist and pulled her achingly against the length of him. Her thighs touched his, her breasts were crushed against his chest, her heartbeat echoed with his in the still night.

His lips caressed her eyelids before moving slowly downward, leaving a moist trail of midnight dew on her cheekbones and the soft skin below her chin. A warm passion uncurling within her made a shudder pass through her body, and her skin quivered under the touch of his hands. His lips moved gently against her throat, and his tongue stroked the white skin, leaving a heated, wet impression. Sheila sighed dreamily into the night, unconsciously asking for more from him.

Her lips quivered when met by his and her gentle moan of pleasure blended warmly with his answering sigh. Their breath mingled and caught, heated by the fires dancing in their bloodstreams. When his tongue touched hers, the tempo of her heartbeat quickened and she opened her mouth in a gasp, wanting all of him, craving more of his bittersweet love.

He felt her surrender, knew the moment when the passion began to thunder in her ears and her bones began to melt. Her tongue stroked his, teasing and flirting with him until he could stand no more of the painless agony. Gently be pushed against her until the weight of his body forced her to fall on the soft bed of grass beneath the towering ponderosa pines. He let his weight fall against her, imprisoning her with the power of his body and the strength of his desire.

The ground felt cool against her back, a welcome relief to a sultry night. Noah's kisses inflamed her blood and awakened a savage beast of passion slumbering quietly within her. She felt hot blood pumping through her racing heart until she thought she would explode from the powerful surge of desire sweeping through her. She wanted him—all of him. There was a desperation to her need, an untamed craving that knew no bounds.

"Make love to me," she pleaded through fevered lips. He lifted his head and slowly extracted himself from her embrace.

After opening one of the buttons of her blouse, he kissed the warm skin between her breasts, tasting the salt of her perspiration on his tongue. His hand shook as he smoothed the hair away from her face. "I thought I'd go crazy," he confessed, watching the play of moonlight on her red-brown hair. "I wanted to follow you back here that first night I met you." His face was grave, his eyes earnest. "It was hell staying away."

"Why didn't you come sooner?" she asked, trying to keep her mind on the conversation. With his free hand he was toying with the collar of her blouse, letting his fingers dip deliciously below the lapels. Her skin still burned where he had planted the wet kiss between her breasts. Heat waves washed over her skin, which flushed a rosy hue.

"You were the one who needed time," he reminded her. "I didn't want to push you into anything you might regret later."

"I could never regret spending time with you," she confessed.

His forefinger circled the hollow of her throat, creating a whirlpool of sensitive longing deep within her. "Is . . . is that why you decided to come now, because you thought I might have come to some decision . . . about our relationship?" Why couldn't she keep her wandering mind on the subject? It was important that she learn more about this man, and yet all of her thoughts were centered on his slow, seductive touch at the base of her throat.

"No . . . I came because I couldn't wait any longer," he admitted. It wasn't a lie; he had felt an urgency to be with her again, but there was that sordid little business about Anthony Simmons's report and her father's implication in the arson. Dear God, how would he be able to tell her? He promised himself that he would find a way to break the news—when the timing was right. Just now, beneath a dusty sprinkling of midnight stars, he could only think of how hopelessly he wanted her.

She grabbed his finger, stopping its wandering journey on her neck. "I can't think when you touch me like that."

"Don't think," he persuaded, but she ignored the husky invitation in his voice.

"Why couldn't you wait?"

"I had to see you again."

She released his finger, and a smile crept slowly across the smooth contours of her face. Shadowy moonlight lingered in her gaze as she looked up at him. "It doesn't matter," she whispered, kissing bis hand. "The only important thing is that you're here, *now*." Her fingers curved around the back of his neck, ruffling his coffee-colored hair and pulling his head down to meet hers in a kiss of naked longing. She willingly parted her lips, inviting him to touch her most intimate reaches.

"Oh, Sheila," he groaned, damning himself inwardly for his deception. How could he make love to her without telling her everything he knew about her, her father, the fire? A bothersome guilt nagged at him like a broken vow, and yet he pushed it savagely aside. "Some other time," he promised himself.

"What?" Her hand stopped caressing his head. "What are you talking about?"

His grip on her tightened. "Nothing, my darling . . . nothing that can't wait."

His lips came to hers in a kiss that dismissed her fears. She was conscious of the hot breeze singing through the trees as it carried the sweet scent of pine and honeysuckle to her. She could taste the salty masculinity that passed from his lips to hers and she felt the protective strength of his hands as they quickly unbuttoned the remaining buttons of her blouse. The fabric parted, letting her breasts caress the night air. Noah pushed the blouse off her shoulders and never took his eyes from hers as he unclasped the filmy bra and tossed it recklessly to the ground.

Sheila's breasts, unbound by clothing, glistening with a dewy film of sweat, were swollen from the flames of passion Noah had aroused within her. They stood out in the darkness as two white globes, small and firm, perfectly proportioned to her petite body. Noah held first one and then the other in his caressing hands. At his softly insistent touch, the dark nipples hardened.

Sheila sighed when he took one of the moonlit mounds of feminine flesh into his mouth. His fingers gripped the soft skin of her back, drawing her closer to him, letting him devour more of her. She felt the tip of his tongue and the ridges of his teeth against her sensitive skin, and she had the sensation of melting deep within her being. His fingers kneaded her back, persuading her muscles to respond to his intimate touch.

"You're gorgeous," he sighed, taking his head away from her breast long enough to capture her passion-drugged gaze with his knowing blue eyes. His hand took one of hers and guided it to the button above the zipper of his cords. "Undress me," he commanded, "and let me make love to you until the sun comes up."

"I want to," she admitted, removing her hand.

Once again he pulled her fingers against him, lifting the edge of his sweater and letting her hand touch the taut muscles of his abdomen. "Trust me," he whispered into her hair. "Come on, love, take my clothes off. Show me that you want me."

"Noah—"

"I'll help." In one quick movement he pulled the sweater over his head and discarded it against the trunk of a tree. Blue fire flamed in his eyes. She let her gaze travel slowly down his chest, taking in the ripple of each muscle, the mat of dark hair, his tanned skin, darker because of the night "Now it's your turn," he coaxed with a wicked smile.

She raised her hand and placed it on his chest. Her fingers tentatively stroked the rock-hard muscles, tracing the outline of his male nipples. He groaned in pleasure and she let her finger slide down his torso to rest on his belt. She told herself she was being wanton, but she didn't believe it, not for a moment. Her love for this man stole all of the guilt from her mind.

The heat in his loins ached with restraint. The fires within him burned with a savage flame, and he had to use all of his willpower to control himself and the urge to rip off the remaining clothes that kept him from taking her. He wanted this night to be as important for her as it was for him. He wanted to love her as she had never before been loved. He wanted to take the time to draw out every feminine urge in her body and satisfy it. Beads of perspiration collected on his forehead and the back of his neck from the frustration of his self-imposed restraint.

"Take them off," Noah pleaded as her fingers hesitated at his belt buckle. Obediently she withdrew his belt and tossed it into the air. It landed silently on the sweater. Her fingers touched the button of his pants—it slid through the hole noiselessly. Every muscle in Noah's body strained with nearly forgotten control.

The zipper tab dropped easily and Noah let out a groan. "Dear God, woman, do you enjoy tormenting me?" He opened his eyes to search hers and saw the reckless gleam of pleasure in her eyes. "You're going to regret this," he warned, and a wicked smile of seduction curved his lips.

Picking up the pieces of his shattered self-control, he began extracting the same sweet agony from her as she did from him. Slowly, with barely concealed deliberation, he lowered her jeans inch by inch over her hips. He let his fingers graze the warm flesh of her inner thighs only to withdraw them. He again took her breast in his mouth and rekindled the passion that had earlier driven her mad with longing.

She arched against him, moaning into the night. Her fingers traced the contours of the lean muscles in his back, pulling him closer to her, letting him know without speaking how much she needed him, how deep the ache within her was. "Please, Noah," she cried into the night, her desire for him chasing away all other thoughts.

Her desperate cry ended the agony. With a groan he settled upon her, letting his weight fall against her, making her feel that the need in him was as great as hers. His lips caressed her and his breath warmed her skin. He threw off the last thin piece of his self-control and found her, became one with her and joined her in the exquisite union of body and soul. His body fused with hers completely, and his rhythm was as demanding as the ceaseless pounding of waves upon the shore. The tempo increased, pushing her to higher crests of rapture as they blended together in a rush of naked passion.

She shuddered beneath him, a quake ripping through her body as the final wave crashed her wildly in sublime surrender. His answering explosion sealed their union, and he let his weight fall gratefully against her body, flattening her breasts. Their arms entwined, the rapid breathing slowed, and they clung together, hoping to capture forever the moment when the two became one.

Words of love, honest thoughts that needed to be shared, came unbidden to her lips. "Noah . . . I . . ."

"Shhh, darling. Just listen to the sounds of the night," he whispered against her hair.

Chapter Nine

"Tell me about yourself," Noah coaxed, whispering into Sheila's ear. They had managed to get dressed and were sitting together, propped by a pine tree. Noah's arms were wrapped protectively around her as she leaned against him, and his chin rested on her head.

"There's not much to tell." She snuggled deeper into his arms while she watched ghostly clouds move across the moon. It was a still night, with a mere hint of a breeze. The soft drone of insects and the occasional cry of an owl were the only sounds she could hear, aside from Noah's steady breathing and the rhythmic beating of his heart.

"Why don't you start by telling me why you want to stay on at the winery?" He felt her body become rigid.

"I think it's obvious."

"Good. Then you can explain it to me."

"It was my father's lifeblood, Noah. He spent his whole life dreaming of producing the best wines possible. I can't just give it up."

"I haven't asked you to."

"Not yet." She could feel the muscles in her jaw tensing. Not now, she thought to herself, don't ruin it now. We just made beautiful, heavenly love. I love you hopelessly. Don't betray me! Not now.

"But you think I will."

She ran a trembling hand through her hair. "You already offered to buy me out."

"And that bothers you. Why?"

He seemed sincere. She didn't want to think that he had the ugly ulterior motives of which her attorney had warned her. She didn't want to believe he was like his infamous father. "It's just too soon . . . after my father's death. I don't want to give up everything he believed in. Not yet."

His thumb persuaded her to turn her head and look at him. "Does it mean that much to you—what your father wanted?"

"We were very close."

Noah rubbed his thumbnail under his lower lip. "Close enough that you're willing to sacrifice everything in order to prolong his dream?"

"It's not a sacrifice. It's what I want to do."

Noah sighed and his breath ruffled her hair as he tightened his grip around her waist and pulled her closer to him. "Oh, beautiful lady—what am I going to do with you?" She was a puzzle to him, an intriguing, beguiling puzzle for which he had no answers.

"Trust me," she replied in answer to his rhetorical question.

"I do," he admitted fervently.

She wanted to believe him, but couldn't forget the dark shadows of doubt she had seen in his clear blue eyes.

"Tell me about your husband," Noah suggested, carefully changing the topic of conversation. The faceless man who had married Sheila, impregnated her and then left her had been eating at Noah since the first night they had been together.

"I don't like to talk about Jeff." It was a flat statement, intent on changing the subject.

"Why not?"

Her fingers curled into tiny fists, and she had to force them to relax. "It still bothers me."

"The divorce—or the marriage?"

"The fact that I made such a big mistake." She pulled herself out of Noah's warm arms.

"Then you blame yourself."

"Partially, I suppose—look, I don't want to talk about it."

"I didn't mean to pry . . ."

Sheila waved his apology aside. "No . . . you didn't. I don't know why it bothers me so much."

"Maybe it's because you're still in love with him."

Sheila's head snapped back as if his words had slapped her in the face. "You're wrong. The answer is probably just the opposite. I don't know if I ever loved him. I thought I did, but if I had loved him enough, perhaps things would be different."

"And you would still be married?"

She nodded mutely, trying to repress the urge to cry.

"Is that what you want—to be married to him?"

Sheila felt as if the blood were being drained from her as she told Noah her innermost thoughts, the secrets she had guarded from the rest of the world. "No, I don't want to be married to him—marrying Jeff might have been my biggest mistake. But, because of Emily, I wonder if I did the right thing."

"By divorcing him?"

"He divorced me," she sighed, rubbing her fingertips pensively over her forehead. "But maybe I should have fought it, tried harder for Emily's sake."

"Oh, so you think that it would be better for the child if the two of you hadn't split up." His voice sounded bitter in the dark night.

"I don't know what would have been right. It was difficult. I thought he was happy."

"Were you?"

"In the beginning, yes. And when I found out I was pregnant, I was ecstatic. Jeff wasn't as thrilled as I was, but I thought his reaction was normal and that he would become more involved with the child once she was born." Sheila paused, as if trying to put her emotions into some kind of order. Noah felt an intense dislike for Jeff Coleridge.

"It didn't happen," Noah guessed.

"It wasn't the baby so much . . . as the added strain on him to support the family. I couldn't work, not even in the part-time job I had kept before Emily was born. The cost of a good sitter would have eaten up all my salary. I guess the financial burden was too much for him." Sheila stopped, and the heavy silence enveloped her. Noah was waiting to hear the end of her story, but she found her courage sadly lacking. What she had hidden from her father and the rest of the world, she found impossible to say to the man whose fingers still touched her arm.

"He left you because of the money? What kind of man would leave a wife and a child when he couldn't support them?"

Sheila felt herself become strangely defensive. "He wasn't born to wealth, like you. He had to struggle every day of his life."

"That has nothing to do with a man's responsibility." His fingers dug into her arm. "What happened? There's something you're not telling me."

Sheila swallowed back her tears. "Jeff . . . he became . . . involved with another woman." She lowered her head, ashamed of what she had admitted.

When confronted with the truth he had suspected, Noah felt a sickening turn in his stomach. He gritted his teeth to prevent a long line of oaths from escaping.

Compelled to continue, Sheila spoke again the barest of whispers, as if the pain were too intense to be conveyed in a normal tone of voice. "This woman—her name was Judith—she was older than Jeff, midforties, I'd guess. Divorced and financially secure. She wanted a younger . . ."

"Stud?" Noah asked sarcastically.

"Man."

"Your husband was no man, Sheila!" he swore. "He's a bastard, and a stupid one at that."

Sheila bravely held her poise together, admitting to Noah what no one else had ever known. She had kept her secrets locked securely within her, hoping to keep any of her pain or anger from tainting Emily's image of her father. "It doesn't matter. Not now. Anyway, Jeff demanded a divorce, and when I realized that there was no hope for the two of us, I agreed. The only thing I wanted was my child. That wasn't much of a problem; Emily would only have gotten in Jeff's way."

Noah's fingers tightened and pulled her closer to his chest. "You don't have to talk about any of this. . . ."

"It's all right. There's not much more to tell, but I think you should hear it," she stated tonelessly. "When the marriage failed, I went off the deep end. I didn't know where to turn. Dad encouraged me to move to California and go to school for my master's."

Sheila smiled wistfully to herself when she recalled how transparent her father had been. "I'm sure that he expected me to find some other man to take my mind off Jeff. So—" she let out the air in her lungs with her confession "—I took money from my dad, a lot of money that he probably couldn't afford to lend to me, and accepted his advice. I didn't know that payment for my out-of-state tuition and living expenses was more than Dad could afford. I thought the winery was profitable.

But, it wasn't, and Dad had to borrow the money he loaned to me."

"From Wilder Investments," Noah guessed. Noah's frown deepened and the disgust churning in his stomach rose in his throat. So this was how Ben had cornered Oliver Lindstrom, by using the man's love of his daughter and capitalizing upon it. The muscles in the back of Noah's neck began to ache with the strain of tension.

"There are two mortgages on the winery," Sheila admitted. "Dad had nowhere else to borrow."

"And of course Ben complied."

"You make it sound as if he instigated the whole thing."

Noah's nostrils flared, and his eyes narrowed. "I wouldn't put it past him."

"Your father had nothing to do with the fact that my marriage fell apart. It's my fault that I hadn't paid back the loan . . . I just thought there was more time. I never even considered the fact that my father was mortal." Her grief overcame her and the tears she had been fighting pooled in her eyes. "I thought he'd always be there."

"Don't," he urged, kissing her lightly on the top of the head. "Don't torture yourself with a guilt you shouldn't bear."

The little laugh that erupted from her throat was brittle with self-condemnation. "If only I could believe that."

"You're being too hard on yourself."

"There's no one else to blame."

"How about your ex-husband to start with?" Noah spat out, surprised at the hatred he felt for a man he didn't know. "Or your father. He should have told you about his financial problems."

She shook her head, and the tears in her eyes ran

down her cheeks. "He didn't want to burden me, and I didn't even ask!"

"Shhh . . . love, don't," Noah whispered, holding her shaking form against him, trying to quiet a rage that burned within him. How did so beautiful a creature, so innocent a woman, get caught in the middle between two men who only meant to hurt her? Her husband was a wretch, and her father, while trying to shield her, had wounded her in the end. The fire and Oliver Lindstrom's part in its conception waged heavy battles in Noah's tired mind. If only he could tell Sheila what he knew about her father, if only he could bare his soul to her. But he held his tongue, fearful lest he reinforce her feelings of guilt.

Noah had never guessed why Sheila's father had borrowed against his interest in the winery. He had assumed that the money was used for personal use or folly, but he didn't doubt the authenticity of Sheila's tale. Too many events correlated with the ledgers at Wilder Investments, ledgers he had studied for hours before coming to the Cascade Valley. If the ledgers weren't evidence enough the guilt-ridden lines on Sheila's face testified to her remorse and self-incrimination.

"Come on," he murmured, rising and pulling her to her feet "Let's go back to the house. You need some sleep."

"Will you stay with me?" she asked, cringing in anticipation of possible rejection. She felt as if her confession would destroy any of the feelings he might have had for her.

"For as long as you want me," he returned, slowly walking up the hill toward the house.

Sheila woke to find herself alone in the bed. The blue printed sheets that she loved seemed cold and mocking without Noah's strong embrace. She knew why he wasn't with her. He had held her and comforted her most of the night, but sometime near morning. when she was drowsily sleeping, he had slipped out of her room to wait for dawn on the uncomfortable couch. It was somewhat hypocritical, but the best arrangement possible because of Emily and Sean.

The day began pleasantly, and even a makeshift breakfast of sausage and pancakes went without much of a hitch. Sean was still sullen and quiet, but at least he seemed resigned to his fate, and for the most part didn't bait Sheila.

After breakfast, while the kids washed the dishes, Sheila took Noah through the rooms of the château. It was a large building; it had originally been built as the country resort of a rich Frenchman named Gilles de Marc. Viticulture had been his hobby; and it was only when he discovered the perfect conditions of the Cascade Valley for growing wine grapes that he began to ferment and bottle the first Cabernet Sauvignon.

Other than a few rooms on the first floor that had been spared, the damage to the main house was dismal. Noah's practiced eyes traveled over the smoke-laden linen draperies and the gritty layer of ash on the carpet. It was obvious that·Sheila had tried to vacuum and shampoo the once-burgundy carpet to no avail. Huge water stains darkened the English wallpaper, and a few of the window panes were broken and covered with pieces of plywood. The elegant European antiques were water stained, and with the grateful exception of a few expensive pieces, would have to be refinished. Everywhere there was evidence that Sheila had attempted to restore the rooms to their original grandeur, but the task had been too overwhelming.

* * *

Later, sitting in the office looking over Oliver Lindstrom's personal records, Noah noted they coincided with the events in Sheila's story. He pondered the entries in Oliver's checkbook, noting dismally when the money borrowed from Wilder Investments had come in. Some of the funds had been sent in quarterly installments to Sheila in California; other money had been used for the day-to-day operation of the winery in lean years. As far as Noah could tell, Oliver had used none of the funds for himself. That knowledge did nothing to ease his mind; it only made it more difficult to explain to Sheila that her father was involved with the arson.

Sheila attempted to help Noah, explaining what she knew of the winery. Noah sat at her father's desk, jotting notes to himself and studying her father's books as if they held the answers to the universe. She felt as if she were growing closer to him, that she was beginning to understand him. She knew that she could trust him with her life, and she quietly hoped that the love she was feeling for him would someday be returned. Perhaps in time the shadows of doubt that darkened his eyes would disappear and be replaced by trust.

Even Emily was beginning to open up to Noah, and the little girl's shyness all but disappeared by mid-afternoon. Though he was busy looking over the books, he always took the time to talk to her and show an interest in what she was doing. By late afternoon Emily seemed completely at ease with Noah.

The most surprising relationship that began to evolve was Emily's attraction to Sean. She adored the teenager and followed after him wherever he went. Though Sean tried vainly to hide his feelings, Sheila suspected that Sean was as fond of the tousled-headed little girl as she was of him. Things were going smoothly—too smoothly.

"Enough work," Sheila announced, breezing into

Oliver's study. Noah was at the desk, a worried frown creasing his brow. One lock of dark hair fell over his forehead. As he looked up from the untidy stack of papers on the desk and his eyes found hers, a lazy grin formed on his lips.

"What have you got in mind?" A seductive glint sparked in his eyes as they caressed her from across the room.

She lowered her voice and dropped her eyelids, imitating his look of provocative jest. "What do you have in mind?"

"You're unkind," he muttered, seeing through her joke.

"And you're overly optimistic."

He leaned back in the leather chair and it groaned with the shifting of his weight. *"Expectant* might be a better word."

"I was hoping to hear that you were hungry."

His smile broadened. "That might apply," he admitted, his voice husky.

"Good." She threw off her look of wicked seduction and winked at him. "We're going on a picnic."

"Alone?"

"Dream on. The kids are joining us."

Before Noah could respond, an eruption of hurried footsteps announced Emily's breathless arrival into the study. "Aren't you ready yet?" she grumbled. "I thought we were going on a hike."

"We're on our way," Sheila laughed. "Did you pack your brownies?"

"Shhh . . ." Emily put her finger to her lips and her face pulled into a pout. "They're supposed to be a surprise!"

"I promise I won't tell a soul," Noah kidded, his voice hushed in collusion with the excited child. "This will be our secret, okay?"

Emily smiled, and Sheila couldn't help but wonder how long it had been since she had seen her daughter so at ease with a man. Emily was shy, and even when her father visited, it took time for her to warm up to him. But with Noah it was different; a genuine fondness existed between the man and child. Or was it her imagination, vain hopes that Emily would take to Noah. . . .

Emily raced out of the room, and Sheila cocked her head in the direction of the retreating child. "I think we'd better get going before Emily's patience wears out."

"I can't believe that little girl would ever lose her temper."

"Just wait," Sheila warned with a warm laugh. "You'll see, only hope that you're well out of range of her throwing arm if you ever cross her."

"Emily? Tantrums?"

"The likes of which haven't been seen in civilization," Sheila rejoined.

Noah rose from the chair. "I wonder where she gets that temper of hers?" he mused aloud. The corners of his eyes crinkled in laughter as he stared pointedly at Sheila. He crossed the room and encircled her waist with his arms. His fingers touched the small of her back, pressing her firmly against him. He pushed an errant lock of copper hair behind her ear as he stared down at her, a bemused smile curving his lips. His clean, masculine scent filled her nostrils.

She lifted an elegant eyebrow dubiously. "Are you accusing me of being temperamental?"

He shook his head. "Temperamental is far too kind. Argumentative is more apt, I think." His lips caressed her forehead and his voice lowered huskily. "What I wouldn't give to have just an hour alone with you," he growled against her ear.

"What would you do?" she asked coyly, playing with the collar of his shirt.

"Things you can't begin to imagine."

She felt a tremor of excited anticipation pierce through her. "Try me."

His eyes narrowed in frustration. "You're unbelievable, you know, but gorgeous. Just wait, you'll get yours," he warned as he released her and gave her buttocks a firm pat. "Let's go—we don't want to keep Emily waiting."

The hike up the steady incline of the surrounding hills took nearly an hour, but Sheila insisted that the view from the top of the knoll was well worth the strain on their leg muscles. Noah appeared openly doubtful, Emily was an energetic bundle of anticipation and Sean had once again donned his role of bored martyrdom.

The picnic spot Sheila had chosen was one of her favorites, a secluded hilltop guarded by a verdant stand of tamaracks and lodgepole pines. After selecting an area that afforded the best view of the surrounding Cascade Mountains, she spread a well-worn blanket on the bare ground and arranged paper plates and sandwiches haphazardly over the plaid cloth. The tension of the previous night was subdued, and Sheila relaxed as she nibbled at a sandwich and sipped from a soft drink. Even Sean began to unwind. letting his mask of rebellion slip.

"I know a good place to catch trout," Emily stated authoritatively. She was still trying to impress Sean.

"You do, do you?" Sean kidded, rumpling Emily's dark curls. A mischievous twinkle lighted his blue eyes. "How would a little kid like you know about catching trout?"

Emily's face rumpled in vexation. "I'm *not* a little kid!"

"Okay," Sean shrugged dismissively. "So how do you know how to fish?"

"My grandpa taught me," Emily declared.

Sean's indifference wavered as he sized up the little girl. She was okay, he decided, for a little kid. His expression was still dubious. "What kind of trout?"

"Rainbow . . . and some brook."

Sean's interest was piqued. "So how do you catch them?"

"With a pole, stupid," Emily replied haughtily.

Once again Sean was defensive. "But we didn't bring any poles."

"You think you know everything, don't you?" Emily shot back. She reached into Sheila's backpack and extracted two tubes; within each was an expandable fly rod.

"You need more than a pole to catch a fish!'

Emily shot him a look that said more clearly than words, *Any idiot knows that much*. Instead she said, "Give me a break, will ya?" Once again she reached into the open backpack and pulled out a small metal box full of hand-tied flies. She flipped open the lid and held it proudly open for Sean's inspection. "Anything else?"

Sean smiled, exposing large dimples as he held his palms outward in mock surrender. "Okay, okay-so you know all about fishing. My mistake. Let's go." He looked toward Noah and Sheila sitting near the blanket to see if he had parental approval.

Sheila, who had been witnessing the ongoing discussion with quiet amusement, grinned at the blond youth. "Sure you can go. Your dad and I can handle the dishes-such as they are. Emily knows how to get to the creek; she and her grandpa used to go up there every evening."

Sheila's smile turned wistful. "Just be sure to be back at the house before it gets too dark."

Emily was already racing down the opposite side of the hill, her small hand wrapped tightly around the fly rod. "Come on, Sean. Get a move on. We haven't got all day," she sang out over her shoulder.

Sean took his cue and picked up the remaining pole and the box of flies before heading out after Emily.

Sheila began to put the leftover fruit and sandwiches into the basket. "You can help, you know," she pointed out, glancing at Noah through a veil of dark lashes.

"Why should I when I can lie here and enjoy the view?" His blue eyes slid lazily up her body. He was lying on his side, his body propped up on one elbow as he studied her. As she placed the blanket into her backpack, his hand reached out to capture her wrist. "Explain something to me."

The corners of her mouth twitched. "If I can."

His dark brows blunted, as if he were curiously tossing a problem over in his mind, but his thumb began to trace lazy, erotic circles on the inside of her forearm. "Why is it that you and that precocious daughter of yours can handle my son when I can't even begin to understand him?"

"Maybe you're trying too hard," Sheila answered. She bit into an apple and paused when she had swallowed. "Do you really think that Emily's precocious?"

"Only when she has to be."

"And when is that?"

"When she's dealing with Sean. He's a handful."

Sheila rotated the apple in her hand and studied it. "She's never had to deal with anyone like Sean before."

Noah seemed surprised. "Why not?"

Sheila shrugged dismissively. "All of my friends have children just about Emily's age. Some are older, some younger, but only by a few years. The winery's pretty remote and she hasn't run into many teenagers. That might be because they tend to avoid younger kids."

"Certainly you've had baby-sitters."

Sheila shook her head, and the sunlight glinted in reddish streaks on her burnished curls. "Not many," she explained, tossing the apple core into the trash. "I usually trade off with my friends, and when that doesn't work out, there's always Marian."

"Marian?"

"Jeff's mother. Emily's grandmother."

Noah's thumb ceased its seductive motion on her inner wrist. "Right," he agreed, as if he really didn't understand. He stood up abruptly and dusted his hands on the knees of his jeans. A dark scowl creased his forehead. As if dismissing an unpleasant thought, he shook his head and let out a long gust of wind. "You're still very attached to your ex-mother-in-law, aren't you?" he observed.

Sheila jammed the cork back in the wine bottle and stashed it in the backpack. "I suppose so," she said. "She's Emily's only living grandparent."

"And that makes her special?"

"Yes."

Noah snorted his disagreement as he picked up his pack and the light basket.

"Marian Coleridge is very good to Emily and to me. She adores the child, and just because Jeff and I split up doesn't mean that Emily should have to sacrifice a good relationship with her grandmother."

"Of course not," was Noah's clipped reply.

"Then why does it bother you?"

"It doesn't."

"Liar."

"I just don't like being reminded that you were married."

"You're reminded of it every time you see Emily."

"That's different."

"How?"

"Your child can't be compared to your ex-husband's mother."

Sheila sighed to herself as they began walking back to the house. "I don't want to argue with you. It's pointless. I'm a thirty-year-old divorced woman with a child. You can't expect me to forget that I was married."

"I don't. But then, I don't expect you to constantly remind yourself of the fact."

"I don't."

They came to a bend in the path, and Noah stopped and turned to face Sheila. He set down the basket and gazed into the gray depths of her eyes. "I think you're still hung up on your ex-husband," he accused.

"That's ridiculous."

"Is it?"

Sheila's anger became evident as she pursed her lips tightly together. "The only reason I don't like to talk about Jeff is that I'm not proud of being divorced. I didn't go into that marriage expecting it to end as it did. I thought I loved him once, now I'm not so sure, but the point is, I had hoped that it wouldn't have turned out so badly. It's . . . as if I've *failed.*" She was shaking, but tried to control her ragged emotions. She sighed as she thought of her daughter. "I am glad I married Jeff, though."

"I thought so." His blue eyes narrowed.

"Because of Emily!" Sheila was becoming exasperated. "If I wouldn't have married Jeff, I would never have had Emily. *You* should understand that."

"I didn't get married to have Sean!"

"And I wouldn't have a baby without a father."

Noah's jaw clenched, and the skin over his cheekbones stretched thin. "So you think Marilyn should have gotten an abortion, as she had planned."

"No!" Didn't he understand what she was saying? "Of course not. I don't even understand the circumstances surrounding your son's birth."

"Is that what you want, to hear all the juicy details?"

"I only want to know what you're willing to tell me and to try and convince you that I'm not in the least 'hung up' on Jeff. That was over long before the divorce."

The anger in Noah's eyes began to fade. His mouth spread into a slow, self-deprecating smile. "It's hard, you know."

"What?"

"Dealing with jealousy." He looked into the distance as he sorted his thoughts. It was late afternoon; a warm sun hung low in the sky, waiting to disappear beneath the ridge of snowcapped mountains, and he was with the only woman who had really interested him in the last sixteen years. Why did he insist on arguing with her? Why couldn't he just tell her everything he felt about her—that he was falling in love with her and couldn't let himself fall victim to her? Why couldn't he find the courage to explain about her father? Why couldn't he ignore the look of pride and love in her eyes when she spoke of her father? What did he fear?

Sheila was staring at him, her eyes wide with disbelief. "You're trying to convince me that you're jealous . . . of what . . . not *Jeff?*" If Noah hadn't seemed so earnest, so genuinely vexed with himself, she might have laughed.

He was deadly serious, his voice low and without humor. "I'm jealous of any man that touched you."

She reached down, picked up the basket and handed it to him. "Now who's exhibiting 'latent Victorian morality'?"

His dimple appeared as he carefully considered her accusation. "Okay, so you're right. I can't help it. I get a little crazy when I'm with you." He reached for her, but because he was hampered by the picnic basket, she managed to slip out of his grasp. A few feet ahead of him, she turned and walked backward up the sloping, overgrown path. "Is that such a crime?"

"That depends," she murmured, tossing her rich chestnut hair before lowering her lashes and pouting her lips provocatively.

He waited, his smile broadening, his dark brows arching. "Upon what?" he coaxed while striding more closely to her.

She touched her finger to her lips and then pressed it fleetingly to his. "On just how crazy you want to get. . . ."

"You're wicked," he accused, "seductively wicked." This time, when he reached for her with his free hand, his steely fingers wrapped possessively over her forearm.

"Only when I'm around you" she promised. A smile quirked on her full lips. "That makes us quite a pair, doesn't it? Crazy and wicked."

"That makes for an indescribably potent attraction," he stated, drawing her closer to him. "Just where are you taking me? Didn't you take the wrong tum back at the fork in the path a little while ago?"

"I wondered if you would notice."

"Did you think that you had captivated me so completely that I would lose my sense of direction?"

"Hardly," she whispered dryly.

"Is it a secret?"

"No."

"Then why are you being so mysterious?"

"Because I've never taken anyone up here before . . . aside from Emily."

"What is it, your private part of the mountains?"

Sheila smiled broadly, slightly embarrassed. "I guess I kind of thought of it that way. It's just a place I used to go, as a kid, when I wanted to be alone."

Noah's hand strengthened its grip on her arm. They followed the path around pine trees that had fallen across it and over a summit, until they entered a small valley with a clear brook running through it. The water spilled over a ledge from the higher elevations of the mountain, creating a frothy waterfall with a pool at its base. From the small lake the stream continued recklessly through the valley and down the lower elevations of the foothills.

They walked around the small pond together, arms linked, eyes taking in the serenity of the secluded valley. Noah helped her cross the stream, nearly slipping on the wet stones peeking from the rushing water. Once on the other side of the brook, Noah spread the blanket. They sat together near a stand of ponderosa pines, close to the fall of cascading water and able to feel the cool mist of water on their skin.

"Why did you bring me here?" Noah asked, his eyes following the path of the winding mountain stream.

"I don't know. I guess I just wanted to share the beauty of this place with you . . . Oh, Noah, I just don't want to lose it."

Grim lines formed at the corner of his mouth. "And you think that I'll take it away from you."

"I think you have that power."

Noah rubbed his thumbnail over his lower lip. "Even if I did, do you honestly think I would use it?"

Her eyes were honest when they looked into his. Lines marred her forehead where her brows drew together. "I don't know."

"Don't you trust me?"

She took in a steadying breath. "Yes . . ."

"But?"

"I don't think you're telling me everything."

Noah tossed a stone into the pond and watched it

skip, drawing circles on the clear surface of the water. "What do you want to know?"

"About Anthony Simmons's report on the fire." "What if it isn't complete?" he heard himself ask, damning himself for hedging. The truth should be so simple.

"It has to be. He hasn't been here in two weeks. He strikes me as the kind of man who doesn't give up until he finds what he's looking for."

"And you think he has?"

"I think that if he hadn't, he would still be knocking on my door, digging through Dad's records, asking his inane questions."

Noah rested his forearms on his knees. "You're right about that much."

"And I'm right that his report is complete?" she asked, barely daring to breathe.

"Right again."

"Well?"

"Well, nothing."

"I don't understand."

"I'm not convinced that Simmons's report was conclusive. There are a few discrepancies."

"Such as?"

Noah found himself lying with incredible ease. Was this how it started, with a single deception that multiplied and compounded until it became an intricate network of lies? Is this what had happened to his father? "Nothing all that important . . . it's just that the insurance company needs some more documents to support his theories. Until PacWest is satisfied, the entire report isn't considered valid."

Doubts darkened her eyes and her confidence in him wavered. The trust he had worked so hard to establish was flowing from her as surely as sand through an hourglass.

"I assume that means that Mr. Simmons and his questions will be back."

"Maybe not"

"Noah." Her voice was amazingly level for the sense of betrayal that was overwhelming her. "You're talking in circles. Just tell me the truth . . . all of it."

One lie begat another. "There's nothing to tell."

"Then why did you come here? I thought you had news about the winery. I thought we could finally put the fire behind us."

This time he didn't have to lie. His eyes were a clear blue, filled with sincerity. "Don't let the fire stand between us. I came here because I wanted to' see you. Can't you believe that?"

"Oh, God, Noah, I want to," she whispered fervently. She let her forehead drop into the open palm of her hand. Noah's heart turned over, as he witnessed her defeat. "It's just that I feel that you're holding back on me. Am I wrong? Aren't there things you know that you should be sharing with me?"

He traced the sculpted line of her jaw with his finger. The curves of her bones neared perfection. "Just trust me, Sheila," he stated, feeling the traitor he was. He tilted her head with the strength of one finger and pressed his lips against hers. His lips were gentle but persuasive. His seduction began to work. Against her will, she thought less of the fire and the damage to the winery and concentrated with a growing awareness of the man. She realized that he was pushing against her, that she was falling backward, but she knew that his strong arm would break her fall and before her back would encounter the plaid blanket and cold earth, he would catch her. She wanted to trust him with her life.

His hands parted her blouse, slipping the cotton fabric easily over her shoulders, and his tongue rimmed her lips, which opened willingly to his moist touch. His fingers grazed her breast and finally settled against it, warming her skin and causing her to moan. She trembled with need of him and felt contentment welling from deep within her when he unclasped her bra and pressed his flesh against hers, molding his skin to hers.

Her nipple hardened under his erotic touch, and he growled hungrily in the back of his throat. "You do make me crazy, you know," he whispered against the pink shell of her ear. "You make me want to do things to you that will bind me to you forever," he admitted raggedly. "I want to make love to you and never stop. . . . Damn it, Sheila, I love you."

She swallowed the lump in her throat that had formed during his tortured admission. How could she possibly sort the fact from fiction? Tears began to collect in her eyes. "You . . . you don't have to say anything," she stammered, bracing herself for the denial that was sure to come once his passion had subsided.

"I don't want to love you, Sheila . . . but I just can't seem to help myself." His black brows knit in confusion as he looked down upon her, witnessing her tears and misreading them. "Oh, no, Sheila, darling, don't cry."

To still him and prevent any more half-truths to form on his lips, she kissed him, holding his head against hers and letting him feel the depth of her desire.

Her heart began to thud in her chest, and the blood rushing through her veins turned molten. His hands smoothed the skin over her breasts and down her rib cage, pressing against her with enough force to mold her skin tightly over her ribs and inflame the skin when his fingers dipped below the waistband of her jeans.

His lips followed the path of his hands, and his hungry mouth caressed each breast moistly as his tongue massaged a nipple. She felt the convulsions of desire rip through her body as he trailed a dewy path of kisses across the soft skin of her abdomen. Still, his hands kneaded her breasts. Involuntarily she·sucked in her breath and arched against him. Her fingers pushed his shirt off his shoulders and dug into the hard, lean muscles of his upper arms.

When he removed her jeans, he tossed them aside and she sighed in contentment. Slowly he rose and took off his jeans, discarding them into a pile near hers. She stared at him unguardedly, devouring the contours of his tanned muscles as if her eyes were starved for the sight of him.

The sun was beginning to set, casting lengthening shadows across the valley. The fading light played over his skin, adding an ethereal dimension to the oncoming evening.

Noah was silent as he settled next to her and began caressing her with his lips and hands. He stroked her intimately, forcing the tide of her desire to crest, making the blood within her throb with fiery need as it pulsed through her body. They lay together, face-to-face, man to woman, alone except for the hungry need that controlled them.

He took her slowly, coupling with her as gently as if she were new to him. He waited until he felt her demand a faster rhythm, until he saw passion glaze her eyes, until the pain in his back where her fingernails had found his flesh forced him to a more violent, savage union.

Her breath came in short, uneven gasps, her body broke into a glow of perspiration, and the ache within her deepest core began to control her until she was rising with him, pushing against him, calling his name into the wilderness.

She began to melt inside, and convulsive surges of

fulfillment forced her to cling to him. He groaned her name against the silken strands of her hair as he shuddered in an eruptive release of frustrated desire that turned his bones to liquid.

"I love you, Sheila," he whispered over and over again. "I love you."

Chapter Ten

"You're out of your mind," Noah stated emphatically. Twilight was rapidly approaching and the last thing he wanted to do was take a quick dip in an icy lake.

"Come on . . . it's not that cold."

"Save that for someone who'll believe it, Sheila. That water is runoff from the spring melt on the Cascades. You've got another thing coming if you think you can talk me into swimming in ice water."

"It could be fun," she suggested. He could see her body through the ripples in the water. The firm contours of her limbs were distorted against the darkening pool. He would catch a glimpse of one breast as she treaded in the water, and then it would be gone, covered by her arm as she kept herself afloat. Her hair was damp and tossed carelessly off her face. Dewy drops of water clung to her eyelashes and cheeks. "Come on."

"I've never done anything this irrational in my life," he admitted, testing the water and withdrawing his foot.

"Then it's time." She shoved her hand through the clear ripples and set a wave of cold water washing over his body. His startled look was replaced by determination as he marched into the lake. Quickly she dove under the water and swam near the bottom, to resurface behind the waterfall. Just as she took in a gulp of air, her legs were pulled out from under her by strong arms.

When she came up again, she was sputtering for air. Noah's arms encircled her waist.

"You lied," he accused. "This lake is *too cold*."

"Refreshing," she bantered back.

"Frigid." He captured her blue lips with his and kissed the droplets of water off her face. His hands and legs touched her intimately beneath the surface of the water; his kiss deepened and their tongues entwined. Her skin heated, but was cooled by the chilly temperature in the water.

His fingers touched her thigh, smoothing the soft skin and caressing her as they stood, waist deep in the pond. The waterfall was their flowing curtain of privacy as Noah kissed a hardened nipple and pushed her against the ledge.

"We should be going," she pleaded.

"Not now, you little witch. You coerced me into this lake with you, and you're going to suffer the consequences."

"And just what consequences are you talking about?"

"I'm going to make you beg me to love you."

"But Sean . . . Emily . . ." His hand continued its exploration, warming her internally while her skin was chilled by the water.

"They'll wait for us."

He kissed her again, his hand still extracting sweet promises from her. Her breasts flattened against him, and he licked the moisture from them.

Despite the temperature of the water, Sheila began to warm from the inside out. She felt her legs part and wanted more than the touch of cold lapping water on her skin. She yearned to be a part of the man she loved, ached for him to join with her. His kisses upon her neck enticed her. The dewy droplets of cold water on her breasts made her skin quiver. And his hands, God, his hands, gently stroking her, driving all thoughts from her mind other than the desire welling deep within her body.

"Oh, Noah," she whispered as she felt the excruciating ache within her beg for release.

"Yes, love," he whispered thickly.

"Please . . ."

"What?"

"Please love me," she murmured against his chest, stroking her tongue against the virile male muscles, wondering if it were possible ever to get enough of him. How long would it be before her love for him would consume her?

"I do love you, Sheila. I will forever," he vowed as he pushed her gently against the ledge beneath the water's surface. He placed his legs between hers and the spray from the waterfall ran in lingering rivulets down her face and neck. The water lapped lazily around her hips and thighs and Noah came to her, burying himself in her with savage strokes.

She found herself clutching him, clinging to him, surging with him over the final barrier until satiation and exhaustion took its toll on her.

"I love you," she whispered, licking a drop of water from his temple, and the strength of his arms wrapped her more tightly to him, as if he were afraid that in releasing her he would lose her.

They shivered as they got dressed, packed their belongings and hiked down the path. Dusk began to shadow the hills in darkness, but when they were within sight of the château, they could see that no lights burned in the windows. It was obvious that Sean and Emily hadn't returned. Sheila became uneasy.

"I thought the kids would be back by now," she said, voicing her thoughts. "I told Emily to be home before dark."

"She might have had trouble convincing Sean," Noah muttered. "It's quite a hike, and the best fly fishing is in the evening."

Sheila wasn't convinced. "They should be home."

"They will be. Don't worry. I bet they'll be here within the next half hour."

"And if they're not?"

"We'll go looking for them. You do know where Emily was headed, don't you?"

Sheila nodded and smiled in spite of her apprehension. "It's the same place Dad used to take me."

"Then let's not worry until we have to. There's something I want to talk about." He settled upon a rope hammock in the yard and indicated with a gesture that he wanted her to lie next to him.

She slid into the rope swing, careful not to lose her balance. "Okay—so talk."

"I think I should tell you about Marilyn."

"Sean's mother?"

Noah's lips twisted wryly. "I don't think of her as his mother, merely the woman who gave him birth."

"You don't have to explain any of this to me." Sheila wanted to know everything about him, and yet was unwilling to know his secrets more intimately. The past was gone; what was the point in dredging up bitter memories?

"I don't have to tell you anything, but I want to. Maybe then you'll understand my feelings for my son . . . and my father."

"Ben was involved."

Noah's entire body became rigid. "Oh, yes, he was involved all right—he couldn't help himself. You don't know my father, but if you did, you'd realize that he tries to dominate everyone or everything he touches.

"Your father's ill," Sheila reminded him gently.

Noah relaxed a little and stared at the stars beginning to peek through the violet-gray dusk. "He wasn't ill sixteen years ago," Noah asserted as he squinted in thought. "As a matter of fact he was in his prime."

Noah paused, conjuring up the period in his life he had tried to forget. "Marilyn was only seventeen when we first met. She came to a fraternity dance with a friend of mine. I thought at the time she was the most beautiful girl I had ever seen. Long blond hair, clear blue eyes and a smile that could melt ice. I was captivated.

"It wasn't long before I was dating her, and Ben told me to 'dump her.' In the old man's opinion, Marilyn wasn't quite up to par, socially speaking." Noah shook his head at his own young foolishness.

"You know that I haven't ever gotten along with Ben?" Sheila nodded, afraid to break the silence. "Well, Ben considered Marilyn a 'gold digger,' after the family fortune. Maybe she was. Hell, she was just a kid, barely seventeen. Anyway, I suppose that because my father was so hell-bent against her, it made her all the more attractive to me . . . at least for a while. We dated for about four months, I guess, and then we started arguing, over stupid little things. We never got along."

Noah absently ran his hand across his chin, rubbing the beard shadow that had begun to appear. "Anyway, just as I decided to break things off with her, she turned up pregnant. She was probably scared, but she didn't have the guts to tell me about it. I heard the news secondhand, through a friend of mine who was dating her sister.

"At first I was angry—furious that she hadn't come to me with the news. When I found out that she intended to have an abortion, I thought I would kill her myself. I drove around for four hours, and I had no idea where I'd been, but I had managed to calm down. By the time I went to her house, I knew that I wanted my child more than anything in the world and that I was willing to pay any price to get it.

"I tried pleading with her to keep the baby, but she didn't even want to talk about it. I told her that I would marry her, give my name to the child, whatever she wanted, if she would reconsider."

Noah closed his eyes, as if hiding from the truth. "She finally agreed and I thought I'd won a major victory because it was pretty evident that she was more concerned about being a cheerleader to the football squad than being a mother to my unborn child. And maybe I'd been too rough on her—she wasn't much older than Sean is now. Just a kid. And I was just as foolish. Although we'd made one mistake, I thought we could correct it. Given time, I was sure that Marilyn would mature and learn to love the baby. I even thought she and I had a chance."

Bitterness made his voice brittle. "But I was wrong. Dead wrong. Ben couldn't leave it alone . . . and maybe it was better that he didn't . . . I don't know. Anyway, Ben was against the marriage from the first, baby or no baby, and he offered Marilyn a decent sum of money to go quietly away and give the baby up for adoption. The offer was attractive to her; she had no other means to afford college,

"I was outraged at my father's proposal and sickened by Marilyn's transparent interest in the money. I tried to talk her out of it and insisted that she marry me and keep the child. If she wanted to go to school, I was sure we could afford it, at least part-time. She was adamantly against any solution I provided. I didn't understand it at the time, not until she told me what she had come up with as an alternative solution."

Sheila was breathless as she watched the angry play

of sixteen-year-old emotions contort Noah's face in pain. "In Marilyn's beautiful, scheming mind, she found the answer. The price was considerably higher of course, but she agreed to give the baby up for adoption to me, his father, for a discreet and large sum of money. Although Ben didn't like the idea of being manipulated by a girl he considered socially off-limits, he seemed to almost . . . enjoy her sense of values.

"It was obvious that a marriage to Marilyn under the best circumstances would be a disaster for both the baby and myself, so I swallowed my pride and pleaded with my father to agree to her demands, in order that I could gain custody of Sean. Sixteen years ago fathers' rights were virtually unheard of, and without Marilyn's written consent, I could never have gotten custody of my son. I wanted the only decent thing I could retrieve from that relationship with Marilyn—my unborn son.

"Ben thought I was completely out of my mind, but finally agreed. In the past sixteen years, every time he and I would disagree, Ben would remind me that it *was his money and his power* that gave me custody of Sean."

Noah ran an angry hand through his dark hair and uttered an oath under his breath. Sheila knew she was witnessing a rare side of him. As she watched the cruel emotions tighten his jaw, she understood that she was learning things about him that he kept hidden from the rest of the world. He was letting her become closer to him, divulging his innermost secrets. She leaned her head against his shoulder and listened to the steady beat of his heart.

"Ben even has the stubborn pride to think that he saved me from an unhappy marriage . . . Maybe he did. Who can say? The point is that he's held it over my head for sixteen years. Finally, I've paid him back in full." He spat the words out with a vehemence that sent a shiver skittering down Sheila's spine.

"Because you've taken over the business while he's been recuperating in Mexico?"

"That's right. It took me this long to get out of the old man's debt." Sheila could see the emotional scars of pain etched on Noah's broad forehead; she could read the agony in his blue eyes.

Her voice caught as she began to speak. "I'm sorry."

"Don't be. It's over."

"It bothers you."

"I said, it's over." He shifted on the hammock and seemed to notice the darkness for the first time. His eyes searched the hillside. "The kids should be home."

Sheila, too, had been caught up in the complexity of his story. Panic began to take hold of her as she realized that night had descended and Emily was missing. "Oh, my God," she whispered, clasping a hand over her mouth. "Where could they be?"

"You tell me. Do you have any flashlights?"

She nodded, and was on her way to the house before he could tell her to get them. She fumbled with the light switch in the kitchen in her hurry. Within two minutes she was back outside, listening for a response to Noah's shout. Nothing interrupted the stillness of the night.

"Damn," Noah muttered as he pinched the bridge of his nose. "I should have listened when you wanted to search for them earlier."

"You didn't know they wouldn't come home."

"But you did;" He turned to look at her as they followed the bobbing circles of lights flashing on the ground before them. "Why were you worried—is it part of being a mother?"

"Emily's never late," Sheila asserted breathlessly. They were climbing the hill at a near run.

"Next time I'll pay more attention when you begin to worry."

"A lot of good that does us now," Sheila snapped back. She knew she was being short with Noah and that it was unfair, but her concern for her daughter made her irritable.

Noah stopped and cupped his hands around his mouth to call Sean's name. From somewhere in the distance they heard his answering shout. Sean's voice sounded rough and frightened.

"Oh, my God," Sheila whispered, listening for Emily's voice and hearing nothing. "Something's happened." Fear took a stranglehold on her throat, and she started running up the path, jumping to conclusions and imagining scenarios of life without her daughter.

She stumbled once on an exposed root. Noah reached for her, but couldn't break the fall that tore her jeans and scraped her knee. Wincing in pain, she continued to race up the hill, mindless of the blood that was oozing from the wound.

Sean's shouts were louder, and within minutes his anxious face came into range of the flashlights. Sheila choked back a scream as she saw Emily in his arms. The child was dripping wet, her face was covered with mud and there were several scratches on her cheeks.

"Mommy . . ." Emily reached her arms out to her mother and tears formed in Sheila's eyes as Emily clung, sobbing to her.

"Hush . . . Emily, it's all right. Mommy's here." Emily burrowed her nose into Sheila's shoulder. The girl was visibly shaking and her teeth were chattering. Noah took off his shirt and placed it on Emily's small shoulders. "Shhh . . . Sweetheart, are you all right . . . Are you hurt?"

"It's her ankle," Sean interrupted. His face was ashen as he looked down at Emily.

"Let's take a look at that." Noah took the flashlight and illuminated Emily's right ankle. Gently he touched the swollen joint. Emily wailed in pain.

"Shhh . . . Em, Noah's just seeing how bad it is," Sheila whispered into Emily's bedraggled curls. Sheila's eyes drove into Noah's with a message that he had better be careful with her daughter.

"I don't think it's broken . . . but I can't really tell," Noah said softly. "Here, Emily, let me carry you back to the house. We'll call a doctor when we get there."

"No! Mommy, you hold me. *Please*." Emily clung to Sheila's neck as if holding on for dear life.

"Emily," Noah's voice was firm as he talked to the little girl.

"Don't, I can handle her."

"Forget it, Sheila." The beam of light swept from Emily's ankle to Sheila's torn, bloody jeans. "You'll be doing well if you can get back to the house on your own. I'll carry Emily."

"Mommy . . ." Emily wailed.

"Really; Noah, I'm sure I can manage," Sheila asserted, her gray eyes glinting like daggers.

"Forget it. . . . Sean, you carry the gear and the flashlights." Noah carefully extracted Emily from Sheila's arms, but still gave orders to his son. "Then you walk with Sheila; she's cut her leg. Now let's go. The sooner we get Emily home, the better."

Not even Emily argued with the determination in Noah's voice. Sheila pursed her lips together and ignored the urge to argue with him. The most important thing was Emily's well-being, and Sheila couldn't find fault with Noah's logic.

"Tell me, son," Noah said sternly, when the lights of the château were visible. "Just what happened?"

"We were fishing."

"And?"

"Well, it was getting dark, and I guess I was in kind of a hurry," Sean continued rapidly. "Emily kept getting behind, and when we crossed the creek, she slipped on a rock. I threw down the gear and reached for her, but the current pushed her off balance and pulled her under the water. It was lucky that the creek was shallow, and I got to her. Then she started crying and screaming about her ankle and, well, I just started carrying her down the hill as fast as I could."

"You should have been more considerate, Sean. If you weren't always hurrying to get where you should have been an hour ago, this might never have happened!" Noah declared gruffly.

"I didn't think . . ."

"That's the problem, isn't it?"

"Noah, don't," Sheila interjected. "It's not Sean's fault. Arguing isn't going to help anything."

It seemed an eternity to Sheila, but eventually they got Emily to the house. While she cleaned and dried the child, Noah called a local doctor who was a friend of Sheila's. Sean paced nervously from the living room to the den and back again until Emily was propped up in bed and the doctor arrived.

Doctor Embers was a young woman who had a daughter a couple of years younger than Emily. She was prematurely gray and wore her glasses on the end of her nose as she examined the child.

"So you took a tumble, did you?" she asked brightly as she looked into Emily's pupils. "How do you feel?"

"Okay," Emily mumbled feebly. Her large brown eyes looked sunken in her white face.

"How about this ankle . . . does this hurt?"

Emily winced and uttered a little cry.

The doctor continued to examine Emily while Sheila looked anxiously at the little girl, who seemed smaller than she had earlier in the day. Lying on the white pillow, Emily seemed almost frail.

Dr. Embers straightened, smiled down at the child and gave her head an affectionate pat. "Well, I think you'll live," she pronounced. "But I would stay off the ankle for a while. And no more jumping in creeks for the time being, okay?"

Emily smiled feebly and nodded. Dr. Embers took Sheila into the kitchen and answered the unspoken question hanging on Sheila's lips. "She'll be fine, Sheila. Don't worry."

"Thank goodness."

"She shouldn't need anything stronger for the pain than aspirin, but I do want you to bring her into the clinic on Monday for X-rays."

Alarm flashed in Sheila's eyes. "But I thought . . ."

Donna Embers waved Sheila's fears away with a gentle smile and a hand on her arm. "I said don't worry. I'm sure the ankle is just a sprain, but, I want to double-check. just in case there's a hairline fracture hiding in there."

Sheila let out a relieved sigh. "I really appreciate the fact that you came over tonight."

"No problem; what are friends for? Besides, you'll get the bill."

Sheila smiled. "Can you at least stay for a cup of coffee?"

Donna edged to the door and shook her head. "I'd love to, really, but I left Dennis with dinner and the kids, which might be just a shade too much responsibility for him.

Sheila leaned against the kitchen door frame and laughed. The last thing she would call Donna Ember's loyal husband was irresponsible. A feeling of warm relief washed over her as she watched the headlights of Donna's van fade into the distance.

"Is Emily going to be all right?" Sean asked when Sheila walked back into the kitchen and began perking a pot of coffee.

"She's fine."

Sean swallowed and kept his eyes on the floor. "I'm really sorry."

"It's not your fault," Sheila maintained.

"Dad thinks so," Sean replied glumly.

"Well, your dad is wrong."

Sean's head snapped upward, and his intense blue eyes sought Sheila's. "But I thought you liked Dad."

"I do . . . I like him very much," Sheila admitted, "but that doesn't mean he can't be wrong some of the time."

Sean sank into a chair near the table. "I should have been more careful."

"Even if you had, the accident might still have occurred. Just be thankful it wasn't any worse than it was."

Sean's face whitened at the thought. "I don't think it could have been worse."

"Oh, Sean, it could have been a dozen times worse." Sheila took a chair near Sean and touched him lightly on the shoulder. "Emily could have struck her head, or you could have fallen down, too . . . a thousand different things could have happened." Sheila fought the shudder of apprehension that took hold of her when she considered how dangerous the accident could have been. "Look, Sean, you did everything right. You got Emily out of the water and carried her to me. Thank you."

Sean was perplexed and confused. "You're thanking me . . . why?"

"For clear thinking, and taking care of my little girl."

"Miss Lindstrom—"

"Sheila."

Sean shifted uncomfortably on the chair. He was still carrying the weight of guilt for Emily's accident and had transformed from a tough punk teenager into a frightened boy. "Okay . . . Sheila . . . I'm . . . sorry for the way I acted last night."

"It's okay."

"But I was crummy to you."

Sheila couldn't disagree. "You were."

"Then why aren't you mad at me?"

"Is that what you want?" Sheila inquired, taking a sip from her coffee.

Noah had heard the end of the conversation and stood in the door awaiting Sean's response to Sheila's question.

Sean looked Sheila in the eye, unaware that his father was standing less than five feet behind him. "I don't know." He shrugged, some of his old bravado resurfacing. "I just didn't want to like you."

Sheila's eyes flicked from Sean to Noah and back again. "Because you were afraid that I might take your father from you?"

Again the blond youth shrugged.

"I would never do that, Sean. I have a daughter of my own, and I know how important it is that we have each other. No one could *ever* take me away from my child. I'm sure the same is true of your father."

Sean looked at Sheila, silently appraising her. His next words shattered the friendliness between them. "My dad still cares for my mom!" His look dared her to argue with him.

"I'm sure he does, Sean," Sheila agreed, silencing Noah with her eyes. "And I don't intend to change that."

Knowing that Noah was about to break in on the conversation, and hoping to avoid another confrontation, Sheila changed the topic. "Emily made some brownies for you earlier, but she must have forgotten them with all of the excitement about fishing." She rose from the table and began putting the chocolate squares on a plate. Noah entered the room, but Sheila ignored him. "Why don't you take this into Emily—cheer her up?"

"Do you think she'll want to see me? She might be sleeping or something.'"

"She's awake," Noah stated. "I just left her, and believe it or not, I think she's hungry."

Sean grabbed the plate of brownies and, balancing them between two glasses of milk, left the kitchen in the direction of Emily's room. Without asking if he wanted any, Sheila poured Noah a cup of coffee.

"How's *your* leg?" Noah asked, eyeing Sheila skeptically.

"Never better. I cleaned it and it's okay. A little of the skin is scraped off, that's all."

Noah took an experimental sip from his coffee as he looked dubiously at her white slacks. "Did Dr. Embers look at it."

"No."

"Why not?"

"I told you I cleaned it and bandaged it. Look, it's really no big deal."

Noah didn't look convinced. "I'm just sorry that you and Emily had to suffer because of Sean's neglect."

"Noah, please. Don't blame him. He's just a child himself."

"He's sixteen and has to learn responsibility some time. He should have been more careful."

"He knows that—-don't reprimand him. It would be

like rubbing salt into his wound. He feels badly enough as it is."

"He should."

"Why? Because he was careless? Noah, accidents will happen. Give the kid a break, will you?"

Noah set his cup down on the table and walked over to the sink. For a few silent moments he stared out the window into the night. "It's not just the accident, Sheila. It's his attitude. You were there the night he came home drunk. It wasn't the first time." He breathed deeply and tilted his head back while squinting his eyes shut. "He's in trouble at school and I've even had to pick him up downtown. Since he's a minor, he hasn't been in jail, but he's been close, damned close. He missed a couple of probation meetings, and so now he's walking a very thin line with the law."

"A lot of kids get into trouble."

"I know. I should count myself lucky that he doesn't use dope, I guess."

Sheila approached Noah and wrapped her arms around his waist. How long had he tortured himself with guilt for his son? "Sean will be all right, Noah. I've seen more kids than you'd want to count in my job, some easier to deal with than Sean, others more difficult. Sean will come through this."

He put his large hands over hers, pressing her fingertips into his abdomen. "Why did you let him lie to you?"

"About what?"

"His mother. You know how I feel about Marilyn."

"Sean probably does, too. But he can't admit it to me, not yet. He still considers me a threat."

"I think you're reading more into this than there really is."

"Adolescence is tough, Noah, or don't you remember?

Add to that the fact that Sean knows his mother rejected him. It makes him feel inferior."

"Lots of kids grow up without one parent . . . even Emily."

"And it's hard on her, too," Sheila sighed against his back.

Noah turned around and faced her. One hand pushed aside her hair as he studied her face and noticed the thin lines of worry that dimmed her smile. He pressed a kiss to her forehead. "You're a very special woman, Sheila Lindstrom, and I love you." He traced the edge of her cheekbones with his finger. "It's times like these that I wonder how I managed to live this long without you."

Sheila warmed under his unguarded stare. "I guess you must have a will of iron," she teased.

"Or maybe it's because I'm a stubborn fool." He draped his arm possessively over her shoulder and guided her out of the kitchen. "Let's go check on Emily."

"In a minute. . . . You go look in on her, I'll be there shortly." She moved out of his embrace and pushed him down the hall. "I've got to make a phone call."

Noah looked at his wristwatch. "Now? To whom?"

She was ready for his question. "I think I'd better call Jeff."

"You're ex-husband?" Noah was incredulous. "Why?"

"He has the right to know about the accident," Sheila attempted to explain. Before she could get any further, Noah cut her off and his mouth pulled into a contemptuous scowl. A thousand angry questions came to his mind.

"Do you think he would even care?"

"Noah, he's Emily's father. Of course he'll care."

"From what you've told me about him, he hasn't shown much fatherly concern for his daughter!"

"Keep your voice down!" Sheila warned in a harsh whisper. "Jeff has to know."

Noah's face contorted with disgust. The skin stretched tightly over the angled planes of his features. "Are you sure the accident isn't some handy excuse?"

Sheila's gray eyes snapped. "I don't need an excuse.

He has to know and I can't have him hear it through the grapevine."

"Why not?"

"How would you feel if it were Sean?"

"That's different. I care about my son. I would have done anything to have him with me. It was a little different with your husband, I'd venture to guess."

"He's still her legal father. This is a rural community, but word travels quickly. I either have to call Jeff or his mother, and I'd prefer not to worry Marian. If I call her now, she'll be over here within a half hour."

"And what about Coleridge? Is that what he'll do— come racing over here to check on his daughter and his ex-wife. Is that what you're hoping for?"

"You're impossible!" Sheila accused. "But you're right about one thing, I would be thrilled to pieces if Jeff came over here."

"I thought so," he commented dryly as he crossed his arms over his chest and leaned against the wall, looking as if he were both judge and jury. She, of course, was the unconvincing defendant.

"But not for the reasons you think," she continued, trying to stem her boiling anger. "Jeff is Emily's father,' for God's sake. She's just been through a very traumatic experience, and I think she could use a little support from Daddy."

"A little is all she'd get, at the very best," Noah pointed out in a calm voice. His blue eyes looked deadly. "Jeff Coleridge is no more Emily's father than Marilyn is

Sean's mother! I can't believe that you're still hanging onto ideals that were shot down years ago when he walked out on you and your kid. Sheila. You don't have to paint the picture any rosier than it really is. It's not good for you, and it's not good for Emily."

"So look who's handing out free advice—*Father of the year!*" The minute her words were out, she wanted to call them back. She hadn't meant to be cruel.

Noah's hands clenched and then relaxed against his rib cage. "Once again, the sharp tongue cuts like a whip, Miss Lindstrom. I'm not trying to hurt you, I'm only attempting to suggest that genetics has nothing to do with being a parent. Oh, sure, Coleridge *sired* your child, but where was he when the chips were down? Or have you conveniently forgotten that he walked out on you and took up with another woman? A man like that doesn't deserve to know that his child was hurt. Face it, Sheila, he just doesn't give a damn."

Sheila's nerves were strung as tightly as a piano string, her voice emotionless. "Each summer Emily spends a few weeks with Jeff. He's expecting her by the end of next week."

"Does she want to see him?"

Sheila wavered. "She's confused about it."

Noah's lips twisted wryly. "What you're saying is that she knows he doesn't want her, and you're hoping that when he learns of the accident, he'll rush to her side and reestablish himself as a paragon of virtue in her eyes. Don't delude yourself, Sheila, and for Emily's sake, don't try to make your ex-husband something he's not. Let her make up her own mind."

"She will," Sheila said softly, "whether I call him or not. But I am going to call, you know. It's his right as a father."

"He has no rights—he gave them up about four years ago, wouldn't you say?"

For a moment they stared across the room at each other, trying to repair the damage their argument had caused, but it was impossible. "Excuse me," Sheila said shakily, "but this is my decision." She turned to the telephone and dialed the long-distance number to Spokane.

Noah turned on his heel, uttered a low oath, and headed down the hall toward Emily's room. Women! Would he ever live to understand them?

Chapter Eleven

Though never mentioned again, the argument hung over Noah and Sheila like a dark. foreboding cloud. Noah had decided to spend another week at the winery to double-check Anthony Simmons's conclusions concerning the fire. Sean was entrusted with Noah's car and sent back to Seattle to pick up a couple of changes of clothes and some documents from the office of Wilder Investments. The boy was back at Cascade Valley as he had promised, the car intact.

For his part, Noah was a whirlwind. He decided it was in the best interests of Wilder Investments to reopen the winery, and he began a full-scale cleanup of the estate. It took some fast talking, but even the local sheriff's department had reluctantly complied with his demands that the west wing be completely reconstructed. By late Friday afternoon D & M Construction, a subsidiary of Wilder Investments, had moved in, and the foreman was working with an architect to redesign the building.

Days at the winery were spent preparing for the autumn harvest; the nights making love. Noah didn't mention Jeff again, and Sheila hoped that the harsh words shouted in the heat of anger would soon be forgotten.

Noah began a furious study of viticulture, with Sheila

and Dave Jansen as his tutors. Dave was a young man whose serious, plain face was offset by laughing brown eyes. He took Noah on a tour of the vineyards and explained, endlessly, the reasons that wine production was suited for the valley.

"Thirty years ago, few people thought that western Washington could hold a candle to California for wine production," he declared, proudly showing off a hillside covered with vinifera wine grapes.

"But you're changing their minds, right?" Noah asked.

"You got it. Everybody thinks it rains all the time in Washington, or that it's overcast, but that's because they haven't seen the eastern part of the state. Over here our summers are warm and dry with extremely low precipitation and cloud cover. This allows for a unique combination of moderate heat, high light intensity and long days that produce vinifera fruit with an excellent sugar-acid balance. All of our wines have a distinctive varietal character."

"But what about the winters? A couple of years ago the late snow just about wiped out the crop."

Dave nodded gravely. "That can happen," he admitted. "We try to select our vineyard sights as close as possible to the Columbia River. We use southern slopes above the valley floor to further decrease the risk of low temperatures. Recently we've been planting a hardier grape, a vinifera that can stand colder temperatures."

Noah's gaze ran skeptically over the vineyards.

"Really, this is a great place to produce wine," Dave stated firmly. "Look, Mr. Wilder—"

"Noah."

Dave smiled and inclined his head. "I know that Sheila's had a run of bad luck here, but for my money, Cascade Valley will produce the best wine in the country."

"That's a pretty broad statement."

Dave pursed his lips and shook his balding head. "I don't think so." He held up his fingers to add emphasis to his point. "Eastern Washington has a good climate, the right amount of light, loamy soils, and is relatively free of pests and disease. I don't think you can do better than that."

Noah squatted and ran his fingers through the soil. "So what's to prevent a competitor from building next to Cascade Valley?"

"Name familiarity and reputation," Dave replied quickly.

"A reputation that has been tarnished over the last few years."

"Yeah. I can't deny that, much as I'd like to," Dave conceded, opening the door to his pickup. "Want a lift back to the house? I'd like you to take a look at our latest investment, French oak barrels for aging instead of American white oak. They were Oliver's idea. He used a few of them several years ago and the end result is our reserve Cabernet Sauvignon, which we hope to market later this year.

"I think I'll walk back to the house," Noah decided. "I'll catch you tomorrow because I would like to see the reserve bottles."

"All right. See you then." The battered old pickup took off, leaving a plume of dust in its wake. Noah placed his hands, palms outward, in the back pockets of his jeans as he walked back to the house. He was lost in thought, considering all of the disasters that had struck Cascade Valley in the past few years. No one could be blamed for the volcanic eruption of Mount Saint Helens. The tonnage of ash and soot that had fallen on Cascade Valley and destroyed the harvest would have to be attributed to an act of God, or natural disaster. But the tampered bottles found in Montana were a different story. The contamination had been planned rather than accidental. Needle marks found in the corks of some of the damaged bottles proved that someone had to have been behind the sabotage.

Originally Noah had assumed that Oliver Lindstrom had executed the poisoning of the bottles; now he wasn't so sure. The image painted by people he had spoken with told him that Oliver Lindstrom wasn't the kind of man who would destroy all that he had worked so hard to build. If, as Sheila and the staff maintained, Cascade Valley Wines and the winery itself were Oliver Lindstrom's lifeblood, why would he want to tarnish a reputation it had taken years to establish?

Noah squinted against the setting sun and kicked a stone out of the rutted dirt road. It just didn't make sense. If a man needed money, he wouldn't consciously taint his product, thereby causing an expensive recall and losing consumer trust. Could Lindstrom really have been as desperate as Anthony Simmons wanted Noah to believe: desperate enough to take his own life in an arson attempt? The damned fire—always that damned fire— continued to plague Noah with doubts. As he walked up the final crest of the hill supporting the château, he stopped to look at the wreckage.

A disappearing sun cast red-gold rays over the charred timbers of the west wing. A yellow bulldozer was parked near the blackened building, waiting to raze the sagging skeleton. Noah ran his fingers through his hair as he studied the destruction. If only he didn't care about Sheila, it would be much easier.

Sheila was tearing the old wallpaper off the walls in the dining room when the doorbell rang.

"Emily," she called, pulling at an obstinate strip,

"could you get that? Emily?" There was no immediate response, and Sheila remembered Emily mentioning something about going outside with Sean. Her ankle was much better, and she was feeling more than a little cooped up in the house.

The doorbell rang again impatiently. "Coming," Sheila called as she wiped her hands on a nearby towel. Who could be calling today? she wondered. It was nearly the dinner hour, and she was a mess. Her jeans and blouse smelled like the sooty walls she had been cleaning, and her hair was piled in a bedraggled twist on the top of her head. She pulled out the pins and ran her fingers through it as she made her way to the door.

Before she could open it, the door swung open and Jeff Coleridge poked his head into the foyer. "So there is someone home after all," he remarked dryly, his eyes giving Sheila a quick head to heels appraisal.

Sheila managed a thin smile. "Sorry—I thought Emily would get the door."

"And I thought she was laid up," he replied with a smirk. "Or was this just one of your rather obvious attempts to see me?"

Sheila's gray eyes didn't waver. "That was a long time ago."

"Not that long."

Sheila stood in the entryway, not letting him pass. "I assume you came here to see Emily."

"Who else?" His smile was as devilish as ever, his dark eyes just as flirtatious. He was still handsome; living the good life seemed to suit him well. His lean torso reflected hours on the tennis courts, and his devil-may-care attitude added to his cunning charm. After all of these years, Sheila was immune to it.

"I hope no one. Emily's outside. I'll go and get her."

"Sheila, baby." He reached out a hand and touched her wrist. "What is our darling daughter doing out of bed—I thought she had some horrible ankle sprain. At least that's the story you gave me."

Trying desperately not to be baited, Sheila withdrew her wrist and pasted a plastic copy of his saccharine smile on her face. "That was no story, and if you would have shown up a few days ago, you would have found her in bed. Fortunately she's young and heals quickly."

"Now, now," he cajoled, noting the sarcasm dripping from her words. "Your claws are showing, sweetheart. You know I couldn't come any sooner."

"You could have called."

"Is that what you wanted?"

"What I wanted was for you to show some interest in your child. She's not a baby anymore, Jeff, and she's beginning to understand how you feel about her."

"I'll just bet she does," he snapped, losing his calm veneer of self-assurance. "With you poisoning her mind against me."

"You know I don't do anything of the kind." Sheila's face was sincere, her gray eyes honest and pained. "You handle that part of it well enough on your own."

Jeff's frown turned to a pout. "I thought we were supposed to have a 'friendly divorce,' isn't that what you wanted?"

"When I was naive enough to believe it."

"I suppose you think that's my fault, too.'

"Not really. We couldn't get along while we were married; I should never have expected that the divorce would change anything."

"You act as if it's carved in stone."

"I wish I thought it wasn't," Sheila sighed, leaning against the door.

"So what do you want now, Sheila?" His eyes narrowed suspiciously as he looked down upon her.

"I want you to be an interested father, Jeff. And I don't want it to be an act. Is that too much to ask?"

Jeff took in a deep breath, attempting to stem the rage that took hold of him every time he saw Sheila and was reminded of her quiet beauty. It unnerved him. Perhaps it was her fiery spirit coupled with her wide, understanding eyes. There had been a time in his life when he had been proud to show her off as *his* wife. But she wanted more—she wanted a child, for God's sake. Not that Emily wasn't a great kid . . . he just didn't like the idea of fatherhood. It made him feel so *old*. If only Sheila would have given a little more, seen things his way, maybe the two of them would have made it.

Even in dusty jeans and a sooty blouse, with a black smudge where her hands had touched her cheek, she looked undeniably beautiful. Her hair fell in a tangled mass around her face, the way he liked it, and she still carried herself with an elegance and grace he had never seen in another woman—even Judith. Whereas Judith's beauty was beginning to fade, Sheila's was just beginning to blossom.

Jeff cleared his throat and tried to ignore Sheila's intent stare. He coughed before answering her question. "You know I care about Emily," he said with a shrug of his shoulders. "It's just that I've never been comfortable with kids."

"You've never tried. Not even with your own."

Jeff shook his head, and he looked at the boards of the porch. "That's where you're wrong, Sheila. I did try, honestly . . ."

"But you couldn't find it in your heart to love her."

"I didn't say that." His eyes lifted to meet the disgust and rage simmering in hers.

"You have never loved anyone in your life, Jeff Coleridge, except yourself."

"That's what I've always liked about you, Sheila: your sweet, even-tempered disposition."

Sheila was shaking, but she attempted to regain her poise. If only she could look at Jeff indifferently. If only she didn't see a man who rejected his infant when she looked into his eyes. "This argument is getting us nowhere," she said through tight lips. The strain of trying to communicate with Jeff was getting to her. "Why don't you come into the kitchen and wait while I get Emily. She's just on the patio."

Jeff hesitated, as if he wanted to say something more, but decided against it. Sheila stepped backward, allowing him to pass, and tried to calm her anxious nerves. When she found Emily, she didn't want to infect the child with her worries about the disintegrating relationship between father and daughter.

She stepped onto the patio and drew in a steadying breath. Emily was watching Noah and Sean trying to outdo one another in a Frisbee throwing contest. Emily was giggling in excitement, Noah was concentrating on the returning Frisbee and Sean was smiling with satisfaction, sure that the plastic disc would elude his father. It was a tender scene, a family scene, and it pulled at Sheila's heartstrings knowing she had to destroy it.

"Emily," she called softly. "Someone's here to see you."

"Who?" Emily demanded, riveted to her spot and eyeing Noah's ungraceful catch. He flipped the Frisbee back at his son.

"Daddy's come to see you."

Emily's smile faded. "My daddy?"

Sheila's grin felt as phony as it was. "Isn't that great?"

"He's not going to take me with him to Spokane, is he?"

"Of course not, honey," Sheila said with unfelt

enthusiasm. "He just came to see how you're doing
with that ankle of yours." Pushing aside an errant curl
around her daughter's face, Sheila continued. "Come
on. He's waiting in the kitchen."

"No, I'm not," Jeff's cheery voice called as he
walked out the door. He smiled down at his daughter.
"It's been a long trip, and I couldn't wait any longer." It
was then, when his eyes lifted from his daughter's serious gaze, that he noticed Noah and Sean. The game had
ended and Noah was staring intently at the man who
had once been Sheila's husband. "Pardon me," Jeff
announced with a wary, well-practiced smile. "I don't
believe we've met."

Noah strode slowly up to the patio, his blue eyes
challenging Jeff's dark ones. Sheila could see that every
muscle in Noah's body had become rigid, the skin
drawn taut. 'The name's Wilder," he stated. "Noah
Wilder. This—" he cocked his head in the direction of
the blond boy in cut-off jeans "—is my son, Sean." He
extended his hand, took Jeff's and gave it a short, but
firm, shake.

"Jeff Coleridge."

Noah's smile twisted as if smiling at a private irony.
"I assumed as much."

"Wilder?" Jeff's eyes followed Noah's movements as
he placed his body between those of ex-husband and
wife. The move was subtle, but not lost on either Sheila
or Jeff. "You're connected with Wilder Investments?"

"My father's company."

"Ben Wilder is *your* father?" A note of genuine respect
and surprise entered Jeff's voice.

"That's right." Noah didn't return Jeff's growing
smile.

"Oh . . . so you're here because of the winery . . . as

a business partner to Sheila?" Jeff assumed. He seemed relieved.

"Partly."

"I don't understand."

"Noah is Mommy's friend," Emily interjected.

"Is that right?" Jeff's thin eyebrows raised, and his accusing dark eyes impaled Sheila.

There was an awkward silence while Sheila struggled with the proper words. Both men regarded her intently. From the corner of her eye, Sheila noticed that Sean was walking toward the orchard, away from the uncomfortable scene. An embarrassed flush crept up her neck, but her eyes never wavered, and her voice was surprisingly steady. "Yes, that's right. Noah is a friend of mine, a very good friend."

The nasty retort forming on Jeff's lips died under the power of Noah's stare and the innocent, wondering eyes of his child He didn't want to appear the fool. "I see," he returned vaguely, as if he really didn't understand at all. Then, as if dismissing the entire conversation as something that should have been swept under the rug, he pulled at the crease in his pants and bent on one knee to talk to his daughter. He took one of Emily's little hands and pressed it between his own. He considered it a very fatherly gesture. "So tell me, Emmy, how're you feeling?"

"Fine." Emily was suddenly shy as she found herself the center of attention.

"You're sure now? How about that ankle?"

"It's okay."

"Good . . . that's good. Are you going to tell me all about your fall in the creek?"

"Do you really want to know?" Emily asked skeptically.

Jeff's thin smile wavered. "Of course I do, precious," he replied, patting the top of her hand nervously. He led her over to the chaise lounge and indicated that she should sit with him. "Why don't you tell me all about it?" He pressed the tip of his finger awkwardly against her nose.

Noah felt his stomach lurch at Coleridge's stumbling attempts at paternity. While the man turned all of his attention upon his child, Noah took his leave, heading in the direction of the west wing.

Sheila watched Noah stride angrily across the yard, and she had to suppress the urge to run after him. Until she was assured that Emily was comfortable with Jeff, Sheila felt her responsibility was to remain with her child.

Noah was soon out of sight and Sheila swung her eyes back toward Jeff and Emily. Her gaze met the brittle dark stare of her ex-husband. "How long has *he* been here?" he sneered.

"About a week."

"Do you think that's such a good idea?"

"He's helping me reestablish the winery."

"I bet he is." The insinuation in Jeff's flat statement couldn't be ignored.

"Look, Jeff. I like Noah. . . . I like him a lot. Not that it's any concern of yours."

"He's an arrogant SOB, don't you think?"

Sheila's eyes flew to Emily's young face and then back to Jeff, silently warning him against any further derogatory remarks while Emily was close at hand.

"I think he's a very kind and considerate man."

"And I'm not?"

"I didn't say that." Sheila shot Jeff another threatening glance. "Would you like a cup of coffee?" Somehow she had to change the course of the conversation, for Emily's sake.

Jeff tried to relax and appear comfortable. "Got

anything stronger?" he inquired, running a shaky hand through his neatly combed hair.

"I think so."

"Good." He let out his breath. "Make it a vodka martini."

"All right. It will take me a few minutes." He didn't argue. He, too, must have been looking for a way to avoid further disagreement. Sheila turned toward the house, her eyes still searching for Noah, when Jeff's voice reached her. "With a twist, okay?"

She nodded curtly without glancing back in his direction, muttering under her breath, "With a twist . . . with a twist." Sheila had forgotten how demanding Jeff could be—a real pain in the neck. Damn him for ruining the peaceful afternoon. Damn him for interrupting what she had hoped would be an intimate *family* meal.

That was the problem, wasn't it? She considered Noah and Sean as part of the family, while she looked upon Jeff as an outsider, an intruder who would only cause trouble.

Her chestnut hair swept across her shoulders as she shook her head at her own foolishness. What had she expected? she asked herself as she walked into the den.

She was startled to find Noah sitting at the desk, going over the original blueprints for the west wing of the château. A pencil was in his hand, its lead point tapping restlessly on the yellowed paper. He didn't move when he heard the sound of Sheila's sandaled feet enter the room, nor did he speak. Instead he stared broodingly at the blueprints, seemingly engrossed in the faded drawing. Sheila could feel the rift between them deepen, and she wondered if she had the courage to bridge it.

"I'm sorry you had to witness all of that," she began as she moved across the room to the bar to pull out a bottle of vodka. The pencil stopped its erratic tapping on the desk.

Noah's voice was controlled to the point of exasperation. "Don't apologize to me. It's none of my concern."

"But it is," she disagreed. "And I didn't mean for it to turn into a circus."

"Didn't you? Don't kid yourself, Sheila. You were the one who invited him here. How could you possibly expect things to turn out differently?" ·

"I had no choice. I had to tell him about Emily and invite him to visit her."

"Save it, Sheila. I've heard all this before."

She could read the anger in the crunch of his shoulders, feel his questions begging for answers, see the pride in the lift of his chin. "Please, Noah," she pleaded, setting the mixed drink aside. "Don't shut me out."

"Is that what I'm doing?" He tossed the pencil down on the desk and rubbed his hands wearily against the back of his neck.

"Aren't you?"

"No!" He got out of the chair and faced her for the first time since she entered the room. Ignoring the pain in her eyes, he wagged an accusing finger in her face. "I'll tell you what I'm doing," he stated hoarsely, "I'm sitting on the sidelines, hoping to hold on to my patience, which isn't exactly my long suit to begin with, while the woman I love clings to some faded, rose-colored memories of a past and a marriage that didn't exist."

"I'm not—"

"I'm trying *not* to throw out a conniving jerk whose fumbling attempts at being a father border on the pathetic, for the sake of holding up appearances!"

"Jeff's just trying to—"

"And," his voice increased in volume, "I'm attempting,

Lord knows I'm not good at this sort of thing, but I'm trying damn it, to understand how a beautiful, sensitive woman like you could have ever gotten tangled up with a creep like Jeff Coleridge in the first place." The cords in Noah's neck were bulging, the muscles in his shoulders tight, the line of his mouth curled in distaste. He looked as if at any moment all of his simmering anger might explode.

Sheila picked up the martini with trembling hands. "I think that's enough," she whispered, her wide eyes unseeing. Her voice shook with the wounded tears of pride that had settled in her throat as she turned toward the door.

Noah was beside her in an instant, and his powerful arm reached out to impede her departure. He twisted her back to face him and the drink fell to the floor, breaking the glass and spilling the colorless liquid.

"No, Sheila," he stated through clenched teeth, "You're wrong." He ignored the shattered glass and the pooling liquid. He gave her arm a shake to make sure she was giving him all of her attention. "I love you," he admitted, the hardness in his gaze beginning to soften. "I didn't want to fall in love with you. I fought it . . . I fought it like hell . . . but I lost." His grip loosened on her arm, but she didn't move as she was spellbound by the honesty in his eyes. "And I have no intention of letting you go—not to that snake you once called a husband. Not to anyone."

Sheila felt her anger beginning to wither. Her gray eyes were colored by her conflicting emotions. "Then, please . . . please try and understand that I'm only putting up with Jeff because of Emily."

"Do you think you're fooling that child?"

"I'm not trying to fool her. I'm just trying not to bias her opinion of her dad."

"By letting him intrude where he's not wanted?" His eyes left hers to stare at the spilled drink. "By jumping at his every whim?" He touched her cheek tenderly. "Or by covering up his mistakes and omissions?"

"By letting her make her own decision."

"Then let her see him as he really is."

The muscles in his jawline tensed. "How important to you is Jeff Coleridge?" he demanded.

"He's the father of my child."

"Nothing more?"

"He once was," she admitted. "I can't deny that, and I wouldn't try to. But that was a long time ago. Please believe me, Noah, I'm not in love with him. I don't know if I ever was."

Noah wrapped his arms tightly around her slim shoulders, and she could feel the warmth of his body where his arms touched her. Tenderly he brushed the smudge of soot from her cheek. "All right, Sheila," he said with a reluctant sigh. "I'll try and tolerate that jerk. But, believe me, if he gets obnoxious with you or Emily, I'm not going to apologize for throwing him out on his ear. Fair enough?"

Sheila's smile spread slowly over her lips, showing just a hint of her white teeth. "Fair enough," she agreed.

"Now, why don't you work on dinner, let Jeff and Emily be alone, and I'll finish up with the blueprints."

"Only if you promise to clean up this mess," she suggested, flipping her open palm toward the spilled drink, "and pour Jeff another vodka martini."

"Not on your life, lady. Doting on that man is where I draw the line. If he wants a drink badly enough, he can damn well come in and mix his own."

Sheila laughed and clucked her tongue. "Not very hospitable, are you?" she teased.

Noah raised an inquiring eyebrow. "Can you blame me?"

"No," she admitted with a trace of wistfulness, "I really can't. But, do *try* to be civil."

"If that's what you want," he conceded. "But for the life of me, I don't understand why."

She wrapped her arms around his neck and stood on her toes. "It won't kill you," she pointed out.

"No, I suppose not. But watching him drool over you might."

"You're imagining things." She kissed him lightly on the lips.

The muscles in his body reached out to hers. She felt his thighs straining against hers, his chest flattening her breasts, his arms pressing against the small of her back. "The kinds of things I imagine with you are very private. They have nothing to do with your ex-husband." His lips brushed against hers and his tongue rimmed her lips. "Let's get rid of him and put the kids to bed early." Sheila laughed against his mouth. "Somehow I don't think Sean would take kindly to going to bed at six thirty."

"Spoilsport." Slowly he released her.

She started toward the door, but paused to look over her shoulder at him and give an exaggerated wink. "Later," she promised throatily.

The rest of the evening was uncomfortable but tolerable. Jeff stayed for dinner and looked stiff and ill at ease with Noah, Sean and Emily. His perfectly pressed suit had become wrinkled, his hair unruly and his eyes begged Sheila to find some excuse to get him away from Noah's intense, uncompromising stare. Noah was polite but quiet, and his blue eyes very rarely strayed from Sheila's ex-husband. It made Jeff uncomfortable; the man's stare bordered on the eerie.

Jeff made his excuses, begged off dessert and was back on his way to Spokane long before eight o'clock. Even Emily seemed relieved that she didn't have to go back to her father's sterile apartment and persnickety old wife, Judith, at least for a few more weeks.

For the first time in over a week the dark cloud of argument between Sheila and Noah had disappeared, and they made impassioned love without the shadow of Jeff Coleridge hanging over their heads.

Chapter Twelve

The end of Noah's stay came much too quickly for Sheila. The fact that he hadn't been clear about his decision concerning the status of the winery worried her. She knew that he wanted to rebuild the west wing—the construction crew that had been razing the old structure was proof enough of that—but still he was hesitant. It was as if he were keeping something from her. She could feel his reluctance whenever she would broach the subject of the fall harvest. As far as she could tell, it had to be something to do with the fire.

It was morning on Noah's final day at Cascade Valley when Sheila summoned the courage to bring up the fire and Anthony Simmons's report. Over the past week Noah had managed to dodge the issue, but this morning Sheila told herself she had to have answers—straight ones.

The first rays of dawn filtered through the terrace doors to bathe Sheila's room in a golden aura of dim morning light. Dewdrops clung to the underside of the green leaves of the clematis that grew against the glass doors, and the chill of the mountain night hadn't disappeared.

Noah was still asleep, his face pressed against the pillow. Sheila slowly extracted herself from his embrace, and while still lying near to him on the antique bed, stared at his sleeping form. The dark profile of his face, etched in relief against the ice blue sheets, seemed innocent in slumber. The powerful muscles were relaxed, the corners of his·eyes soft. His near-black hair was unruly and would seem almost boyish if it hadn't been for the contrast of his shadowy beard.

Sheila felt her throat tighten at the sight of him sleeping, oblivious to any of the anxieties that aged his face. He seemed incredibly vulnerable, and it touched the deepest, most feminine part of her. She wanted to smooth back his hair and comfort him. *I love him*, she thought to herself. I love him too much. This is the kind of blind love that can be dangerous, the kind of self-sacrificing, unreturned love that can only cause pain. It's a love that causes dependency and inspires jealousy, like a drug addiction. More than anything else in the world. I want to be with this man, to be a part of him. I want my life to blend with his, my family to be one with his, my blood to run in his body.

She bent over and kissed him softly on the forehead. I know he cares for me—he says he loves me—but I know that he is hiding something from me. He won't let himself trust me.

She drew herself away from him and got out of the bed. After snuggling into the downy folds of a cream-colored velour bathrobe, she once again sat on the edge of the bed, content to watch the even rise and fall of Noah's chest as he lay entwined in the sheets. Why won't you tell me, she wondered. Why won't you tell me everything about the fire? What are you hiding from me?

Noah rolled over onto his back and raised an exploratory eyelid against the invading morning sunlight. His dimpled smile slowly emerged as his gaze focused on her. "God, you look incredible," he growled as he wrapped an arm around her waist and pulled her down beside him on the bed.

"Noah," she whispered, trying to ignore the deliciously warm feel of his lips against her throat. "We have to talk."

"Later." His fingers found the zipper on her bathrobe and slowly lowered it.

Against the yearnings of her body, she put her hand over his to impede the zipper's progress. "Now."

"Let's not waste time with talk," he grumbled as he kissed the exposed tops of her breasts. The zipper slid lower, and the downy robe parted. "This is my last morning here," he murmured against her bared skin. Sheila felt her pulse jump and the blood begin to heat in her veins.

She attempted to clutch the robe together. "Precisely why we have to talk now." She tossed her hair away from her face and looked him steadily in the eye as she disentangled herself from his persuasive grip. Her breath was uneven as she eased her body off the bed.

After somewhat shakily taking a seat in one of the chairs near the terrace, she nervously ran her fingers over the open neckline of her robe. Noah propped himself on one elbow, raked his fingers through his dark hair and stared at her with amused, but smoldering, blue eyes. The sheet was draped across his body, exposing the hard muscles of his chest and leaving his lower torso covered. "All right, Sheila, out with it."

"What?" She really didn't know where to begin.

"The inquisition."

"You're expecting one?" She was surprised.

"I'd have to be a fool not to know that before I went back to Seattle, you and I would have a showdown about the fire. That is what this is all about, isn't it?"

Sheila's eyes narrowed suspiciously, and her fingers

stopped toying with the collar of her robe. "I just want to know why you've been avoiding the issue of the fire and the rebuilding of the west wing."

"Because I hadn't made a decision." His honest blue eyes begged her understanding and patience.

"But you have now?"

"I think so."

"Well?"

The corners of Noah's eyes twitched. I'm going to transfer a quarter of a million dollars into an escrow account from Wilder Investments when I get back to Seattle. The money will be in escrow for the express purpose of rebuilding Cascade Valley."

Sheila's smile froze on her face as she read the hesitation in his gaze. "But what about the insurance company . . . and that report by Anthony Simmons?"

Noah waved off her questions as if they were bothersome insects. "Don't worry about that end of it; that's my problem."

Sheila held back a million questions, but the one nagging doubt in her mind refused to die. Her voice was hoarse. "But what about my father's name? Will you be able to clear it?" she asked cautiously. The look of sincere concern in her light gray eyes pierced him to the soul, and he found his deception entrapping him. He had decided not to tell her anything about the fire or Simmons's report, knowing full well that what he would have to disclose to her would only cause her more pain. In his mind she had borne more than her share. He couldn't add to it.

"I hope so," he whispered, damning himself for his duplicity.

She sighed with relief and closed her eyes.

"We do have another problem to consider."

She smiled wryly and opened her eyes to study him. "Only one?" she asked sarcastically.

He laughed aloud. How long had it been since he'd laughed in the dawn? The thought of leaving Sheila sobered him, and he realized it was an impossible task. She sat across the room from him, her toes peeking out from the folds of creamy fabric, her hair beautiful in its coppery disarray. And her eyes, a warm gray, the color of liquid silver, surrounded by thick, sexy black lashes, watched his every movement. "Maybe we have two problems," he acquiesced with a slow smile. "The first is simple. If construction of the west wing is incomplete by harvest time, I'll lease a facility nearby and we'll still bottle under the Cascade label. It will be expensive, but better than selling our crop to the competition."

Sheila thoughtfully nodded her silent agreement.

"So that brings us to our next dilemma."

"If you come up with another blockbuster solution, like you did for the first problem, I doubt that there will be any dilemma at all," she quipped, smiling radiantly. At last she knew for certain that the winery would reopen. She couldn't help but smile.

Noah rubbed the edge of his chin before he tossed off the sheet, stood up and strode over to the chair in which she was sitting. Positioning his hands on either arm of the chair, he imprisoned her against the peach-colored cushions. "The solution depends entirely on you."

The corners of her mouth twitched, and a light of interest danced in her eyes. She cocked her head coquettishly and let the chestnut sheen of her hair fall over one cheek. "On me? How?"

His voice was low and serious, his gaze intent as it probed her eyes. "Sheila, I want you to marry me. Will you?"

Her playful smile disappeared as the meaning of his words sunk in. An overwhelming sense of ecstasy overtook her as her heart flipped over. "You want to get married?" she repeated, her voice filled with raw emotion.

"As quickly as possible."

Her self-assurance wavered. "Of course . . . I mean, I'd love to . . ." She shook her head. "This is coming out all wrong. I guess I just don't understand what's going on here."

"What's to understand?" His lean muscles entrapped her, and his lips nuzzled softly behind her ear. When he spoke, she could feel his warm breath against her hair. "Because I love you, Sheila. Haven't you been listening to what I've been saying to you for the better part of the week?"

"But . . . married?" she stammered. Visions of her first marriage filled her mind. She remembered the hope and the love, a gorgeous ivory lace gown that had yellowed with the lies and the faded dreams. She had rushed into marriage once, and though she loved Noah with all her heart, she was wary of making the same mistake again. The thought of losing him was too agonizing to her. "I . . . I don't know," she said, and the confusion she felt was reflected in the gray depths of her eyes.

The muscles of his arms tensed as he gripped the chair more savagely. "Why not?"

There were probably more than a dozen reasons, but Sheila couldn't think of them. Memories of Jeff closing the door in her face kept closing in on her. "Have you thought about the kids? How is this going to affect them?" She was grasping at straws, and they both knew it. He provided the perfect response.

"Can you honestly think of any better arrangement for Sean or Emily?"

"But that's no reason to get married . . . to provide another parent for your child."

"Of course it isn't. Think of it as a fringe benefit," he suggested. His hand had been touching the collar of her robe, gently rubbing the delicate bones surrounding her neck. Suddenly he stopped touching her and took a step backward. "Are you trying to find a polite way of telling me no?" he challenged, his features growing hard.

Sheila shook he head, tears of happiness welling in her eyes. He misread them.

"Then what is it? Certainly you're not satisfied with a casual *affair?*"

"No, no, of course not."

He crossed his arms over his chest, his blue eyes intent on hers. "Has this got something to do with Coleridge? Damn it! I knew he was still in your blood."

"He isn't. . . . It's just that I'm overwhelmed, Noah. I didn't expect any of this . . . I don't know what to say."

"A simple yes or no will do."

"If only it were simple." She wrapped her arms around herself as if protecting her body from a sudden chill. "I'd love to marry you . . ."

"But?"

"But I think it's all a little sudden." Why was she making up excuses? Why couldn't she just accept his vow of love?

As she looked into Noah's brooding eyes and honest, angular face, Sheila's doubts fled. If she knew nothing else, she realized that Noah Wilder wasn't the kind of man who would stoop to deceit. She shook her head as if shaking out the cobwebs of unclear thought that had confused her. "I'm sorry," she apologized shakily as she touched her fingertips to the solid wall of his chest. "It's just that you surprised me. The truth is that I love you and I can't think of anything I'd rather do than spend the rest of my life with you."

"Thank God," be declared prayerfully. He folded her into the strength of his arms and pressed his hungry lips to hers. A warm glow of happiness began to spread through her as her lips parted to accept the promise of his love. She closed her eyes and sighed against his mouth as she felt the robe slip off her shoulders and the chill of morning touch her skin when Noah guided her to the bed.

"Woman," he groaned against her skin, "I need you so desperately." She shivered in anticipation as she fell against the cool sheets and was warmed only by the gentle touch of the man she loved.

Sheila's life became a whirlwind. Between scanning blueprints submitted by architects, attempting to organize the interior designers sent by Wilder Investments and working with Dave Jansen on the fall harvest, Sheila had little time to dwell on the distance that kept her apart from Noah. She fell into bed exhausted each night and was up at the crack of dawn each morning. One hot summer day bled into another as June flowed into July.

Though Sheila was working herself to the bone, it was worth it. Everything seemed to be going her way. Jeff had called earlier in the week, and when Sheila had explained that Emily had reservations about visiting with him in Spokane, Jeff didn't press the issue. In fact, he had almost sounded *relieved* that he wouldn't have to entertain his child until later in the summer.

Emily missed Sean, but Sheila took that as a positive sign. She prayed that the two children would continue to get along after the marriage, whenever that was. Noah had been pressing Sheila for a date, even had gone so far as to suggest eloping. Sheila admitted to herself that running off to get married might be the best solution for all involved. She had once been married in an elaborate ceremony; it hadn't guaranteed success.

Perhaps this weekend, she mused to herself as she pressed her foot more heavily on the throttle of the car. The auto responded and climbed the Cascade Mountains more quickly. For the first time in four weeks, there had been a break in the work. The interior of the château was nearly completely restored to its original regal design. Only a few details remained unfinished. The fabric for the draperies was woven in Europe, hence the delay. But the walls had been resurfaced and painted, new wallpaper hung and the old stained burgundy carpet replaced by a new, elegant champagne-colored pile.

Emily was spending the weekend with her grandmother, and Sheila decided to visit Noah. He would be surprised, no doubt, as he hadn't expected to see her until all of the legal papers surrounding the refurbishing of the winery were complete, but when she hadn't been able to reach him by telephone, Sheila had thrown caution to the wind, packed a few clothes and jumped in her car·

It was a beautiful summer day, the mountain air fresh with the scent of wildflowers and pine trees, and Sheila had the confident feeling that nothing could ruin the feeling of exhilaration that claimed her. The prospect of spending a quiet weekend alone with Noah made her smile to herself and hum along to the pop music coming from the radio.

Nothing can possibly go wrong, she thought to herself as she turned up the circular drive of the Wilder estate. This weekend is going to be perfect. She smiled when she saw the familiar silver Volvo sitting near the garage. At least she had caught Noah at home.

She knocked on the door and waited for it to be answered. The mysterious smile that had spread across her face froze in place when the door was opened by a well-mannered, gray-haired man of near fifty. He was dressed in formal livery and displayed not one shred of emotion as he inquired as to the nature of her call.

A butler, Sheila thought wildly, not really understanding. Noah employed a butler? He hadn't mentioned hiring any servants in his telephone conversations. An uneasy feeling began to grip Sheila. Something was wrong.

"I'm here to see Mr. Wilder," Sheila explained to the outwardly skeptical butler.

"Is he expecting you?"

"No. You see, this is kind of a surprise."

The butler cocked a dubious gray eyebrow and his lips pressed into a thin, firm line. "You do know that Mr. Wilder isn't well. He isn't seeing visitors."

Sheila's eyes widened, and her heart leapt to her throat. What was this man saying? "What's wrong with him?" she demanded, fear claiming her emotions.

"Pardon me?"

Sheila forgot all sense of civility. "What's wrong with Noah? Was he hurt in an accident?" Her hands were shaking. "What happened?" How could this character out of *Upstairs Downstairs* take Noah's health so casually? She looked past the butler into the stone house, her eyes searching for some evidence that Noah was all right "Miss, if you will calm down! I wasn't speaking of Noah Wilder, but his father."

Sheila's eyes flew back to the butler. "Ben? Ben's here?"

The man in the doorway raised his nose a bit higher, but Sheila sensed kindliness in his sparkling hazel eyes. "Would you kindly state your name and business?"

"Oh, I'm sorry. I'm Sheila Lindstrom," she replied rapidly. Thank God Noah was safe. Her breath released slowly. "I'm . . . a friend of Noah's. Is . . . is he in?"

"Yes, of course, Miss Lindstrom. This way please." The butler seemed pleased that he had finally made sense of her appearance. He turned on a well-polished heel and escorted her into a formal living room.

It was a cold room, not at all like the warm den where she had met Noah. It was decorated in flat tones of silver and white, with only a sprinkling of blue pillows on the expensive, modern furniture. White walls, icy gray carpet and tall, unadorned windows. In the middle of it all, sitting near the unlit flagstone fireplace, was a man Sheila guessed to be Ben Wilder. He didn't bother to rise when she entered the room, and his smile looked forced, as cold as the early morning fog that settled upon Lake Washington.

"Miss Lindstrom," the butler announced quietly. "She's here to see your son."

At the mention of her name, Ben's interest surfaced. His faded eyes looked over her appraisingly, as if she were a thoroughbred at auction. Sheila felt an uncomfortable chill.

"Pleased to meet you, Miss·Lindstrom. I'm Noah's father.

"I thought so. I think I met you once, years ago . . ."

Ben was thoughtful for a moment. "I suppose you did. I came to the winery to see Oliver—by the way, please accept my condolences."

"Thank you." Sheila anxiously fingered the clasp on her purse. Where was Noah? The man sitting in the snowy chair was not anything she had expected. When she had met Ben Wilder he was robust and bursting with energy. Though it had only been nine years, Ben Wilder had aged nearly thirty. The pallor of his skin was gray, and his·hair had thinned. He still appeared tall, but there was a gauntness to his flesh that added years to his body. Ben Wilder was gravely ill.

"Did I hear someone at the door?" a female voice asked. Sheila turned to see a woman, younger than Ben by several years, walk into the room. She was graceful, and the smile that warmed her face seemed sincere. "This is Sheila Lindstrom," Ben said. "My wife, Katharine."

Katharine's smile wavered slightly. "Noah's mentioned you," she stated vaguely. "Would you care to have a seat?"

"Thank you, but I really did come to see Noah."

"Of course you did. He was outside with Sean. I think George has gone to find him."

Thank God, Sheila thought to herself as she settled onto the uncomfortable white couch. Katharine attempted to make conversation. "I was sorry to hear about your father, Sheila." Sheila nodded a polite response. "But I hear from Noah that you've made marvelous strides toward rebuilding the entire operation."

"We're getting there," Sheila replied uncomfortably.

"A big job for a young woman," Ben observed dryly.

Sheila managed a brave smile and turned the course of the conversation away from Cascade Valley. "I didn't know that you had come back from Mexico," she explained. "I should have called and let Noah know that I was planning to visit him here."

The silence was awkward, and Katharine fidgeted with the circle of diamonds around her thin neck while she studied the young woman in whom her son had shown such an avid interest. An interest that had taken him away from his duties of managing the business. Sheila Lindstrom was pretty, she thought to herself with amusement, but beautiful women had held no interest for her only son. What was so special about this one? She heard herself responding hollowly to Sheila's vague apology. "Don't worry about that," Katharine stated with a dismissive wave of her slim, fine-boned hand. "Noah's fond of you. Therefore, you're welcome anytime. No invitation is necessary."

"Did Noah tell you all the details that Anthony Simmons dug up on the fire?" Ben asked, bored with social amenities. It was time to get down to business. He reached for a cigar and rotated it gently in his fleshless hand.

Sheila felt her spine stiffen. "Only that the report was inconclusive," she replied, meeting his gaze squarely.

Ben smiled, still watching her over the cigar. He reached for a match, but was halted by his wife's warning glare. "I figured as much."

"Pardon me?" Sheila inquired, pressing the issue.

"I didn't think he told you everything "

"Ben!" Katharine's smooth voice held a steely note of caution. She lowered it slightly. "Let's not bore Miss Lindstrom with all this talk about business. Sheila, would you like to stay for dinner? It really would be no imposition. . . ."

Her voice faded as the sound of heavy, quick footsteps caught her attention. A wavering smile broadened her lips. "Noah, guess who dropped by?" she asked.

"What are you doing here?" Noah asked fiercely. Sheila turned to see if his question was intended for her. It was. His face was hard, set in rigid lines. A muscle near his jaw pulsed.

"I wanted to surprise you."

"You did!"

Sheila felt something wither inside her under his uncomfortable stare. He appeared more gaunt than the last time she had been with him. The circles under his blue eyes gave his face a harsh, angular appearance. His inflamed gaze moved from her face to that of his father's. Ben's old lips twisted with private irony. "What have you been telling her?" he demanded, advancing upon his father.

"Noah, please . . ." Katharine interjected.

"I asked you a simple question," Noah said through tightly clenched teeth. "If you won't answer it, then fine. I'd like to talk to her . . . alone." He looked away from his father to meet Sheila's confused gaze. For a moment his face softened, and the defeat in his eyes seemed to fade. "Let's go into the den and talk," he suggested softly.

Sheila understood. He had changed his mind about her and the winery and the marriage. He was going to tell her that all of her dreams had turned to dust. A sinking sensation of doom, like that of falling into a bottomless black hole, enveloped her. Noah's persuasive hand was on her shoulder, encouraging her to her feet. Slowly, she rose. She felt dizzy, sick.

"No reason to shuffle her out of here, son," Ben said with sarcastic familiarity. "One way or another, she's got to know."

"I'll handle it," Noah spat. The pressure on Sheila's back increased as he tried to guide her out of the sterile living room.

"I'm sure you will, my boy," Ben agreed with a mirthless laugh.

"What's he talking about?" Sheila asked impatiently.

"Tell her," Ben demanded.

"Ben . . . let Noah handle this his own way," his wife whispered.

The pressure in Sheila's head got to her. She stopped her exit from the long living room with the cold carpet and announced in a calm, hushed voice. "Don't talk as if I can't hear you, because I can. What's this all about?"

She had to know, had to hear his words of rejection, waited with head held high for the final blow. Noah's lips compressed into a thin, uncompromising line. "I'll tell you everything, but it will be best if we're alone."

"Oh, hell, boy! Stop pussyfootin' around, for God's sake." The old man rose shakily from his chair and rubbed his freckled scalp. "What Noah is trying to tell you, honey, is that your father started that damned fire and it cost the company one helluva lot of money, let me tell you. The insurance company hasn't paid us a dime; there's a doubt that they ever will!"

Sheila's face turned ashen, her stomach lurched and she thought she might faint. She turned her eyes to Noah's and read the guilt and remorse in his look. He had known. From the time that Anthony Simmons had turned in his preliminary report Noah Wilder had known about her father and the fire.

"No!" she attempted to shout. But no sound escaped from her constricted throat. His deceit was too much for her to accept.

Ben enjoyed the scene. It was hard for an old man with a heart condition to get many thrills out of life. He enjoyed the intrigue of passions and deceit. It didn't matter that it was his own son. The sanctimonious heir had been looking down his nose at his father's morals for the last sixteen years—even to the point of refusing to work for the company, until he was forced to by Ben's most recent attack. It did old Ben's failing heart good to see the tables turned for once.

"Sheila." Noah said softly, touching her chin. She drew away, repelled by his touch. "Things aren't exactly what they seem."

"But you knew about Dad!" she accused.

"Yes," he admitted loudly.

"And you didn't tell me!"

"I thought I could prove the report wrong . . . I was convinced that with a little time, I could sort things out, and the results would be different."

"But you knew!" Her heart sank to the blackest depths of despair. "And you wouldn't tell me. . . ."

"I didn't want to hurt you."

"So you lied to me?"

His response was quick. "I've never lied to you."

"Just omitted the facts, avoided the issues. . . ."

"Tried to stop your pain."

"I don't want a man to *protect* me from the truth. I don't want anyone who can't trust me. . . ." The ugliness of the situation became blindingly apparent to her, and another wave of nausea took all of the color from her pale face. *"You thought I was involved, didn't you?"*

"No."

"Didn't you?"

"No!" he screamed. He shook his head, and his blue eyes pleaded with her to understand him. "Not after I met you. I couldn't."

"Oh, Noah," she whispered, shaking her head, running her fingers through her long, chestnut hair. "What has happened to us?"

She had forgotten there were other people in the

room. When she looked up, she met Katharine's sorrowed gaze. "I'm sorry," Katharine murmured. "Come on, Ben, let's leave them alone." She tried to help her husband out of the living room, but he refused.

Ben yanked his arm out of Katharine's grasp. "I think you should understand something, Miss Lindstrom." Sheila raised her head to meet his cool, laughing eyes. It was as if he were enjoying some private joke at her expense. "I'm a businessman, and I can't let you continue to operate the winery."

"What do you mean?"

"I mean that I'm not prepared to invest the money Noah promised you to rebuild the winery."

"Don't worry about it," Noah interjected. "I'll handle it."

Ben continued, unruffled by his son's visible anger. "The most prudent thing for you to do, Sheila, would be to sell out your portion of Cascade Valley to Wilder Investments."

"I can't do that. . . . I won't."

Ben's toothy smile slowly turned into a frown. "I don't think you'll have much of a choice, considering the information in Mr. Simmons's report—"

"Stop it!" Noah shouted, taking Sheila by the arm and nearly dragging her out of the living room. "Don't listen to him . . . don't pay any attention to any of his suggestions."

She pulled what little shreds of dignity she could find and turned her cold eyes on Noah. "I won't," she assured him coolly, while extracting her arm out of his fingers. Her eyes burned, her throat ached, her heart bled, but she held her face as impassive as possible. "Nothing you or your father can say will convince me to sell my father's winery."

"I know that," he admitted softly.

"But you were the first one to suggest that I sell."

"At that time I thought it would be best."

The unhappy smile that twisted on her lips was filled with self-defeat. "And now you expect me to believe that you don't?"

"You know that, Sheila." His fingers reached out to cup her chin, and they trembled as he sought to rub his thumb along her jawline. She had to turn away from him; she was too numb to feel the tenderness in his caress.

"Leave me alone, Noah," she whispered tonelessly. "I'm tired."

"Don't go," he begged, his hand dropping impotently to his side. The pain in his eyes wasn't hidden as he watched her move slowly toward the door. "Don't let the old man get to you."

"The 'old man' isn't the one that got to me."

"Sheila!" He reached for the bend of her elbow, clutching at her arm and twisting her to him. He held her so savagely that she wondered for a moment if she could breathe . . . or if she really cared. The tears that had slid over her lips to warm them with drops of salt told her she was crying, but she couldn't feel them. She didn't feel *anything*. Empty. Hollow. It was as if the spirit she had once owned had been broken.

"Let go of me," she said through her sobs.

"You can't go. You don't understand. . . ."

"I understand perfectly! You may have been able to get what you wanted from Marilyn by paying her off, but you can't buy me, Noah Wilder! No man can. I'll go bankrupt before I'll sell you one bottle of my cheapest wine!" She wrenched free of his hold on her and backed toward the door.

He watched her leave, not moving from the foyer where he had held her in his arms. They felt strangely empty as his eyes followed the path of her flight. The door slammed ·shut, closing her out of his life. He fought the vain urge to follow her and tried to convince himself that everything was for the best. If she trusted him so little, he was better off without her.

Chapter Thirteen

For five long weeks Sheila tried futilely to get the image of Noah Wilder out of her mind. It had been an impossible task. Everywhere on the estate she was reminded of him and the bittersweet love they had shared. There wasn't a room in the château where she could hide from him or the memories of the nights of surrendered passion they had shared together. She couldn't even find solace in her own room, the sanctuary where they had held each other dear until the first stirrings of dawn. Now the room seemed pale and empty, and Sheila was alone. She attempted to convince herself that she never had really loved him, that what they had shared was only a passing fancy, an affair to forget. It was a bald-faced lie, and she couldn't deceive herself for a minute. She had loved Noah Wilder with a passion time and deceit couldn't erase. She loved him still.

The winery had become a ghost town. Reconstruction of the west wing had been halted by one fell stroke: an executive order from Ben Wilder himself. Gone was the whine of whirring saw blades consuming wood, vanished were the shouts and laughter from the construction crew. The air was untainted with the smell of burning diesel or the scent of freshly cut lumber. The west wing of the winery was as defeated as her dreams.

Sheila had tried, ineffectively, to tell Emily about Noah. As comfortingly as possible she had mentioned that Noah and Sean wouldn't be back to Cascade Valley as they had originally planned and that her marriage to Noah would probably never happen. If Sheila had hoped not to wound her child, she had failed miserably. Emily was heartbroken. When Sheila had explained that she doubted if Noah and Sean would return to the winery, Emily had burst into tears, screamed that it was all her mother's fault and raced from the dinner table to hide in her room. It had taken several hours for Sheila to get through to her and calm her down. The child had sobbed on her shoulder bitterly, and it was difficult for Sheila to hold back the tears stinging the backs of her eyes.

Part of Emily's reaction was due to incredibly bad timing. The girl had just returned from a dismal trip to visit her father, a vacation that was to have lasted a week and was cut down to five regretful days. It seemed as if Jeff and his wife Judith just didn't have the time or the inclination to take care of a busy eight-year-old. Emily felt rejected not only by her father but by Noah as well.

The final blow to Sheila's pride had come from a local banker she had dealt with for years. Regardless of the winery's past record, Mr. Stinson couldn't justify another loan to Cascade Valley. It had no reflection on Sheila, but the winery just didn't qualify. There was simply not enough collateral to back up a quarter of a million dollars of the bank's money. He was kind and told her that he would talk to his superiors, although he was sure that her request was next to impossible. There was a distinct note of inflexibility in his even voice.

Sheila found it increasingly difficult to sit idle. Time seemed to be slipping by without purpose or meaning. Within a few short weeks Emily would be enrolled in the fall semester of school and the autumn harvest of grapes would be ripe. Sheila had no alternative but to sell the crop despite Dave Jansen's protests. He was convinced that this was the best year Cascade Valley had seen in a decade. The yield per acre was ten percent better than the previous year's, and the grapes held the highest sugar and acid content he had seen in several years. All in all it looked like a bumper crop. But Sheila had no choice. She was backed into a corner by Ben Wilder and his son.

She sighed wearily and ran her fingers through her hair as she picked up the telephone and dialed the number of Mid-Columbia Bank. A cheery receptionist put Sheila through to Jim Stinson. Sheila could envision the perplexed look of dismay that must have crossed his features when he learned that she was calling. He probably wanted to avoid this conversation as much as she did.

"Good afternoon, Sheila," Jim greeted heartily. "How've you been? Busy, I'll bet."

Sheila was taken aback at his friendly response to her call. "It's about that time of the year," she agreed.

"How's the construction going?" Jim asked good-naturedly. "Are you going to get the west wing finished before harvest?"

Sheila choked on her response. Jim, better than most people, knew of her plight, and it wasn't like him to rub salt into a wound. He actually sounded as if he thought she were running the winery as she had planned. "I can't do that, Jim, because construction has stopped on the west wing."

There was a moment's hesitation before Jim laughed. "Is this some kind of a joke? Haven't you begun to re-build yet?"

"As a matter of fact, no. I was hoping that Mid-Columbia would give me a loan, remember?"

"But that was before you got your other loan."

Once again silence.

"Other loan?" What the devil was Jim talking about? He wasn't usually one to talk in circles.

He acted as if she were incredibly dense. "You know, the quarter of a mil."

"The loan I requested from you."

She heard an exasperated sigh. "Just a minute." She was put on hold for a minute and then he was on the phone again. "Is there some mistake?"

Before she could ask what in the world he was muttering about, he spoke again. "No . . . no, everything looks right. You do know that a deposit of two hundred and fifty thousand dollars was made to the winery's account on the thirtieth of August, don't you?"

Sheila's mind was reeling, her voice faint. "What deposit?" she asked.

"Let's see . . . it was a cashier's check drawn on Consolidated Bank of Seattle. Didn't you get a loan from them . . . Sheila?"

Sheila felt as if she were melting into the kitchen floor. Noah! Noah had deposited the money. From somewhere in her conscious mind, she was able to respond to Jim Stinson. "Of course I did. I just wasn't aware that they had transferred the money so quickly. My statement hasn't come yet."

"But didn't they call you?" Stinson asked.

"I've been out a lot lately . . . down in the vineyards." She lied, trying to find a way to get off the phone politely. "Thank you very much."

"No trouble, but you might think about putting some of that money into savings or another account. Deposits aren't insured for that large a sum."

"You're right. I will. Thanks, Jim."

She hung up the phone and leaned against the wall.

Hot beads of perspiration dampened the back of her neck. "That bastard!" she muttered between her teeth. Why couldn't he leave her alone? He must have deposited the money out of a guilty conscience from the coffers of Wilder Investments, perhaps as incentive for her to sell. But that didn't explain everything. Why would she have to sell anything? The money was hers, or so it appeared.

Her anger grew white hot. Ben Wilder might have bought Marilyn Summers sixteen years ago, but no man, not even Noah, could purchase her or her father's dream. She balled a small fist and slammed it into the wall. "Emily," she called as she raced to the back door.

Emily was playing distractedly with a fluffy white kitten. She turned her head to watch her mother nearly run out of the back door. "What?"

Sheila tried to hold her fury in control. "Get your overnight case and pack your pajamas and a change of clothes. We're going to Seattle."

"Seattle?" The girl's dark eyes glittered with expectations. "To see Noah and Sean?" she asked hopefully.

"I . . . I don't know if we'll see Noah, honey." The trembling in her voice belied her calm. "And I really doubt that Sean will be where we're going."

The smile on Emily's face fell "Then why are we going to Seattle?"

"I have some business to discuss with Noah and his father."

Emily's brows drew together, and her rosy cheeks flushed. "Then why can't we see Sean? Won't he be with Noah?" She was genuinely concerned . . . and expectant.

"Another time. But we're going to Noah's office. Sean's probably at home."

Emily's lower lip stuck out in a pouty frown. "Can't we go see him? We don't go to Seattle very often."

Sheila shook her head but muttered a quick "We'll see," hoping to change the subject. "Hurry up and get your things." She left Emily in her room, packing, and did the same herself. She was out the door before she remembered the checkbook. Cascade Valley's checkbook. The one with a balance of over a quarter of a million dollars in it.

She tried to smile as she imagined herself self-righteously scribbling out a check for two hundred and fifty thousand dollars and dropping it theatrically on Noah's desk. Her smile faded as she visualized the scenario. Where was the justice she would feel? Where the triumph? And why, dear God, why wouldn't this ache leave her heart?

It was nearly five o'clock when they arrived in Seattle. The drive had been tedious due to the combination of roadwork on the winding mountain roads and Sheila's thinly stretched nerves. Her palms were damp on the steering wheel, her lips tight over her teeth. Emily had been quiet for most of the trip, but as they got closer to the heart of the city and she caught a few glimpses of Puget Sound, she began to chatter, asking Sheila questions about Seattle. The questions were intended to be innocent. Each one wounded Sheila anew.

"Where does Sean live?"

"Not down here. His house is near Lake Washington."

"Have you been there?"

"A couple of times."

"Can we go to Sean's house together?"

A pause. The lump in Sheila's throat made speech impossible. She tried to concentrate on shifting down as the car dipped along the hillside streets.

"Can we? Will you take me?" Emily repeated, looking

at her mother with the wide-eyed innocence of only eight years.

"Maybe someday."

The water of Puget Sound shimmered in the brightness of the warm summer sun. Seagulls dipped and dived over the salty water; huge, white-hulled ferries with broad green stripes down their sides plowed through the water, churning up a frothy wake and breaking the stillness with the sound of their rumbling engines.

Sheila parked the car across from the waterfront and stared out at the open water. Perhaps when all of this business with Wilder Investments was over, she would be able to take Emily out to dinner on one of the piers. Perhaps . . .

"Come on, Em," she stated with renewed determination. "Let's go."

The Wilder Building was an imposing structure. A concrete and steel skyscraper that towered over the neighboring turn-of-the-century buildings, it proudly boasted smooth modern lines and large, reflective windows. Sheila's stomach began to wind into tight, uncomfortable knots as she and Emily rode the elevator to the thirtieth floor.

The elevator doors parted, and they stepped into a reception area. A plump woman of about sixty greeted Sheila and Emily with a cool but efficient smile.

"Good afternoon. May I help you?"

Sheila gathered in her breath. "I'm looking for Mr. Wilder . . . *Noah* Wilder. Is he in?"

The secretary, whose nameplate indicated that her name was Margaret Trent, shook her perfectly coiffed red tresses. "I'm sorry Miss . . ."

"Lindstrom," Sheila supplied hastily. "I'm Sheila Lindstrom, and this is my daughter, Emily." The daughter smiled frailly.

Maggie showed just the hint of a dimple. So this was the Lindstrom woman all the fuss was about "I'm Maggie Trent," she said warmly. Then, remembering Sheila's request, continued, "I'm sorry, Miss Lindstrom, but Noah doesn't work here any longer." Her reddish brows drew together behind her glasses. "Didn't you know? Things haven't . . ." Maggie quickly held her tongue. She had been on the verge of divulging some of the secrets of Wilder Investments to this slender young woman with the intense gray eyes, but she quickly thought better of it. She hadn't gotten to be Ben Wilder's personal secretary by idly wagging her tongue at anyone who walked through the door. Quite the opposite. Maggie was a good judge of character and could tell from the looks of the determined woman in the soft blue dress and the well-mannered child that she could trust them, but prudence held her tongue.

The look of disappointment in Sheila's eyes did, however, give her pause. "I think that Noah was planning to go back to Portland," she offered, leaving the rest of the sad story unsaid. It wouldn't do to gossip.

Sheila had to swallow back a dozen questions that were determined to spring to her lips. Intuitively she knew that Maggie was privy to the workings of the Wilder household. The thought that Noah actually left staggered her, and the blood drained from her face. She had to know more. Suddenly it was incredibly important that she see him. "Is it possible to speak with Noah's father?" she asked, tonelessly.

The secretary looked as if Sheila had hit her. "Ben?" she repeated, regaining her composure. "No . . . Mr. Wilder isn't in." The warmth in the woman's eyes faded as she turned back to her typewriter. She looked at Sheila over the top of her glasses. "Was there anything else? Would you like to leave your name and number?"

"No," Sheila said, her voice beginning to quiver. "Thank you."

Together she led Emily to the elevator, and they began the descent. "Mom, are you okay?" Emily asked as they walked back to the car.

"Sure I am."

"You don't look so good."

Sheila forced a smile and gave her daughter a playful pat on the shoulders. "Is that any way to talk to your mother?"

They slid into the car simultaneously, and Sheila turned the key to start the engine. Emily looked out the passenger window, but Sheila saw the trace of a tear in the corner of her daughter's eye. "Emily?" she asked, letting the engine die.

"What?" Emily sniffed.

"What's wrong?"

Emily turned liquid eyes to her mother and her small face crumpled into a mask of despair. "He's gone, really gone, isn't he?"

"Honey . . . what?"

"Noah!" Emily nearly shouted, beginning to lose all control. "I heard that lady at his office. She said he's gone, and I know that he took Sean, too! He left, Mommy, just like Daddy did. He doesn't love me either . . ." Her small voice broke, and her shoulders began to heave with her sobs.

Sheila reached out for her child and wrapped comforting arms around the limp form. "Hey, Em, shhh . . . don't cry." Her own voice threatened to break. "It's not like that, you know. Noah loves you very much."

"No, he doesn't. He doesn't call. He doesn't come see us. Just like Daddy!"

"Honey, no. Noah's not like Daddy at all." Sheila

kissed her daughter on the forehead and wiped the tears from the round, dark eyes.

"Then why doesn't he call?"

Sheila closed her eyes and faced the truth, the damning truth. "Because I asked him not to."

Emily's body stiffened in Sheila's arms. "Why, Mommy I thought you liked him."

"I did . . . I do."

"Then why?"

"Oh, Em, I wish I knew. . . . We had a fight. A very big fight and . . . I doubt that we'll ever get it straightened out."

Sheila attempted to comfort Emily as she guided the car out of the heart of the city. Emily's accusations reinforced her own fears, and her mind was swimming by the time that she reached the stone pillars flanking the long driveway of the Wilder estate. She drove without hesitation, knowing that she had to speak to Ben. Surely he would know how to get in touch with his son. Her purpose had shifted. Though her checkbook was still in her purse, its significance diminished and the only thoughts in her mind centered on Noah and the cruel insinuations she had cast upon him the last time they were together. No matter what had happened in the past, Sheila was now face-to-face with the fact that she still loved him as desperately as ever. She also realized that her love wasn't strong enough to bring them together again—nothing was. Too much mistrust held them away from each other. Too much deceit had blackened their lives.

Sheila pulled on the emergency brake, and Emily eyed the massive stone house suspiciously. "Who's house is that—it's creepy." Her voice steady, she was once again composed. Her young eyes traveled up the cornerstones of the house and the brick walk that led to the large double doors.

"It's not creepy," Sheila countered, and added, "Ben Wilder lives here."

"Sean's grandpa?" Emily asked, not hiding her enthusiasm.

"That's right."

"Maybe Sean will be here!" Emily was out of the car in a flash, and Sheila had to hurry to catch up with her.

"I don't think so, honey," she said as they both stood on the arched porch. Emily ignored her mother's doubts and pressed the doorbell, which chimed inside the house. Sheila prepared herself to meet George the butler's disapproving glare.

Hurried footsteps echoed in the house, and the door was thrust open to expose Sean on the other side. He wore a sneer, but it quickly faded into a brilliant smile of clean, white teeth. He was dressed, as usual, in cutoff jeans and a well-worn football jersey that had once been blue.

"Hi ya, pipsqueak," he greeted Emily. "How're ya?" His grin widened as he pretended to punch her in the arm.

"Good . . . real good," Emily piped back delightedly. An "I told you so" expression covered her face as she turned to look at Sheila. "See, Mom, Sean *is* here, just like I thought," she declared with a triumphant gleam in her eyes.

Sean's face sobered slightly as he looked at Sheila. She thought he seemed older-more mature-than he had when they were all living at the winery. She couldn't help but notice how similarly featured he was to his father. The sadness and maturity that had entered his gaze reminded her of Noah, and her throat became dry. "Hi, Sheila. You lookin' for Dad?"

Sheila's heart leapt to her throat. "Is he here?"

Sean nodded silently.

"I expected to find your grandfather."

Sean's eyes darted from Sheila to Emily and back again. He bit at his lower lip, scratched his neck and seemed to ponder what he was about to say. It was as if he were hesitant to trust her, and Sheila felt a knife of doubt twist in her heart. What had Noah told his son about their breakup? "Ben isn't here now," Sean explained. "He's . . . at the hospital. I'm not supposed to say anything about it, you know, in case some reporters come nosin' around here, but I suppose it's all right to tell you about it." He didn't seem sure of his last statement.

"Is it serious?" Sheila asked quietly.

Sean shrugged indifferently, but worried lines scarred his flawless forehead. He pushed his hands into the pockets of his ragged shorts. "I think so. Dad doesn't talk about it much."

Sheila felt a deep pang of sadness steal into her heart. "Where is your father, Sean?"

Sean cocked his head toward the back of the house. "He's down at the lake, just walkin' and thinkin', I guess." His blue eyes met the sober expression in Emily's. "Hey, pipsqueak, don't look so down. . . . Maybe you and I can walk down to the park and grab an ice cream cone. What do ya say?"

Sheila recognized and appreciated Sean's rather obvious way of giving her some time alone with Noah.

"Can I go, Mom, *please?*" The look of expectation on Emily's face couldn't be denied.

"Sure you can, but come back in a couple of hours, okay?"

Sheila doubted if Emily heard her. The child was already racing across the wooded lawn, her dark curls escaping from the neat barrettes over her ears. Sean was loping along beside her, seemingly as excited as Emily.

When the dangerous duo was out of sight, Sheila took in a deep breath of air, hoping to fortify herself against the upcoming confrontation with Noah. As she closed the door behind her and headed through the elegant main hallway of the manor, she wondered if Noah would listen to what she had to say. He had lied to her, it was true, but her reaction had been vicious and cold, entirely without reason. If only she had trusted him a little.

She walked through the den and a pang of remorse touched her heart as she remembered her first night with Noah, the dying fire and the heated love they had shared. Tears burned the back of her eyes as she opened the French doors and stood upon the veranda from which she had attempted to make her escape into the night several months before.

As she leaned against the railing she looked down the rocky cliff on which the veranda was perched. Nearly a hundred feet below her, standing at the edge of the water, was Noah. He stared out at the gray blue water as if entranced by the distant sailboats skimming across the lake. Sheila's throat became dry at the sight of him; her love tore her soul in two.

Without thinking about how she would approach him, she half ran across the flagstones, her fingers slipping upon the railing, her eyes glued to Noah's unmoving form. The old cable car had seen better years, and it groaned when Sheila pressed the call button. It shuddered and then steadily climbed the cliff to dock at the end of the deck. Sheila climbed inside the cab and pressed against the lever that released the brakes and slowly took the old car back to its original position at the base of the cliff. Noah didn't seem to notice; he didn't glance toward her, but continued to stare out at the cold lapping water.

He seemed to have aged since she last saw him. Deep lines outlined his eyes; his jaw was more defined, his face more sharply angled. Either he hadn't been eating properly or he wasn't able to sleep. Perhaps both. Her heart bled silently for the man she loved and the guilt he bore so proudly. How could she have accused him of everything she had? How could she have been so cruel as to add to his torment? A man who had given up everything to claim his unborn son; a man who had bucked tradition and raised that son alone; a man who had grieved when he thought he had failed with that same precious son.

The wind off the lake blew his hair away from his face, displaying the long lines of anxiety etching his brow. It was cool as it pushed the soft fabric of her dress against her legs and touched her cheeks to chill the unbidden tears that slid from her eyes.

He stood with his feet apart, his hands pressed palms out in the back pockets of his jeans. At the sound of her footsteps in the gravel, he cocked his bead in her direction, and when his blue gaze clashed with hers, the expression of mockery froze on his face.

What was there to say to her? Why was she here? And why did she look more beautiful in person than she had in the sleepless nights he had lain awake and imagined her?

Tentatively she reached up and pushed a wayward lock of black hair from his forehead and stood upon her toes to kiss him lightly on the lips. He didn't move.

She lowered herself but continued to rest her fingertips on his shoulders.

"You must have come here because of the money," he said, his voice breaking the thin stillness.

Sheila's voice was firm. "I just found out that you deposited the money in my account, and I decided to come and throw it back in your face."

His smile was still distrustful. "I knew you would."

"You expected me to give it back to you?"

He shook his head at his own folly. "I hoped that you would come and see me face-to-face. If you hadn't, I had decided to come back to Cascade Valley and try and talk some sense into you. I only waited because I thought we both needed time to cool off."

"You knew we could work things out . . . after all that's happened?"

He looked away from her and out at the lowering sun. "I didn't know anything," he admitted, "except that I couldn't live without you."

"But why didn't you tell me about the fire? Why did you lie?"

"I didn't lie to you, and I just needed more time to look into the cause of the fire. You have to believe that I would never intentionally hurt you, nor would I deceive you."

"Only when you thought it was for my own good."

"Only *until* I had all the answers," he replied quietly.

"And do you?"

He closed his eyes and sighed. "Oh, woman, if only I did!"

When he opened his eyes to look at her again, some of his hostility seemed to have melted. His gaze traveled from her windswept chestnut hair, down the column of her throat and past the swell of her breasts, draped loosely in a soft blue dress.

"Then why did you want to see me?"

"A few things have changed around here," he responded cryptically.

"Because of Ben's illness?"

Noah nodded and his eyes grew dark. "He's in the hospital again, and the doctors are concerned that he won't get out."

"I'm sorry. . . ."

Noah waved her condolences aside. "Maybe it's better this way." His dark expression didn't falter.

"What do you mean?"

"It's a long story. Basically, the doctor in charge of my father, Dr. Carson, has ordered Ben to give up working. Not only must he step down as president of Wilder Investments, but Ben's got to give up even going into the office."

"And that would kill your father?" she asked, trying to follow Noah's line of reasoning.

"Ben's not the kind of man to sit idle."

"I suppose not."

"He likes to be in the middle of things. Anyway," he continued with an expression of indifference, "the old man asked me to take over as head of the business, sell out my operation in Portland to Betty Averill and move to Seattle. I wasn't too hot for the idea."

Sheila tried to hide her disappointment. "Then you are moving back to Portland," she surmised.

"I thought so, but things have changed." Sheila's heart turned over, and her throat went dry. "Anthony Simmons's report was invalid."

"What?"

Sheila didn't know that she was shaking until Noah placed a steadying hand on her shoulder. "What are you saying?" she asked in a hoarse whisper.

"Pac-West Insurance Company continued with its investigation on the fire." Sheila held her breath. "You were right about your father, Sheila; there is no evidence that he started the fire."

"How do you know this?' Tears once again began to slide down her cheeks.

"Because the insurance company found out that Ben hired Simmons to start the fire. Ben's confirmed all this and he's cleared your father's name. Therefore the insurance company is refusing to pay the claim."

"But the money . . . in my account."

"I took it from Wilder Investments to rebuild the winery, as I'd promised. And as far as I'm concerned, the note against the winery has been satisfied. Within a few weeks you should get the legal papers that will acknowledge and guarantee that you are sole owner of the winery."

"Oh, Noah," she whispered hoarsely, her emotions strangling her.

"It's all right, Sheila," he said, wrapping his arms around her and kissing the top of her head. "I'm just sorry that my family had anything to do with your father's death or his financial worries." His voice had lowered. "Ben even admitted that he had been behind the tampered bottles in Montana, in a move to force your father out of business. It looks as if he will be prosecuted for the arson and involuntary manslaughter."

"Oh, God, Noah . . . but he's ill. . . ."

"That's no excuse for the things he's done."

"What are you going to do?" Her tears were running freely.

"I've agreed to run the company since Ben's given me sole authority, and I'm going to try and right my father's mistakes." His mouth twisted into a line of disgust. "I don't know if it's possible. That's why I started with you. Ben tried to cheat you out of the winery rather than just continue to share the profits with you. It's all yours now. Wilder Investments is out of it."

He watched her reaction, gauged her response. "You don't understand, do you?" she whispered. "Nothing . . . not the winery . . . not my father's reputation . . . none of it means anything unless you're with me."

"You were the one who left."

"But only because I didn't understand." His arms tightened around her.

His voice caught. "Dear God, Sheila, if only you knew how much I love you . . . if only you could feel the emptiness I've had to deal with."

"I do," she vowed, "every night that I'm alone."

"Never again," he promised, "you'll never be alone again. Promise me that you'll marry me."

Sobs of joy racked her body. "Oh, Noah, I've been such a fool. I love you so dearly and I tried to convince myself that I could forget you. . . . I thought I wanted to."

"Shhh . . . it's all right. We're together now, and we will be forever. And we're going to have our own family—Sean, Emily and as many more children as you want."

"Do you mean it?"

"Of course I do, love. More than anything I've ever said. Will you marry me?"

"Do you have to ask?" she sighed, tipping her head to look at him through the shimmer of unshed tears. A slow, satisfied smile curved his lips, and his eyes caressed hers.

"I love you, Sheila," he vowed. "I promise that I always will."

"But what about the winery?"

"We'll work that out later. If you want, I'll move the headquarters of Wilder Investments to Cascade Valley.

It doesn't matter where we live, just as long as we're together."

"Noah . . ."

"Shhh . . . don't worry about anything. Just love me."

"Forever," she vowed against his chest before his lips claimed hers in a kiss filled with the promise of a blissful future they would share.

DEVIL'S GAMBIT

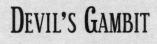

Chapter One

Tiffany heard the back door creak open and then shut with a bone-rattling thud. *It's over,* she thought and fought against the tears of despair that threatened her eyes.

Hoping to appear as calm as was possible under the circumstances, she set her pen on the letter she had been writing and placed her elbows on the desk. Cold dread slowly crept up her spine.

Mac's brisk, familiar footsteps slowed a bit as he approached the den, and involuntarily Tiffany's spine stiffened as she braced herself for the news. Mac paused in the doorway. Tonight he appeared older than his sixty-seven years. His plaid shirt was rumpled and the lines near his sharp eyes were deeper than usual.

Tiffany knew what he was going to say before Mac had a chance to deliver his somber message.

"He didn't make it, did he?" she asked as her slate blue eyes held those of the weathered ex-jockey.

There was a terse shake of Mac's head. His lips tightened over his teeth and he removed his worn hat. "He was a good-lookin' colt, that one."

"They all were," Tiffany muttered, seemingly to herself. "Every last one of them." The suppressed rage of three sleepless nights began to pound in her veins, and for a moment she lost the tight rein on her self-control. "Damn!" Her fist crashed against the desk before the weighty sadness hit and her shoulders slumped in defeat. A numb feeling took hold of her and she wondered if what was happening was real. Once again her eyes pierced those of the trainer and he read the disbelief in her gaze.

"Charlatan is dead," he said quietly, as if to settle the doubts in her mind. "It weren't nobody's fault. The vet, well, he did all he could."

"I know."

He saw the disappointment that kept her full lips drawn into a strained line. *She can't take much more of this,* he thought to himself. *This might be the straw that breaks the camel's back.* Everything that was happening to her was a shame—a damned shame.

"And don't you go blaming yourself," he admonished as if reading her thoughts. His crowlike features pinched into a scowl before he dropped his wiry frame into one of the winged side chairs positioned near the desk. Thoughtfully he scratched the rough stubble of his beard. He'd been awake for nearly three days, same as she, and he was dog-tired. At sixty-seven it wasn't getting any easier.

Tiffany tried to manage a smile and failed. What she felt was more than defeat. The pain of witnessing the last struggling breaths of two other foals had drained her. And now Charlatan, the strongest of the lot, was dead.

"It's just not fair," she whispered.

"Aye, that it's not."

She let out a ragged sigh and leaned back in the uncomfortable desk chair. Her back ached miserably and all thoughts of her letter to Dustin were forgotten. "That makes three," she remarked, the skin of her flawless forehead wrinkling into an uncomfortable frown.

"And two more mares should be dropping foals within the next couple of weeks."

Tiffany's elegant jaw tightened. "Let's just hope they're healthy."

Mac pushed his hands through his thinning red hair. His small eyes narrowed suspiciously as he looked out the window at the group of large white buildings comprising Rhodes Breeding Farm. Starkly illuminated by the bluish sheen from security lights, the buildings took on a sinister appearance in the stormy night.

"We've sure had a streak of bad luck, that we have."

"It almost seems as if someone is out to get us," Tiffany observed and Mac's sharp gaze returned to the face of his employer.

"That it does."

"But *who* and *why* . . . and *how?*" Nothing was making any sense. Tiffany stretched her tired arms before dropping her head forward and releasing the tight clasp holding her hair away from her face. Her long fingers massaged her scalp as she shook the soft brown tresses free of their bond and tried to release the tension in the back of her neck.

"That one I can't answer," Mac replied, watching as she moved her head and the honey-colored strands fell to her shoulders. Tiffany Rhodes was a beautiful woman who had faced more than her share of tragedy. Signs of stress had begun to age her fair complexion, and though Tiffany was still the most regally beautiful and proud woman he knew, Mac McDougal wondered just how much more she could take.

"That's just the trouble—no one can explain what's happening."

"You haven't got any enemies that I don't know about?" It was more of a statement than a question.

Tiffany's frown was pensive. A headache was beginning to nag at her. She shrugged her shoulders. "No one that would want to ruin me."

"You're sure?"

"Positive. Look, we can't blame anyone for what's happened here. Like you said, we've just had a string of bad luck."

"Starting with the loss of Devil's Gambit four years ago."

Tiffany's eyes clouded in pain. "At least we got the insurance money for him," she whispered, as if it really didn't matter. "I don't think any of the foals will be covered, not once the insurance company gets wind of the problems we're having."

"The insurance money you got for Devil's Gambit wasn't half of what he was worth," Mac grumbled, not for the first time. Why had Ellery Rhodes been so careless with the most valuable stallion on the farm? The entire incident had never set well with Mac. He shifted uncomfortably on the chair.

"Maybe not, but I'm afraid it's all water under the bridge." She pushed the letter to Dustin aside and managed a weak smile. "It really doesn't matter anyway. We lost the horse and he'll never be replaced." She shuddered as she remembered the night that had taken the life of her husband and his most treasured Thoroughbred. Images of the truck and horse trailer, twisted and charred beyond recognition, filled her mind and caused her to wrap her arms protectively over her abdomen. Sometimes the nightmare never seemed to go away.

Mac saw the sadness shadow her eyes. He could have kicked himself for bringing up the past and reminding her of the god-awful accident that had left her a widow. The last thing Tiffany needed was to be constantly reminded of her troubles. *And now there was the problem with the foals!*

The wiry ex-jockey stood and held his hat in his hands. He'd delivered his message and somehow Tiffany had managed to take the news in stride. But then she always did. There was a stoic beauty and pride in Ellery Rhodes's widow that Mac admired. No matter how deep the pain, Tiffany Rhodes always managed to pull herself together. There was proof enough of that in her marriage. Not many women could have stayed married to a bastard the likes of Ellery Rhodes.

Mac started for the door of the den and twisted the brim of his limp fedora in his gnarled hands. He didn't feel comfortable in the house—at least not since Ellery Rhodes's death—and he wanted to get back to the foaling shed. There was still unpleasant work to be done.

"I'll come with you," Tiffany offered, rising from the desk and pursing her lips together in determination.

"No reason—"

"I want to."

"He's dead, just like the others. Nothing you can do."

Except cry a few wasted tears, Tiffany thought to herself as she pulled her jacket off the wooden hook near the French doors that opened to a flagstone patio.

Bracing herself against the cold wind and rain blowing inland from the coast, Tiffany rammed her fists into the pockets of her jacket and silently followed Mac down the well-worn path toward the foaling shed. She knew that he disapproved of her insistence on being involved with all of the work at the farm. After all, Ellery had preferred to leave the work to the professionals. But Tiffany wanted to learn the business from the ground up, and despite Mac's obvious thoughts that a woman's place was in the home or, at the very least, in the office doing book work, Tiffany made herself a part of everything on the small breeding farm.

The door to the shed creaked on rusty hinges as Tiffany entered the brightly lit building. Pungent familiar odors of clean straw, warm horses, antiseptic and oiled leather greeted her. She wiped the rain off her face as her eyes adjusted to the light.

Mac followed her inside, muttering something about this being no place for a woman. Tiffany ignored Mac's obvious attempt to protect her from the tragic evidence of Charlatan's death and walked with determination toward the short man near the opposite end of the building. Her boots echoed hollowly on the concrete floor.

Vance Geddes, the veterinarian, was still in the stall, but Felicity, the mare who just two days earlier had given birth to Charlatan, had already been taken away.

Vance's expression was grim and perplexed. Weary lines creased his white skin and bracketed his mouth with worry. He forced a weak smile when Tiffany approached him and he stepped away from the small, limp form lying in the straw.

"Nothing I could do," Vance apologized, regret and frustration sharpening his normally bland expression. "I thought with this one we had a chance."

"Why?" She glanced sadly at the dead colt and a lump formed in her throat. Everything seemed so . . . pointless.

"He seemed so strong at birth. Stood up and nursed right away, not like the others."

Tiffany knelt on the straw and touched the soft neck of the still-warm foal. He was a beautiful, perfectly formed colt—a rich chestnut with one white stocking and a small white star on his forehead. At birth his dark eyes had been keenly intelligent and inquisitive with that special spark that distinguished Moon Shadow's progeny. Tiffany had prayed that he would live and not fall victim to the same baffling disease that had killed the other recently born foals sired by Moon Shadow.

"You'll perform an autopsy?" she asked, her throat tight from the strain of unshed tears.

"Of course."

After patting the soft neck one last time, Tiffany straightened. She dusted her hands on her jeans, cast one final searching look at the tragic form, and walked out of the stall. "What about Felicity?"

"She's back in the broodmare barn. And not very happy about it. We had a helluva time getting her away from the foal. She kicked at John, but he managed to get her out of here."

"It's not easy," Tiffany whispered, understanding the anxious mare's pain at the unexplained loss of her foal. Tiffany looked around the well-kept foaling shed. White heat lamps, imported straw, closed-circuit television, all the best equipment money could buy and still she couldn't prevent the deaths of these last three foals.

Why, she wondered to herself. *And why only the off-spring of Moon Shadow?* He had stood at stud for nearly eight years and had always produced healthy, if slightly temperamental, progeny. Not one foal had died. Until now. *Why?*

With no answers to her question, and tears beginning to blur her vision, Tiffany reluctantly left the two men to attend to the dead colt.

The rain had decreased to a slight drizzle, but the wind had picked up and the branches of the sequoia trees danced wildly, at times slamming into the nearby buildings. The weather wasn't unusual for early March in Northern California, but there was something somber and ominous about the black clouds rolling over the hills surrounding the small breeding farm.

"Don't let it get to you," Tiffany muttered to herself.

She shivered as she stepped into the broodmare barn and walked without hesitation to Felicity's stall.

The smell of fresh hay and warm horses greeted her and offered some relief from the cold night. Several mares poked their dark heads out of the stalls to inspect the visitor. Tiffany gently patted each muzzle as she passed, but her eyes were trained on the last stall in the whitewashed barn.

Felicity was still agitated and appeared to be looking for the lost foal. The chestnut mare paced around the small enclosure and snorted restlessly. When Tiffany approached, Felicity's ears flattened to her head and her dark eyes gleamed maliciously.

"I know, girl," Tiffany whispered, attempting to comfort the anxious mare. "It wasn't supposed to turn out like this."

Felicity stamped angrily and ignored the piece of apple Tiffany offered.

"There will be other foals," Tiffany said, wondering if she were trying to convince the horse or herself. Rhodes Breeding Farm couldn't stand to take many more losses. Tears of frustration and anxiety slid down her cheeks and she didn't bother to brush them aside.

A soft nicker from a nearby stall reminded Tiffany that she was disturbing the other horses. Summoning up her faltering courage, Tiffany stared at Felicity for a moment before slapping the top rail of the stall and walking back to the house.

Somehow she would find the solution to the mystery of the dying foals.

The first inquiry came by telephone two days later. Word had gotten out about the foals, and a reporter for a local newspaper in Santa Rosa was checking the story.

Tiffany took the call herself and assured the man that though she had lost two newborn colts and one filly, she and the veterinarian were positive that whatever had killed the animals was not contagious.

When the reporter, Rod Crawford, asked if he could come to the farm for an interview, Tiffany was wary, but decided the best course of action was to confront the problem head-on.

"When would it be convenient for you to drive out to the farm?" she asked graciously, her soft voice disguising her anxiety.

"What about next Wednesday? I'll have a photographer with me, if you don't mind."

"Of course not," she lied, as if she had done it all her life. "Around ten?"

"I'll be there," Rod Crawford agreed.

Tiffany replaced the receiver and said a silent prayer that the two mares who were still carrying Moon Shadow's unborn foals would successfully deliver healthy horses into the world, hopefully before next Wednesday. A sinking feeling in her heart told her not to get her hopes up.

Somehow, she had to focus Rod Crawford's attention away from the tragedy in the foaling shed and onto the one bright spot in Rhodes Breeding Farm's future: Journey's End. He was a big bay colt, whose career as a two-year-old had been less than formidable. But now, as a three-year-old, he had won his first two starts and promised to be the biggest star Rhodes Farm had put on the racetrack since Devil's Gambit.

Tiffany only hoped that she could convince the reporter that the story at Rhodes Breeding Farm was not the three dead foals, but the racing future of Journey's End.

The reputation of the breeding farm was on the line. If the Santa Rosa papers knew about the unexplained deaths of the foals, it wouldn't be long before reporters from San Francisco and Sacramento would call. And then, all hell was sure to break loose.

* * *

The doorbell chimed at nine-thirty on Wednesday morning and Tiffany smiled grimly to herself. Though the reporter for the *Santa Rosa Clarion* was a good half an hour early, Tiffany was ready for him. In the last four years she had learned to anticipate just about anything and make the most of it, and she wouldn't allow a little time discrepancy to rattle her. She couldn't afford the bad press.

Neither of the broodmares pregnant with Moon Shadow's offspring had gone into labor and Tiffany didn't know whether to laugh or cry. Her nerves were stretched as tightly as a piano string and only with effort did her poise remain intact. Cosmetics, for the most part, had covered the shadows below her eyes, which were the result of the past week of sleepless nights.

She hurried down the curved, marble staircase and crossed the tiled foyer to the door. After nervously smoothing her wool skirt, she opened the door and managed a brave smile, which she directed at the gentleman standing on the porch.

"Ms. Rhodes?" he asked with the slightest of accents.

Tiffany found herself staring into the most seductive gray eyes she had ever seen. He wasn't what she had expected. His tanned face was angular, his features strong. Raven-black hair and fierce eyebrows contrasted with the bold, steel-colored eyes staring into hers. There was a presence about him that spoke of authority and hinted at arrogance.

"Yes . . . won't you please come in?" she replied, finally finding her voice. "We can talk in the den. . . ." Her words trailed off as she remembered the photographer. Where was he? Hadn't Crawford mentioned that a photographer would be with him this morning?

It was then she noticed the stiff white collar and the expensively woven tweed business suit. A burgundy silk tie was knotted at the stranger's throat and gold cuff links flashed in the early-morning sunlight. The broad shoulders beneath his jacket were square and tense and there was no evidence of a note pad, camera, or tape recorder. Stereotyping aside, this man was no reporter.

"Pardon me," she whispered, realizing her mistake. "I was expecting someone—"

"Else," he supplied with a tight, slightly off-center smile that seemed out of place on his harsh, angular face. He wasn't conventionally handsome; the boldness of his features took away any boyish charm that might have lingered from his youth. But there was something about him, something positively male and sensual that was as magnetic as it was dangerous. Tiffany recognized it in the glint of his eyes and the brackets near the corners of his mouth. She suspected that beneath the conservative business suit, there was an extremely single-minded and ruthless man.

He extended his hand and when Tiffany accepted it, she noticed that his fingers were callused—a direct contradiction of the image he was attempting to portray.

"Zane Sheridan," he announced. Again the accent.

She hesitated only slightly. His name and his face were vaguely familiar, and though he looked as if he expected her to recognize him, she couldn't remember where she'd met him . . . or heard of him. "Please come in, Mr. Sheridan—"

"Zane."

"Zane," she repeated, slightly uncomfortable with the familiarity of first names. For a reason she couldn't put her finger on, Tiffany thought she should be wary of this man. There was something about him that hinted at antagonism.

She led him into the den, knowing instinctively that this was not a social call.

"Can I get you something—coffee, perhaps, or tea?" Tiffany asked as she took her usual chair behind the desk and Zane settled into one of the side chairs. Placing her elbows on the polished wood surface, she clasped her hands together and smiled pleasantly, just as if he hadn't disrupted her morning.

"Nothing. Thank you." His gray eyes moved away from her face to wander about the room. They observed all the opulent surroundings: the thick pile of the carpet, the expensive leather chairs, the subdued brass reading lamps and the etchings of Thoroughbreds adorning the cherrywood walls.

"What exactly can I do for you?" Tiffany asked, feeling as if he was searching for something.

When his eyes returned to hers, he smiled cynically. "I was an acquaintance of your husband."

Zane's expression was meant to be without emotion as he stared at the elegant but worried face of Ellery Rhodes's widow. Her reaction was just what he had expected—surprise and then, once she had digested his statement, disbelief. Her fingers anxiously toyed with the single gold chain encircling her throat.

"You knew Ellery?"

"We'd met a few times. In Europe."

Maybe that was why his face and name were so familiar, but Tiffany doubted it. A cautious instinct told her he was lying through his beautiful, straight white teeth.

She was instantly wary as she leveled her cool blue gaze at him. "I'm sorry," she apologized, "but if we've met, I've forgotten."

Zane pulled at the knot of his tie and slumped more deeply and comfortably into his chair. "I met Ellery Rhodes before he was married to you."

"Oh." Her smile was meant to be indulgent. "And you're here because . . . ?" she prompted. Zane Sheridan unnerved her, and Tiffany knew instinctively that the sooner he stated his business and was gone, the better.

"I'm interested in buying your farm."

Her dark brows arched in elegant surprise. "You're kidding!"

"Dead serious." The glint of silver determination in his eyes emphasized his words and convinced her that he wasn't playing games.

"But it's not for sale."

"I've heard that everything has a price."

"Well in this case, Mr. Sheridan, you heard wrong. The farm isn't on the market. However, if you're interested in a yearling, I have two colts that—"

"Afraid not. It's all or nothing with me," was the clipped, succinct reply. Apparently Zane Sheridan wasn't a man to mince words.

"Then I guess it's nothing," Tiffany replied, slightly galled at his self-assured attitude. Who the hell did he think he was, waltzing into her house uninvited, and offering to buy her home—Ellery's farm?

Just because he had been a friend of Ellery's—no, he hadn't said friend, just acquaintance.

It didn't matter. It still didn't give him the right to come barging in as if he owned the place. And there was more to it. Tiffany sensed that he was here for another reason, a reason he hadn't admitted. Maybe it was the strain in the angle of his jaw, or the furrows lining his forehead. But whatever the reason, Tiffany knew that Zane Sheridan was hiding something.

Tiffany stood, as if by so doing she could end the conversation.

"Let me know if you change your mind." He rose and looked past her to the framed portrait of Devil's Gambit;

the painting was mounted proudly above the gray stone fireplace.

Just so that Mr. Sheridan understood the finality of her position on the farm, she offered an explanation to which he really wasn't entitled. "If I change my mind about selling the place, I'll give Ellery's brother Dustin first option. He already owns part of the farm and I think that Rhodes Breeding Farm should stay in the family."

Zane frowned thoughtfully and rubbed his chin. "If the family wants it—"

"Of course."

Shrugging his broad shoulders as if he had no interest whatsoever in the Rhodes family's business, he continued to gaze at the portrait over the mantel.

"A shame about Devil's Gambit," he said at length.

"Yes," Tiffany whispered, repeating his words stiffly. "A shame." The same accident that had claimed the proud horse's life had also killed Ellery. Mr. Sheridan didn't offer any condolences concerning her husband, the man he'd said he had known.

The conversation was stilted and uncomfortable, and Tiffany felt as if Zane Sheridan was deliberately baiting her. But why? And who needed it? The past few weeks had been chaotic enough. The last thing Tiffany wanted was a mysterious man complicating things with his enigmatic presence and cryptic statements.

As she walked around the desk, shortening the distance between the stranger and herself, she asked, "Do you own any horses, Mr. Sheridan?" His dark brows quirked at the formal use of his surname.

"A few. In Ireland."

That explained the faint accent. "So you want to buy the farm and make your mark on American racing?"

"Something like that." For the first time, his smile

seemed sincere, and there was a spark of honesty in his clear, gray eyes.

Tiffany supposed that Zane Sheridan was the singularly most attractive man she had met in a long while. Tall and whip-lean, with broad shoulders and thick, jet-black hair, he stood with pride and authority as he returned her gaze. His skin was dark and smooth, and where once there might have been a dimple, there were now brackets of strain around his mouth. He had lived a hard life, Tiffany guessed, but the expensive tweed jacket suggested that the worst years had passed.

It would be a mistake to cross a man such as this, she decided. Zane Sheridan looked as if he were capable of ruthless retribution. This was evidenced in the tense line of his square jaw, the restless movement of his fingers against his thumb and the hard glint of determination in those steel-gray eyes. Zane was a man to reckon with and not one to deceive.

The doorbell rang, and Tiffany was grateful for the intrusion.

"If you'll excuse me," she said, taking three quick steps before pausing to turn in his direction.

"We're not through here."

"Pardon me?" Tiffany was taken aback. She expected him to show some civility and leave before Rod Crawford's interview. Instinctively Tiffany knew that having Zane in the same room with the reporter would be dangerous.

"I want to talk to you—seriously—about the farm."

"There's no reason, Mr. . . . Zane. You're wasting your time with me. I'm not about to sell."

"Indulge me," he suggested. He strode across the short distance separating them and touched her lightly on the arm. "Hear what I have to say, listen to what my offer is before you say no."

The doorbell chimed again, more impatiently this time.

"I really do have an appointment," she said, looking anxiously through the foyer to the front door. The grip on her arm tightened slightly.

"And I think you should listen to what I have to say."

"Why?"

He hesitated slightly, as if he weren't sure he could trust her and the skin tightened over his cheekbones. His rugged features displayed a new emotion. Anger and vengeful self-righteousness were displayed in the thrust of his jaw. All traces of his earlier civility had disappeared. Tiffany's heart began to pound with dread.

"Why are you here?" she asked again, her voice suddenly hoarse.

"I came to you because there is something I think that you should know."

"And that is?" Her heart was pounding frantically now, and she barely heard the doorbell chime for the third time.

"I'm not so sure that Devil's Gambit's death was an accident," he stated, gauging her reaction, watching for even the slightest trace of emotion on her elegant features. "In fact, I think there's a damned good chance that your horse is still alive."

Chapter Two

The color drained from Tiffany's face. "You . . . you think that Devil's Gambit might be alive?" she repeated, her voice barely a whisper. "You're not serious. . . ."

But she could tell by Zane's expression that he was dead serious.

"Dear God," she whispered, closing her eyes. She wanted to dismiss what he was saying as idle conjecture, but he just didn't seem the type of man who would fabricate anything so bizarre. "I don't know if I can deal with this right now. . . ." Devil's Gambit alive? But how? She'd been to the site of the accident, witnessed the gruesome truth for herself. Both the horse and the driver of the truck had been killed. Only Dustin had survived.

It was difficult to speak or to think rationally. Tiffany forced herself to look into Zane's brooding gaze and managed to clear her throat. "Look, I really do have an interview that I can't get out of. Please wait. . . . I . . . I want to talk to you. Alone." She extracted her arm from his grasp and made her way to the door. Her mind was running in crazy circles. What did he mean? Devil's Gambit couldn't possibly be alive. And Ellery—what about Ellery? Dear Lord, if what Zane was suggesting was true, there might be a chance that Ellery was still alive. But how? *Don't think like this,* she told herself. *What this man is suggesting can't possibly be true.*

Her knees were weak, and she leaned against the door for several seconds, trying to recover her lost equilibrium before the bell chimed for the fourth time. "Get hold of yourself," she murmured, but she was unable to disguise the clouds of despair in her eyes. Why now? Why did Zane Sheridan pick this time when everything at the breeding farm was in turmoil to enter her life with rash statements about the past? Forcing her worried thoughts to a dark corner of her mind, she straightened and braced herself for the interview.

With a jerk, she tugged on the brass handle and the door swung inward. Despite the storm of emotions raging within her, she forced what she hoped would appear a sincere and pleasant smile. Only the slightest trembling of her full lips hinted at her ravaged emotions.

"Mr. Crawford?" Tiffany asked the agitated young man slouching against a white pillar supporting the roof. "Please accept my apologies for the delay. My housekeeper isn't in yet and I had an unexpected visitor this morning." Her voice was surprisingly calm, her gaze direct, and she disguised the trembling in her fingers by hiding her hands in the deep pockets of her wool skirt.

The bearded, blond man eyed her skeptically, motioned to someone in the car and then handed her a card that stated that he was Rod Crawford of the *Santa Rosa Clarion.*

A petite, dark-haired woman climbed out of the car and slung a camera over one shoulder. Tiffany stepped away from the door to let the two people enter her home. In the distance she heard the familiar rumble of Louise's old Buick. The noise was reassuring. Once the housekeeper took charge of the kitchen, some of the disorder of the morning would abate. *Except that Zane Sheridan was in the den, seemingly convinced that Devil's Gambit and, therefore, Ellery, were still alive.*

"Could I offer you a cup of coffee . . . or tea?" Tiffany asked with a weak smile.

"Coffee—black," Crawford stated curtly, withdrawing a note pad from his back pocket.

Tiffany trained her eyes on the photographer. "Anything," the pleasant-featured woman replied. She flashed Tiffany a friendly grin as she extended her small hand. "Jeanette Wilkes." Jeanette's interested eyes swept the opulent interior of the house and she noted the sweeping staircase, gleaming oak banister, elegant crystal chandelier, and glossy imported floor tiles. "I was hoping to get a couple of pictures of the farm."

"Wonderful," Tiffany said with a smile that disguised her inner turmoil. "Please, have a seat in the living room." She opened the double doors of the formal room and silently invited them inside.

"You have a beautiful home," Jeanette stated as she looked at the period pieces and the Italian marble of the fireplace with a practiced eye. Everything about the house was first class—no outward sign of money problems.

"Thank you."

"Is this where you work?" Crawford asked skeptically.

"No . . ."

"If you don't mind, Jeanette would like to get some shots of the inside of the farm as well as the outbuildings. You know, give people a chance to see whatever it is you do when you're working. Don't you have an office or something?" He eyed the formal living room's expensive formal furniture with obvious distaste.

"Of course." The last thing Tiffany could afford was any bad press, so she had to accommodate the nosy reporter. She decided she would have to find a way to get rid of Zane Sheridan. His story was too farfetched to be believed; and yet there was something forceful and determined about him that made her think the Irishman wasn't bluffing.

Zane was still in the den and Tiffany wanted to keep Rod Crawford, with his probing questions, away from the visitor with the Irish accent. If the two men with their different perspectives on what was happening at Rhodes Breeding Farm got together, the results would be certain disaster. Tiffany shuddered when she envisioned the news concerning Moon Shadow's foals and a rumor that Devil's Gambit was still alive being splashed across the front page of the *Santa Rosa Clarion*. The minute the combined reports hit the front page, she would have reporters calling her day and night.

Tiffany's mind was spinning miles a minute. What Zane had suggested was preposterous, and yet the surety of his gaze had convinced her that he wasn't playing games. But Devil's Gambit, alive? And Ellery? Her heart was beating so rapidly she could barely concentrate. She needed to talk to Zane Sheridan, that much was certain, just to find out if he were a master gambler, bluffing convincingly, or if he really did mean what he was saying and had the facts to back him up. But she had to speak to him alone, without the watchful eyes and ears of the press observing her.

Holding her back stiffly, she led Rod and Jeanette back through the foyer to the den, which was directly opposite the living room. Zane was standing by the fireplace, his eyes trained on the painting of the horse over the mantel. He had discarded his jacket and tossed it over the back of one chair, and the tight knot of his tie had been loosened. He looked as if he intended to stay. That was something she couldn't allow, and yet she was afraid to let him go. There were so many questions whirling in her mind. Who was he? What did he want?

How did he know Ellery? Why did he want her to believe that Devil's Gambit might still be alive after four long years?

Without hesitation, Tiffany walked toward him. He turned to face her and his eyes were as cool and distant as the stormy, gray Pacific Ocean. If he had been lying a few moments before, he showed no trace of deceit. Yet his story couldn't possibly be true; either it was a total fabrication or he just didn't know what he was talking about.

The steadiness of his glare suggested just the opposite. Tiffany knew intuitively that Zane Sheridan rarely made mistakes. Cold dread took hold of her heart.

"Mr. Sheridan, would it be too much trouble to ask you to wait to finish our discussion?" she asked with an unsteady smile. *What if he wouldn't leave and caused a scene in front of the reporter from the* Santa Rosa Clarion? *His story was just wild and sensational enough to capture Rod Crawford's attention.*

Zane's eyes flickered to the other two people and quickly sized them up as reporters. Obviously something was going on, and the widow Rhodes didn't want him to know about it. His thick brows drew together in speculation.

"How long?"

"I'm not sure. . . . Mr. Crawford?"

"Call me Rod."

Tiffany made a hasty introduction, while the bearded man came to her side and shook Zane's outstretched hand. The image of the reporter's hand linked with Zane's made her uneasy.

"I don't know," Rod was saying, rubbing his bearded chin. "I suppose it will take . . . what?" He eyed Jeanette for input. "An hour, maybe two. I want to ask you some questions and then we need a quick tour of the buildings."

Tiffany's throat went dry. No matter how crazy Zane's story seemed, she had to talk to him, find out what he wanted and why he thought that Devil's Gambit might still be alive.

"I have a meeting at noon," Zane stated, his calculating gaze never leaving the worried lines of her face. There was something in Tiffany Rhodes's manner that suggested it would be to his advantage to stay. But he needed to be with her alone in order to accomplish everything he had planned for six long years. He'd given her the bait, and she'd swallowed it hook, line, and sinker. The satisfaction he had hoped to find was sadly lacking, and he felt a twinge of conscience at the worry in her clouded eyes.

"Look, Ms. Rhodes—can we get on with it? We've got another story to cover this afternoon," Crawford interjected.

"Of course." Tiffany returned her attention to Zane's proud face. She hoped that she didn't sound nearly as desperate as she felt. "Could you come by tomorrow, or would it be more convenient to meet you somewhere?"

"I have to catch an early flight." His angular jaw was tense, his muscles rigid, but there was the glimmer of expectancy in his eyes. *He's enjoying this,* she thought and she had to work to control her temper. She couldn't blow up now, not with Rod Crawford in the room, but there was something infuriating in Zane's arrogant manner.

Trying not to sound condescending she asked, "Then tonight?" He couldn't just waltz into her life, make outrageous statements, and then disappear as if nothing had happened. She had to know the truth, or what he was attempting to portray as the truth. She wanted to forget about him and his wild imaginings, but she couldn't dismiss him as just another publicity seeker. What did he want—*really want* from her?

Zane's gray eyes narrowed a fraction. "All right. What time?"

"How about dinner—seven-thirty?"

"I'll be here."

He picked up his jacket and flung it over his arm. Tiffany escorted him to the door and let out a long sigh of relief when he was gone. At least he had no inkling why the reporter was there, although it wouldn't be too hard to figure out, especially once the article was printed. "Maybe he'll be back in Ireland where he belongs by then," she muttered with false optimism.

Louise was serving coffee and scones when Tiffany returned to the den. After accepting a cup of black coffee, Tiffany seated herself at her desk, feeling uncomfortably close to Rod Crawford, who sat across the desk. While Jeanette snapped a few "candid" shots of Tiffany at work, Rod began the interview.

"How long have you actually managed the farm?" he asked.

"About four years."

"Ever since your husband's death?"

Tiffany felt her back tighten. "That's right. Before that I helped Ellery on the farm, but he ran it."

"I don't mean to bring up a sore subject," the wily reporter went on, "but ever since you took over, you've had quite a few bad breaks."

Tiffany smiled grimly. "That's true, but I don't like to dwell on them. Right now I'm concentrating on Journey's End."

"The three-year-old, right?"

"Yes. He has all the potential of being one of the greatest horses of the decade."

Rod Crawford laughed aloud. "I doubt if you're all that objective about your own colt."

"Obviously you've never seen him run,"Tiffany replied with a slow-spreading grin. The tense air in the room dissolved, as she talked at length about Journey's End's impressive career.

"What about the recent string of deaths in the foaling shed?" Rod asked when the conversation waned. Though Tiffany had been bracing herself for the question, she found no easy answer to it.

"Three foals died shortly after birth," she admitted.

"And you don't know why?" Skepticism edged Rod's question.

Tiffany shook her head. "So far the autopsies haven't shown anything conclusive, other than that the cause of death was heart failure."

Rod settled into his chair and poised his pencil theatrically in the air. "Were the foals related?"

Here it comes, Tiffany thought. "They had different dams, of course, but both colts and the filly were sired by Moon Shadow."

"And he stands at stud here, on the farm."

"Yes, although we're not breeding him . . . until all this is cleared up." Tiffany's hands were beginning to shake again, and she folded them carefully over the top of the desk.

"You think he might be the cause?"

"I don't know."

"Genetic problem?"

Tiffany pursed her lips and frowned thoughtfully. "I don't think so. He's stood for almost eight years, and until now he's proved himself a good sire. Devil's Gambit and Journey's End are proof of that."

"Moon Shadow was the sire of both stallions?"

"And many more. Some not as famous, but *all* perfectly healthy and strong horses."

"So, what with Journey's End's success, you must be getting a lot of requests for Moon Shadow's services."

"That's right. But we're turning them down, at least for a while, until we can prove that whatever is happening here is not a genetic problem."

"That must be costing you—"

"I think it's worth it."

"Then you must think he's the cause."

"I don't know what's the cause. It may just be coincidence."

Rod snorted his disbelief, and Tiffany had to press her hands together to keep from losing her temper. To Rod Crawford, Moon Shadow was just another story, but to Tiffany he was a proud stallion with an admirable reputation as a racehorse and a sire. She would do anything she had to—short of lying—to protect him and the reputation of the farm.

"Have you had him tested?" Rod asked.

"Moon Shadow?" When Rod nodded, Tiffany replied, "Of course. He's been given a complete physical, and we've taken samples of his semen to be analyzed."

"And?"

"So far, nothing."

Rod twirled his pencil nervously. "What about mares that were brought to Moon Shadow and then taken home?"

Tiffany felt a headache beginning to pound. "As far as I know, only the horses on this farm have been affected. However, it's still early in the year and there are several mares who haven't yet dropped their foals."

"Have you been in contact with the owners of the mares and explained the problem to them?"

"Mr. Crawford," Tiffany stated evenly, "I'm not

certain there is a problem, or exactly the nature of it. I'm not an alarmist and I'm not about to warn other owners or scare them out of their wits. What I have done is written a letter inquiring as to the condition of the foals involved. I've had seven responses, and all of them indicate that they have beautiful, healthy horses. Two owners want to rebreed their mares to Moon Shadow."

Rod frowned. "And have you?"

"Not yet."

"Because you're afraid?"

"Because I want to be certain of what is happening before I do anything that might cause any stress or trauma to the horses or the owners." Tiffany looked him squarely in the eye. "This is more than a business for me. It's a way of life, and there's more at stake than money." Rod's blank stare told Tiffany that he didn't understand anything she was saying. Perhaps no one did. Rod Crawford, or anyone else for that matter, couldn't know about the agonizing years she had spent growing up in musty tack rooms and dingy stables where the smell of ammonia had been so strong it had made her retch. No one knew that the only comfort she had found as an adolescent child was in working with the Thoroughbreds her father had been hired to train.

Before her thoughts became too vivid and painful, Tiffany spread her hands expressively over the desk and forced a frail smile at the reporter. "Look, until I know for certain what exactly it is that's happening, I'm not about to make any rash statements, and I would appreciate your cooperation—"

Rod raised a dubious blond brow. "By withholding the story?"

"By not sensationalizing the deaths and *creating* a story. I agreed to this interview because I know of the *Clarion's* reputation."

"I have to report the truth."

Tiffany smiled stiffly. "That's all I can ask for. Now, if you have any further questions about the horses involved, you can call Vance Geddes, the veterinarian who was with the mares when they delivered the foals."

"Fair enough," Rod replied.

Tiffany led the reporter and his assistant through the broodmare barn and the foaling shed, before returning outside to the brisk March air. While Rod asked questions, Jeanette took some outside shots of a field where mares grazed and spindly-legged foals ran in the shafts of late-morning sunlight.

Tiffany's face lifted with pride as she watched the dark foals run and shy behind the safety of their mothers' flanks. The newborns always held a special place in her heart. She loved to watch them stand and nurse for the first time, or run in the fields with their downy ears pricked forward and their intelligent eyes wide to the vast new world. Maybe that was why the deaths of the foals affected her so deeply.

"I'll send you a copy of the article," Rod promised just before he and Jeanette left.

"Thank you." Tiffany watched in relief as the sporty Mazda headed out the long drive. The interview hadn't been as bad as she had expected, but nonetheless, she felt drained from the ordeal.

After changing into comfortable jeans and a sweatshirt, Tiffany returned to the den and pulled out the checkbook. But before she could concentrate on the ledgers, she let her eyes wander to the portrait of Devil's Gambit, the horse that Zane Sheridan insisted was alive.

"It can't be," she murmured to herself. Devil's Gambit had been a beautifully built colt with a short, sturdy back, and powerful hind legs that could explode into a full stride of uncanny speed and grace. Jet-black, with one distinctive white stocking, Devil's Gambit had taken the racing world by storm, winning all of his two-year-old starts by ever-increasing margins. As a three-year-old his career had taken off with a flourish, and he had been compared to such greats as Secretariat and Seattle Slew.

Then, a month before the Kentucky Derby, it had all ended tragically. Devil's Gambit suffered a horrible death while being transported from Florida to Kentucky.

Tiffany had learned that Ellery had been driving and had apparently fallen asleep at the wheel. Dustin, his brother, had been a passenger in the truck. Miraculously Dustin had survived with only minor injuries by being thrown out of the cab as the truck tumbled end over end, down an embankment, where it exploded into flames that charred beyond recognition the bodies of Ellery Rhodes and his fleet horse. Dustin's injuries had included a broken leg and minor concussion, which were treated at a local hospital. He had been out of the hospital in time to stand by Tiffany's side at Ellery's funeral.

Tiffany swallowed against the painful memory and shook her head. It had taken her several months to come to accept the death of her husband and his brave horse. And now a total stranger, a man by the name of Zane Sheridan, was trying to make her believe that it had all been a treacherous mistake.

But he didn't state that Ellery was alive, she reminded herself with a defeated smile, only Devil's Gambit. And when Zane had mentioned Ellery, it had been with a look of barely veiled contempt on his rugged black-Irish features.

What can it all mean? She slanted a glance at the portrait of Devil's Gambit and frowned. How could someone hide a horse of such renown? And who could have come up with such a scheme? And why? Certainly not for kidnapping ransom. *Get hold of yourself,* she cautioned, *you're letting your imagination run away with you, all because of some stranger's outlandish remarks.*

With a grimace she turned her attention back to the check book and finished paying the month-end bills. She wasn't exactly strapped for money, but each month her assets seemed to diminish. There was still a large, outstanding mortgage against the property, and several major repairs to the barns couldn't be neglected much longer.

If she regretted anything, it was allowing Ellery to build the expensive house. "You can't be a horse breeder unless you look the part," he had said with the confidence of one who understands the subtleties in life. "No one will bring their mares here if we don't *look* like we know what we're doing."

"It's not the house that counts, it's the quality of the stallions and the care of the horses," Tiffany had argued uselessly. In the end, Ellery had gotten his way. After all, it had only taken a quick signature at the bank—his signature—to get the loan to rebuild the house into a grand, Southern manor.

"This is California, not Kentucky," she had reminded him. "No one cares about this sort of thing." But her protests had fallen on deaf ears and Ellery had taken up wearing suits with patches on the sleeves and smoking a pipe filled with blended tobaccos.

The house was finished only six months before the accident. Since that time she had lived in it alone. It was beautiful and grand and mortgaged to the hilt. Ellery hadn't seen fit to purchase mortgage insurance at the time he took out the loan. "Money down the drain," he had commented with a knowing smile.

"I must have been out of my mind to have listened to

him," Tiffany thought aloud as she pushed the ledgers aside and stood. How many years had she blindly trusted him, all because he had saved her life? She shuddered when she remembered the time she had seen Ellery, his face contorted in fear, as he dived in front of the oncoming car and pushed her out of its path.

Maybe it had been gratitude rather than love that she had felt for him, but nonetheless they had been married and she had depended upon him. And *now there was a chance that he was still alive.* The thought made her heart race unevenly.

After grabbing her jacket, she sank her teeth into her lower lip, walked outside and turned toward the broodmare barn. A chilly wind was blowing from the west and she had to hold her hair away from her face to keep it from whipping across her eyes. Mac was leaning over the railing of one of the stalls in the barn. His sharp eyes turned in her direction when she approached.

"I was just about to come up to the house," he stated, a worried expression pinching his grizzled features.

"Something wrong?"

"No . . . but it looks like this lady here—" he cocked his head in the direction of the black mare restlessly pacing her stall "—is gonna foal tonight."

Instead of the usual expectation Tiffany always felt at the prospect of new life, she now experienced dread. The mare in question, Ebony Wine, was carrying another of Moon Shadow's foals.

"You're sure?" she asked, surveying the mare's wide girth.

"Aye. She's a week overdue as it is, and look." He pointed a bony finger at the mare's full udder. "She's waxed over and beginning to drip."

"Has she starting sweating?"

"Not yet. It will be a while—sometime after midnight unless I miss my guess."

"But everything else looks normal?" Tiffany asked, her knowing gaze studying the restless horse.

"So far."

"Let me know when the time comes," Tiffany ordered, patting the mare fondly.

"You're not going to wait up again?"

"Of course I am."

Mac took off his hat and dangled it from his fingers as he leaned on the railing of the stall. "There's nothing you can do, you know. What will be, will be."

"You can't talk me out of this. I'll give Vance a call and ask him to come over." She took one last glance at the heavy-bellied mare. "Come up to the house and get me if anything goes wrong, or if it looks like the foal will be early."

Mac nodded curtly and placed his frumpy fedora back on his head. "You're the boss," he muttered, placing his hands in the back pockets of his trousers. "I'll be in the tack room if ya need me."

"Thanks, Mac." Tiffany walked outside but didn't return to the house. Instead, she let herself through a series of gates and walked through the gently sloping paddocks away from the main buildings.

When she neared the old barn, she halted and studied the graying structure. Once the barn had been integral to the farm, but the vacant building hadn't been used for years. Ellery had insisted that the horses needed newer, more modern facilities, and rather than put money into modernizing the old barn, he had erected the new broodmare barn and foaling shed.

The weathered building with the sagging roof was little more than an eyesore, and Tiffany realized that she should have had it torn down years before. Its only function was to store excess hay and straw through the winter.

She walked toward the barn and ignored the fact that blackberry vines were beginning to ramble and cling to the east wall. The old door creaked on rusty rollers as she pushed it aside and walked into the musty interior.

It took a few minutes for her eyes to adjust to the dim light. How many years had it been since she had first seen Ellery? She had been standing near the stalls, making sure that the horses had fresh water when he had startled her.

Before that fateful day, she had seen him only from a distance. After all, she was only a trainer's daughter. A nobody. Tiffany doubted that Ellery Rhodes realized that when he hired Edward Chappel, he took on Edward's eighteen-year-old daughter, as well.

Perhaps her mistake had been to stay with her father, but Edward Chappel was the only family she had known. Her mother, Marie, had abandoned them both when Tiffany was only five. She could remember little of Marie except that she had thick, golden hair and a beautiful but weary face that very rarely smiled.

Fragments of life with her mother had come to mind over the years. Tiffany remembered that Marie insisted that her daughter's hair always be combed and that her faded clothes always be neatly starched. And there was a tune . . . a sad refrain that Marie would sing when she helped Tiffany get dressed in the morning. Twenty years later, Tiffany would still find herself humming that tune.

The day that her mother had walked out of her life was still etched vividly in her mind. "You must remember that Mommy loves you very much and I'll come back for you," Marie had whispered to Tiffany, with tears gathering in her round, indigo eyes. "I promise, pumpkin."

Then Marie had gathered her daughter close to her breast, as if she couldn't bear to walk out the door.

Tiffany had felt the warm trickle of her mother's tears as they silently dropped onto the crown of her head.

"Mommy, don't leave me. *Please*. . . . Mommy, Mommy, don't go. I'll be good . . . Mommy, I love you, please . . ." Tiffany had wailed, throwing her arms around her mother's neck and then sobbing with all of her heart for hours after Marie's car had disappeared in a plume of dust.

Her father's face was stern, his shoulders bowed. "Don't blame her, Tiffy," he had whispered hoarsely, "it's all my fault, you know. I haven't been much of a husband."

Tiffany had never seen Marie Caldwell Chappel again.

At first she couldn't believe that her mother had left her, and each night she would stare out the window and pray that the tall man with the big car would bring her mother home. Later, in her early teens, Tiffany was angry that she didn't have a mother to help her understand the changes in her body and the new emotions taking hold of her. Now, as an adult, Tiffany understood that a woman who had been brought up with a taste for the finer things in life could never have been happy with Edward Chappel.

Edward had always been irresponsible, going from job to job, breeding farm to breeding farm, working with the animals he loved. But each time, just when Tiffany thought they had settled down for good and she had made one or two friends in the local school, he would lose his job and they would move on to a new town, a new school, a new set of classmates who would rather ignore than accept her. To this day, she had never made any close friends. She had learned long ago that relationships were fragile and never lasted for any length of time.

After Marie had left him, Edward had sworn off the bottle for nearly three years. Tiffany now realized that his abstinence was because of the hope that Marie would return to him rather than because of his new responsibility as a single parent.

When she was just eighteen and trying to save enough money to go to college, they'd moved to the Rhodes Farm. Edward was off the bottle again and he had promised his daughter that this time he would make good.

It was in this very barn that her life had changed. While she'd been softly talking to one of the yearlings, Ellery Rhodes had walked in on her.

"Who are you?" he'd asked imperiously, and Tiffany had frozen. When she'd turned to face him, the look on his even features was near shock.

"I'm Tiffany Chappel," she had replied, with a faltering smile.

"Ed's daughter?"

"Yes."

Ellery had been flustered. "I thought that you were just a little girl." His eyes moved from her face, down the length of her body and back again. An embarrassed flush crept up his neck. "Obviously, I was mistaken."

"Dad seems to think that I'm still about eleven," she explained with a shrug and turned back to the horses.

"How old are you?"

"Eighteen."

"Why aren't you out on your own?" It was a nosy question, but Ellery asked it with genuine concern in his gold eyes. His brows had pulled together and a thoughtful frown pulled at the corners of his mouth. For a moment Tiffany thought that he might fire her father because of her. Maybe Ellery Rhodes didn't like the idea of a girl—young woman—on his farm. Maybe one of the grooms had complained about a woman on the farm. She had already had more than her share of male advances from the stable boys.

Tiffany couldn't explain to her father's employer that she had to look after him, or that a good share of his work was done by her strong hands. Edward Chappel would be fired again. Instead she lied. "I'm only helping him out for a little while. Until I go back to college—"

Ellery's practiced eyes took in her torn sweatshirt, faded jeans and oversized boots. Tiffany knew that he saw through her lie, but he was too much of a gentleman to call her on it.

Two days later, she was called into his office. Her heart pounded with dread as she entered the old farmhouse and sat stiffly in one of the chairs near his desk.

Ellery looked up from a stack of bills he had been paying. "I've got a proposition for you, young lady," he stated, looking up at her and his gold eyes shining. "Your father has already approved."

"What do you mean?"

Ellery smiled kindly. It wasn't a warm smile, but it was caring. He explained that he had worked out a deal with her father. He liked the way she handled the horses, he claimed, and he offered to send her to school, if she promised to return to the farm and work off the amount of money her education would cost once she had graduated.

Tiffany had been ecstatic with her good fortune, and Edward, feeling that he had finally found a way to rightfully provide for his daughter, was as pleased as anyone.

She had never forgotten Ellery's kindness to her, and she had held up her part of the bargain. When she returned to the farm two years later, she found that her father was drinking again.

"You've got to leave," he said, coughing violently. The stench of cheap whiskey filled the air in the small room he had been living in on the farm.

"I can't, Dad. I've got a debt to pay."

Edward shivered, though he was covered by several thick blankets. "You should never have come back."

"Why didn't anyone tell me you were sick—"

Edward raised a feeble hand and waved away her concerns. "It wouldn't help anything now, would it? You were so close to finishing school, I didn't want you to know."

"I think you should be in a hospital."

Edward shook his head and another fit of racking coughs took hold of him. "I want you to leave. I've got a little money. Get away from this farm, from Ellery Rhodes—"

"But he's been so good to me."

Her father's faded blue eyes closed for a second. "He's changed, Tiff. . . ." Another fit of coughing took hold of him, and he doubled up in pain.

"I'm getting you to a hospital, right now."

Despite her father's protests, Tiffany managed to get him out of the stifling room and to the main house. When she knocked on the door, Stasia, the exotic-looking woman Ellery was living with, answered the door.

"My father needs help," Tiffany said.

Stasia's full lips pulled into a line of disgust at the sight of Tiffany and her father. Her dark eyes traveled over Tiffany, and she tossed her hair off her shoulders. "He needs to dry out—"

"He's sick."

"Humph."

Pulling herself to her full height, Tiffany looked the older woman directly in the eye. "Please. Call Ellery."

"He's not here."

"Then find someone to help me."

Edward's coughing started again. His shoulders racked from the pain. "I don't know why Ellery keeps him around," Stasia muttered, as she reached for her coat and begrudgingly offered to drive them into town.

Tiffany remained at her father's side for two days until the pneumonia that had settled in his lungs took his life.

"You stupid, lovable old fool," Tiffany had said, tears running down her face. "Why did you kill yourself—why?" she asked, as her father's body was moved from the hospital room to the morgue.

Refusing help from the hospital staff, Tiffany had run out of the building, blinded by tears of grief and guilt. If she hadn't gone away to school, if she had stayed on the farm, her father would still have been alive.

She didn't see the oncoming car as she crossed the street. She heard the blast from an angry horn, smelled the bum of rubber as tires screamed against the dry asphalt and felt a man's body push her out of the way of the station wagon.

The man who had saved her life was Ellery. He'd gathered her shaken form into his arms and muttered something about being sorry. She didn't understand why, and she didn't care. Ellery Rhodes was the only person she had ever known who had been kind to her with no ulterior motives.

Within two weeks, Stasia was gone and Ellery asked Tiffany to marry him.

Tiffany didn't hesitate. Ellery Rhodes was the first person she had met whom she could depend on. He cared for her, and though he seemed distant at times, Tiffany realized that no relationship was perfect.

She wondered now if she had married him out of gratitude or grief. The love she had hoped would bloom within her had never surfaced, but she supposed that was because passionate, emotional love only existed in fairy tales.

Inexplicably, her thoughts returned to Zane Sheridan, with his knowing gray eyes and ruggedly hewn features. He was the last person she needed to complicate her life right now, and the idea that he could shed any light on what had happened to Devil's Gambit or Ellery was preposterous.

But what if there's a chance that Ellery's alive?

Without any answers to her questions, Tiffany headed back to the house to remind Louise that there would be a guest for dinner.

"You're asking the impossible!" John Morris stated as he eyed his client over the clear rims of his reading glasses.

"It's a simple document," Zane argued, rubbing the back of his neck and rotating his head to relieve the tension that had been building ever since he had met Tiffany Rhodes. He'd known she was beautiful; he'd seen enough pictures of her to understand that her exotic looks could be any man's undoing. But he hadn't counted on the light of intrigue and mystery in her intense gaze or the serene beauty in the curve of her neck. . . .

"A deed of sale for a breeding farm? You've got to be joking."

Zane's eyes flashed like quicksilver. He pulled at the bothersome knot in his tie and focused his eyes on the attorney. "Just get me a paper that says that for a certain amount of money—and leave that blank—I will purchase all of the assets and the liabilities of Rhodes Breeding Farm."

The lawyer let out a weary sigh. "You're out of your mind, Zane. That is if you want anything legal—"

"I want it to be binding. No loopholes. It has to be so tight that if the buyer decides she wants out of the deal, she has no legal recourse. None whatsoever." His square jaw tightened, and the thin lines near the corners of his eyes deepened with fresh resolve. Revenge was supposed to be sweet. So where was the satisfaction he had been savoring for nearly six years?

"You're asking the impossible. We're not talking about a used car, for God's sake."

"It can't be that difficult." Zane paced in the prestigious San Francisco lawyer's office and ran impatient fingers through his raven-black hair in disgust. "What about a quitclaim deed?"

The lawyer leaned back in his chair and held on to his pen with both hands. "I assume that you want to do this right."

"Of course."

"No legal recourse—right?"

"I already told you that."

"Then be patient. I'll draw up all the legal documents and do a title search . . . take care of all the loose ends. That way, once you've agreed upon a price, you can wrap it up and it *will* be binding. You can't have it both ways, not here anyway. You're not just talking about real estate, you know. There is personal property, equipment, the horses. . . ."

"I get the picture." Zane stared out the window and frowned. The trouble was he wanted to get away from Tiffany Rhodes. Do what he had to do and then make a clean break.

There was something about the woman that got under his skin, and he didn't like the look of honesty in her slate-blue eyes. It bothered him. A lot. Whatever else he had expected of Ellery Rhodes's widow, it hadn't been integrity.

Zane shrugged as if to shake off the last twinges of guilt. "So how long will it take you?" he asked, hiding some of his impatience.

"Four weeks—maybe three, if we're lucky. I'll work out something temporary for the interim. Okay?"

"I guess it will have to be. Doesn't seem that I have much of a choice."

John drummed his fingers on the desk. "You're sure that this woman wants to sell? I've read a little about her. She seems to be . . . the plucky type. Not the kind to sell out."

"She just needs a little convincing."

John scowled at the blank piece of paper in front of him. "That sounds ominous—right out of a bad B movie."

Zane smiled despite his discomfiture. It was a rare smile, but genuine, and he flashed it on his friend in a moment of self-mockery. "I guess you're right."

"Aren't I always?"

"And humble, too," Zane muttered under his breath. "Come on, counselor, I'll buy you a drink."

"On one condition—"

Zane's brows quirked expectantly.

"That you quit calling me counselor. I hear enough of that in the courtroom."

"It's a deal."

John slipped his arms into his jacket and then straightened the cuffs before bending over his desk and pressing a button on the intercom. "Sherry, I'm going out for a few minutes with Mr. Sheridan. I'll be back at—" he cocked his wrist and checked his watch "—three-thirty."

John reached for the handle of the door before pausing and turning to face his friend. "There's just one thing I'd like to know about this transaction you requested."

"And that is?"

"Why the hell do you want to buy a breeding farm? I thought you learned your lesson in Dublin a few years back."

Zane's eyes grew dark. "Maybe that's exactly why I want it." With a secretive smile he slapped his friend fondly on the back. "Now, how about that drink?"

Chapter Three

Tiffany's fingers drummed restlessly on the desk as she stared at the portrait of Devil's Gambit. For so long she had believed that Ellery and his proud horse were dead. And now this man, this stranger named Zane Sheridan, insisted just the opposite. Her blue eyes were shadowed with pain as she studied the portrait of the horse. *Was it possible? Could Ellery still be alive?*

Shaking her head at the absurdity of the situation, she got up and paced restlessly, alternately staring at the clock and looking out the window toward the foaling shed. Ebony Wine would be delivering a foal tonight, Moon Shadow's foal. Would he be a normal, healthy colt or would he suffer the same cruel fate as three of his siblings?

She listened as the clock ticked off the seconds, and her stomach tightened into uneasy knots. Mac hadn't come to the house this afternoon, and Tiffany was beginning to worry. Between her anxiety for the unborn foal and worries about Zane Sheridan and his motives for visiting her, Tiffany's nerves felt raw, stretched to the breaking point.

Seven-thirty-five. Though Zane would arrive any minute, Tiffany couldn't sit idle any longer. She jerked her jacket off the wooden peg near the French doors and hurried outside, oblivious to the fact that her heels sank into the mud of the well-worn path. The darkness of the night was punctuated by the sharp wind that rattled the windowpanes and whistled through the redwoods.

Tiffany found Mac in the broodmare barn, examining the black mare. His face was grim, and Tiffany's heart nearly stopped beating.

"How's it going?" she asked, hoping that she didn't sound desperate.

Mac came to the outside of the stall and reached down to scratch Wolverine, the farm's border collie, behind the ears. Wolverine thumped his tail against the concrete floor in appreciation, but Tiffany had the impression that Mac was avoiding her gaze.

"So far so good," the ex-jockey replied, straightening and switching a piece of straw from one side of his mouth to the other. But his sharp brown eyes were troubled when they returned to Ebony Wine. The mare shifted uncomfortably in the large stall, and Tiffany noted that everything was ready for the impending birth. Six inches of clean straw covered the concrete floor, and a plastic bucket containing towels, antibiotics, scissors and other equipment necessary to help the mare give birth, had been placed near the stall.

"Might be a little earlier than I thought originally," Mac suggested. He took off his hat and straightened the crease with his fingers.

"Why?"

"This is her second foal. If I remember right, the last one came before midnight." He rammed the hat back on his head. "Could be wrong . . . just a feeling I've got."

"Have you called Vance?"

Mac nodded curtly. "He'll be here around eleven, earlier if we need him."

"Good."

Tiffany cast one final look toward the mare and then

returned to the house. Wolverine padded along behind her, but she didn't notice. Her thoughts were filled with worry for the mare and anxiety about meeting Zane Sheridan again. He couldn't have picked a worse time to show up.

All afternoon her thoughts had been crowded with questions about him. Who was he? What did he want? How did he know Ellery? Why would he concoct such an elaborate story about Devil's Gambit being alive?

There was something about the man that was eerily familiar, and Tiffany felt that she had heard Ellery speak of him at least once. But it was long ago, before they were married, and she couldn't remember the significance, if there was any, of Ellery's remarks.

She had just returned to the house and stepped out of her muddied shoes when headlights flashed through the interior of the manor as if announcing Zane's arrival. "Here we go," she muttered to herself as she slipped on a pair of pumps and attempted to push back the tides of dread threatening to overtake her. "He's only one man," she told herself as the doorbell chimed. "One man with a wild imagination."

But when she opened the door and she saw him standing in the shadowy porch light, once again she experienced the feeling that Zane Sheridan rarely made mistakes. He was leaning casually against one of the tall pillars supporting the porch roof, and his hands were thrust into the front pockets of his corduroy slacks. Even in the relaxed pose, there was tension, strain in the way his smile tightened over his teeth, a coiled energy lying just beneath the surface in his eyes.

In the dim light, his mouth appeared more sensual than she had remembered and the rough angles of his face seemed less threatening. His jet-black hair was without a trace of gray and gleamed blue in the lamplight.

Only his eyes gave away his age. Though still a sharp, intense silver, they were hard, as if they had witnessed years of bitterness. The skin near the corners of his eyes was etched with a faint webbing that suggested he had stared often into the glare of the afternoon sun.

"Sorry I'm late," he said, straightening as his bold gaze held hers.

"No problem," she returned and wondered what it was about him that she found so attractive. She'd never been a woman drawn to handsome faces or strong physiques. But there was an intelligence in Zane's eyes, hidden beneath a thin veneer of pride, that beckoned the woman in her. It was frightening. "Please come in."

I can't be attracted to him, she thought. *He can't be trusted. God only knows what he wants from me.*

He walked with her to the den. "I'm sorry for the interruption this morning—" she began.

"My fault. I should have called." A flash of a brilliant smile gleamed against his dark skin.

Tiffany didn't bother to wave off his apology. Zane's surprise appearance on her doorstep had thrown her day into a tailspin. It had been a wonder that she could even converse intelligently with the reporter from the *Santa Rosa Clarion* considering the bombshell that this man had dropped in her lap.

"Could I get you a drink?" she inquired as she walked toward a well-stocked bar disguised in the bookcase behind her desk. Ellery had insisted on the most modern of conveniences, the bar being one of his favorites. Tiffany hadn't used it more than twice since her husband's death.

"Scotch, if you have it."

She had it all right. That and about every other liquor imaginable. "You never can guess what a man might drink," Ellery had explained with a knowing wink. "Got to be prepared . . . just in case. I wouldn't want to blow a potential stud fee all because I didn't have a bottle of liquor around." Ellery had laughed, as if his response to her inquiry were a joke. But he had filled the bar with over thirty bottles of the most expensive liquor money could buy. "Think of it as a tax deduction," he had joked.

"Oh, I'm sure I've got Scotch," she answered Zane. "It's just a matter of locating it." After examining a few of the unfamiliar labels, Tiffany wiped away some of the dust that had collected on the unused bottles. *What a waste.*

It didn't take long to find an opened bottle of Scotch. She splashed the amber liquor into a glass filled with ice cubes and then, with a forced smile, she handed Zane the drink. "Now," she said, her voice surprisingly calm, "why don't you tell me why you think Devil's Gambit is alive?"

After pouring herself a glass of wine, she took an experimental sip and watched Zane over the rim of her glass. "That is, if you haven't changed your mind since this morning."

A gray light of challenge flashed in his eyes and his facade of friendly charm faded slightly. "Nothing's changed."

"So you still think that the horse is alive . . . and you're still interested in buying the farm, right?"

"That's correct."

Tiffany let out a ragged sigh and took a chair near the desk. "Please, have a seat."

Zane was too restless to sit. He walked over to the window and stared into the black, starless night. "I didn't mean to shock you this morning." Why the hell was he apologizing? He owed this woman nothing more than a quick explanation, and even that stuck in his throat. But there was something intriguing about her—a feminine mystique that touched a black part of his soul. Damn it all, this meeting was starting off all wrong. Ellery Rhodes's widow turned his thinking around. When he was with her, he started forgetting his objectives.

"Well, you did."

"Like I said—I should have called to make sure that we would have some time to talk."

Tiffany shifted uneasily in the chair. "We have all night," she said, and when a flicker of interest sparked in his eyes she quickly amended her statement. "Or however long it takes to straighten out this mess. Why don't you explain yourself?"

"I told you, I have reason to believe that Devil's Gambit is alive."

Tiffany smiled and shook her head. "That's impossible. I . . . I was at the scene of the accident. The horse was killed."

Zane frowned into the night. "*A* horse was killed."

"Devil's Gambit was the only horse in the trailer. The other two horses that had been stabled in Florida were in another truck—the one that Mac was driving. They were already in Kentucky when the accident occurred." She ran trembling fingers through her hair as she remembered that black, tragic night. Once again she thought about the terror and pain that Ellery and his horse must have gone through in those last agonizing moments before death mercifully took them both. "Devil's Gambit died in the accident." Her voice was low from the strain of old emotions, and she had to fight against the tears threatening her eyes.

"Unless he was never in that truck in the first place."

Tiffany swallowed with difficulty. "What are you suggesting, Mr. Sheridan?"

"I think that Devil's Gambit was kidnapped."

"That's crazy. My husband—"

Zane's eyes flashed silver fire. "Was probably involved."

Tiffany stood on trembling legs, her hands flattened on the desk to support her. A quiet rage began to burn in her chest "This conversation is absurd. Why would Ellery steal his own horse?"

Zane shrugged. "Money? Wasn't Devil's Gambit insured?"

"Not to his full value. After he won in Florida, we intended to increase the coverage, as he proved himself much more valuable than anyone had guessed. I had all the forms filled out, but before I could send them back to the insurance company as Ellery had suggested, I had to wait until I saw him again. Several of the documents required his signature." She shook her head at her own foolishness. "Why am I telling you all of this?" After releasing a weary sigh, she rapped her knuckles on the polished desk and clasped her hands behind her back.

"Because I'm telling you the truth."

"You think."

"I know."

Tiffany's emotions were running a savage gauntlet of anger and fear, but she attempted to keep her voice steady. "How do you know?"

"I saw your horse."

She sucked in her breath. "You saw Devil's Gambit? That's impossible. If he were alive, someone would have told me—"

"Someone is."

There was a charged silence in the air. "It's been four years since the accident. Why now?"

"Because I wasn't sure before."

Tiffany shook her head in denial, and her honey-colored hair brushed her shoulders. "This is too crazy—where did you see the horse? And how did you know it was Devil's Gambit? And what horse was killed in the trailer—and . . . and . . . what about my husband?" she whispered. "His brother Dustin was with him. Dustin knows what happened."

"Dustin claimed to be sleeping."

Tiffany flinched. How did this man, this virtual stranger, know so much about her and what had happened that night? If only she could remember what Ellery had said about Zane Sheridan. Ellery had spent some time in Ireland—Dublin. Maybe that was the connection. Zane still spoke with a slight brogue. Ellery must have known Zane in Dublin, and that's why he was here. Something happened in Ireland, years ago. Any other reason was just a fabrication, an excuse.

"Dustin would have woken up if the truck was stopped and the horses were switched. Dear God, do you know what you're suggesting?" Tiffany took a calming swallow of her wine and began to pace in front of the desk. Her thoughts were scattered between Zane, the tragic past, and the tense drama unfolding in the foaling shed. "Ellery would never have been involved in anything so underhanded."

"Didn't you ever question what happened?" Zane asked suddenly.

"Of course, but—"

"Didn't you think it was odd that Dustin had taken sleeping pills? Wasn't he supposed to drive later in the night—switch off with Ellery so that they wouldn't have to stop?"

Tiffany was immediately defensive. "Dustin's an insomniac. He needed the rest before the Derby."

"The Derby was weeks away."

"But there was a lot of work—"

"And what about your husband? Why did he decide to drive that night? Wasn't that out of the ordinary?" Bitterness tightened Zane's features, and he clutched his drink in a death grip.

"He was excited—he wanted to be a part of it." But even to her, the words sounded false. Ellery had always believed in letting the hired help handle the horses. Before that night, he had always flown—first class—to the next racetrack.

Zane saw the doubts forming in her eyes. "Everything about that 'accident' seems phony to me."

"But there was an investigation—"

"Thorough?"

"I—I don't know. . . . I think so." At the time she had been drowning in her own grief and shock. She had listened to the police reports, viewed the brutal scene of the accident, visited Dustin in the hospital, and flown home in a private fog of sorrow and disbelief. After the funeral, Dustin's strong arms and comforting words had helped her cope with her loss.

"Were Ellery's dental records checked?"

Tiffany's head snapped up, and her eyes were bright with righteous defiance. "Of course not. Ellery was driving. Dustin was there. There didn't need to be any further investigation." Her eyes narrowed a fraction, and her voice shook when she spoke again. "What are you suggesting, Mr. Sheridan? That my husband is still alive—hiding from me somewhere with his horse?"

Zane impaled her with his silvery stare and then ran impatient fingers through his hair. "I don't know."

A small sound of disbelief came from Tiffany's throat and she had to lean against the desk for support. "I—I don't know why I'm even listening to this," she whispered hoarsely. "It just doesn't make any sense. Devil's Gambit is worth a lot more as Devil's Gambit—in terms of dollars at the racetrack and stud fees. Anything you've suggested is absolutely beyond reason." She smiled grimly, as if at her own foolhardiness. "Look, I think maybe it would be better if you just left."

"I can't do that—not yet."

"Why not?"

"Because I intend to convince you that your horse was stolen from you."

"That's impossible."

"Maybe not." Zane extracted a small manila envelope from his breast pocket and walked back to the desk. "There are some pictures in here that might change your mind." He handed Tiffany the envelope, and she accepted it with a long sigh.

There were three photographs, all of the same horse. Tiffany scanned the color prints of a running horse closely, studying the bone structure and carriage of the animal. The similarities between the horse in the photograph and Devil's Gambit were uncanny. "Where did you get these?" she asked, her breath constricting in her throat.

"I took them. Outside of Dublin."

It made sense. The horse, if he really was Devil's Gambit, would have to be hidden out of the country to ensure that no one would recognize or identify him. Even so, Zane's story was ludicrous. "This isn't Devil's Gambit," she said, her slate-blue eyes questioning his. "This horse has no white marks . . . anywhere." She pointed to the portrait above the fireplace. "Devil's Gambit had a stocking, on his right foreleg."

"I think the stocking has been dyed."

"To hide his identity?"

"And to palm him off as another horse, one of considerably less caliber."

"This is ridiculous." Tiffany rolled her eyes and

raised her hands theatrically in the air. "You know, you almost convinced me by coming in here and making outlandish statements that I nearly believed. Heaven knows why. Maybe it's because you seemed so sure of yourself. But I can tell you without a doubt that this is not Devil's Gambit." She shook the prints in the air before tossing them recklessly on the desk. "Nothing you've said tonight makes any sense, nor is it backed up with the tiniest shred of evidence. Therefore I have to assume that you're here for another reason, such as the sale of the farm. My position hasn't altered on that subject, either. So you see, Mr. Sheridan, any further discussion would be pointless."

Louise knocked softly on the door of the den before poking her head inside. "Dinner's ready." She eyed Tiffany expectantly.

"I don't think—"

"Good. I'm starved," Zane stated as he turned his head in the housekeeper's direction. A slow-spreading, damnably charming grin took possession of his handsome face. Gray eyes twinkled devilishly, and his brilliant smile exposed a dimple on one tanned cheek.

"Whenever you're ready," Louise replied, seemingly oblivious to the tension in the room and returning Zane's smile. "I have to be getting home," she said apologetically to Tiffany, who nodded in response. Louise slowly backed out of the room and closed the door behind her.

"I didn't think you'd want to stay," Tiffany remarked, once Louise had left them alone.

"And miss a home-cooked meal? Not on your life."

Tiffany eyed him dubiously. "Something tells me this has nothing to do with the meal."

"Maybe I'm just enjoying the company—"

"Or maybe you think you can wear me down and I'll start believing all this nonsense."

"Maybe."

"There's no point, you know."

Zane laughed aloud, and the bitterness in his gaze disappeared for a second. "Try me."

"But we have nothing more to discuss. Really. I'm not buying your story. Not any of it."

"You're not even trying."

"I have the distinct feeling that you're attempting to con me, Mr. Sheridan—"

"Zane."

"Whatever. And I'm not up to playing games. Whether you believe it or not, I'm a busy woman who has more important things to do than worry about what could have happened. I like to think I deal in reality rather than fantasy."

Zane finished his drink with a flourish and set the empty glass down on the corner of the desk. "Then you'd better start listening to me, damn it. Because I'm not here on some cock-and-bull story." His thick brows lifted. "I have better things to do than spend my time trying to help someone who obviously doesn't want it."

"Help?" Tiffany repeated with a laugh. "All you've done so far is offer me vague insinuations and a few photographs of a horse that definitely is *not* Devil's Gambit. You call that help?"

Zane pinched the bridge of his nose, closed his eyes and let out a long breath. "If you weren't so blind, woman," he said, his black-Irish temper starting to explode.

"Look—"

Zane held up one palm and shrugged. "Maybe you just need time to think about all of this."

"What I don't need is someone to march into my life and start spewing irrational statements."

Zane smiled, and the tension drained from his face to be replaced by genuine awe of the woman standing near the desk. In the past six years, he'd imagined coming face to face with Ellery Rhodes's widow more often than he would like to admit, but never had he thought that she would be so incredibly bewitching. His mistake. Once before Ellery Rhodes and Zane Sheridan had been attracted to the same woman, and that time Zane had come out the loser, or so he had thought at the time. Now he wasn't so sure.

"Come on," he suggested, his voice becoming dangerously familiar. "I wasn't kidding when I said I was starved."

Tiffany backed down a little. "I won't change my mind."

With a nonchalant shrug, Zane loosened the knot of his tie and unbuttoned the collar of his shirt. His chin was beginning to darken with the shadow of a day's growth of beard, and he looked as if he belonged in this house, as if he had just come home from a long, tiring day at the office to share conversation and a drink with his wife. . . . The unlikely turn of her thoughts spurred Tiffany into action. As a slight blush darkened the skin of her throat, she opened the door of the den. Knowing it to be an incredible mistake, she led Zane past a formal dining room to a small alcove near the kitchen.

Louise had already placed the beef stew with gravy on the small round table.

"Sit," Tiffany commanded as she pulled out a bottle of wine and uncorked it before pouring the rich Burgundy into stemmed glasses. Zane did as he was bid, but his face registered mild surprise when Tiffany took the salads out of the refrigerator and set them on the table.

After Tiffany sat down, Zane stared at her from across a small maple table. "Your housekeeper doesn't live in?"

"No."

"But she manages to keep the place up?"

Tiffany released an uneasy laugh. "I'm not that messy. I do pick up after myself, even do my own laundry and cook occasionally," she teased. What must he think of her? That she was some princess who wouldn't get her fingers dirty? Did his preconceived notions stem from his relationship—whatever that was—with Ellery? "Actually, Louise only comes in twice a week. Today I asked her to come over because of the interview with Rod Crawford. I thought I might need another pair of hands. But usually I can handle whatever comes up by myself."

"That surprises me," Zane admitted and took a sip of his wine. Tiffany arched her elegant dark brows. "Why?"

"Because of the house, I suppose. So formal."

"And here you are stuck in the kitchen, without the benefit of seeing the crystal and silver," Tiffany said with a chuckle. "Disappointed, Mr. Sheridan?"

His gray eyes drove into hers and his voice was low when he spoke. "Only that I can't persuade you to call me by my first name."

"I don't think I know you that well—"

"Yet." He raised his glass in mock salute and his flinty eyes captured hers. "Here's to an independent woman," he announced before taking another long drink.

She was more than a little embarrassed by the intimate toast, and after a few silent moments when she alternately sipped the wine and twirled the glass in her fingers, she decided she had to level with him. Against her wishes she was warming to him, and that had to stop. "Look, *Zane*. As far as I'm concerned, you're close enough to certifiably crazy that I doubt if I'll associate with you again," she said half-seriously as she poured them each another glass of wine and then began to attack her salad. "There's no reason for first names."

"I'm not crazy, Ms. Rhodes—"

"Tiffany." Gentle laughter sparkled in her eyes. "Just concerned, right?" Her smile faded and she became instantly serious. "Why? Why are you here, now, telling me all of this?"

"It took me this long to be sure."

"Then you'll understand why I'm having trouble accepting what you're suggesting as the truth. You've had four years to think about it. I just found out this morning."

Tiffany pushed her plate aside, crossed her arms over her chest and leveled serious blue eyes in his direction. "Let's quit beating around the bush," she suggested. "So what's in this for you? You don't impress me as the kind of man who would go traipsing halfway around the world just to set the record straight and see that justice is served."

"I'm not."

"I didn't think so."

"I have an interest in what happens here."

Dread began to hammer in her heart. "Which is?"

"Personal."

"What does that mean? A grudge—revenge—vendetta—what?" She leaned on one hand and pointed at him with the other. "This morning you said you knew Ellery. I got the impression then, and now again, that you didn't much like him." Her palm rotated in the air as she collected her scattered thoughts. "If you ask me, all this interest in my horse has to do with Ellery. What's the point, Mr. Sheridan? And why in the world would you want to buy this farm? There must be a dozen of them, much more profitable than this, for sale."

Zane set aside his fork and settled back in the chair. As he pondered the situation and the intelligent woman staring beguilingly at him, he tugged on his lower lip. "The reason I want this farm is because it should have been mine to begin with. That your husband got the capital to invest in this parcel of land was a . . . fluke."

"Come again," she suggested, not daring to breathe. What was he saying? "Ellery's family owned this land for years."

"I don't think so. The way I understand it, he was a tenant farmer until a few years ago. The two hundred thousand dollars that your husband put into this farm as a down payment—"

"Yes?" Tiffany asked.

"He stole it from me."

"Oh, dear God," Tiffany whispered, letting her head fall forward into her waiting hands. She didn't know whether to laugh or to cry. Obviously Zane thought he was telling the truth, and he didn't seem like a dangerous psychotic, but what he was saying was absolutely ridiculous. Ellery might have been many things, but Tiffany knew in her heart he wasn't a thief.

"I think it's time for you to leave, Mr. Sheridan," she said, her voice as cold as ice. "You've been saying some pretty wild things around here—things that could be construed as slander, and—"

Footsteps on the back porch interrupted her train of thought. Panic welled in Tiffany's mind and she snapped her head upward as the familiar boot steps drew near. Within a minute, Mac was standing in the kitchen, worrying the brim of his fedora in his fingers, his dark eyes impaling hers. "You'd better come, Missy," he said, his voice uncommonly low.

"Ebony Wine?"

"Aye."

"The foal is here?"

"Will be soon, and . . ." His eyes shifted from Tiffany to Zane and back again. Tiffany's heart began to thud painfully in her chest. She could read the silent message in Mac's worried gaze.

"No . . ." she whispered, pushing the chair back so hard that it scraped against the hardwood floor. Her fearful eyes darted to Zane. "If you'll excuse me, we have an emergency on our hands." She noticed the glimmer of suspicion in Zane's eyes, but didn't bother to explain. Time was too imperative.

In seconds she was away from the table and racing toward the den. "Have you called Vance?" she called over her shoulder.

Mac pushed his hat onto his head and nodded. "He's on his way. Damn, but I should have seen this coming. I'll meet you in the shed."

Tiffany kicked off her pumps, pulled on a pair of boots and yanked her jacket off the wooden hook. Mindless of the fact that she was dressed in wool slacks, angora vest and silk blouse, she opened the French doors and raced into the dark night. She had taken only three breathless strides, when she felt the powerful hand on her arm, restraining her in its hard grasp.

"What's going on?" Zane demanded as Tiffany whirled to face the man thwarting her. Her hair tossed wildly around her face, and even in the darkness Zane could see the angry fire in her wide eyes. He hadn't been able to decipher the silent messages passing from Mac to Tiffany in the kitchen, but Zane knew that something horrible was taking place and that Tiffany felt she could do something about it.

Tiffany didn't have time to argue. She was trying to free herself. "A mare's gone into labor."

"And that upsets you?"

She jerked her arm free of his imprisoning grasp. "There might be complications. If you'll excuse me—" But he was right beside her, running the short distance from the house to the foaling shed with her, his strides long and easy.

With a sinking feeling, Tiffany realized that there was no way she could hide her secret from him any longer, and she really didn't care. The only thing that mattered was the mare in labor and the unborn colt.

Chapter Four

The soft overhead lights of the foaling shed were reflected in the sweat-darkened coat of Ebony Wine. As the mare paced restlessly in the stall, she alternately snorted in agitation and flattened her dark ears against her head in impatience.

Mac's arms were braced on the top rail of the gate to the foaling stall and his anxious brown eyes studied the horse. A matchstick worked convulsively in the corner of his mouth.

He spoke softly in quiet tones filled with years of understanding. "Simmer down, lady." His gravelly voice was barely audible as the distressed mare shifted under the intense pressure of an abdominal contraction.

Tiffany's heart was pounding more rapidly than her footsteps on the cold concrete floor as she walked rapidly down the length of the corridor to the foaling stall. The acrid smells of sweat and urine mingled with antiseptic in the whitewashed barn. One look at Mac's tense form told her that the birth of Ebony Wine's foal was going no better than he had expected.

Zane was at Tiffany's side, matching her short strides with his longer ones. His dark brows were drawn over his slate gray eyes. He kept his thoughts to himself as he tried to make head or tail of the tense situation. Something was very wrong here. He could feel it. Though it hadn't been stated, he had witnessed fear in Tiffany's incredible blue eyes when Mac had entered the kitchen and made the announcement that one of the mares had gone into labor. Zane had noticed something else in Tiffany's worried expression—determination and pride held her finely sculpted jaw taut, but worry creased her flawless brow. A sense of desperation seemed to have settled heavily on her small shoulders.

"Has her water broken?" Tiffany asked as she approached Mac and leaned over the railing of the stall.

Mac shook his head and ran bony fingers over the stubble on his jaw. "Not yet."

Ebony Wine was moving restlessly in the stall. Her sleek body glistened with sweat, and her ears twitched warily.

"Come on, lady," Mac whispered softly, "don't be so stupid. Lie down, will ya?"

"She didn't get off her feet the last time," Tiffany reminded the trainer.

"She'd better this time," Mac grumbled, "or we'll lose this one, sure as I'm standing here." He shifted the matchstick from one side of his mouth to the other. "Moon Shadow's colts need all the help they can get. Come on, Ebony, be a good girl. Lie down."

"Moon Shadow?" Zane asked. "He's the sire?"

Mac's troubled gaze shifted from the horse to Tiffany in unspoken apology. 'That he is."

Zane's eyes narrowed as he studied the anxious mare. "Where's the vet?"

"He was at another farm—said he'd be here on the double," Mac replied.

At that moment, Ebony Wine's water broke and the amniotic fluid began cascading down her black legs.

"Looks like he might be too late," Zane observed wryly.

Without asking any further questions, he rolled up

his shirt sleeves, walked to a nearby basin and scrubbed his arms and hands with antiseptic.

"What're you doing?" Tiffany demanded.

His gaze was steady as he approached her. "I'm trying to help you. I've spent most of my life with horses and seen enough foals being born to realize when a mare's in trouble. This lady here—" he cocked his dark head in the direction of the anxious horse "—needs a hand."

Mac looked about to protest, but Tiffany shook her head to quiet him. "Let's get on with it."

Ebony Wine stiffened as Mac and Zane entered the stall. Her eyes rolled backward at the stranger. Mac went to Ebony Wine's head and talked to the horse. "Come on, Ebony, girl. Lie down, for Pete's sake."

Zane examined the horse and the bulging amniotic sac beginning to emerge below her tail. "We've got problems," he said with a dark frown. "Only a nose and one leg showing. Looks as if one leg has twisted back on itself."

"Damn!" Mac muttered. His hands never stopped their rhythmic stroking of Ebony Wine's head.

Tiffany felt her heart leap to her throat. Moon Shadow's foals were having enough trouble surviving, without the added problems of a complicated birth. Against the defeat slumping her shoulders, Tiffany forced her head upward to meet the cruel challenge fate had dealt the mare. Her vibrant blue eyes locked with Zane's. "What do you want me to do?"

"Help with supplies." He pointed in the direction of the clean pails, scissors and bottles of antiseptic. "We've got to get that foal out of there, and my guess is that this lady isn't going to want our help."

The sound of the door to the foaling shed creaking open caught her attention and brought Tiffany's head around.

Vance Geddes, his round face a study in frustration, let the door swing shut and hurried down the corridor to Ebony Wine's stall.

He took one look at the horse and turned toward the basin. "How long has she been at it?" he asked, quickly washing his hands.

"Over half an hour," Mac replied.

"And she won't lie down?"

"Not this one. Stubborn, she is."

"Aren't they all?" Vance's gaze clashed with the stranger attending to Ebony Wine. Zane responded to the unspoken question. "Zane Sheridan."

"'Evening," Vance said.

"I was here on other business, but I thought I'd help out. I've worked with Thoroughbreds all my life, and I think we've got problems here. One leg's twisted back. The foal's stuck."

"Great," Vance muttered sarcastically, entering the stall as quietly as possible. "Just what we need tonight." His eyes traveled over the mare. "How're ya, gal? Hurtin' a little?" he asked as he studied the glistening horse.

"How can I help?" Tiffany asked, forcing her voice to remain steady as she noticed the tightening of Vance's jaw.

"Be ready to hand me anything I might need," Vance replied and then positioned himself behind the mare to confirm what Zane had told him. "Damn." He shook his blond head and frowned. "All right, let's get him out of there."

Ebony Wine moaned as her womb contracted, and the foal remained stuck in the birth canal.

"This is gonna be touchy," Vance whispered, as warning to the tall man standing next to him.

Zane's body tensed and he nodded curtly, before he

helped Vance carefully push the foal back into the mare so that there was less danger of breaking the umbilical cord and to give more room to coax the bent leg forward. Time was crucial, and both men worked quickly but gently, intent on saving the mare and her offspring.

Tiffany assisted with the towels and antiseptic, silently praying for the life of the unborn horse. Her throat was hot and tight with the tension in the confining stall. Sweat began to bead on Zane's forehead, and his intent eyes never left the mare. The muscles in his bronze forearms flexed as he worked on righting the foal. Tiffany's heart was hammering so loudly, it seemed to pound in her ears.

Ebony Wine pushed down hard with all the muscles of her abdomen. As the mare pushed, Vance and Zane stood behind her and pulled down steadily toward her hocks in rhythm with the birth contractions.

With the first push, the tiny hooves and the head of the foal emerged. On the second contraction, the mare gave a soft moan, and the men were able to pull the shoulders, the broadest part of a foal's body, through Ebony Wine's pelvis. Once the shoulders emerged, the rest of the foal followed.

The umbilical cord broke.

Zane dropped to the floor and, mindless of the fluid pooling at his knees, he ripped open the tough amniotic sac. Vance was beside him and worked on the colt's nose, so that it could breathe its first breaths of air.

Tiffany brought towels and held them near the foal so that Vance could take them as he needed them. Her eyes watched the little black colt's sides as she prayed for the tiny ribs to move. *Dear Lord, don't let him die. Please don't take this one, too.*

Because the colt had to be pulled out of the mare, the umbilical cord had broken early, and he was shortchanged of the extra blood in the placenta that should have passed into his veins. Both men worked feverishly over the small, perfect body.

The foal's lips and eyelids looked blue as it lay wet and motionless in the straw.

"Oh, God, no," Tiffany whispered, as she realized that it had been far too long already since the birth. She dropped the towels and her small hands curled into impotent fists. "Not this one, too."

Ebony Wine nickered, ready to claim her foal. Mac gently held the frustrated mare as she tried to step closer to the unmoving black body lying on the floor of the stall.

Zane held his hands near the colt's nose to feel for breath. There was none. "He's not breathing," he whispered, looking up for a second at Tiffany before bending over the colt and pressing his lips to the nostrils, forcing air into the still lungs.

Vance knelt beside Zane, checking the colt for vital signs, while Zane fruitlessly tried to revive the colt.

"It's no use," Vance said at last, restraining Zane by placing a hand on his shoulder. "This one didn't have a prayer going in."

"No!" Tiffany said, her voice trembling and tears building in her eyes. "He's got to live. He's got to!"

"Tiff . . ." Vance said wearily. The vet's voice trailed off. There were no adequate words of condolence. For a moment the only sounds in the building were the soft rain beating against the roof and the restless shifting of the mare's hooves in the straw.

Mindless of the blood and amniotic fluid ruining her clothes, Tiffany fell into the straw beside the inert body of the beautifully formed black colt. Her throat was swollen with despair, her eyes blurred with fresh tears. "You have to live, little one," she whispered in a voice filled with anguished desperation. She touched the foal's warm, matted coat. "Please . . . live."

Her fingers touched the small ears and the sightless eyes. "Don't die. . . ."

"Tiffany." Zane's voice was rough but comforting as he reached forward and grabbed her shoulders. He felt the quiet sobs she was trying to control. "He was dead before he was born—"

Tiffany jerked herself free. "No!" Her hands were shaking as she raised them in the air. "He was alive and healthy and . . ."

"Stillborn."

That single word, issued softly from Zane's lips, seemed to echo against the rafters.

A single tear wove a solitary path down her cheek. Tiffany let her arms fall to her sides. "Oh, God," she whispered, pulling herself to her full height and shaking her head. Blood discolored her silk blouse, and straw stuck in her angora vest as well as her hair. "Not another one." Her small fist clenched and she pounded it on the rough boards of the stall. "Why? Why is this happening?" she demanded, hopelessly battling an enemy she couldn't see . . . didn't understand.

Ebony Wine snorted, and Tiffany realized she was disturbing the already distraught mare. She let her head drop into her palm, leaned against the wall and closed her eyes against the truth. *Why the foals? Why all of Moon Shadow's foals?*

"Come on, let's go back to the house," Zane suggested, placing his strong arms gently over her shoulders.

"I should stay," she whispered as cold reality began to settle in her mind. She felt a raw ache in her heart as she faced the tragic fact that another of Moon Shadow's foals was dead before it had a chance to live. It just wasn't fair; not to the mare, not to the farm, and not to the poor lifeless little colt.

"We'll take care of things," Mac assured her, giving Zane a look that said more clearly than words, "Get her out of here." Mac was holding the lead rope to Ebony Wine's halter, and the anxious horse was nickering to the dead foal.

"I'll make some coffee . . . up at the house," Tiffany murmured, trying to pull herself together. She was shaking from the ordeal but managed to wipe the tears from her eyes.

"Don't bother for me," Vance said, working with the afterbirth. "I'll stay with the mare until Mac can watch her and then I'll call it a night."

"Same goes for me." Mac's kind eyes rested on Tiffany. "You just take care of yourself, Missy. We'll handle the horses."

"But—"

"Shh, could be three, maybe four hours till I'm finished with this old gal here," Mac said, cocking his head sadly in the black mare's direction. "After that, I think I'll hit the hay. I'm not as young as I used to be, ya know, and the missus, she'll be looking for me." He winked at Tiffany, but the smile he tried to give her failed miserably.

Numbly, leaning against Zane's strong body, Tiffany slowly walked out of the foaling shed and into the night. The rain was still falling from the darkened sky. It splashed against the sodden ground, and the large drops ran through her hair and down her neck.

She felt cold all over, dead inside. Another of Moon Shadow's foals. Dead. Why? Her weary mind wouldn't quit screaming the question that had plagued her for nearly two weeks. She shuddered against the cold night and the chill of dread in her heart. Zane pulled her closer to the protective warmth of his body.

Hard male muscles surrounded her, shielded her from the rain as well as the storm of emotions raging in her mind. Lean and masculine, Zane's body molded perfectly over hers, offering the strength and security she needed on this dark night. For the first time in several years, Tiffany accepted the quiet strength of a man. She was tired of making decisions, weary from fighting the invisible demons that stole the lifeblood from innocent newborns.

The house was still ablaze with the lights she had neglected to turn off. Zane led her into the den and watched as she slumped wearily into the chair near the fireplace. The sparkle in her blue eyes seemed to have died with Ebony Wine's foal. Her arms were wrapped protectively over her breasts, and she stared sightlessly into the smoldering embers of the fire.

"I'll get you a drink," he offered, walking to the bookcase that housed the liquor.

"Don't want one."

He picked up a bottle of brandy before looking over his shoulder and pinning her with his intense gray gaze. "Tiffany, what happened?" he asked quietly. She continued to gaze dully at the charred logs in the stone fireplace. He repeated his question, hoping to break her mournful silence. "Just what the hell happened out there tonight?"

"We lost a colt," she whispered, tears resurfacing in her eyes.

"Sometimes that happens," he offered, waiting patiently for the rest of the story as he poured two small glasses of the amber liquor.

She lifted her gaze to meet his and for a moment he thought she was about to confide in him, but instead she shrugged her slim shoulders. "Sometimes," she agreed hoarsely as she watched his reaction.

How much could she trust this stranger? True, he had tried to help her with the unborn colt and in a moment of weakness she felt as if she could trust her life to him. But still she hesitated. She couldn't forget that he was here on a mission. Not only did he want to buy the farm, but he was filled with some insane theory about Devil's Gambit being alive.

Zane's stormy eyes glanced over her huddled form. Her soft honey-brown curls were tangled with straw and framed her elegantly featured face. Her tanned skin was pale from the ordeal. Dark, curling eyelashes couldn't hide the pain in her wide, innocent eyes.

She's seen more than her share of pain, Zane guessed as he walked over to her and offered the drink that she had declined.

"I don't want—"

"Drink it."

She frowned a little. "Just who do you think you are, coming in here and giving me orders?"

He smiled sternly. "A friend."

Tiffany found it difficult to meet the concern in his eyes. She remained rigid and ignored the glass in his outstretched hand.

With an audible sigh, Zane relented. Dealing with this beautiful woman always seemed to prove difficult. "All right, lady. Drink it. *Please.*"

Tiffany took the glass from his hand and managed an obligatory sip. The calming liquor slid easily down her throat, and as she sipped the brandy she began to warm a little. *Who was this man and why did he care?*

Zane walked over to the fireplace and stretched the tension out of his shoulders, before stoking the dying fire and finally taking a seat on the hearth. He propped his elbows on his knees and cradled his drink in his large hands.

She didn't follow his actions but kicked off her shoes, ignoring the mud that dirtied the imported carpet. Then she drew her knees under her chin as if hugging herself for warmth against an inner chill.

Zane's eyes never left her face. As he watched her he felt a traitorous rush of desire flooding his bloodstream and firing his loins. As unlikely as it seemed, he suddenly wanted Ellery Rhodes's beautiful widow and wanted her badly. The urge to claim her as his own was blinding. In a betraying vision, he saw himself kissing away the pain on her regal features, lifting the sweater vest over her head, slipping each button of her blouse through the buttonholes.

Zane's throat tightened as he imagined her lying beneath him, her glorious, dark-tipped breasts supple and straining in the moonlight. . . .

"Stop it," he muttered to himself, and Tiffany looked upward from the flames to stare at him.

"Stop what?" she whispered, her eyes searching his.

Zane's desire was thundering in his ears, and he felt the unwelcome swelling in his loins. "Nothing," he muttered gruffly as he stood, walked across the room and poured himself another drink. He downed the warm liquor in one long swallow as if the brandy itself could quell the unfortunate urges of his body.

For God's sake, he hadn't reacted to a woman this way since Stasia. At the thought of his sultry Gypsy-like ex-wife, Zane's blood went ice-cold, and the effect was an instant relief. The ache in his loins subsided.

He set his glass down with a thud, jarring Tiffany out of her distant reverie. "Do you want to talk?" he asked softly, walking back across the close room to face her. He placed himself squarely before her, effectively blocking her view of the fire.

She shook her head and ran trembling fingers through her hair. "Not now . . ."

His smile was sad, but genuine. "Then I think you should get cleaned up and rest. It's after midnight—"

"Oh." For the first time that night, Tiffany was aware of her appearance. She looked down at her vest and saw the bloodstains discoloring the delicate gray wool. The sleeves of her pink blouse were rolled over her arms and stained with sweat and blood. She felt the urge to cry all over again when she looked up from her disheveled clothing and noticed the concern in Zane's gentle gray eyes.

Instead of falling victim to her emotions, she raised her head proudly and managed a stiff smile. "I'll be fine in the morning. This night has been a shock."

"Obviously."

"If you'll excuse me . . ."

When she rose from the chair, her knees felt unsteady, but she managed to stand with a modicum of dignity despite her disheveled appearance.

Zane picked up her barely touched glass. "I don't think you should be alone."

Involuntarily she stiffened. Ellery's words from long ago, just after her father had died, echoed in her mind. "You shouldn't be alone, Tiffany," Ellery had insisted. "You need a man to care for you." In her grief, Tiffany had been fool enough to believe him.

She lifted her chin fractionally. "I'll be fine, Mr. Sheridan," she assured him with a calm smile. "I've been alone for over four years. I think I can manage one more night."

He noticed the slight trembling of her fingers, the

doubt in her clear blue eyes, and realized that she was the most damnably intriguing woman he had ever met.

"I'll stay with you."

"That won't be necessary."

"The mare's not out of the woods yet."

Tiffany hesitated only slightly. Zane's presence did lend a certain security. She remembered his quick, sure movements as he tried to revive Ebony Wine's dead colt. With a shake of her head, she tried to convince herself that she didn't need him. "Mac can take care of Ebony Wine."

"And it wouldn't hurt to have an extra pair of hands."

She was about to protest. She raised her hand automatically and then dropped it. "Don't get me wrong, Zane," she said softly, her tongue nearly tripping on the familiarity of his first name. "It's not that I don't appreciate what you've done tonight. I do. But the foal is dead." She shuddered and hugged her arms around her abdomen. "And Mac will attend to Ebony Wine." She shook her head at the vision of the dead little colt lying on the thick bed of straw. "I . . . I think it would be best if you would just leave for now. I know that we still have things to discuss, but certainly they'll wait until morning."

"I suppose." Zane glanced at the portrait of Devil's Gambit hanging proudly over the mantel. He had the eerie feeling that somehow the tense drama he had witnessed earlier in the foaling shed was linked to the disappearance of the proud stallion. *Impossible.* And yet he had a gut feeling that the two tragic events were connected.

As if Tiffany had read his thoughts, she shuddered. Zane was across the room in an instant. Tiffany wanted to protest when his strong arms enfolded her against him, but she couldn't. The warmth of his body and the protection of his embrace felt as natural as the gentle rain beating softly against the windowpanes. He plucked a piece of straw from her hair and tenderly let his lips press a soft kiss against her forehead. The gesture was so filled with kindness and empathy that Tiffany felt her knees buckle and her eyes fill with tears.

"I . . . I think you should go," she whispered hoarsely, afraid of her response to his masculinity. Damn him! She wanted to lean on him. What kind of a fool was she? Hadn't she learned her lessons about men long ago from Ellery?

"Shh." He ignored her protests and led her gently out of the den, through the foyer and up the stairs. "Come on, lady," he whispered into her hair. "Give yourself a break and let me take care of you."

She felt herself melt inside. "I don't think, I mean I don't need—"

"What you need is to soak in a hot tub, wrap yourself in one of those god-awful flannel nightgowns and fall into bed with a glass of brandy."

It sounded like heaven, but Tiffany couldn't forget that the tenderness of the man touching her so intimately might be nothing more than a ploy to extract information from her. At this moment she was too tired to really give a damn, but she couldn't forget her earlier instincts about him. He was engaged in a vendetta of sorts; she could feel it in her bones. Try as she would, Tiffany couldn't shake the uneasy feeling that Zane Sheridan, whoever the hell he was, would prove to be the enemy.

Zane left Tiffany in the master bedroom. Once she was certain he had gone downstairs, she peeled off her soiled clothes, threw them in a hamper and walked into the adjacent bathroom.

As she settled into the hot water of the marble tub,

her mind continued to revolve around the events of the past few weeks. If the first foal's death had been a shock, the second had been terrifying. Now two more foals by Moon Shadow had died mysteriously. Each foal had been only a few hours old, with the exception of Charlatan, who had survived for a few hope-filled days.

Just wait until Rod Crawford gets hold of this story, she thought as she absently lathered her body. The wire services would print it in a minute and she'd have more reporters crawling all over the place than she could imagine. If that wasn't enough, Zane Sheridan's theories about Devil's Gambit's fate would stir up the press and get them interested all over again in what was happening at Rhodes Breeding Farm. *And the scandal. Lord, think of the scandal!*

Tiffany sank deeper into the tub, and didn't notice that her hair was getting wet.

What about Zane Sheridan? Was he here as friend or foe? She sighed as she considered the roguish man who had helped her upstairs. One minute he seemed intent on some vague, undisclosed revenge, and the next his concern for her and the farm seemed genuine. *Don't trust him, Tiffany,* the rational side of her nature insisted.

"Men," she muttered ungraciously. "I'll never understand them." Her frown trembled a little as she thought about Ellery, the husband she had tried to love. Marrying him had probably been the biggest mistake of her life. The moment she had become Mrs. Ellery Rhodes, he seemed to have changed and his interest in her had faded with each passing day. "Dad warned you," she chided herself. "You were just too bullheaded to listen."

The distance between her and her husband had become an almost physical barrier, and Tiffany had foolishly thought that if she could bear Ellery a child, things might be different. He might learn to love her.

What a fool! Hadn't she already known from her own agonizing experience with her mother that relationships between people who loved each other were often fragile and detached? In her own naive heart, she had hoped that she would someday be able to reach Ellery. Now, if what Zane Sheridan was saying were true, Ellery might still be alive.

"Oh, God," she moaned, closing her eyes and trying to conjure Ellery's face in her mind. But try as she would, she was unable to visualize the man she had married. Instead, the image in her mind had the forceful features of a virtual stranger from Ireland. "You bastard," she whispered and wondered if she were speaking to Zane or Ellery.

Her tense muscles began to relax as she rinsed the soap from her body and then turned on the shower spray to wash her hair.

Once she felt that all of the grime had been scrubbed from her skin, she turned off the shower, stepped out of the tub and wrapped herself in a bath sheet. After buffing her skin dry, she grabbed the only nightgown in the room, an impractical silver-colored gown of thin satin and lace.

Just what I need, she thought sarcastically as she slipped it over her head and straightened it over her breasts. She smiled to herself, grabbed her red corduroy robe and cinched the belt tightly around her waist. She was still towel-drying her hair when she stepped into the bedroom.

As she did, her gaze clashed with that of Zane Sheridan.

"What are you doing here?" she asked, lowering the towel and staring at him with incredulous slate-blue eyes.

"I wanted to make sure that you didn't fall asleep in the tub."

She arched an elegant brow suspiciously. "Didn't you hear the shower running?" When a slow-spreading smile grew from one side of his face to the other, Tiffany's temper snapped. "I don't need a keeper, you know. I'm a grown woman."

His eyes slid over her body and rested on the gap in her overlapping lapels. "So I noticed."

Angrily, she tugged on the tie of her robe. "You're insufferable!" she spit out. "I could have walked in here stark naked."

"Can't blame a guy for hoping—"

"I'm in no mood for this, Zane," she warned.

He sobered instantly and studied the lines of worry on her beautiful face. "I know. I just thought I could get you to lighten up."

"A little difficult under the circumstances."

"You lost a foal. It happens."

Her lips twisted wryly. "That it does, Mr. Sheridan. That it does." She sat on the corner of the bed and supported herself with one straight arm while pushing the wet tendrils of hair out of her face with her free hand. "It's been a long day."

"I suppose it has." He strode across the room, threw back the covers of the bed and reached for a drink he had placed on the nightstand. "I checked on Ebony Wine."

Tiffany watched his actions warily. Why was he still here and why was she secretly pleased? She raised her head in challenge and ignored her rapidly pounding heart. "And?"

"You were right. Mac took care of her. She's a little confused about everything that went on tonight, still calling to the foal. But she's healthy. The afterbirth detached without any problem and Mac had already cleaned her up. He thinks she'll be ready to breed when she shows signs of foal heat, which should be the middle of next week. The veterinarian will be back to check her tomorrow and again before she goes into heat."

Tiffany nodded and accepted the drink he offered. "It's a little too much for me to think about right now," she admitted, swirling the brandy in her glass before taking a sip.

"It's the business you're in."

Tiffany stared into the amber liquor in her glass and moved her head from side to side. "And sometimes it seems like a rotten way of life."

Zane ran his hand around the back of his neck. "It's never easy to lose one, but it's the chance you take as a breeder."

"And the living make up for the dead?"

Zane frowned and shrugged. "Something like that. If it bothers you so much, maybe you should get out of the business," he suggested.

"By selling the farm to you?" Her eyes lifted and became a frigid shade of blue.

"I didn't think we would get into that tonight."

"You brought it up."

"I just voiced your concerns."

"Oh, God," she whispered, setting her unfinished drink aside. "Look, I'm really very tired and I can't think about all this tonight."

"Don't. Just try and get some sleep."

She managed a wan smile and walked around to her side of the bed. "I guess I owe you an apology and a very big thank you. I . . . really appreciate all the help you gave in the foaling shed."

Zane frowned. "For all the good it did."

Tiffany raised sad eyes to meet his questioning gaze.

"I don't think there was anything anyone could have done."

"Preordained?"

She sighed audibly and shook her head; The wet hair swept across her shoulders. "Who knows?" She sat on the edge of the bed, her fingers toying with the belt holding her robe together. "Goodbye, Zane. If you call me in the morning, we can find another time to get together and talk about your hypothesis concerning Devil's Gambit and my husband."

"I'll be here in the morning," he stated, dropping into a chair facing the bed and cradling his drink in his hands.

"Pardon me?" she asked, understanding perfectly well what he meant.

"I'm staying—"

"You can't! Not here—"

"I just want to check with Mac once more, and then I'll sleep downstairs on the couch."

Visions of him spending the night in her house made her throat dry. She couldn't deny that he had been a help, but the thought of him there, in the same house with her, only a staircase away, made her uneasy. Her fingers trembled when she pushed them wearily through her hair. "I don't know," she whispered, but she could feel herself relenting.

"Come on, Tiff. It's after two. I'm not about to drive back to San Francisco now, just to turn around and come back here in six hours."

Tiffany managed a smile. "I don't suppose that makes a whole lot of sense." Her blue eyes touched his. "You don't have to sleep in the den. There's a guest room down the hall, the first door to the left of the stairs."

He returned her hint of a smile and stood. For a

moment she thought he was about to bend over the bed and kiss her. She swallowed with difficulty as their eyes locked.

Zane hesitated, and the brackets near the corners of his mouth deepened. "I'll see you in the morning," he said, his eyes darkening to a smoky gray before he turned out the lamp near the bed and walked out of the room.

Tiffany expelled a rush of air. "Oh, God," she whispered, her heart thudding painfully in her chest. "I should have made him leave." He was too close, his rugged masculinity too inviting.

Maybe he would come back to her room, or maybe he would sift through the papers in the den looking for something, anything, to prove his crazy theories. But all the important documents, the computer data disks and the checkbook were locked in the safe; even if Zane rummaged through the den, he would find nothing of value.

That's not why you're concerned, her tired mind teased. *What scares you is your response to him.* She rolled over and pushed the nagging thoughts aside. Despite all of her doubts, she was comforted that Zane was still with her. Somehow it made the tragedy of losing the foal easier to bear.

Zane hiked his quickly donned jacket around his neck and felt the welcome relief of raindrops slide under his collar. He needed time to cool off. Being around Tiffany, wanting to comfort her, feeling a need to make love to her until the fragile lines of worry around her eyes were gone, unnerved him. The last thing he had expected when he had driven to Rhodes Breeding Farm was that he would get involved with Ellery Rhodes's widow.

He heard the roar of an engine as he started to cross the parking lot. Turning in the direction of the sound, Zane walked toward Mac's battered truck. Mac rolled down the window as Zane approached. Twin beams from the headlights pierced the darkness, and the wipers noisily slapped the accumulation of rain from the windshield.

"Everything okay?"

"Aye," Mac replied cautiously. "The mare's fine."

"Good." Zane rammed his fists into the jacket of his coat. "What about the colt?"

"Vance will handle that." The wiry trainer frowned in the darkness. "He'll give us a report in a couple of days."

"Good." Zane stepped away from the truck and watched as Mac put the ancient Dodge pickup into gear before it rumbled down the driveway.

Wondering at the sanity of his actions, Zane unlocked his car and withdrew the canvas bag of extra clothes from the backseat. He always traveled with a change of clothes, his briefcase and his camera. He slung the bag over his shoulder and considered the briefcase. In the leather case were the papers his attorney had toiled over. According to John Morris, every document needed to purchase Rhodes Breeding Farm was now in Zane's possession. So why didn't owning the farm seem as important as it once had?

Zane cursed angrily and locked the briefcase in the car. Knowing that he was making a grave error, he walked back into the house, locked the doors and mounted the stairs. After throwing his bag on the guest bed, he took off his shoes and turned down the covers.

Then, on impulse, he went back to her room. He

paused at the door and then strode boldly inside. His blood was thundering in his eardrums as he lowered himself into the chair near the bed. It took all of his restraint not to go to her.

Zane watched the rounded swell of her hips beneath the bedclothes, and the smoldering lust in his veins began to throb unmercifully. *You're more of a fool than you thought,* Zane chastised himself silently.

He noticed the regular rhythm of her breathing and realized that she had fallen asleep. The urge to strip off his clothes and lie with her burned in bis mind. He fantasized about her response, the feel of her warm, sleepy body fitted to his, the agonizing glory of her silken fingers as they traced an invisible path down his abdomen. . . .

A hard tightening in his loins warned him that his thoughts were dangerous; still he couldn't help but think of slowly peeling off her bedclothes and letting the shimmery nightgown peeking from the edges of her robe fall silently to the floor. He wanted to touch all of her, run his tongue over the gentle feminine curves of her body, drink in the smell of her perfume as he touched her swollen breasts. . . .

Quietly he placed his drink on the table and walked over to the bed.

Tiffany moaned in her sleep and turned onto her back. In the dim light from the security lamps, with the rain softly pelting against the windows, Zane looked down at her. How incredibly soft and alluring she appeared in slumber. All traces of anxiety had left the perfect oval of her face. Her still-damp hair curled in golden-brown tangles around her shoulders and neck.

The scarlet robe had gaped open to display the silvery fabric of a gossamer gown and the soft texture of her breasts beneath. Tiffany shifted slightly and the hint of a dark nipple shadowed the silvery lace covering it.

Zane clenched his teeth in self-restraint. Never had he wanted a woman more, and he told himself that she was there for the taking. Hadn't he seen her vulnerability? Hadn't he witnessed the way she stared at him? Deep within her, there was a need to be taken by him; he could sense it.

He closed his eyes against the pain throbbing in his loins and dropped to his knees by the bed. "What have you done to me?" he whispered as he lovingly brushed a strand of hair from her eyes.

This woman was once the wife of Ellery Rhodes, a person he had intended to destroy. Zane couldn't help but wonder, as he stared into the sleep-softened face of Ellery Rhodes's widow, if just the opposite were true.

Would he be able to carry forth his plans of retribution, or would Ellery Rhodes's wife reap her sweet vengeance on him?

Chapter Five

When Tiffany opened her eyes she noticed that the first purple light of dawn had begun to filter into the room. With a muted groan, she stretched between the cool sheets and rolled over, intent on returning to sleep.

Her cloudy vision rested on the chair near the bed and her breath got lost somewhere in her throat.

Zane was in the room. The realization was like an electric current pulsing through her body, bringing her instantly awake. What was he doing here?

He was slumped back in the chair, his head cocked at an uncomfortable angle, his stocking feet propped against the foot of the bed. He had thrown a spare blanket over himself, but it had slipped to the floor. His unfinished drink sat neglected on the bedside table.

"You wonderful bastard," she whispered quietly, before a silent rage began to take hold of her. Why hadn't he left as he had promised? Why had he decided to stay here—in her bedroom? Conflicting emotions battled within her. On the one hand, she was pleased to see him. It was comforting to watch his beard-darkened face relaxed in quiet slumber. There was something slightly chivalrous in the fact that he had stayed with her on the pretense of caring for her. She supposed that in all honesty she should consider his actions a compliment, an indication that he cared for her—if only a little.

On the other hand, she was quietly furious that he would force himself so boldly into her life. Whatever it was that he wanted at Rhodes Breeding Farm, he obviously wanted very badly. Badly enough to pretend interest in Tiffany and her horses.

The smile that had touched the corners of her mouth began to fade. Zane stirred in the chair, and Tiffany knew that he would soon be awake. No better time than the present to take the bull by the horns! She slipped out of the bed and cinched her robe tightly under her breasts before planting herself in front of his chair.

"Liar!" she whispered loudly enough to disturb him.

The muscles in Zane's broad shoulders stiffened slightly. He grumbled something indistinguishable and his feet dropped to the floor as he tried to roll over.

"What the hell?" he mumbled, before opening his eyes. He awoke to find himself staring up at Tiffany's indignant blue gaze. Stretching in the uncomfortable chair, he tried to rub the stiffness from his neck and cramped shoulders. "What're you going on about?" he asked.

"You said you'd sleep downstairs or in the guest room."

A devilish grin stole across his features. "So I did."

Her blue eyes narrowed. "Don't you have any shame?"

"None." He pulled himself out of the chair and stretched his aching muscles. God, he hurt all over. It had been years since he'd slept sitting up; and never in his thirty-six years had he kept vigil on a beautiful woman, a woman who obviously didn't appreciate his efforts.

"I should have known."

"Known what?" He rubbed his hands over the stubble of his beard and then threw his head back and rotated his neck to relieve the tension at the base of his skull.

"Don't you have any coffee around here?" he asked once he'd stretched.

Tiffany crossed her arms self-righteously over her breasts and glared up at her unwelcome visitor. She was still wearing her robe, Zane noticed, though the gap of the lapels had been pulled together when she had tied the belt around her small waist. "Known you'd end up here."

"It's too early in the morning for this outraged virgin routine, Tiff," he said, rubbing the stubble on his chin. "We're both adults."

Her lips pressed together in anger. "Virginity isn't the issue."

He raised a brow in overt disbelief. "Then what is? Morality?"

"Sanity," she shot back. "Your being in here borders on the insane. I don't know who you are, what you want, where you live, why you're here in the first place. . . . God, Zane, for all I know you could be married with a dozen kids."

His dark glare silenced her. "I'm not married," he said gruffly.

"Good. Because I certainly wouldn't want some outraged wife calling me and demanding to talk to her husband." He looked as if she had slapped him.

"I came in here to check on you last night and you're acting as if I'm some kind of criminal, for God's sake."

She let out a ragged breath and her hands dropped to her sides. "It's just that I don't really know you," she said softly.

"Sure you do," he cajoled, his slate-colored eyes warming slightly when he noticed the flush of indignation on her cheeks.

Tiffany attempted to remain angry, but it was nearly impossible as she stared into Zane's incredible gray eyes.

They were a reflection of the man himself, sometimes dark with anger, other times filled with a compelling intimacy that touched her heart and caused her pulse to jump. Slowly, by calculated inches, this man was working his way into her heart. She felt more vulnerable and naked than she had in years. The emotions beginning to blossom within her had to be pushed aside. She couldn't chance an involvement with him; it was far too dangerous.

Zane rubbed his eyes and stretched before smiling lazily. "Has anyone ever told you you're beautiful when you're angry?"

"Dozens," she returned sarcastically.

"Or that you're gorgeous when you wake up?"

Tiffany swallowed back a lump in her throat. "Not quite as many." She ran her long fingers through her knotted hair and slowly expelled a sigh. Arguing with him would get her nowhere. "I guess I haven't been very hospitable this morning," she conceded, lowering herself to a corner of the bed.

"Some people wake up in a bad mood."

"Especially if they find a stranger in their room?"

His gray eyes touched hers and his voice lowered to an intimate whisper. "We're not strangers."

Her elegant brows arched skeptically. "No?"

"No." He shook his head and frowned decisively.

"Then tell me," she suggested as one long, nervous finger began tracing the line of delicate stitching on the hand-pieced quilt. "Just how would you describe our relationship?"

A mischievous light gleamed in his eyes and his voice lowered suggestively. "How about two strong-willed people thrown mercilessly together by the cruel tides of fate?"

Tiffany couldn't help but laugh. "Seriously—"

"Seriously?" He sobered instantly. "Why don't we start as friends?"

She nodded silently to herself as if agreeing with an earlier-drawn conclusion. "Ah. Friends." Looking up, she found Zane staring intensely at her. "Friendship isn't formed in one night. Not when one of the 'friends' doesn't know anything about the other."

"Or suspects that he's holding out on her?"

She stiffened slightly. "Right." Folding her hands in her lap, she forced her eyes to meet the stormy gray of his. "You came here yesterday and announced that you intended to buy this farm. You also insisted that Devil's Gambit was alive. These aren't the usual kinds of statements to kick off an amiable relationship."

Before he could respond, she pointed an accusing finger up at him and continued, "And there's more to it than you've told me. I get the distinct impression you're here for other reasons, that you were probably involved with Ellery in the past and you're holding a grudge against him . . . or what used to be his before he died. . . ."

Zane didn't deny it, but the mention of Ellery's name caused his face to harden. An unspoken challenge flashed from his eyes.

"My husband is dead—"

"You think." He rammed his fists into his pockets and walked over to one of the tall, paned windows. Leaning one shoulder against the window frame, he surveyed the farm. From his vantage point he could look past the white buildings near the house to the gently rolling hills in the distance. It was barely dawn. A gentle drizzle was falling, and wisps of fog had settled in the pockets between the hills to color the lush green meadows a hazy shade of blue.

Standing apart from the main buildings, its shape

barely visible in the clinging fog, was the sagging skeleton of an old weather-beaten barn, the one structure on the farm that was in sharp contrast to the rest of the modern facilities. The old relic was out of sync with the times. Why had Ellery kept it?

Tiffany watched Zane with new fear taking hold of her heart. What was he saying? Did he really believe that Ellery could still be alive after all these years?

Her voice was suddenly hoarse and she was forced to clear her throat. "Look . . ."

He continued to stare at the rain-washed countryside.

"If you think that Ellery is alive, I want to know about it and I want to know now. This minute. No more stalls."

Zane lifted his hands dismissively. "I don't really know. The only thing I'm certain about is the horse."

"But you said—"

He whirled to face her, his burning hatred resurfacing in his eyes. "What I said was that I don't know what happened to your husband, but I wouldn't rule out the possibility that he could very well be alive and hiding out somewhere."

Tiffany's dark brows drew together, and she shook her head as if she could physically deny the doubts and fears beginning to plague her. "That doesn't make any sense!"

Zane's scathing eyes slowly traveled up her body to rest on her troubled face. He shook his head as if he couldn't begin to understand what was happening between himself and Ellery Rhodes's wife. "If your husband did leave you, then he's not only a crooked bastard, he's crazy to boot."

"You didn't much like him, did you?"

"I didn't like him at all." Zane uttered the words without any trace of emotion, as if he were simply stating a fact. He noticed the worry clouding her gaze, the weariness in the slump of her shoulders, and he silently wondered how such a beautiful woman could have linked up with the likes of Ellery Rhodes. Stasia's passion for money was understandable, but Tiffany? The bitter thought of Stasia heightened his curiosity and got the better of him. "Tell me, what kind of a marriage did you have?"

"Pardon me?"

"How was your relationship with Ellery?"

Searching gray eyes probed hers and seemed to pierce her soul. Just how much did this man want from her? "I don't think this is the time or the place—"

"Cut the bull, Tiffany."

"It's really none of your business—"

"Like hell! I just spent the night with you, lady, and I think that counts for something." His skin tightened over his cheekbones and his jaw hardened. An unspoken challenge flared in his intense gaze.

"Wait a minute. You didn't 'spend the night' with me. You merely sat in a chair in my room."

"Tell that to the rest of the people on the farm."

"I really don't give a rip what anyone else thinks, Zane," she replied, coloring only slightly. "What I do with my life is my own business."

He quirked a disbelieving brow.

"By the same token, I expect that you wouldn't go around to the workers and brag that you slept in the boss lady's room." Her heart was pounding wildly, but she managed to keep her voice steady.

Zane rammed fingers through his dark hair. "But I did."

"No reason to brag about it, especially since nothing happened."

"Not for any lack of wanting on my part," he admitted

with a sigh of frustration. His eyes had darkened, and a tiny muscle worked furiously in the corner of his jaw. The tension that sleep had drained from his body resurfaced, and Tiffany realized for the first time just how badly this man wanted her. Her pulse jumped, and she had to force herself to stand and face him. Things were moving too rapidly, and she couldn't begin to deal with the bold desire written on Zane's rugged features.

"This conversation isn't getting us anywhere," she whispered, her voice becoming thick as her eyes lingered in the smoky depths of his. "I . . . I'm going to clean up and get dressed and then I'll fix you that cup of coffee. It's the least I can do since you helped out here last night . . . and were such a gentleman in the bargain." She motioned with a suddenly heavy hand toward the door of the room. "There's a bath down the hall, if you'd like to shave or change. . . ."

He noticed her hesitation. "I brought a change of clothes."

"You did? Why?" Tiffany demanded. Had he intended to spend the night? Was he using her? If so, then why hadn't he tried to force himself upon her last night? Surely he had sensed her attraction to him. Zane Sheridan was a very fascinating man, and it had been a long time since she had been with a man . . . so very long.

"I thought I was going straight to the airport from here," he replied, abruptly bringing her back to the present.

She flushed from her wanton thoughts and smiled. "I see. Then I'll meet you downstairs later."

Without any further protests, Zane left the room. Tiffany waited until she heard him on the stairs, then she slowly closed the door to the bedroom and locked it.

A few minutes later she heard water running in the guest bathroom at the other end of the hall, and she smiled. "You're a fool," she whispered to herself as she stripped off the vibrant red robe, flung it carelessly on the foot of the bed and walked into her private bathroom. "A stranger just spent the night in your room, and if you had your way, he would be back here in a minute malting furious, passion-filled love to you."

After turning on the shower, she shook her head and smiled at her unfamiliar and traitorous thoughts. "Tiffany, my friend," she warned her reflection in the steamy mirror, "this fascination with Zane Sheridan can only spell trouble."

Dropping her silvery nightgown on the floor, she stepped into the hot spray of water.

After braiding her hair into a single plait, applying just a little makeup and dressing in her favorite pair of faded jeans and a loose sweater, Tiffany headed downstairs to the kitchen. The airy room was bright with copper pots and pans suspended over the stove, plants arranged strategically on the gleaming tile counters, and oversized windows offering a view of the pasture near the broodmare barn.

The coffee was perking, muffins were baking in the oven and the previous night's dishes had been placed in the dishwasher before she heard Zane on the stairs. The inviting aromas of baking bread, coffee and cured ham wafted through the large kitchen.

"Efficient, aren't you?" he stated, offering her a lazy grin.

"I try to be." She glanced over her shoulder and felt her heart begin to pound irregularly as her eyes were caught in the silvery web of his gaze. Zane's black hair was still wet from his shower, his shadow of a beard had been shaved off to reveal the hard angle of his jaw and he was dressed casually in tan cords and a teal-blue sweater. Without his formal attire, he appeared more rakishly handsome than ever. Looking at him caused an uneasy fluttering in Tiffany's stomach.

He leaned against the counter, seemingly content to watch her work. Turning back to the coffee, she poured a cup and tried to hide the fact that her hands were unsteady.

"Cream or sugar?"

"Black is fine." He took an experimental sip, all the while observing Tiffany over the rim of the stoneware mug. "What happened to your cook?"

"She doesn't come in every day—remember? Only a couple of days a week to keep the house up, and on special occasions."

Zane observed her sure movements. God, she wasn't what he'd expected in Ellery Rhodes's wife. "You're a bit of a mystery," he thought aloud as his eyes wandered from her braid, past her slim waist to the inviting swell of her jean-clad hips.

"Ha. And what about you? Appearing on my doorstep with an offer on the farm and a wild tale about Devil's Gambit being kidnapped by Ellery. . . ." She let her voice trail off. She couldn't think that Ellery was alive, couldn't deal with it now. Ellery wouldn't have left. He couldn't have. Not when he knew that she would think he was dead! Though their marriage had been less than ideal, certainly Ellery cared for her in his own, distant way. He wouldn't have put her through the pain of the funeral, the adjustment to widowhood, the problems of running the farm alone. . . .

"Not to mention dead husbands," he offered, as if reading her thoughts.

Tiffany's shoulders flexed, and she held back the hot retort forming on her tongue. It wouldn't be wise to anger him, not yet. She had to find out what he wanted, what kind of game he was playing with her. With an effort, she turned her attention to the boiling water on the stove. Carefully she cracked and added the eggs.

"My husband isn't alive," Tiffany whispered, as if to convince herself.

"You're sure?"

She didn't answer him right away. She removed the muffins from the oven, and, when they were cooked, spooned the poached eggs from the pan. Only then did she say, "Ellery wouldn't let me think he was dead—he wouldn't put me through that kind of pain," she insisted, her quiet dignity steadfastly in place.

"Ellery Rhodes was a bastard." Zane's words were soft, but they seemed to thunder in the small kitchen.

"Your opinion."

"Granted, but correct nonetheless."

"And one I think you should keep to yourself!"

His bitter smile grew slowly from one side of his arrogant face to the other. He took a long swig of his coffee and noticed that Tiffany had paled. "Did you love him so much?"

"I don't understand," she began, but under his direct gaze, she changed the course of her thoughts. "Of course I loved him."

"Enough to cover up for him?"

Her simmering anger ignited, and pride took control of her tongue. "Wait a minute, Sheridan. You're way out of line."

He studied the honesty in her deep blue eyes and frowned into his mug. "My apologies," he muttered, before downing the rest of his coffee.

"If I had any brains at all, I'd throw you and your outlandish stories out of this place—"

"But you can't."

"Why not?"

He settled into the cane-backed chair he had occupied at the table the night before and flashed her a devastating smile that seemed to touch the darkest corners of her soul. "Because you believe me—" She raised her hands as if to protest and he silenced her with a knowing glare. "At least you believe a little."

Tiffany's chest was incredibly tight. She found it difficult to breathe. "I think, Mr. Sheridan, the only reasons I haven't asked you to leave are, one, because we didn't finish our discussion last night—a discussion that I have to admit piqued my curiosity about you—and two, because you helped out here last night when I was desperate." *And because I find you the most incredibly interesting man I've ever met,* she added silently to herself as she put the muffins in a basket and set them on the table next to the platter of ham and eggs. The attraction she felt to him was as crazy as the stories he spun about Devil's Gambit, and yet she couldn't fight it.

They ate in silence, neither breaking the unspoken truce while they consumed the hearty breakfast Tiffany had prepared.

After the table had been cleared, Tiffany heard Mac's footsteps on the back porch. Automatically she reached for the pot of coffee and poured a large mug of the dark liquid before adding both sugar and cream to the cup.

"Momin'," Mac grumbled as he accepted the mug Tiffany offered. He took off his hat and placed it on top of the refrigerator. His eyes swept the interior of the kitchen and rested on Zane. The frown that began on Mac's crowlike features was quickly disguised as he took a long swallow of coffee.

So Sheridan had spent the night, Mac thought. He didn't much like the idea, didn't trust the Irishman. But Tiffany did what suited her, and if Zane Sheridan suited her, then it was none of Mac's business what went on between them. Tiffany had been alone too long as it was, and if he was uncomfortable in the Irishman's presence, Mac silently told himself it was his own problem.

"It's late for you to be getting in," Tiffany teased the ex-jockey with a warm grin.

"Not after a night that ended at three this morning."

Winking fondly at Mac, Tiffany moved toward the stove. "How about some breakfast?"

"Thanks much, but no." Mac eyed the leftover blueberry muffins but shook his head. 'The missus, she made me eat before I left." He patted his lean stomach. "Couldn't hold anything else." He propped an elbow against the pantry door, finished his coffee and fidgeted. "I checked Ebony Wine this morning."

"I was about to go out there myself."

"No need. She's fine." Mac stared out the window toward the foaling shed and scowled. "She wasn't much of a mother the last time she foaled, so I don't reckon she'll miss this one much. . . ." He shifted his weight from one foot to the other and set his empty cup on the blue tiles. "She should go into foal heat soon—next week, maybe. You plan on breeding her when she docs?"

"If Vancé says she's all right," Tiffany replied.

"To Moon Shadow?" Mac asked, and at the look on Tiffany's face he knew he'd made a monumental mistake saying anything in front of Zane Sheridan. He could have kicked himself for his lack of tact, but then he'd supposed that Sheridan knew what was going on. Apparently Tiffany hadn't confided in Sheridan, and Mac had let the cat out of the bag. Damn it all to hell anyway. Moving his slim shoulders in a gesture of indifference, Mac tried to undo the damage he'd caused before it was too late. "No reason to worry about it now, we've got a few days."

"I . . . I think I'll look in on Ebony Wine," Tiffany stated, wiping her hands on a towel hanging near the stove and steering the conversation toward safer ground. "She had a rough night."

"Didn't we all?" Mac frowned but a good-natured twinkle lighted his faded eyes. In his opinion, Tiffany Rhodes was as smart as she was pretty. "I've got to go into town—check with a guy about some alfalfa. Need anything else?"

"Just a few groceries, but I can get them later."

"Suit yourself." He nodded in Zane's direction, forced his rumpled fedora back onto his head and walked out the door.

Zane's silvery eyes rested on Tiffany's face. The near perfect features were slightly disturbed. Obviously something the old man said bothered her. It was as if she was hiding something from him. Zane had experienced that same sensation yesterday morning when the reporter was at the house, and again last night while attending to the stillborn colt. Something was bothering Tiffany Rhodes, and Zane suspected that it was more than his remarks about Devil's Gambit.

"Are you coming with me?" Tiffany asked as she walked down the short hallway to the den, slipped on her boots and pulled a worn suede jacket from the wooden hook near the French doors.

"Nothing better to do," Zane admitted, striding with her.

"Good." She scooped some envelopes from the top drawer of the desk, stuffed them into her pocket and headed outside. "I just want to drop these in the mail and pick up the paper before I go back to the foaling shed." She unlocked the French doors and stepped outside into the brisk morning air.

The world smelled fresh and new from the morning

rain. Birds twittered in the trees, and the fog had begun to lift. Though the drizzle had let up, raindrops still clung tenaciously to the branches of the maple trees lining the drive. Shallow pools of water rested on the uneven surface of the asphalt.

Despite the problems with the foals and Zane's outlandish remarks about Devil's Gambit, Tiffany felt refreshed, as if the gentle morning rain had washed away the fears of the night. She noticed the dewy, crystal-like web of a spider in the rhododendrons, and the woodsy scent of the earth beginning to warm from the first rays of a partially hidden sun.

It seemed the most natural thing in the world when Zane's fingers linked with hers, warming her hand. When he pulled on her hand, forcing her to stop near a thicket of oaks close to the end of the drive, she turned to face him and offered a smile. "What?"

"You don't know that you're driving me crazy, do you?" he asked gently, his gray gaze probing the vibrant blue depths of her eyes.

"And all the while I thought your wild stories and insane ideas about Devil's Gambit were genetic. Now it's my fault." Her blue eyes sparkled in the morning sunlight.

"Be serious," he suggested, his voice low and raspy. "I've wanted you from the first moment I laid eyes on you."

Tiffany laughed softly. "Now it's time for you to be serious."

"I am."

"You don't even know me—"

"I know you well enough to realize that we're good together."

"In what way?"

"All ways."

"Just because you helped Ebony Wine and you . . . saw to it that I fell asleep last night, it isn't enough to—"

"Shh." He tugged on her arm, forcing her closer. As he looked down upon her she felt as if he were stripping her of the barriers she had so carefully placed around herself, around her heart. She smelled the clean, masculine scent of him, felt the warmth of his body, knew in a minute that he intended to kiss her and that she wouldn't do a damn thing about it.

When his lips touched hers, she closed her eyes and couldn't withhold the moan that came from her throat. Both of his hands reached upward to cup her face. Strong fingers held her cheeks while his lips moved slowly, provocatively over her mouth. He touched the underside of her jaw, gently stroking the delicate pulse in her neck. When he lifted his head, his eyes had grown dark with unspoken passion.

Tiffany swallowed with difficulty, and her blood began to throb wildly in her veins. Feminine urges, long dormant, began to heat and swirl within her, captivating her mind as well as her body.

"Tiffany," he whispered hoarsely against the shell of her ear as his hand slowly found and removed the band at the end of her braid of hair. His fingers worked the shimmery golden brown strands until her hair tumbled free of its bond to frame her face in soft brown curls.

Her arms wound around his waist as his mouth dipped once again to the invitation of her parted lips. This time the kiss deepened, and Tiffany felt the thrill of his tongue as it sought out and mated with hers.

Liquid fire seemed to engulf her as desire flooded her veins and throbbed in her ears. *I can't want this man,* she reasoned with herself, but logic seemed to slip away. *He's using me. . . .* But she found that she didn't care.

Beneath the still-naked branches of the towering oaks, she returned his passionate kiss and sighed in contentment when he pressed up against her and the evidence of his desire strained against the fabric of his cords.

Dear God, I don't want to love you, she thought as his arms encircled her and held her tightly to him. *I can't let myself fall for you. . . . I don't even know who you are or what you want from me. Is this moment just a diversion, an intricate part of your plan, or are your feelings real?*

Logic began to cool her blood, and he felt her withdrawing from him. "Let me love you," he whispered, refusing to let her go, his powerful arms holding her a willing captive.

She shook her head and tried to deny the traitorous feelings burning in her breast. "I can't . . . I just . . . can't."

"Because you still love your husband." His voice was low and damning. Dark fire smoldered in his eyes.

Her clear eyes clouded and her teeth sunk into her lower lip. When she shook her head, sunlight caught in the honeyed strands of her hair. "Because I don't know you well enough," she countered.

"You never will, unless you take a chance."

"I am. Right here. Right now. With you. Please . . . try to understand."

His arms dropped. "Understand what? That you don't know me?" He stepped away from her, granting a small distance between their bodies. "Or is it that you're suspicious of my motives?" His dark eyes searched her face. "Or maybe it's because you think I might be just slightly off my rocker."

She laughed despite the tension in the crisp morning air. "That just about says it all," Tiffany admitted, tossing her tangled hair away from her face. "Except that I think things are moving a little too fast for me," she said, her breathing still irregular. "Yesterday we were strangers, earlier this morning, 'friends,' and now you're suggesting that we become lovers. I'm not ready for all of this—not yet."

"Don't play games with me."

"It takes two to play," she reminded him, holding her head high, her gaze steady.

"You're a mature woman, Tiffany, not some seventeen-year-old girl. You've been married—"

"And I don't have casual affairs."

"There's nothing casual about what I feel for you." His arms encircled her waist, his warm hands splaying naturally against the small of her back.

"Give it time, Zane," she pleaded in a raspy whisper. He was so near she could feel the warmth of his breath in her hair, sense the desire heating his veins, witness the burning passion in his eyes. Her expression clouded with the indecision tormenting her mind. *How easy it would be to lie naked with him in the morning sun. . . .*

With a sound of frustration he released her and leaned against the scaly trunk of one of the larger oaks in the thicket. Lethargic raindrops fell from the branches of the tree and glistened in his dark hair. He cocked his head to the side and forced a ragged but devastating smile. "Okay—so why not give me a chance to prove myself?"

"I am. You're still here, aren't you?"

She turned on her heel, walked the short distance to the road, extracted the envelopes from her pocket and placed them in the mailbox. Then, almost as an afterthought, she retrieved the morning paper from the yellow cylinder nailed to the fence post.

Rather than consider the implications of her mixed

emotions toward Zane, she opened the paper and stared down at the headlines. Her breath froze in her throat. "Oh, dear God," she whispered as her eyes scanned the front page.

The bold headline seemed to scream its message to her in powerful black and white:

LOCAL BREEDER PLAGUED BY MYSTERIOUS DEATHS.

Chapter Six

Tiffany felt as if the wet earth were buckling beneath her feet. She stared at the two pictures on the front page of the *Clarion*. One photograph had been taken yesterday. It was a large print of Tiffany sitting at her desk. The other, slightly smaller picture was of Moon Shadow after his loss in the Kentucky Derby.

Tiffany read the scandalous article, which centered on the mysterious deaths of the foals. Not only did Rod Crawford imply that there was something genetically wrong with Moon Shadow, who had sired all of the colts, but he also suggested that Tiffany, in an effort to save her reputation as a horse breeder, had hidden the deaths from the public and the racing commission. Crawford went on to say that any horse bred to Moon Shadow was likely to produce foals with genetic heart defects.

The article reported that since Tiffany had assumed control of Rhodes Breeding Farm, she had encountered more problems than she could handle. From the time her husband and the legendary Devil's Gambit had died, and Tiffany had been in charge of the farm, she had experienced nothing but trouble. It appeared that either Tiffany Rhodes was the victim of fate or her own gross incompetence.

"No!" Tiffany whispered, forcing the hot tears of indignation backward. She crumpled the damning newspaper in her fist. No mention had been made of Journey's End or any other of Moon Shadow's living, healthy progeny. Rod Crawford had twisted and butchered her words in a piece of cheap sensational journalism. Nausea began to roil in her stomach. "Damn it, nothing is wrong with him! Nothing!"

Her words sounded fragile into the late morning air, as if she were trying to convince herself.

Zane had watched as Tiffany read the article. She had paled slightly before anger settled on her elegant features. Now she was clenching the newspaper in her small fist and trembling with rage.

"What happened?" he demanded.

"Rod Crawford wrote his article," Tiffany explained.

"The reporter who was here just yesterday?"

Tiffany let out a furious sigh and looked upward to the interlaced branches of the oak and fir trees. Shafts of sunlight passed through the lacy barrier to dapple the wet ground. "I didn't think the article would be printed this soon," she replied, somehow stilling her seething rage, "but I guess in the case of a scandal, even the *Clarion* holds the presses."

She expelled an angry breath and coiled her fist. "Damn it all, anyway!" She had trusted Rod Crawford and the *Clarion's* reputation, and her trust had backfired in her face. The slant of the article was vicious, a personal attack intended to maim Tiffany's reputation. It was the last thing she had expected from a paper with the reputation of the *Santa Rosa Clarion*.

Zane touched her lightly on the shoulder in an attempt to calm her. "What are you talking about?"

"This." Her breasts rose and fell with the effort as she handed him the newspaper.

As Zane quickly scanned the article, his dark brows drew together in a savage scowl and his skin tightened over his cheekbones. A small muscle worked furiously in the corner of his jaw, and his lips thinned dangerously.

After reading the story and looking over the photographs, he smoothed the rumpled paper and tucked it under his arm. Every muscle had tensed in his whip-lean body. He was like a coiled snake, ready to strike. "Is there any truth in the article?"

"Enough to make it appear genuine."

"Great." He frowned and pinched the bridge of his nose with his thumb and forefinger, as if attempting to ward off a threatening headache. "Why didn't you tell me about this?"

Tiffany clenched her impotent fists. "I had enough to worry about with you and your crazy theories about Devil's Gambit. I didn't want to cloud the issue with the problem with Moon Shadow's foals."

"Even after last night, when I was with Ebony Wine?"

"There wasn't time." Even to her own ears, the excuse sounded feeble.

"And that's why you didn't want me near Rod Crawford. You were afraid I'd tell him what I knew about Devil's Gambit, he would report it and something like this—" he held up the newspaper and waved it in her face angrily "—might happen."

"Only it would be much worse."

He shook his head in disbelief. "I wouldn't have, you know." He could read the doubts still lingering in her eyes and silently damned himself for caring about her.

As if physically restraining his anger at her lack of trust in him, he handed the paper back to Tiffany. "I guess I can't blame you—I did come storming in here yesterday."

He managed a stiff smile and pushed his hands into the back pockets of his cords. After taking a few steps, as if to increase the distance between them, he turned and faced her. Thoughtful lines etched his brow, but the intense anger seemed to dissolve. "So tell me—the colt that was born last night—he was sired by Moon Shadow. Right?"

"Yes."

Zane raked frustrated fingers through his hair. "Then the death last night will only support the allegations in Crawford's newspaper column."

Tiffany felt as if everything she had worked for was slowly slipping through her fingers. "I suppose so," she admitted with a heavy sigh. Dear God, what was happening to her life? Suddenly everything seemed to be turning upside down. Zane Sheridan, a man whom she barely knew, whom she desired as a man but knew to be an enemy, was clouding her usually clear thinking at a time when she desperately needed all of her senses to prove true. He was voicing her worst fears, and she had trouble keeping the worried tears at bay.

"You should have told me."

"I couldn't."

"Because you didn't trust me and you thought that I might use the information on Moon Shadow against you," he said flatly, as if reading her thoughts.

So close to the truth! Was she so transparent to this man she had met only yesterday? Or was it because he knew more about her than he was willing to admit? "Something like that," she allowed, raising one suddenly heavy shoulder. "It really doesn't matter now."

"Look, woman," he said, barely able to contain his simmering anger. "You'd better start trusting me, because it looks like you're going to need all the friends you can get."

Her eyes took on a suspicious light. "But that's the problem, isn't it? I'm not quite sure whether you're on my side or not—friend or foe."

"Wait a minute—" He looked at her incredulously, as if she'd lost her mind. "Didn't I just tell you that I'm attracted to you? Wasn't I the man trying to make love to you just a few minutes ago?"

Tiffany elevated her chin fractionally. Now was the time to see exactly where Zane stood. Her dark brows arched suspiciously. "Sleeping with the enemy isn't something new, you know. It's been documented throughout history."

"Oh, give me a break," he spat, his palms lifting upwards as if he were begging for divine interference. "Did Ellery scar you so badly that you can't trust any man?"

"Ellery has nothing to do with this."

"The hell he hasn't!" Zane thundered, shaking his head in disbelief. His arms fell to his sides in useless defeat. "You're not an easy woman to like sometimes," he said softly as he approached her. He was close enough to touch. He was offering his strength, his comfort, if only she was brave enough to trust him.

"I haven't asked you to like me—"

He reached out and grabbed her arm. "Oh, yes, you have. Every time you look at me with those wide, soul-searching eyes, you beg me to like you. Every time you smile at me, you're inviting me to care about you. Every time you touch me, you're pleading with me to love you."

Tiffany listened in astonishment, her heart beginning to pound furiously at his suggestive words. She closed her eyes in embarrassment. How close to the truth he was! His fingers wrapped more tightly over her upper arms, leaving warm impressions on her flesh.

"Look at me, dammit," he insisted, giving her a shake. When she obeyed, Zane's flinty eyes drilled into hers. "Now, lady, it looks as if you've got one hell of a problem on your hands. There's a good chance that I won't be able to help you at all, but I don't think you're in much of a position to pick and choose your friends."

She tossed her hair away from her face and proudly returned his intense stare. "Maybe not."

"So let's try to figure out why those foals are dying, right now."

"How?"

"First I want to take a look at Moon Shadow."

Tiffany hesitated only slightly. Zane was right. She needed all the allies she could find. She checked her watch and discovered that it was nearly noon. No doubt the telephone was already ringing off the hook because of the article in the morning paper. There was no time to waste. Straightening her shoulders, Tiffany cocked her head in the direction of the stallion barns.

"Mac usually takes him outside about this time. He's probably getting some exercise right now."

Moon Shadow was in a far corner of the field. His sleek black coat shimmered in the noonday sun and he tossed his arrogant ebony head upward, shaking his glossy mane and stamping one forefoot warily.

Zane studied the nervous stallion. As a three-year-old, Moon Shadow had been impressive. He boasted a short, strong back, powerful hindquarters and long legs that could propel him forward in an explosion of speed at the starting gate that had been unmatched by any of his peers. He'd won a good percentage of his starts including two jewels of the Triple Crown. His most poignant loss was the Kentucky Derby, in which he had been jostled and boxed in near the starting gate and hadn't been able to run "his race," which had always been to start in front, set the pace and stay in the lead.

Zane blamed Moon Shadow's Derby disaster on several factors, the most obvious being that of a bad jockey. Moon Shadow's regular rider had been injured the day of the race, and his replacement, Bill Wade, was a green, uncaring man who had later lost his license to ride.

Mac was leaning over the fence, a piece of straw tucked into a corner of his mouth. Suddenly the black horse snorted, flattened his ears to his head, lifted his tail and ran the length of the long paddock. His smooth strides made the short dash appear effortless.

"He knows he's got an audience," Mac said as Tiffany approached. Wolverine was resting at the trainer's feet. At the sight of Tiffany, he thumped his tail on the moist ground. She reached down and scratched the collie's ears before propping her foot on the lowest board of the fence and resting her arms over the top rail.

"He's going to have more," Tiffany said with a sigh.

Mac's eyes narrowed. "More what?"

"More of an audience."

"What d'ya mean?" Instantly Mac was concerned. He read the worry in Tiffany's eyes.

"I'm afraid Moon Shadow is going to get more than his share of attention in the next couple of weeks. Take a look at page one." Tiffany handed Mac the paper before shading her eyes with her hand.

"Son of a bitch," Mac cursed after reading the article. He pushed his hat back to the crown of his head. "A pack of lies—nothing but a goddamn pack of lies." His eyes flickered from Zane to Tiffany before returning to Moon Shadow. "Damn reporters never have learned to sort fact from fiction." After smoothing the thin red hair over his scalp, he forced the frumpy fedora back onto his head. "A good thing you and Vance already told the Jockey Club about the dead colts."

"Yeah, right," Tiffany agreed without much enthusiasm. "But wait until the owners who have broodmares pregnant with Moon Shadow's foals get wind of this."

Mac frowned and rubbed the toe of his boot in the mud. "You'll just have to set them straight, Missy. Moon Shadow's a good stud. He's got the colts to prove it. Why the hell didn't that bastard of a reporter write about Journey's End or Devil's Gambit?"

Tiffany's eyes moved from Mac to Zane and finally back to the stallion in question. "I don't know," she answered. "Probably because he needed a story to sell papers." And he'd get one, too, if Zane decided to publicize his conjectures about Ellery and Devil's Gambit.

"How many foals were affected?" Zane asked.

"Three—no, Ebony Wine's colt makes four," Tiffany replied softly. "Three colts and a filly. Two died shortly after birth, the colt last night was stillborn and Charlatan . . . well, he lived longer, a couple of days, but . . ." Her voice faded on the soft afternoon breeze.

The silence of the afternoon was interrupted only by the wind rustling through the fir needles and the sound of Moon Shadow's impatient snorts.

"And they all died from heart failure?" Zane asked, staring at the proud stallion as if he hoped to see the reasons for the tragic deaths in the shining black horse.

Tiffany nodded, and Mac shifted the piece of straw from one corner of his mouth to the other.

"Seems that way," Mac muttered.

"Unless Vance discovers something different in the autopsy of the colt born last night," Tiffany added and then shook her head. "But I doubt that he'll find anything else."

"What about other horses bred to Moon Shadow?"

"Fortunately, none of the foals of mares from other owners have been affected—at least not yet. I've corresponded with all of the owners. So far, each mare has delivered a strong, healthy foal."

"Thank God for small favors," Mac mumbled ungraciously.

"Some owners even want to rebreed to Moon Shadow," Tiffany said, almost as an afterthought.

"But you're not breeding him?"

"Not until we find out what's going on."

"I don't blame you." Zane's gaze returned to the imperious stallion, who was tossing his head menacingly toward the spectators.

"He knows we're talkin' about him," Mac said fondly. "Always did like a show, that one." He rubbed the back of his weathered neck. "Should've won the Triple Crown, ya know. My fault for letting that son of a bitch ride him."

"Mac's been blaming himself ever since."

"I should've known the boy was no good."

"Quit second-guessing yourself. Ellery thought Bill was a decent jockey. Moon Shadow didn't win and that's that."

Mac frowned as he stared at the horse. "The closest I've come to a Triple Crown. Moon Shadow and Devil's Gambit were the finest horses I've ever seen race."

Tiffany stiffened at the mention of Devil's Gambit. "Mac's prejudiced, of course. The owners of Secretariat, Seattle Slew and a few others would have different opinions. But Moon Shadow sure used to be a crowd-pleaser," Tiffany remarked thoughtfully as she stared at the fiery black stallion.

"Aye. That he was," the old trainer agreed sadly as he rubbed the stubble on his chin. "That he was."

Tiffany spent the rest of the day showing Zane the farm. As Mac had stated, Ebony Wine seemed none the worse from her trauma the night before, and if Vance Geddes gave his okay, Tiffany wanted to breed her as soon as the mare was in heat.

As much as it broke her heart, Tiffany decided that Moon Shadow couldn't be allowed to sire any more foals until it was proved beyond a doubt that the cause of his foals' deaths wasn't genetic.

By the time she and Zane headed back to the house, it was late afternoon. The March sun was warm against Tiffany's back. As they walked toward the back porch, she slung her jacket over her shoulder. Zane had been with her all day, and it seemed natural that he was on the farm, helping with the chores, offering her his keen advice, and flashing his devastating smile.

"So you've already had him tested," Zane remarked as he held open the screen door to the broad back porch.

"Yes. And so far the semen samples have shown nothing out of the ordinary. I've asked for additional tests, but Vance Geddes seems to think that nothing will be discovered."

"What about the mares?"

She frowned and sighed. "Each horse has been examined by several vets. Blood samples, urine samples . . . every test available. The mares seem perfectly healthy.

"So all of the evidence points to Moon Shadow."

Tiffany nodded as she wedged the toe of one boot behind the heel of the other and kicked it off. She placed the scarred boots in the corner of the porch near the kitchen door. "It looks that way," she admitted.

"But you don't believe it."

"A good stud just doesn't go bad overnight." She pursed her lips together and ran weary fingers through her unruly hair. "Something has to have happened to him—I just don't know what."

"All the mares were bred to him around the same time?"

"Within a few weeks—I think. However, there are still mares who haven't dropped their foals."

"And you think they may have problems?"

Her blue eyes clouded with worry. "I hope to God they don't," she whispered as she started toward the door to the house. Zane's hand on her arm restrained her.

"I need to ask you something," he said quietly. The tone of his voice sent a prickle of fear down her spine.

"What?"

"Do you have any enemies, anyone who would want to hurt you?" His eyes had darkened as they searched her face.

"None that I can think of."

"What about this Crawford, the guy who wrote the article? Why would he want to distort the truth?"

"I couldn't begin to hazard a guess." She looked at the paper Zane was still carrying under his arm. "I guess the *Clarion* is into sensationalism these days."

"No personal reasons?"

"No."

His eyes drove into hers. "How about someone else who might want to see you exposed as incompetent?"

Tiffany stiffened, and cold dread settled between her shoulder blades. "Like whom?"

"I don't know—a competitor maybe?" When she shook her head in disbelief, her hair tumbled over her shoulders. He tightened his fingers around her arms. "A spurned lover?"

"Of course not!"

His grip relaxed a little. "You can't think of anyone who would want to hurt you? Someone with a big enough grudge against you or this farm to want to see your dirty laundry in black and white?" He was staring at her boldly, daring her to reply. "It would have to be someone with inside information."

Tiffany's eyes grew cold, and she felt a painful constricting of her heart. "The only person who remotely fits that description is you."

Zane stiffened. Tiffany saw the anger flash in his eyes, but he didn't bother to refute her accusation. His lips thinned until they showed white near the corners. "You know there was no love lost between myself and your husband. If Ellery were alive today, I'd probably do what I could to ruin him." He looked away from her and for a moment, pain was evident in the rugged planes of his face. "I despised the man, Tiffany, but you have to believe that I would never intentionally hurt you."

"Even if Ellery is still alive?" she whispered.

He closed his eyes against the possibility. The craving for vengeance that had festered in his blood still poisoned him, but as he gazed down upon Tiffany's face, Zane knew that he was lost to her. His hatred for Ellery couldn't begin to match the intensity of his feelings for this proud, beautiful woman. "If Ellery Rhodes walked through the door tonight, I would still detest him. But—" he reached out and gently stroked her chin "—because of you, I would leave."

Tiffany swallowed the uncomfortable lump forming in her throat and ignored the hot sting of tears against her eyelids. How desperately she longed to believe him. "Even if I asked you to stay?"

"What are you saying, Tiffany?" he asked, his face close to hers. "If Ellery is alive, would you leave him for me?"

"I . . . I don't know," she admitted, confused at the emotions warring within her. She ached to say yes and fall into Zane's arms, never to look back. If only she could love him for now, this moment, and cast away any thought to the future, or the past.

Slowly he pulled her to him, and Tiffany felt his larger body press urgently against hers. She leaned on him, and he kissed her forehead. "I can't make things different between us," he said, gently smoothing her hair away from her face.

"Would you, if you could?"

"Yes," he replied quickly as he had a vision of her lying naked in Ellery Rhodes's bed. "I wish I'd known you long ago."

In the privacy of the screened porch, with the fragrance of cherry blossoms scenting the air, nothing seemed to matter. It was a private world filled with only this one strong, passionate man. Tears pooled in Tiffany's eyes and clung to her lashes. "I think that it's better not to dwell on the past . . . or wish for things that could never be."

He tilted her face upward with his hands, and his lips claimed hers in a kiss that was filled with the desperation of the moment, and the need to purge all thoughts of her husband from her mind.

Her lips parted willingly for him, and his tongue touched the edges of her teeth before slipping into her mouth and plundering the moist cavern she so willingly offered.

A raw groan of frustrated longing escaped from his lips as he molded his hungry body to hers. She wound her arms around him, held him close, clinging to him as if afraid he would leave her empty and bereft.

"Tiffany," he whispered into her hair and let out a ragged breath. "Oh, Tiffany, what am I going to do with you?"

Whatever you want, she thought, returning his kiss with a bursting passion that had no earthly bounds.

His hands found the hem of her sweater and slipped underneath the soft fabric to press against the silken texture of her skin. Her breath constricted in her throat, and when his fingers cupped the underside of her breast she felt as if she were melting into him. A soft moan came from her throat as his fingers softly traced the lacy edge of her bra. She felt the bud of her nipple blossom willingly to his touch as his fingers slid slowly upward.

Zane's breathing became labored, a sweet rush of air against her ear that caused tantalizing sparks of yearning to fire her blood. "Let me love you, sweet lady," he pleaded, fanning her hair with his breath.

If only I could! Her desire throbbed in her ears, burned in her soul, but the doubts of the night filtered into her passion-drugged mind, and before she lost all sense of reason, she pulled away from him, regret evidenced in her slumberous blue eyes. "I . . . I think it would be best if we went inside," she said raggedly, hoping to quell the raging storm of passion in her blood.

The tense lines along the edge of his mouth deepened. "You want me," he said, holding her close, pressing the muscles of her body to his. "Admit it."

Her heart was an imprisoned bird throwing itself mercilessly against her rib cage. She lost her sense of time and reason. "I want you more than I've ever wanted a man," she whispered, trying to pull free of his protective embrace. "But wanting isn't enough."

"What is?"

Love, her mind screamed, but the word wouldn't form on her lips. How often before had she felt love only to see it wither and die? The love of Tiffany's mother had been so fragile that Marie had left her only daughter in the care of a drunken father. Edward's love hadn't been strong enough to conquer the drink that eventually killed him, and Ellery . . . Ellery probably didn't know the meaning of the word.

"I . . . I'm not sure," she admitted, her voice quavering unexpectedly.

"Oh, hell," Zane swore in disgust, releasing her. "Neither am I." He looked thoroughly disgusted with himself, and he rammed his hands into his pockets, trying to quiet the fury of desire straining within him. The heat in his loins seemed to sear his mind. Never had he wanted a woman so painfully. He felt as if his every nerve was raw, charged with lust.

Tiffany stared at Zane until her breathing had silenced and her racing pulse had slowed to a more normal rate. She entered the house, and the smells of roast and cinnamon filled her nostrils. "Louise?" she called as she went into the kitchen. The plump woman with graying hair and a ready smile was extracting a deep-dish apple pie from one of the ovens. "I thought you were going out of town for the weekend."

"Not until tomorrow." Louise set the hot pie on the tile counter and turned to face Tiffany. "I thought maybe you could use a little help around here today."

"You read the article in the *Clarion*."

Louise's full mouth pursed into an angry pout. "Yep. I read it this morning and canceled my subscription before noon. That was the trashiest piece of journalism I've ever read. Rod Crawford should be strung up by his—" her eyes moved from Tiffany to Zane "—hamstrings."

Tiffany smiled at the angry housekeeper. "You shouldn't have canceled your subscription."

"Humph. What I should have done was write a letter to the editor, but I suppose that would only make the situation worse, what with the publicity and all."

At that moment the phone rang, and Tiffany reached to answer it.

"It's been ringing off the hook all afternoon." When Tiffany hesitated, Louise continued. "Reporters mostly. A couple of other breeders, too. The messages are on your desk."

"I'll take the call in the den," Tiffany decided, straightening her shoulders.

"Vultures," Louise muttered as she opened the oven and checked the roast.

Tiffany answered the phone in the den on the sixth ring.

"Tiffany, is that you?" an agitated male voice inquired.

"Yes."

"This is Hal Reece." Tiffany's heart sank. Reece had bred one of his mares to Moon Shadow. Was he calling to tell her that the foal was dead? Her palms began to sweat and her pulse jumped nervously.

"What can I do for you, Mr. Reece?"

The stuffy sixty-year-old paused before getting to the point. "I read an article about your farm in the *Clarion*. No one told me there was any genetic problem with Moon Shadow."

"There isn't."

"But the article stated—"

"What the article stated was only half the story." Tiffany's eyes clashed with Zane's as he entered the den.

"Then you're saying that those foals didn't die?" he questioned, relief audible in his voice.

"No," Tiffany replied, bracing herself by leaning on the desk. "It's true we've lost a few foals—"

"Moon Shadow's foals," he clarified.

"Yes. But there is no reason to think that the problem is genetic. I've had Moon Shadow tested by several veterinarians. You're familiar with Vance Geddes, aren't you?"

"Why, yes. Good man, Geddes."

"He's been involved with the problem from day one. He's concluded that there's no evidence that the deaths were genetically related."

"But certainly they were linked."

"It appears that way."

"And the natural assumption is that it was the sire, as all the foals were his."

Tiffany heard the hopeful note in Hal's voice. She hated to discourage him. Forcing herself to remain calmly professional, she held her voice steady as she clutched the receiver in a deathlike grip. "Moon Shadow has proved himself a good stud. Journey's End and Devil's Gambit are proof enough of that. Most of the foals that he sired this year had no problems."

"No other owner has complained?" Reece asked, sounding dubious.

"None, and I've been in contact with each of them. So far, Moon Shadow has sired twenty-three perfectly healthy foals—something Mr. Crawford neglected to print."

"But three have died."

There was no use in hiding the truth from Reece or any of the other owners who had bred their expensive mares to Moon Shadow. It would only look worse later. Tiffany gritted her teeth and closed her eyes. "Four. We lost another colt last night."

"Oh, God!" His voice sounded weak.

Zane was standing near the fireplace, one shoeless stockinged foot propped against the stone hearth.

"When is your mare due to foal?" Tiffany asked.

"Any day now."

"I'm sure you'll find that you have a healthy Thoroughbred on your hands."

"I'd better, Tiffany," Hal said softly. "I'm not a rich man, I can't afford a loss like this. I'm sure the insurance company wouldn't cover the cost of my stud fee—"

"Mr. Reece, if you do happen to lose the colt and we discover that the problem stemmed from breeding your mare to Moon Shadow, I'll refund the stud fee."

"And then what? My mare's lost nearly a year of prime breeding time."

Tiffany's face became rigid. "I won't be able to do anything about that, Mr. Reece. It's the chance we take as breeders." She heard herself repeating Zane's advice of the night before. "When your mare does foal, I'd appreciate a call from you."

"You can count on it. Good day," he replied frostily, and Tiffany replaced the receiver. As soon as she set it down the phone rang again.

"Don't answer it," Zane advised, seeing the way she had paled during her lengthy conversation.

"I have to."

"The calls can wait."

"I don't think so. I have ten or twelve owners who are probably in a state of panic."

The phone rang again.

"It could be the press," Zane argued.

"Then I'll have to deal with them as well. I can't just hide my head in the sand. This was bound to happen sooner or later." She reached for the phone and answered it. A male voice demanded to speak to Tiffany Rhodes.

"This is she," Tiffany replied. The man identified himself as a reporter for a San Francisco paper. The telephone call was a short interview, and by the time it was over, Tiffany felt drained.

Zane sat on the edge of the desk, his worried gaze studying her as she turned around, clicked on a small computer in the bookcase and started typing onto the keyboard when luminous green letters appeared on the screen.

"What're you doing?"

"Getting a printout of all the owners who still have broodmares pregnant with Moon Shadow's foals. I think it would be best if I called them, rather than having them read a story like the one in the *Santa Rosa Clarion.*"

"This can wait until morning."

Tiffany shook her head and refused to be deterred. "I'd just as soon get it over with. The sooner the better." The printer began rattling out the list of owners as Tiffany checked the phone messages Louise had stacked on her desk. "Great," she mumbled. She held up one of the messages and handed it to him. "A reporter for a television station in San Francisco wants an interview." She smiled grimly. "What do you bet that it's not to talk about Journey's End's career?"

Zane frowned. "No wager from me, lady. I learned a long time ago not to bet money unless it was a sure thing—and then only when the man you're betting against is honest." His voice was low, and edged in anger. From the look on Zane's face, she knew that he was somehow referring to Ellery.

The printer stopped spewing out information, and the silence in the small room seemed deafening.

At that moment, Louise appeared, balancing a tray in

her plump hands. "I thought you two could use a cup of coffee," she explained. Noticing the tension in the room and the silent challenge in Tiffany's eyes, Louise pursed her lips together thoughtfully and amended her offer. "Or I could get you something stronger—"

"Coffee's fine," Zane replied, turning to watch her and sending a charming grin in her direction.

"Yes, thank you," Tiffany said, once Zane's gaze had released her.

"Dinner will be in about an hour."

Tiffany managed a frail smile. "Louise, you're a life-saver."

The large woman chuckled. "I'm afraid you'll need more than a hot meal before the evening's done."

"Don't be so optimistic," Tiffany remarked cynically.

"Just my nature," Louise replied before leaving the room.

"What else have you got on that computer?" Zane asked, studying the list of owners.

"Everything."

"Like what?"

"Health records on the horses, the price of feed, the stud fees we charged, equipment. Everything."

"Including a profile of your Thoroughbreds?"

"Every horse that's been a part of the farm."

"Can you get me a printout on Moon Shadow?"

She managed a tight smile. "Sure."

"How about the mares he was bred to, especially the four that lost their foals?"

Tiffany sat down at the keyboard. "This has already been done, you know."

"Humor me. I need something to do while you're tied up with the phone. I may as well be doing something constructive since I canceled my flight."

"Can't argue with that." Tiffany requested the information from the computer, and when the printer started spewing out profiles of the horses in question, Tiffany started with the first of what promised to be several uncomfortable telephone calls to the owners of mares bred to Moon Shadow.

Chapter Seven

"Here, drink some of this," Zane suggested. He handed Tiffany a glass of white wine. "Maybe it will improve your appetite."

"And my disposition?" She accepted the glass and took a sip of the white Burgundy. The cool liquid slid easily down her throat, and she eyed her plate of forgotten food with a sigh.

"They really got to you, didn't they?" Zane asked as he leaned back in his chair and frowned into his glass. He had finished Louise's dinner of roast beef, parslied potatoes and steamed broccoli before noticing Tiffany's neglected plate.

"Let's just say I'm glad it's over," she replied and then amended her statement, "or I hope to God it is."

What if any of the unborn foals were to die shortly after birth? What would happen to her and the farm? The telephone conversations with the owners who had mares bred to Moon Shadow hadn't gone well at all. By the time she had contacted or left messages with all the owners, Tiffany had felt as if every nerve in her body had been stretched as tightly as a piano wire. During two of the more difficult calls, she had been threatened with lawsuits, should the foals be born with life-threatening heart problems.

She couldn't begin to do justice to Louise's delicious

meal. With a weary shake of her head, she pushed her plate aside, leaned back in the chair and ran tense fingers through her hair.

Zane offered her a sad, understanding smile. "Come on, the dishes will wait. Let's finish this—" he held up the opened bottle of wine "—and relax in the study."

"I don't think that's possible."

"Come on, buck up." He got up from the table and placed a comforting hand on her shoulder. "Things are bound to get better."

"That's a strange statement, coming from you," she stated. He shrugged his broad shoulders and his smile faded. "But I guess you're right," she continued, slapping the table with new resolve. "Things can't get much worse." *Unless another foal dies.*

The den seemed warm and intimate. The glowing embers of the fire and the muted illumination from a single brass lamp with an emerald-colored shade softened the corners of the room and reflected on the finish of the cherry-wood walls. The thick Oriental carpet in hues of green and ivory, the etchings of sleek horses adorning the walls and the massive stone fireplace offered a sense of privacy to the room.

Zane stoked the smoldering coals in the fireplace. *As if he'd done it a hundred times. Here. In her home.* His actions seemed so natural, as if he were an integral part of the farm. As he knelt before the fire, he lifted a chunk of oak from the large basket sitting on the warm stones of the hearth. "This should do it," he mumbled to himself as he placed the mossy log on the scarlet embers. Eager flames began to lick the new fuel and reflect in golden shadows on Zane's angular face. His shirt was stretched over his back, and Tiffany watched his fluid movements as he worked. When the fire was to his satisfaction, he dusted his hands together and studied the ravenous flames.

As she sipped her wine and observed him, Tiffany felt the long dormant stirring of feminine desire. Urges that were better denied began to burn in her mind. *I won't let myself fall for him,* she promised but knew that her efforts would prove futile. He was already an integral part of her life. Ever since last night, when he had bent over the lifeless foal and tried to force air into the still lungs, Zane Sheridan had become a part of Rhodes Breeding Farm. Whether she liked it or not.

She dragged her eyes away from his strong physique and concentrated on the clear liquid in her wineglass. "Don't you have some place you have to be?" she asked.

The lean frame stiffened. He hesitated for just a moment before turning to face her. "Later."

"Tonight?" she asked in attempted nonchalance. Her tongue caught on the solitary word.

He nodded curtly. "I've got some early appointments in San Francisco tomorrow." He noticed the slight tensing in her shoulders. *Damn her, that strong will and pride will be her downfall . . . or mine.* "Things I can't put off any longer." He finished his wine and stared at her. "Is that a hint?"

"No . . . I mean, I just think it's strange that you've been here—" she made a big show of checking her watch "—over twenty-four hours and still haven't gotten down to the reason you came."

"The time of reckoning—right?" His eyes met her gaze boldly before glancing at the portrait of the horse.

She took a seat on the edge of the gray corduroy couch. "Close enough. But first I want to thank you for helping last night. I really appreciate everything you did. . . ."

"You're sure about that?"

She remembered waking up and finding him sleeping in the uncomfortable chair with his feet propped on her bed. "Yes," she whispered. "For everything."

"And now you want to know about Devil's Gambit," Zane thought aloud as he stood and stretched his arms over his head. It was an unconscious and erotic gesture. His sweater rose, displaying all too clearly his lean abdomen. His belted cords were slung low over his hips and Tiffany glimpsed the rock-hard muscles near his navel. She imagined the ripple of the corded muscles of his chest, his muscular thighs and lean flanks. . . . She had to look away from him and force her mind from the sexual fantasy she was envisioning. What was wrong with her? She'd never reacted this way to a man, not even Ellery. Until Zane Sheridan had walked into her life, she had considered herself nearly uninterested in the opposite sex.

One look from Zane's steely gray eyes had drastically altered her entire perception of her own sexuality. Her new feelings were at once exciting and frightening. Zane was the one man she couldn't begin to trust . . . not with her body or her soul. He had already admitted that he was waging a vendetta of sorts, and she didn't doubt for a minute that he was the kind of man who would use and destroy her because of his hatred of Ellery.

Zane took a final sip of his wine and then set the empty goblet on the mantel. "I meant to tell you about Devil's Gambit last night," he explained, "but Ebony Wine had other things on her mind."

Tiffany nodded and clutched the stem of her crystal glass more tightly as she remembered the agonizing scene in the foaling shed and the innocent stillborn colt. Had it been only last night? So many things had changed, including her respect and feelings for Zane. "So what about now?"

Zane angled his head to the side and studied the wariness in her eyes. She was sitting on the edge of the gray cushions, waiting for him to explain his reasons for being there. "No time like the present, I suppose." He walked over to the bar and splashed three fingers of Scotch into an empty glass. "I think your horse—"

"You mean Devil's Gambit?"

"Right. I think he's in Ireland, using an alias."

"Now I know you're crazy." What did he mean about Devil's Gambit being in Ireland? His story was getting more far-fetched by the minute.

If she had any guts at all, she would tell him to get out of her house . . . her life, take his wild stories and shove them. Instead she twirled the stem of the wine-glass in her fingers and stared up at him.

"Just hear me out. Have you ever heard of a horse named King's Ransom?"

"Yes," she admitted, recalling the Irish Thoroughbred. "But I really don't keep up on the European horses, not as much as I should, I suppose. There just isn't enough time. Dustin handles that end of the business."

"I'm not surprised," Zane replied with obvious distaste.

"What does that mean?"

"Only that sometimes it's hard to tell Ellery and Dustin apart." He paced across the room before sitting on the warm stones of the hearth.

"So you know Dustin?" That knowledge came as a shock to her and she felt a new wariness steal over her heart. *Hadn't Dustin mentioned King's Ransom to her— something about the horse's fame as a stud?* Tiffany couldn't recall the conversation. . . .

"We've met." Zane leaned his elbows on his knees and cradled his drink with both of his hands.

"And you don't like him any more than you liked Ellery."

"As I said, they're too much alike to suit my taste."

Tiffany was stunned. Dustin had his faults, of course, but she'd come to rely on her brother-in-law and his savvy for horses. It seemed as if Zane were determined to destroy anything and anyone who was solid in her life.

"Not much does, does it?" she countered.

"What?"

"Suit your taste."

He hesitated. His eyes darkened and for a moment she imagined that he might suggest that she suited him. Instead he lifted an appreciative dark brow. "You're right—not much."

Tiffany's throat constricted, and she sipped her wine to clear the tight lump that made it difficult to breathe.

If he noticed her discomfort, Zane chose to ignore it and get to the point. "Anyway, this horse, King's Ransom, was a disappointment when he raced. He had all the qualities to perform on the track—great bloodlines, perfect conformation and a long, easy stride. He had the look of a winner about him, but he just didn't seem to have the grit . . . or heart to be a champion. He never finished better than fifth, and consequently he was retired about seven years ago and put out to stud.

"The first of his offspring began running about four years ago, and even though they inherited all his physical characteristics, none of the colts and fillies were anything to write home about. It seemed as if they all ended up with his lack of drive."

"So what does this have to do with Devil's Gambit?" Tiffany asked. Her blue eyes mirrored her worry. Despite her arguments to the contrary, she was beginning to understand what Zane was hinting at.

"I'm getting to that. All of a sudden, less than two years ago, when that year's two-year-olds and three-year-olds hit the track, look out! Overnight, King's Ransom was producing some of the fastest horses in Europe."

"That's not impossible," Tiffany said uneasily. She felt a sudden chill and shivered before getting up and walking closer to the fire . . . to Zane.

"But highly improbable. It's the same principle as what's happening here with Moon Shadow, in reverse. Just as a good stud won't go bad overnight, the reverse is true. A mediocre stallion doesn't become the greatest stud in Ireland by a fluke." Zane was looking up at her with his magnetic gray eyes. He knew that he had Tiffany's full attention. Her glass of wine was nearly untouched, her troubled blue eyes reached into the blackest corners of his soul. *God, she was beautiful.* He swirled his drink and stared into the amber liquor, trying to still the male urges overcoming him.

"I own a mare that I bred about five years ago to King's Ransom," Zane continued. "The colt that was born from that union was just what I expected—a solid horse, a plodder, but nothing that would compare to his recent foals. I rebred that same mare to King's Ransom three years ago, and the resulting filly has already won two races and come in second in another. This horse is a full sister to the first."

Tiffany's dark honey-colored brows drew together pensively as she tried to remember what it was about King's Ransom . . . Vaguely she recalled a conversation with Dustin. Dustin had been going on and on about King's Ransom and his ability as a sire. At the time, it hadn't seemed all that important. Dustin was always raving about one horse or another—comparing his current favorite to the horses he and Tiffany owned.

"It might be worth it to breed one of the mares, say Felicity, to King's Ransom," Dustin had insisted.

"But the cost of shipping her would be prohibitive," Tiffany had replied. "The insurance alone—"

"I tell you, that stud's got what it takes!" Dustin had been adamant. "He could sire the next Devil's Gambit!"

Now, as Dustin's words came back to her, Tiffany paled. If what Zane was suggesting was true, then Dustin must have been involved! "I . . . I don't believe it," Tiffany said, taking a sip of her wine and trying to ignore the chilling implications running through her mind.

This was absurd. Ludicrous. Her relationship with Dustin had always been solid, and after Ellery's accident it had been Dustin who had helped her over the rough spots, given her his ear, offered a strong shoulder to cry on.

"Believe it, Devil's Gambit is siring foals and King's Ransom is getting all the credit. Your horse is being used, Tiffany!"

She squared her shoulders and trained disbelieving eyes on Zane. "I don't know why you came here," she said. "If it was to trick me into selling the farm, then you may as well leave now. All of this—" she moved both arms in a sweeping gesture meant to encompass everything that had transpired between them "—has been a very entertaining show, but I don't believe any of it. You're wasting your breath."

Zane pursed his lips together in frustration. With a frown he got up, crossed the room and picked up his briefcase.

"God, Tiffany, you don't make it easy," he muttered as he set the leather case on the wooden desk and silently wondered why it bothered him so much that he had to prove himself to this woman. He could hardly expect that she would believe his story without proof. After snapping the case open and extracting a white envelope, he handed the slim packet to her.

With trembling fingers Tiffany opened the envelope and extracted a faded photograph of a black stallion.

"This," he said angrily while pointing at the horse in the photo, "is a picture of King's Ransom. He looks a lot like Devil's Gambit, don't you think?"

The resemblance was eerie. Tiffany couldn't deny what was patently obvious. Even though the photograph was old and faded it was glaringly evident that the stallion's size and conformation were incredibly like that of the dead horse.

Zane reached inside his briefcase again. This time he took out the manila envelope he had given her the night before. It still contained the photographs he had insisted were those of Devil's Gambit. Tiffany might have believed him last night except for the fact that the white stocking on the horse's foreleg was missing.

"Are those two horses the same?" he demanded. His jaw was rigid, his gaze blistering as he searched her face.

She studied the photographs closely. A cold chill of dread skittered down her spine. The horses were nearly identical, but definitely not one and the same. Only by placing the photographs side by side was Tiffany able to discern the subtle differences between the two horses. The slope of the withers was different, as was the shape of the forehead. Only a professional would notice the small dissimilarities.

Tiffany closed her eyes against Zane's damning truth.

"Are they the same horse?" he repeated, his voice low. Slowly, she shook her head.

Zane set the pictures on the desk and expelled a heavy sigh. Finally, he had gotten through to her! He poked a long finger at the more recent photograph. "This," he said, "is the stallion that's supposed to be King's Ransom. I say he's Devil's Gambit."

Tiffany swallowed against the dryness settling in her throat. Here was the proof that her husband had lied to her, that her proud stallion was still alive, that everything she had believed for four years was nothing more than an illusion created by her husband. *Devil's Gambit and Ellery were alive!* "How did you know?" she finally asked in a forced whisper.

He rubbed his hand over his chin and closed his eyes. "I didn't really know, not for a long time. I guess I became suspicious when the second foal, the filly, exhibited such a different temperament from her brother."

"When she started racing as a two-year-old, I was certain she was the fastest horse on the farm, though her bloodlines weren't nearly as good as several other horses."

He walked over to the fire and looked into the golden flames, as if searching for easy answers to his life. "I didn't think too much about it until I got to talking to several other owners who had noticed the same phenomenon on their farms: all of King's Ransom's latest offspring were markedly different from his first foals." Zane smiled to himself, amused by a private irony. "No one was really asking questions—all the owners were thrilled with their luck, and of course, King's Ransom's stud fees have become astronomical since the latest colts and fillies have begun racing."

Tiffany lifted her hands and shook her head in silent protest. "It still could be a coincidence," she whispered. Her suggestion was a desperate attempt to right her crazily spinning world, to hold on to what she had believed to be true for four long years, and both she and Zane knew it.

"Look at the pictures, Tiffany," Zane quietly insisted. "You're knowledgeable enough to realize those two stallions are different. Something isn't right at Emerald Enterprises."

"Pardon?"

"Emerald Enterprises owns the farm."

"And therefore King's Ransom."

"If that's what you want to call him."

Still the connection to her horse wasn't completely clear. "And you think Devil's Gambit is somehow involved?"

"I know he is."

"Because . . . someone switched horses, planned the accident, thereby killing the replacement horse and Ellery? Then what about Dustin? How did he manage to escape with his life?"

"Maybe he planned it."

The words settled like lead in the room. Only the occasional crackle and hiss of the fire disturbed the thick, condemning silence. "Dustin wouldn't . . ." she said, violently shaking her head. "He couldn't kill Ellery . . . they were brothers . . . very close. . . ."

"Maybe it wasn't intentional. I told you I think Ellery was in on the swindle."

Her frigid blue eyes held Zane's gaze. "That doesn't make a hell of a lot of sense, you know," she rasped, her body beginning to shake from the ordeal of the past two days. "Ellery owned the horse. Devil's Gambit was worth a lot more alive than he was dead!" She raised a trembling hand in the air to add emphasis to her words, but Zane reached for her wrist and clutched it in a deathlike grip.

"Just hear me out. Then you can draw your own conclusions."

"I already—"

He broke off her protests by tightening his fingers over her arm. "Please listen." His grip relaxed but his stormy eyes continued to hold her prisoner.

"All right, Zane. I'll listen. But in the end, if I don't believe you, you'll have to accept that."

"Fair enough." He released her and took a seat on the corner of the desk. His stormy eyes never left the tense contours of her elegant face. "When I requested a third breeding to King's Ransom, at the high stud fee, I was granted it. But because of the stallion's 'temperamental state' I wasn't allowed to witness my horse being bred."

"And you didn't buy that excuse?" Tiffany guessed.

"It sounded like bull to me. It just didn't make a lot of sense. I'd witnessed the first breeding but was out of the country when the second foal was conceived."

"So what happened?"

"I began asking a lot of questions. Too many to suit the manager of the farm. All of a sudden I was told that King's Ransom's services were, after all, unavailable. He was booked to cover far too many mares as it was, and I was asked to pick up my mare and leave."

"Before she was bred?"

"Right."

Tiffany began to get a glimmer of the truth, and it was as cold as a winter midnight.

Zane walked over to the hearth. As he sat on the warm stones he studied the amber liquor in his glass. "I picked up the mare, and the manager didn't bother to hide his relief to be rid of me. As I was leaving I saw a horse I recognized as King's Ransom running in a distant field. I thought it odd, since the manager had told me not five minutes before that King's Ransom was supposedly in the breeding shed."

"So you took these pictures!" she said breathlessly, the scenario becoming vivid in her confused mind.

"I'm a camera buff and happened to have my camera and telephoto lens with me. I grabbed what I needed from the glove box and photographed the horse. I took several shots and noticed that the stallion was running with a slight misstep. I hadn't heard about any injury to King's Ransom, and that's when I began to suspect that there might be two horses using the same name."

Tiffany's eyes were wide and questioning. "And from that you just deduced that one of the horses was Devil's Gambit?"

"It wasn't that difficult, really," Zane stated, his silvery eyes delving into hers. "Black Thoroughbreds are fairly uncommon, much rarer than bay or chestnut."

Tiffany nodded, her heart freezing with the fear that he was telling the truth. Dear God, what had Ellery done?

"Because of King's Ransom's age and coloring, it was relatively easy to discover what horse was being used in place of him to cover his mares. I did some research, and once I saw the pictures of Devil's Gambit again, I knew that he was the sire responsible for the faster offspring in the past few years."

"This is all still conjecture, you know," she said, trying to find any way possible to refute what he was saying. Even as she did so, she knew that she was grasping at straws.

"You're right. Except for one fact."

Tiffany steeled herself. "Which is?"

"That six years ago the ownership of the breeding farm where King's Ransom is standing at stud changed hands. A corporation now owns the farm. It took a lot of digging, but I finally found out that the primary stockholder in Emerald Enterprises is none other than your brother-in-law."

"Dustin?" Tiffany gasped, hoping with all her heart

that Zane would come up with another name, any other name.

"One and the same."

Tiffany felt weak but outraged. Her knees buckled and she leaned against the desk for support. Even if everything Zane told her was the truth, she had to settle it herself with Dustin and Ellery . . . *if* Ellery was alive. *If* she could. Two very big "ifs." For a moment her voice failed her. When at last she could speak, all she could manage was a hoarse whisper. "I think, Mr. Sheridan," she suggested, "that you'd better leave."

"Are you so afraid of the truth?"

Tiffany closed her eyes, and her finely arched brows drew together. *Yes, Zane,* she thought, *I am afraid. I'm afraid that what you're telling me is reality. I'm afraid the man I trusted as a brother-in-law lied to me, I'm afraid that my husband has betrayed me and I'm afraid, so afraid of you—and what you do to me!*

She reached for her wineglass with shaking fingers. Her voice was husky. "You seem to have done your homework," she admitted. "But just because Dustin owns part of the farm in Ireland—"

"Did you know about it?" he demanded.

She managed to shake her head, and the golden light from the fire caught in the soft brown silk of her hair. Zane fought against the sudden tightness in his chest.

"Don't you think that's odd—since you're still business partners here in the States?"

Odd as hell, she thought to herself as she pushed the hair from her face and stared at the ceiling. Her brother-in-law had been the one solid thing in her life when her world had shattered in pain and desperation on the night that Ellery and Devil's Gambit were killed. Becoming a widow had been a new and frightening experience, and the scandal about Ellery and his tragic horse had only made facing widowhood worse. Reporters hadn't left her alone for over two weeks. If it hadn't been for Dustin and his strength . . . "I don't know everything about Dustin's business. He's just my brother-in-law, not my . . ."

"Husband?"

Her throat was parched, and the words forming in her mind were difficult to say. "Have you . . . did you . . . see any evidence to indicate that Ellery might still be alive?" she asked, her fingers tightening over the edge of the desk fiercely enough that her knuckles showed white.

"No."

A lump formed in her throat. "But you can't be sure?" she insisted in a breathless whisper.

Zane frowned darkly. "Oh, lady, I wish I could answer that one for you," he said fervently.

She felt the sting of tears and forced them back. "If Ellery was alive, he wouldn't have let me believe that he was dead," she said as much to convince herself as Zane. Her small hands balled into fists, and she pounded them against the varnished surface of the desk she had used for four years . . . Ellery's desk. "You know that you're destroying everything I've worked for, don't you? In two days, everything I've believed in is slowly being torn apart . . . and I don't understand why."

"Don't you want to know if your husband is alive?"

"Yes!"

"And if he is?"

"Oh, God." She clasped her hand over her mouth before she managed to steady herself. "I . . . I don't know."

"Would you divorce him?"

She shook her head and pressed back the tears threatening her eyes. "No. Not until I heard his side of the story."

"And when you did?" Zane asked, his features becoming harsh.

Tiffany let out a ragged breath. "I don't know. It's all so unbelievable—I don't have all the answers."

Zane's eyes bored into her as if searching for her soul. *Damn Ellery Rhodes and what he had done to his beautiful wife!* Despite the desire for revenge seeping through his blood, Zane knew as he watched Tiffany battle against tears that he could never hurt her. It would be easy to make love to Rhodes's wife, but Zane knew instinctively that she would never forgive him if he took advantage of her vulnerable state and she later found out that her husband was alive.

She managed to slowly get hold of herself. "Why does all this matter to you, and why on earth would you want to buy this farm?" she questioned, her voice a whisper. "You have your choice of every breeding farm on the market—so why this one?"

"I'm not interested in just any farm. I already have one in Ireland."

"And that's what you do—breed horses, when you're not bothering widows?"

His lips thinned in disgust. Against his better judgment, Zane crossed the room and stood near the desk, near the attractive woman leaning against the polished surface. Her head was thrown back, her white throat exposed, her silken hair falling in a reckless tumble of honey-brown that touched the desk.

"Have I bothered you so much?"

"More than you'll ever guess," she admitted, straightening. She rubbed her arms, hoping to warm the inner chill of dread settling between her shoulders. After glancing up at the portrait of Devil's Gambit, she turned cold, suspicious eyes on Zane.

"You really believe everything you've told me, don't you?"

"It's the truth."

"And is that why you want the farm? Do you want to buy me out, and then blow this whole thing wide open about Devil's Gambit? That way there would be an investigation and you would have a chance, as owner of Rhodes Breeding Farm, of recovering him?"

"I don't think it would work that way," Zane said stiffly. "You would still own the horse. That's not the reason I want this farm."

"Then what is, Zane? Why did you come here in the first place?" He was much too close, but she didn't give in an inch. Proudly she faced him, her soft lips pressed into a frown, her skin stretched tightly over the gentle curve of her cheek.

Zane's dark eyes drove into her very soul. "Ellery Rhodes stole from me."

"What are you talking about?"

Deciding to distance himself from her, Zane walked over to the bar and splashed another drink into his glass. *How much could he confide to Ellery Rhodes's widow without blowing everything?* "It's not a subject I like to discuss," Zane admitted after taking a long swallow of the warm Scotch. "But about six years ago Ellery won a large amount of cash from me."

"And you hate him for that?" Tiffany was incredulous. What kind of a man was Zane?

"Not until I found out that the game was rigged. Oh, by the way, your brother-in-law, Dustin, was in on it, too."

"I don't believe it."

"Believe it. Your husband was little more than a thief."

Tiffany was numb from the tattered state of her emotions. "And you've waited all this time, just to get even with him," she guessed, her voice without inflection. "It didn't matter that he was dead—you just had to do something, *anything* to get even."

Zane saw the disbelief and silent accusations in Tiffany's eyes. He wanted to purge himself, tell all of the story, but couldn't. Stasia's betrayal had been long ago, but it was still an open wound that continued to bleed. He'd accused himself of still loving his ex-wife, even after she'd run off with Ellery Rhodes. But Zane knew better. He doubted if he had ever loved Stasia, but his battered pride was still raw from her deceit.

"I want this farm," he said as thoughts about Stasia gave him renewed conviction. The look on his face was intense, slightly threatening.

"I'm sorry, Zane. I told you yesterday that if I ever decided to sell, the first option would be Dustin's."

"Even when you know that he deliberately lied to you?"

"If he did, you mean. I can't believe—"

Zane cut her off by slicing the air with his hand. He strode over to the desk, reached inside his briefcase and handed her a thick packet of legal documents.

"What are these?" she asked, slowly scanning the complicated pages.

"Corporate documents, ownership papers."

"How did you get them?"

"It doesn't matter. Just read." He hated to put the damning evidence in front of her, but she'd been so bull-headed about Ellery and Dustin, he'd had no choice. Tiffany didn't strike him as the kind of woman who would live in a fantasy world, but maybe when a woman loved a man as passionately as Tiffany loved Rhodes . . . He frowned darkly and finished his drink in one swallow. His inner vision of Tiffany entwined in Ellery Rhodes's arms turned his thoughts back, and a senseless anger took hold of his mind.

Tiffany sifted through the documents, and as she did her heart contracted painfully. Dustin's signature was scrawled all over the legal papers concerning Emerald Enterprises and the purchase of the farm in question. Without a doubt, some of Zane's story was true. Just how much, she would have to determine on her own, when issues such as the dead foals and her feelings for Zane didn't clutter her mind. Pursing her lips together she handed the papers back to Zane.

"They're yours," he said.

"I don't want them."

"I have extra copies, and I think you might want to go over these more carefully while I'm gone."

"You're leaving?" *Oh, God, not now. Not when I need your arms to protect me . . .*

"Have to," he admitted with obvious reluctance.

"I see," she replied, stunned. How long did she expect him to stay? He'd already mentioned that he had business back in San Francisco. It was only a matter of time until they went their separate ways.

She stared sightlessly down at the documents she still held in her hands. Since Zane had been with her, she had avoided thinking about the time he would leave. *This is crazy, let him go, before you do something you'll regret later. . . .*

His hands molded over her upper arms. The warmth of his touch made her knees weaken, and she had to fight the urge to fall against him for support.

"While I'm gone, I want you to consider selling the farm to me," he said sharply, his gentle fingers in stark contrast to his harsh words.

He was a man of contradictions, ruthless one moment, kind the next; sensitive to her desires as a woman, yet insensitive to her needs as a person. She told herself she couldn't possibly fall in love with him and yet she knew that fate had already cast the die. She was falling desperately and hopelessly in love with the stranger from Ireland.

"It's just not that easy, Zane. Dustin still owns twenty-five percent—I can't make a decision without him."

"Then consider selling out your portion. I'll deal with Dustin later." The tone of his voice was harsh, his jaw hard.

"It's just not possible."

"Anything's possible, Tiffany. Don't you know that?"

As possible as falling in love with you? Dear Lord, what has happened to my common sense?

As if reading her unspoken question, Zane smiled gently. The tense line of his jaw relaxed as slumberous eyes embraced hers. One long finger traced the elegant curve of her neck. "I'll be back in a few days," he promised.

Her lips trembled beguilingly. "There's no need. You know my position on selling the farm—"

"And what about Devil's Gambit?"

She frowned and pushed an errant lock of golden hair over her shoulder. "I . . . I don't know," she admitted, eyeing the portrait of the proud stallion. She needed time alone, time to think and sort out everything Zane had stated. How much of his story was fact and how much was pure fiction?

"You'll need a contact in Ireland."

The thought that Zane might be leaving the country shocked her. For this short time she'd had with him, she felt as if they'd grown incredibly close.

"I'll have to think about that—"

"Tiffany?"

"Yes?" She looked up and found him staring at her. For most of the evening he had forced himself to stay away from her physically. But standing next to her with the warmth of the fire against his back, smelling the scent of her perfume, seeing the honest regret in her blue eyes, was too much to bear. The restraint he had placed upon himself began to dissolve into the shadowy room.

He touched the seductive contour of her jaw, and she closed her eyes. His hands were gentle as they lingered near her throat. "Come with me to San Francisco," he suggested impulsively as his blood began to heat and he forgot his earlier promise to himself. He wanted Tiffany Rhodes as he'd never wanted a woman.

"Oh, Zane, I can't."

"Why not?" His fingers had wrapped around her nape, under the curtain of her hair. She had trouble thinking clearly as his hands drew her near to him, and his lips touched her eyelids.

"I have . . . too many things to do . . . too much to think about. . . ."

'Think about me—"

"That, I can assure you, I will," she promised fervently, her words the barest of whispers.

When his lips touched hers, he tasted more than the flavor of rich Burgundy. His tongue skimmed the soft surface of her mouth, gently prying her lips apart. Tiffany had no desire to stop him. She felt reckless, daring. Her raw emotions had pushed rational thought aside. Though she barely knew him, her body trembled at his touch, thrilled at his gentle caress.

His fingers slid down her arms to wrap securely over her waist, pulling her willing body to his. He moaned when he felt her hands, which had been gently touching his shoulders, grip the corded muscles more tightly. She was warm, pliable, yielding. . . .

Silently cursing the doubts in his mind, he crushed her body to his. He felt the heat in her blood, tasted her need when her mouth opened willingly to him, smelled the heady scent of perfume mingling with burning pitch. The ache in his loins began to pound with the need of this woman—Ellery Rhodes's wife.

Tiffany let her arms hold him close. She knew he would be leaving soon, and she had to savor each sweet second she had with him. When she felt the weight of his body gently push her to the floor, she didn't resist. Her hands linked behind his head, and she let herself fall until the soft cushion of the carpet broke her fall and was pressed against her back.

"I want you," he whispered, his face taut with desire. "God forgive me, but I want you."

Her blue eyes reflected the golden flames of the fire, and her hair was splayed in tangled curls on the deep, green carpet. Passion darkened her gaze and lingered in her eyes. "There's no need for forgiveness," she murmured, her fingers stroking the back of his neck, his tensed shoulder muscles.

Her blood was pulsing violently through her veins, heating the most intimate parts of her. Her heart felt as if it would burst with need, want. It continued to beat an irregular rhythm in her ears, making her oblivious to anything but the desire of this man . . . this stranger. As she gazed into his silvery eyes, she wondered if what she was feeling was love or lust and found she didn't care.

"Tiffany," he whispered against her hair. He was lying over her, his chest crushing her breasts as if he were afraid she would escape, his long legs entangled with hers. "I didn't want this to happen." His ragged breathing was filled with reluctance.

"I know," she whispered.

He kissed the curve of her neck and tingling sensations raced wildly down her body. Dear Lord, she couldn't think when he was touching her, couldn't reason. . . .

Before she could try to explain her feelings, his rugged face loomed over hers. He gazed down upon her and passion darkened his eyes. *Think of Ellery,* she told herself, *there is a slim chance that he might be alive. Though he betrayed you, he is still your husband.*

Zane's lips captured hers, and despite the arguments in her mind she wrapped her arms around his neck and let her fingers wander in his thick, obsidian hair. His touch was electric, and all the nerves in her body screamed to be soothed by him.

I can't do this, she thought wildly, when his hands rimmed the boat neck of the sweater and teased the delicate skin near her collarbone. He lowered his head and pressed his moist tongue to the hollow of her throat, extracting a sweet torment that forced her pulse to quiver.

He kissed her again, more savagely this time, and she responded with a throaty moan. When he lifted his head, he gazed into her eyes, then pulled the sweater over her head, baring her breasts to the intimate room. A primitive groan slid past his lips as he looked down at her. The lacy bra, the sheerest of barriers to him, displayed the ripeness of her breasts and their pink tips. Already the nipples were rigid, thrusting proudly against the silky fabric and offering the comfort to soothe him if he would only suckle from them. "God, you're beautiful," he said, running first his eyes and then his tongue over the delicious mounds of white and feeling the silken texture of her skin beneath the sheer lace. She trembled with the want of him.

The wet impression of his tongue left a dewy path from one rose-tipped peak to the next. Tiffany struggled beneath him, arching up from the carpet and pulling him to her with anxious fingers digging into the thick muscles of his shoulders.

In a swift movement he removed his sweater and

tossed it beside Tiffany's on the floor. She stared at him with love-drugged eyes. His chest was lean and firm; dark skin was covered when she lifted a hand to stroke him, and his nipples grew taut as she stared at him.

He lowered himself over her and covered her mouth with his. His tongue tasted of her, dipping seductively into her mouth only to withdraw again. The heat within her began to ache for all of him. She wanted him to touch her, fill her, make long, passionate love to her until the first shafts of morning light filtered through the windows.

When his mouth moved slowly down her neck to pause at the shadowy valley between her breasts, she cried out his name. "Zane, please," she whispered, begging for his touch. Thoughts of a distant past with Ellery infiltrated her mind. *I couldn't feel this way with Zane if Ellery were still alive. . . . I couldn't!*

In response to her plea, he unclasped the bra and removed it from her, staring at the blushing beauty of her breasts.

"What do you want, sweet Tiffany?" he asked, his slumberous gray eyes searching hers.

Her throat tightened and she closed her eyes. Her dark lashes swept invitingly downward. "I want you— all of you."

He dipped his head and ran his tongue over one proud nipple. "Do you want me to love you?"

"Please . . . Zane . . . yes!" *Didn't he know? Couldn't he see the love in her eyes as she opened them to search his face?*

"All of you?" He kissed the other nipple, but his eyes locked with hers for an electrifying instant. His teeth gently teased the dark point, and she quivered from the deepest reaches of her soul.

"All of me," she replied and groaned when he began

to suckle hungrily at one delicious peak. His large hands held her close, pressing against her naked back and warming her exposed skin. Tiffany felt waves of heat move over her as he kissed her, caressed her, stroked her with his tongue. She cradled his head, holding him close, afraid he would leave her bereft and longing. As his mouth and tongue tasted her, drew out the love she felt, the hot void within her began to throb with desire.

"Make love to me, Zane," she whispered when the exquisite torment was more than she could bear. "Make love to me and never let me go. . . ."

It was the desperate cry of a woman in the throes of passion. Zane knew that Tiffany had unwittingly let her control slip. He positioned himself above her and his fingers toyed with the waistband of her jeans, slipping deliciously on her warm abdomen. She contracted her muscles, offering more of herself, wanting his touch. Her body arched upward eagerly, her physical desire overcoming rational thought.

Her fingers strayed to the button on his cords and he felt it slide easily through the buttonhole. Her hands did delightful things to him as she slid the zipper lower. He squeezed his eyes shut against his rising passion. His need of her was all-consuming, his desire throbbing wildly against his cords. His fingers dipped lower to feel the smooth skin over her buttocks, and he had to grit his teeth when she began to touch him.

"Tiffany," he whispered raggedly, forcing himself to think straight. He remembered all too vividly that Ellery Rhodes could very well be alive. If Zane took her now, and Ellery was alive, Tiffany would never forgive him. "Wait." His voice was hoarse. With gentle hands he restrained her fingers. She stared up at him with hungry, disappointed blue eyes.

God, what he wouldn't give to forget all his earlier vows to himself. If he made love to her now, before the mystery surrounding Devil's Gambit was resolved, before he had purchased the farm, she would end up hating him.

"I . . . had no intention . . ." *Of what? Making love to Ellery Rhodes's woman? As just revenge for what he did to you?* ". . . of letting things get so out of hand."

She read the doubts on his face and closed her eyes. "Forgive me if I don't believe you," she murmured, trying to roll away from him. "But I seem to recall a man who, this very morning, matter-of-factly insisted that we become lovers." Tears of embarrassment flooded her eyes.

"It's not for lack of any wanting on my part," he replied.

That much she didn't doubt. She'd felt the intensity of his desire, witnessed the passion in his eyes, felt the doubts that had tormented him. "Then what?" she asked, reaching for her sweater. "Are you teasing me, trying to find a way to convince me to sell the farm to you?" she accused.

He flinched as if she had physically struck him, and his entire body tensed. "You know better than that."

"I don't think I know you at all. I think I let my feelings get in the way of my thinking."

His fist balled impotently at his side and his face hardened. "Would you feel better about it, if we resumed what we started and I took you right here . . . even though Ellery might still be alive?"

"Of course not," she gasped. Her blood had cooled and reason returned.

He reached out and tenderly pushed her hair from her eyes. "Then wait for me," he asked, his voice low. "I just want to make sure that you won't regret anything that might happen."

"Are you sure you're concerned for my feelings, or your own?"

"Oh, lady," he whispered, forcing a sad smile. His fingers trembled slightly when he brushed a solitary tear from her eye. "Maybe a little of both." He reached for her and his fingers wrapped possessively around her neck. Closing his eyes against the passion lingering in his blood, he kissed her sensuously on the lips. "I'll be back. . . ."

Chapter Eight

"This isn't the smartest thing you've ever done, Missy," Mac warned as he finished his coffee and pushed his hat onto his head. He scraped his chair back from the table and placed the empty cup on the tile counter, not far from the area where Louise was rolling dough.

"The least you could do is show a little support," Tiffany teased. She smoothed the hem of her cream-colored linen suit and smiled at Mac's obvious concern.

"After that newspaper article in the *Clarion,* I'd think you'd have more sense than agree to another interview."

"Can't argue with that," Louise chimed in as she placed a batch of cinnamon rolls in the oven.

"Okay, so the interview with Rod Crawford was a mistake. This one will be different." Tiffany leaned against the counter and attempted to look confident.

"How's that?" Mac's reddish brows rose skeptically on his weathered face.

"The reporter from the *Times* is Nancy Emerson, a roommate of mine from college."

"Humph." Louise was busily making the second batch of rolls and didn't look up as she spread the cinnamon and sugar over the dough. "How do you know she won't do the same thing that Crawford did? In my book a reporter's a reporter. Period."

"Nancy's a professional."

"So was Crawford."

"I talked about the interview. I told her I would only do it if it didn't turn out to be a hatchet job."

"I bet she liked that," Louise remarked sarcastically as she began furiously rolling the dough into a long cylinder. "It's none of my business, mind you, but didn't you bank on the reputation of the *Clarion?*"

"Yes," Tiffany said with a sigh.

Mac noted Tiffany's distress. "Well, if you think you can trust her—"

"I just know that she won't print lies," Tiffany insisted. "She's been with the *Times* for over six years and written dozens of articles on horse racing in America and abroad. She's extremely knowledgeable and I figured she'd give an unbiased, honest report." Tiffany lifted her palms in her own defense. "Look, I had to grant an interview with someone. I've had over a dozen calls from reporters in the past three days."

"I can vouch for that," Louise agreed as she sliced the rolls and arranged them in a pan.

Louise had insisted on working at the farm every day since Zane had left and Tiffany was grateful for the housekeeper's support. Life on the farm had been hectic in the past few—had it only been four?—days. It seemed like a lifetime since she'd been with Zane.

"Well, I guess you had no choice," Mac allowed.

"None. The longer I stall, the more it seems as if we're hiding something here."

"Aye. I suppose it does," Mac mumbled as he sauntered to the back door. "I'll be in the broodmare barn if you need me." He paused as his fingers gripped the doorknob, glanced back at Tiffany, and shifted uncomfortably from one foot to the other. "It looks like Alexander's Lady's time has come."

Tiffany felt her heart fall to the floor. Alexander's

Lady was pregnant with Moon Shadow's foal. Tiffany closed her eyes and gripped the edge of the table. Louise stopped working at the counter.

"Oh, Lord," the large cook muttered, quickly making a sign of the cross over her ample bosom. Then, with a knowing eye in Tiffany's direction, she smiled kindly. "This one will be all right, honey . . . I feel it in my bones."

"I hope to God you're right," Tiffany whispered.

"It's in His hands now, you know. Not much you can do 'bout it," Mac advised with a scowl. "Worryin' ain't gonna help."

Tiffany studied Mac's wrinkled brow. "Then maybe you should take your own advice."

"Naw—I'm too old and set in my ways to stop now. Anyway, worryin's what I do best." The trainer raised his hand in the air as a salute of goodbye and opened the door to the back porch, just as the doorbell chimed. Mac's frown deepened. "Looks like your friend is here."

Tiffany managed a thin smile. "Good. We may as well get this over with."

"Good luck," Louise muttered, once again hastily making the sign of the cross with her flour-dusted hands as Tiffany walked out of the kitchen.

"Tiffany! You look great," Nancy said with heartfelt enthusiasm as Tiffany opened the door.

The slim, dark-haired woman with the bright hazel eyes appeared no different than she had six years ago. Dressed in navy-blue slacks and a crisp red blouse and white jacket, Nancy looked the picture of efficiency. Short dark-brown curls framed a pixie-like face filled with freckles and smiles.

"It's good to see you, Nance. Come in." Tiffany's grin was genuine as she hugged her friend. It had been years since she'd seen Nancy. Too many years. The two women had parted ways right after college. Tiffany's father had died, and Nancy had moved to Oregon to marry her high school boyfriend.

"And what a beautiful house," Nancy continued, her expressive hazel eyes roving over the sweeping green hills surrounding the white-clapboard and brick home. "This is something right out of *Gone with the Wind!*"

"Not quite, I don't think."

"All you need is a couple of mint juleps, a porch swing and—"

"Rhett Butler."

Nancy laughed. "I suppose you're right. But, God, Tiff, this is *fabulous!*"

"The house was Ellery's idea," Tiffany admitted as Nancy's eager eyes traveled up the polished oak banister and marble stairs to linger on the crystal chandelier. "He thought the farm would appear more genuine if it had a Southern atmosphere."

"This is beyond atmosphere, Tiffany, this is flair!"

Tiffany blushed a little under Nancy's heartfelt praise. She'd forgotten what it was like to be around the exuberant woman. Though Nancy had to be thirty, she didn't look a day over twenty-five, and part of her youthful appearance was due to her enthusiasm for life.

Tiffany showed Nancy the house and grounds of the farm. "This is heaven," Nancy insisted as she leaned against a redwood tree and watched the foals romp in the late-morning sun.

"I like it."

"Who wouldn't? Let me tell you, I'd give an arm and a leg to live in a place like this."

Tiffany laughed. "And what would you do? You're a city girl by nature, Nance."

Nancy nodded in agreement. "I suppose you're right."

"You'd miss San Francisco within the week."

"Maybe so, but sometimes sharing a two-bedroom apartment with two kids and a cat can drive me up the wall. The girls are five and four, and you wouldn't believe how much energy they have."

"They probably get it from their mother. Genetics, you know."

"Right. Genetics. The reason I'm here."

Tiffany ignored the comment for now. "So why don't you bring the kids out here for a weekend sometime?"

Nancy's bright eyes softened. "You mean it?"

"Of course."

"They're a handful," the sprightly reporter warned.

"But they'd love it here, and I adore kids."

Nancy was thoughtful as she stared at the horses frolicking in the lush grass of the paddock. "So why didn't you have any?"

Tiffany shrugged. "Too busy, I guess. Ellery wasn't all that keen on being a father."

"And you?"

"It takes two."

Nancy sighed and lit a cigarette. A small puff of blue smoke filtered toward the cloudless sky. "Boy, does it. Raising the kids alone is no picnic. Ralph has them every other weekend, of course, but sometimes . . . Oh, well. Look, I'm here for an interview, right? Tell me what you've been doing since you took over the farm."

Nancy took a tape recorder from her purse and switched it on. For the next hour and a half Tiffany answered Nancy's questions about the farm—the problems and the joys.

"So what's all this ruckus over Moon Shadow?" Nancy asked, her hazel eyes questioning.

"Hype."

"What's that supposed to mean?"

"Come on, I'll show you." Tiffany led Nancy to the

stallion barn and Moon Shadow's stall. Moon Shadow poked his ebony head out of the stall, held it regally high and flattened his ears backward at the sight of the stranger. "Here he is, in the flesh, the stallion who's been getting a lot of bad press."

"What you referred to as 'hype'?"

"Yes. He's fathered over a hundred Thoroughbreds in the past eight years, several who have become champions."

"Like Devil's Gambit?"

Tiffany's heart seemed to miss a beat. She didn't want to discuss Devil's Gambit with anyone, including Nancy. "Yes, as well as Journey's End."

"Rhodes Breeding Farm's latest contender. He promises to be the next Devil's Gambit," Nancy observed.

"We hope so."

Moon Shadow's large brown eyes wandered from Tiffany to the reporter and back again. Tiffany reached into the pocket of her skirt and withdrew a piece of carrot. The proud stallion nickered softly and took the carrot from Tiffany's hand.

"He's been a good stud," Tiffany emphasized while rubbing the velvet-soft black muzzle.

Tiffany continued to talk about Moon Shadow's qualities and the unfortunate incidents with the dead foals. Whenever Nancy posed a particularly pointed question, Tiffany was able to defend herself and her stallion by pointing to his winning sons and daughters.

Nancy had snapped off her tape recorder and stayed through lunch. Tiffany felt more relaxed than she had in days when she and Nancy reminisced about college.

"So what happened between you and Ralph?" Tiffany asked, as they drank a cup of coffee after the meal.

Nancy shrugged. "I don't really know—it just seemed

that we grew in different directions. I thought that the kids would make a difference, but I was wrong." When she saw the horrified look in Tiffany's eyes, she held up her hand. "Oh, don't get me wrong, Tiff. It wasn't that Ralph wasn't a good father—" she shrugged her shoulders slightly "—he just wasn't comfortable in the role of breadwinner. Too much responsibility, I suppose. Anyway, it's worked out for the best. He's remarried, and I'm dating a wonderful man."

"And the girls?"

Nancy sighed and lit a cigarette. "It was rough on them at first, but they seem to be handling it okay now."

"I'm glad to hear it."

"It's hard to explain," Nancy said softly. "It just seemed that the longer we lived together, the less we knew each other or cared. . . ."

"That happens," Tiffany said. Hadn't she felt the same doubts when Ellery was alive? Hadn't there always been a distance she was unable to bridge?

"Yeah, well . . ." Nancy stubbed out her cigarette. "As I said, I think it's for the best. Oh, God, look at the time! I've got to get out of here."

Tiffany watched as Nancy gathered her things, and then she walked her friend to the car. "I was serious when I told you to bring the kids out for a weekend. Just give me a call."

"You don't know what you're asking for."

Tiffany laughed. "Sure I do. It'll be fun. Come on, Nance, those girls could use a little fresh country air, and they'd love being around the horses."

Nancy eyed the rolling hills of the farm wistfully. "Be careful, Tiff, or I just might take you up on your offer."

"I'm counting on it."

Nancy's car was parked in the shade of a tall maple

tree near the back of the house. When they reached the car, Nancy turned and faced Tiffany. "This has been great," she said. "The best interview I've done in years."

"Do you do many stories about Thoroughbreds?" Tiffany asked.

"Some—mainly from the woman's angle," Nancy replied. "Most of the time I write human interest stories—again, from the woman's perspective. The reason I got this assignment is that I read the article in the *Clarion* and stormed into my editor's office, insisting that since I knew you, I would be the logical person to write a more in-depth article for the *Times*. He really couldn't argue too much, since I used to cover all the local and national races." Her hazel eyes saddened a little. "I think you, and not your horse, were the victim of bad press, my friend."

Tiffany shrugged, but smiled. "Maybe." A question formed in her mind, and she had to ask. "When you were working on the races, did you ever hear of a stallion named King's Ransom?"

"Sure. But he wasn't much of a champion, not until recently. From what I understand his services as a stud are the most sought-after in Ireland."

"Who owns him?"

Nancy smiled. "That's the interesting part. It's kind of a mystery. He's syndicated of course, but the largest percentage of the stallion is owned by Emerald Enterprises." Tiffany's heart felt as if it had turned to stone. *Zane had been telling the truth!*

"Which is?"

"A holding company of sorts," Nancy replied.

"I see," Tiffany said, her heartbeat quickening. "What about a man by the name of Zane Sheridan?" she asked.

Nancy was about to get into the car but paused. "Now there's an interesting man."

"Oh?" Tiffany cocked her head to the side and the smile on her lips slowly faded. "Do you think he's somehow involved with Emerald Enterprises?"

"I don't really know, but I doubt it. He owns a farm near the one owned by Emerald Enterprises. Why are you so interested?"

"I'm not . . . not really." Tiffany lied in ineffectual nonchalance. "He was here a couple of days ago, looking at some horses."

"He's a bit of a mystery," Nancy said. She leaned against the car door and stared up at the blue sky as she tried to remember everything she could about the breeder from Ireland. "He's a tough guy, from what I hear. Ruthless in business. He grew up on the streets of Dublin. Had several scrapes with the law and ended up working as a stable boy at an Irish Thoroughbred farm in the country. The owner of that particular farm took a liking to him, sent him to school, and once educated, Sheridan made a small fortune breeding horses." She sighed as she tried to remember the fuzzy details of a scandal that had occurred in the past.

"And then, well, it's kind of foggy, but from what I remember, he was in some sort of trouble again. A scandal, and he lost his fortune and his wife. I can't remember all the details right now."

The news hit Tiffany like a bolt of lightning. Though stunned, she managed somehow to ask, "His wife is dead?"

"No—she ran off with this guy named . . . God, what was it? Rivers, I think. Ethan Rivers, an American. . . . Like I said, it's kind of a mystery. No one really knows what happened to this Rivers character or Sheridan's wife."

The thought of Zane being married did strange things to Tiffany. "How long ago was this?" she asked.

"Geez, what was it? Five years, maybe more like seven, I'm really not sure." She pursed her lips as she thought and then, when she checked her watch, nearly jumped out of her skin. "Look, I've got to go. Deadlines, you know. I'll call you soon."

"Good. I'd like that."

Nancy got into her car and settled behind the wheel. The engine started, and Nancy rolled down the window. "The article on the farm should be in the paper no later than Thursday. I'll send you a copy." With a brilliant smile, she fingered a wave at Tiffany and forced the little car into gear.

Tiffany watched the car disappear down the tree-lined drive, but her mind was miles away. Nancy's visit had only increased her restlessness. Where was Zane and why hadn't he called?

Hours later, Tiffany was walking back from the half-mile track near the old barn when she heard a familiar voice.

"Tiffany!"

A tall man wearing a Stetson was running toward her. Tiffany shielded her eyes from the ever-lowering sun and smiled when she recognized her brother-in-law.

"Dustin!" She hadn't expected him back for another week.

"Hello, stranger," he said as he reached her and gathered her into his arms to twirl her off the ground. How had she ever doubted him? "What's this I hear about you getting some bad press, little lady?"

"Some?" Tiffany repeated with a shake of her head. "How about truckloads of it."

"You can't be serious." He flashed her a brilliant smile.

"Four of Moon Shadow's foals have died—all from heart failure."

Dustin lifted his hat, pushed a lock of brown hair out of his eyes and squinted into the setting sun toward the exercise track, where Mac was still working with a yearling. "So I read."

"You and the rest of the world." Tiffany pushed her hands into the pockets of her jeans. Her conversation with Zane came hauntingly back to her, and she wondered just how much she could confide in Dustin. He did own twenty-five percent of the farm and was entitled to know everything that was going on . . . well, almost everything. "I have owners who are threatening me with lawsuits if the mares they bred to Moon Shadow drop foals that die."

"How many mares are involved?" Dustin's hand reached out and took hold of her arm. They had been walking toward the old barn where Tiffany had been headed. Near the building, Dustin stopped her.

"About twelve," she said. "Some of them took the news fairly well. The others, well . . . they weren't so understanding."

"In other words they're ready to rip your throat out."

"Close enough."

"Damn!" Dustin let out an angry blast. "This is the last thing we need right now. Okay, so what about the mares that have already foaled?"

"The foals that eventually died were from our mares. So far, every mare bred to Moon Shadow from another farm has dropped a healthy colt or filly."

"So much for small favors."

"I guess we should consider ourselves lucky that this isn't a contagious virus," she said.

"You're sure?" Dustin didn't sound convinced.

"Um-hm. Vance checked everything carefully. At first he thought it might be sleepy foal disease, but fortunately it wasn't."

"Yeah, fortunately," Dustin muttered sarcastically.

Tiffany pushed open the door to the old barn and checked the supply of grain stacked in sacks in the bins. The interior was musty and dark, the only light filtering through the small window on the south side of the building and the open door. Dustin leaned against a post supporting the hayloft and watched her make notes in a small notebook.

Once she had finished counting and was satisfied that the inventory of feed was about what it should be, she started back toward the door.

Dustin's hand on her arm stopped her. His topaz-colored eyes pierced into hers. "So what happened to those foals?"

Tiffany shook her head and her honey-brown tresses glowed in the shadowy light from the windows. "Your guess is as good as mine."

"What does Vance say?"

"Nothing good, at least not yet."

He leaned against the post, shoved the hat back on his head so he could see her more clearly and drew Tiffany into the circle of his arms. His voice was low with concern, his gold eyes trained on her lips. The intimate embrace made Tiffany uncomfortable. All Zane's accusations concerning Dustin began to haunt her. Maybe she should ask him flat out about the circumstances surrounding Devil's Gambit's death, but she hesitated. There was just enough of the truth woven into Zane's story to give her pause.

Dustin read the worry on her features. "Do you think there's a possibility that Moon Shadow's to blame for the deaths?"

Tiffany frowned and tried to pull away from him. "No."

"But all the evidence—"

"Is circumstantial."

"I see." Dustin released her reluctantly and cleared his throat. "So what are you doing with him?"

"Nothing. I can't breed him. Not until I know for certain that the problem isn't genetic."

"Then you do have reservations?"

Tiffany bristled slightly. "None, but what I don't have is proof. Unfortunately, Moon Shadow has already been tried and convicted by the press. He's as good as guilty until proved innocent."

"Bitter words . . ."

"You haven't been here trying to talk some sense into the reporters, the owners, the television people."

"No," he conceded with obvious regret. "But I bet you handled them."

Tiffany lifted a shoulder. "As well as I could. I had an interview with Nancy Emerson from the *Times* this morning."

Dustin smiled. "Your old roommate?"

"Uh-huh."

He breathed deeply. "Good. It never hurts to know someone in the press."

Tiffany decided to set her brother-in-law straight. "I didn't buy her off, you know."

"I know, I know, but at least she's on our side. She should be objective. Thank God for small favors."

Something in Dustin's attitude made Tiffany uneasy. *You're overreacting*, she told herself, all because of Zane Sheridan and his wild accusations.

Dustin smoothed back his wavy hair. "I've got to hand it to you, Tiff. You've come a long way," he said appreciatively. "There was a time when I didn't think you would be able to pull yourself together."

"I have you to thank for getting me back on my feet," she replied, uncomfortable with the personal tone of the conversation. She was reminded of Zane and the accusations he had made about Dustin. Today, in the fading sunlight, those allegations seemed positively absurd. Dustin was her brother-in-law, her friend, her partner. The man who had pulled her out of the depths of despair when Ellery and Devil's Gambit had been killed.

Then what about the farm in Ireland, the one owned by Emerald Enterprises? What about Dustin's signature on the ownership papers? What about King's Ransom?

She decided to broach the difficult subjects later, once she had learned the reason for Dustin's unexpected visit. Was it possible that he knew Zane had been here? Had someone tipped Dustin off, possibly Zane himself?

Tiffany felt a growing resentment and anger at Zane. Single-handedly he had destroyed her trust in the only family she had ever known.

"Come on," she suggested, pushing her worrisome thoughts aside as she walked through the open door of the barn. "I'm starved. Louise made some cinnamon rolls this morning, and I bet we can con her out of a couple."

Dustin looked as if he had something he wanted to say but held his tongue. Instead he walked with Tiffany to the house and waited patiently while she kicked off her boots and placed them on the back porch.

"Are you staying long?" she asked, once they were in the kitchen and seated at the table.

Dustin hedged slightly. "Just a couple of days."

"And then?"

"Back to Florida."

"To check on Journey's End?"

"Right." He took a long swallow of his coffee, and his golden eyes impaled her. "You think you could spare the time to come with me?" he asked, his voice uncommonly low.

Tiffany ignored the hidden innuendoes in his tone. They'd covered this territory before, and Dustin obviously hadn't taken the hint. The scene in the old barn emphasized the fact. Dustin had never hidden the fact that he would like to pursue a more intimate relationship with her, but Tiffany just wasn't interested. Dustin seemed to assume that her lack of interest was due in part to loyalty to Ellery, and Tiffany didn't argue the point. He just couldn't seem to get it through his thick skull that she wasn't interested in a relationship with a man—any man.

Except Zane Sheridan, her mind taunted. Would she ever be able to get him out of her mind? In four days, he hadn't phoned or stopped by the farm. All of his concern for her while he was here must have been an act, a very convincing act. Still, she couldn't forget him.

"Tiff!"

"Pardon?"

Dustin was frowning at her. He'd finished his coffee, and the cup was sitting on the table. His empty plate showed only a few crumbs and a pool of melted butter where his cinnamon rolls had sat. "You haven't heard a word I said," he accused.

"You're right."

"So where were you?"

"What?"

"You looked as if you were a million miles away."

"Oh, I guess I was thinking about Moon Shadow," she lied easily, too easily. "Mac thinks another one of his foals will be born tonight."

Dustin leaned back in his chair and let out a low whistle. "No wonder you're worried. If this one dies, the press will be crawling all over this farm again. Maybe I'd better stay a few extra days."

Waving off his offer, she shook her head. "No reason.

You know you're welcome to stay as long as you like, but if you have things to do, go ahead and do them. I can handle everything here."

He walked around the table, stood behind her and placed his hands on her shoulders. "You're sure?"

Tiffany tensed. "Of course I am."

As if receiving her unspoken message, he dropped his hands to his sides. "You know that's one of the qualities I admire about you, Tiff, your strength."

"I guess I should be flattered."

Dustin stepped away from her and rested his hips against the counter. All the while his eyes rested on her worried face. "Is something else bothering you?" he asked.

"Isn't that enough?"

"I suppose so." He shrugged his broad shoulders and folded his arms over his chest. Silent reproach lingered in his eyes. The air in the kitchen became thick with tension.

Tiffany heard the screen door bang shut. Within minutes Mac was in the kitchen.

"Don't tell me, you smelled the coffee," Tiffany guessed, reaching for a cup and feeling relieved that the inquisition with Dustin was over for the moment.

"Aye, that I did."

"Well, pull up a chair, sit yourself down and help yourself to a roll, while I get you a mug."

Mac's faded eyes rested on Dustin. Not bothering to hide a frown, he cocked his head toward the younger man. "'Evenin', Dustin. Didn't expect you back for a while."

Tiffany handed Mac the cup.

Dustin managed a tight grin as he offered the older man his hand. "I read an article about the foals dying and thought I should come back—" his gold eyes moved to Tiffany "—since no one bothered to tell me what was going on."

"I thought I'd wait until Vance had something concrete to go on," Tiffany stated.

"And how long would you have waited?"

"Not much longer."

"It was a hell of a way to find out, you know," Dustin said, his anger surfacing, "by reading about it in the paper." He rammed his fingers through his hair in frustration. For a moment he appeared haunted.

"You're right. I should have called, but I didn't because there wasn't a damned thing you or I or anyone else could do."

"I suppose you're right about that," Dustin conceded with a frown and then turned his attention to Mac. "I was just trying to convince Tiffany here that she ought to come to Florida and see for herself how Journey's End is doing."

"Not a bad idea," Mac agreed, though there were reservations in his eyes. He removed his hat and took a chair at the table. "That way she could check up on Bob Prescott, see that he's doing a good job of training the colt."

Prescott was a young trainer who traveled with the horses while they were racing. He was a damned good man around a horse, but there was something shifty about him that Mac didn't like. The missus called it jealousy. Mac wasn't so sure, but he couldn't put his finger on the problem, and Bob Prescott had molded Journey's End into a fine racing machine.

Dustin's smile froze. "See, Tiffany, even Mac agrees that you could use a vacation. A little Florida sun might do you a world of good."

Tiffany managed a thin smile for both men and finished her coffee. "It'll have to wait until we're over this crisis." She leaned back in the chair and held up a finger. "However, you can bet I'll be at the Derby this year."

"You think Journey's End will make a good show of it?" Dustin asked as he placed his empty cup in the sink and wiped an accumulation of sweat from his brow.

"Not a show nor a place, but a win," the crusty old trainer predicted.

"High praise coming from you," Dustin observed.

"Journey's End is a fine colt. He's got the heart, the look of eagles if you will, but his temperament's got to be controlled . . . guided." He lifted his wise old eyes to Dustin's face. "I just hope that Bob Prescott knows what he's doing."

"He does."

"Then Journey's End should win the Derby," Mac stated without qualification. "He's the best horse I've seen since Devil's Gambit or Moon Shadow."

Dustin nearly choked on his final swallow of coffee and turned the subject away from Devil's Gambit. "We all know why Moon Shadow lost the Derby, don't we?" Dustin asked pointedly.

Mac's faded eyes narrowed. "Aye, that we do. I haven't made any excuses about it, either. I should never have let that jockey ride him."

"He was Ellery's choice," Tiffany intervened, sensing an argument brewing between the two men.

"And I shouldn't have allowed it." Mac straightened his wiry frame from the chair, and his fedora dangled from his fingers as he turned to Tiffany. "I called Vance. I'm sure we'll have another foal before morning."

Tiffany took in a ragged breath. "Let me know when the time comes."

"Aye. That I will." With his final remarks, Mac walked out of the room and the screen door banged behind him.

Tiffany whirled on Dustin. "That was uncalled for, you know," she spit out.

"What?"

"Those remarks about Moon Shadow and the Derby."

"Serves the old man right. I never have figured why you keep that old relic around, anyway."

Tiffany was furious and shaking with rage. "Mac's not old, nor a relic, and he's the best damned horseman in this state, maybe the country. He knows more about Thoroughbreds than you or I could hope to know in a lifetime. Let's just hope, brother-in-law, that he doesn't take your remarks to heart and quit on us. We'll be in a world of hurt, then, let me tell you!"

Dustin had visibly paled but scoffed at Tiffany's remarks. "You're giving him too much credit," he said with a shrug as he stared out the window. "You're genuinely fond of the old goat, aren't you?"

"Mac's been good to me, good to this farm, good to Ellery and good to you. Why you continue to ridicule him is beyond me. Unless you'd secretly like to see him leave."

"It wouldn't affect me one way or the other."

"Like hell, Dustin. We had an agreement, remember?" she reminded him. "I run the operations of the farm, you handle the PR. Right now, because of all the adverse publicity with Moon Shadow's foals, it seems to me that you've got more than your share of work cut out for you!"

With her final remark Tiffany stormed out of the kitchen, tugged on her boots and went off to make amends with Mac. Why did Dustin have to provoke the trainer now when she needed Mac's expertise the most?

* * *

Mac was already at his pickup when Tiffany caught up with him. "I'm sorry," she apologized. She was out of breath from her sprint across the back lawn and parking lot.

"No need for that, Missy," Mac said with a kindly smile as he reached for the door handle on the old Dodge. "What Dustin said was the truth."

"No, it wasn't. Even with his regular jockey, there was no assurance that Moon Shadow would win."

"He was the odds-on favorite."

"And we all know how many long shots have won when it counted. Besides, it's all water under the bridge now," she assured him. "We'll just pin our hopes on Journey's End. And maybe this time, we'll win the Derby."

"I hope so," Mac said, pursing his lips together thoughtfully as he studied the lush Northern California countryside that made up the pastures of Rhodes Breeding Farm. "It's time you got a break." He opened the door to the truck. "I'll be back after dinner to check on Alexander's Lady. My guess is she'll foal around midnight."

"See you then." Tiffany stepped away from the old truck and Mac started the engine before shoving it into gear. Tiffany felt her teeth sink into her lower lip as she watched the battered old pickup rumble down the long driveway.

Three hours later Tiffany was in the foaling shed, watching, praying while the glistening chestnut mare labored. The air was heavy with the smell of sweat mingled with ammonia and antiseptic.

Vance and Mac were inside the stall with the horse

while Tiffany and Dustin stood on the other side of the gate. Alexander's Lady was lying on her side in the thick mat of straw, her swollen sides heaving with her efforts.

"Here we go," Vance said as the mare's abdomen contracted and the foal's head and shoulders emerged. A few minutes later, the rest of the tiny body was lying beside the mare.

Vance worked quickly over the newborn, clearing the foal's nose. As Tiffany watched she noticed the small ribs begin to move.

Tiffany reached for the switch that turned on the white heat lamps to keep the precious animal from catching cold.

"Let's leave the lamps on for two or three days," Vance suggested, his round face filled with relief as the filly tested her new legs and attempted to stand. "I don't want to take any chances."

"Neither do I," Tiffany agreed, her heart warming at the sight of the struggling filly. She was a perfect dark bay, with only the hint of a white star on her forehead.

Tiffany slipped into the stall and began to rub the wet filly with a thick towel, to promote the filly's circulation. At that moment, the mare snorted.

"I think it's time for Mom to take over," Vance suggested, as he carefully moved the foal to the mare's head. Alexander's Lady, while still lying on the straw, began to nuzzle and lick her new offspring.

"Atta girl," Mac said with the hint of a smile. "'Bout time you showed some interest in the young-un." He stepped out of the stall to let mother and daughter get acquainted.

Vance stayed in the stall, watching the foal with concerned eyes. He leaned against the wall, removed his glasses and began cleaning them with the tail of his coat, but his thoughtful gaze remained on the horses, and deep furrows lined his brow.

"Is she all right?" Tiffany asked, her heart beating irregularly. Such a beautiful filly. She couldn't die!

"So far so good." But his lips remained pressed together in an uneasy scowl as he attended to the mare. Alexander's Lady groaned and stood up. She nickered softly to the filly.

As if on cue, the little newborn horse opened her eyes and tried futilely to stand.

"Come on, girl. You can do it," Tiffany whispered in encouragement. The filly managed to stand on her spindly, unsteady legs before she fell back into the straw. "Come on . . ."

"Good lookin' filly," Mac decided as the little horse finally forced herself upright and managed the few steps to the mare's side. "Nice straight front legs . . . good bone, like her dad." Mac rubbed his hand over the stubble on his chin.

Tiffany's heart swelled with pride.

"She looks fine," Vance agreed as he watched the filly nuzzle the mare's flanks and search for her first meal.

"So did Charlatan," Tiffany reminded him, trying her best not to get her hopes up. The filly looked strong, but so had Felicity's colt. And he had died. A lump formed in Tiffany's throat. She couldn't imagine that the beautiful little filly might not live through the night.

"Keep watch on her," Vance stated, his lips thinning.

"Round the clock," Tiffany agreed. "We're not going to lose this one," she vowed, oblivious to the worried glances being exchanged between the veterinarian and the trainer.

"What have you decided to name her?" Dustin asked, seemingly entranced by the healthy young horse.

"How about Survivor?" Tiffany replied. "Better yet, how about Shadow's Survivor?"

"As in Moon Shadow?" Dustin inquired.

"Yes." Tiffany glanced at the suckling baby horse. The fluffy stub of a tail twitched happily. "I like it."

"Isn't it a little premature for a name like that?"

"I hope not," Tiffany whispered. "I hope to God, it's not."

"Missy," Mac said gently, touching her sleeve.

"Don't say it, Mac," Tiffany said, holding up her hand. "This little filly is going to make it. She's got to!" Tiffany's lips pressed together in determination, as if she could will her strength into the little horse.

"I just don't want you to be too disappointed."

"I won't be." Tiffany's jaw tensed, and her blue eyes took on the hue of newly forged steel. "This horse is going to live."

"I'll stay overnight in the sitting-up room, watching the monitor. If anything goes wrong, I'll call," Mac volunteered.

"Good." Vance washed his hands and removed his bloodied white jacket. "I want this filly babied. I want her to stay inside for a full three days, under the lamps. We're not out of the woods yet, not by a long shot. And as for the mare, make sure she gets bran mash for three days."

"You got it," Mac agreed, casting one last worried glance at the filly. "Now, Missy, why don't you go up to the house and get some sleep? You can take over in the morning."

Tiffany glanced at the two horses. "Gladly," she whispered.

As she walked out of the foaling shed and into the windy night, Tiffany felt the sting of grateful tears in her eyes. Large crystalline drops began to run down her cheeks and catch the moon glow. *Everything would be perfect,* she thought to herself as she shoved her hands into the pockets of her jacket and started walking on the path to the house, *if only Zane were here to see for himself the strong little daughter of Moon Shadow.*

Chapter Nine

Zane cradled his drink in his hands as he stared at the two other men in the office. His attorney, John Morris, sat behind the oiled teak desk. The other fellow, a great bear of a man, had been introduced by John as Walt Griffith. He was staring out the window at the black San Francisco night.

Walt Griffith wasn't what Zane had expected. When Zane had asked John to hire the best private investigator in California, he'd expected to meet a slick L.A. detective, a man who was street smart as well as college educated. Instead, John had come up with Griffith, a semiretired investigator nearly seventy years old, with thick, gray hair, rotund waistline, clean-shaven jowls and an eye-catching diamond ring on his right hand.

Griffith made Zane slightly uneasy, but he managed to hide his restlessness by quietly sipping his bourbon and water.

"So you want to locate your ex-wife," Griffith said at last while frowning at the city lights illuminating that particular section of Jackson Square.

"That's right." Zane shifted uncomfortably in his chair, and his lips tightened at the corners.

"Maybe she doesn't want you to know where she is."

"She probably doesn't." Zane cocked his head and studied the large man. What was he getting at?

Griffith clasped his hands behind his back. "I wouldn't do this for anyone, you know, but John and I—" he looked at the worried attorney "—we go way back. He says you're straight."

"Straight?" Zane repeated, turning his eyes to the attorney. John took off his reading glasses and frowned.

"I assume that John knows you well enough," Griffith continued. "He told me you weren't a wife-beater or some other kind of psycho."

Zane cocked a dubious dark brow at his friend. "Thanks," he said with a trace of sarcasm.

Griffith turned and leaned against a bookcase filled with leather-bound law books. He withdrew an imported cigar from the inside pocket of his suit coat and studied the tip. "Let me tell you, boy," he said, pointing the cigar in Zane's direction. "I've seen it all, and I'm not about to do anything that smacks of brutality." His small, brown eyes glittered from deep in their sockets, and Zane had the distinct impression that Griffith had gotten himself into trouble more than once from something "smacking of brutality." "If I didn't owe John a favor, I wouldn't have bothered to take your case at all. You seem to have somewhat of a checkered past yourself."

Zane forced a severe smile and his gray eyes met Griffith's intense stare. "I wouldn't physically abuse a woman, any woman. Including Stasia."

"Abuse doesn't have to be physical."

Zane's anger got the better of him, and his fingers tightened around his drink. "There's no love lost between Stasia and me," he admitted, his eyes sparking furiously. "But I have no intention of hurting her. Actually, the less I have to do with her, the better. The only reason I want to locate her is because I think she'll be able to help me with some answers I need." Zane smiled at the irony of it all. "Believe me, Griffith, if there was another way to deal with this problem, I'd be glad to hear it. I don't relish the thought of confronting my ex-wife any more than you want this assignment."

Griffith struck a match and lit his cigar. As he puffed, a thick cloud of pungent smoke rose to the ceiling. "Answers?" he asked, rolling Zane's words over in his mind. "About the other woman?"

Zane nodded.

Griffith's thick gray brows rose questioningly as he became interested in the Irishman's case. "Does she know you're checking up on her?"

Zane was cautious. He had to be with this man. "Tiffany?"

"Right."

Zane shook his head and scowled into his drink. "No."

"Humph." Griffith drew in on the cigar until the tip glowed red. "This other woman—this Rhodes lady, what's she to you?" he demanded.

"A friend."

Griffith shook his great head, and his eyes moved from Zane to John. "I thought you said he'd put all his cards on the table."

"He will." John glared severely at Zane. "You wanted the man." He motioned to indicate the investigator. "So help him."

At that moment, Zane realized he'd run out of options. He hesitated only slightly, and the smile that curved his lips appeared more dangerous than friendly. "All right, counselor, I'll level with Griffith, if he promises that everything I tell him will be kept in the strictest confidence."

"Goes without saying," Griffith grumbled, lowering himself into the chair next to Zane and folding his hands over his round abdomen. "Now, Mr. Sheridan, kindly explain why you're so interested in these two women, your wife and your . . . 'friend.'"

As she came downstairs the morning after Alexander's Lady had foaled, Tiffany felt as if a great weight had been lifted from her shoulders. She had slept soundly, and only once, at about four, had she woken up. After turning on the monitor in the den and assuring herself that both the mare and the filly were alive and resting as well as could be expected, she trudged back up the stairs and fell into her bed. She had gone to sleep again instantly and had awakened refreshed.

"Good morning," Tiffany said with a cheery smile as Louise entered the kitchen and placed her purse on the table.

Louise's eyes sparkled. "It must be, from the looks of you," she decided. "Don't tell me—that Sheridan fella is back again."

"No," Tiffany quickly replied. She avoided the housekeeper's stare by pulling a thermos out of the cupboard near the pantry, and managed to hide the disappointment she felt whenever she thought about Zane. "Alexander's Lady is now the mother of a healthy filly," Tiffany stated, forcing a smile.

"Thank God!" Louise removed her coat and hung it in the closet. "This calls for a celebration!"

"Champagne brunch maybe?" Tiffany suggested.

Louise thought for a moment and then nodded. "Why not? It's about time we had some good news around here." She pulled her favorite apron out of the closet, tied it loosely around her waist and began rummaging through the drawers looking for the utensils she needed. After grabbing a wooden spoon, she tapped it thoughtfully against her chin and said, "I can fix something for when? Say around noon?"

"That would be perfect," Tiffany agreed. "Vance should be back by then and maybe we can persuade him to stay."

At that moment the telephone rang, and without thinking Tiffany reached for the receiver and settled it against her ear. "Hello?" she said into the phone, hoping for a fleeting second that the caller would be Zane.

"Tiffany? Hal Reece, here."

Tiffany's heart fell to the floor, and her stomach tightened painfully. Obviously his mare had foaled. Her fingers tightened around the receiver. "Yes?"

"I just wanted to report that Mile High delivered."

Tiffany braced herself for the worst. She was already imagining how she would deal with the press, the lawsuit, the other owners. . . . "When?"

"Three nights ago."

"And?" Tiffany's heart was thudding so loudly she was sure Hal could hear it.

Louise stopped rattling in the cupboards; the serious tone of Tiffany's voice warned her of impending doom. Usually she wouldn't eavesdrop, but this time, under the circumstances, the kindly housekeeper couldn't hide her interest in the strained conversation.

"And, I'm glad to say, we have three-day-old colts— healthy ones," Hal announced.

"Colts? Plural?"

"That's right, Tiffany," Hal said, his voice nearly bursting with pride. "Can you believe it? After everything we worried about, I end up with twins—and beauties at that."

"Wonderful," Tiffany replied as she sagged against the pantry doors and tried desperately to keep her voice professional. Louise's worried face broke into a wide grin.

"I knew it all along, you know," the proud owner went on, "but we did have a few tense moments during the labor. From the look on the trainer's face while Mile High was delivering, I thought the colt was stillborn, but that wasn't his concern at all! He just hadn't expected number two." Hal went on to describe in minute detail all the physical characteristics of each of his new horses and ended by saying, "Look, Tiffany, I would have called you a couple of days ago, but, well, I wanted to be sure that . . . you know, we didn't have any problems."

"I understand," Tiffany replied, remembering Charlatan's short life. "I'm just pleased that it turned out so well."

"Yes, yes. And, uh, look, I'm sorry about the things I said the other night. I was . . . well, there's just no excuse for my behavior."

"It's okay," Tiffany said with a sigh.

"Have you heard from any of the other owners?" Hal asked.

"You're the first."

"Well, good luck. And mind you, if anyone tries to give you any trouble, let me know. Maybe I'll be able to help."

"Thank you."

He was about to ring off, but changed his mind. "One other thing, Tiffany."

"Yes?"

"As soon as all this . . . ballyhoo over Moon Shadow passes, I'd like to breed a couple of mares to him again."

Tiffany smiled. Hal Reece's words were the final olive branch offered to bridge the rift between them. "Thank you," she said gratefully, "I'll be in touch."

Tiffany hung up the phone and grinned at Louise.

"Good news?" Louise guessed with a knowing smile.

"The best. Hal Reece's mare gave birth to twins. *Healthy* twin colts. Three nights ago. They've been examined by a vet, given a clean bill of health and even have been insured by the insurance company."

"That does it," Louise said with a toss of her head. "We'll have that celebration brunch after all."

"Hal is only one owner," Tiffany murmured as if to herself, "but at least it's a start." After pouring herself a hot cup of coffee, she filled the thermos, pushed open the door with her shoulder and started down the steps of the back porch. Wolverine, who had been lying beneath a favorite juniper bush near the brick stairs, trotted over to greet her.

"How's it going, boy?" Tiffany asked, checking to see that he had food and fresh water in the appropriate dishes. The collie tilted his head to the side, and his tail wagged slowly as she spoke. Tiffany set the thermos on the top step, took a sip from her coffee and scratched the old dog behind the ears. "Haven't you been getting enough attention lately?" she asked in an understanding voice. "All those horses are kind of stealing the show right now, aren't they?"

Wolverine whined and placed a furry paw on her bent knee.

Tiffany laughed and shook her head. "You're still the boss, though; aren't you?" As she picked up her things and turned toward the foaling shed, Wolverine trotted behind her, content with the little bit of attention he'd received.

The hinges on the door creaked as Tiffany entered the whitewashed building. Mac was standing at Alexander's Lady's stall and writing on a white card that Tiffany recognized as the foaling record.

"Good mórning, Missy," the trainer said, without bothering to look up. When his job was finished, he placed the foaling record back on the post near the stall. Once the card was complete, Tiffany would enter the appropriate information into the farm's computer.

"That it is," she said, mimicking Mac's speech pattern.

Mac's brown eyes twinkled. "What's got you in such good spirits?" Forcing a tired smile, he leaned over the railing of the foaling box. "Could it be this little lady, here?"

"She's got a lot to do with it," Tiffany admitted. The little filly hid behind the protection of her mother's flank. At the filly's skittish behavior, Alexander's Lady's ears flattened to her reddish head, and she positioned herself between the intruders and her foal.

"Mama's takin' her job seriously," Mac decided.

"Good."

The newborn poked her inquisitive nose around the mare's body and stared at the strangers through intelligent brown eyes.

"I told you she'd make it," Tiffany said. The precocious little bay looked so healthy. *The filly couldn't die. Not now.*

Mac's knowing eyes traveled over the mare and foal, but he didn't offer his thoughts to Tiffany. She read the hesitation in his gaze. It's still too early to tell, he was saying without uttering a word.

As Tiffany watched the two horses, she realized that the stall had already been cleaned. The smell of fresh straw and warm horses filled the small rooms attached to the broodmare barn, which were used for the express purpose of foaling.

"You didn't have to stay in the sitting-up room," Tiffany remarked, knowing that she was wasting her breath. Mac was from the old school of horse training. "There's a monitor in the den."

"Aye, and what good does it do ya?"

"I used it last night."

Mac laughed. "As if you don't trust me." She was about to protest, but he stilled her with a wave of his arm. "I like to be close, especially since we've had so much trouble. If anything goes wrong, I'm right next door." He cocked his head in the direction of the sitting-up room positioned between the two foaling boxes. "It's what I'm used to."

Tiffany didn't argue. Mac had been around horses long before the introduction of video cameras and closed-circuit television. "There's fresh coffee up at the house, and Louise is in the process of whipping up a special brunch, if you can stick around."

"The missus—"

"Is invited, too."

Mac rubbed a hand over the stubble on his chin and cracked a wide smile. "She might like that, ya know. She's always grumblin' 'bout cookin' for me," he teased.

"I'll bet." Tiffany laughed in reply. Emma McDougal positively doted on her husband of over forty years, but Mac was none the worse for his wife's spoiling. "Why don't you grab a cup of coffee, or take this thermos and then go home for a while? Bring Emma back with you around eleven."

"And what about you?"

"I'll stay here until Vance arrives." Tiffany checked her watch. "And then, if Vance approves, we'll let John watch the horses."

"If you think you can trust him—"

Tiffany waved Mac off. "John's only nineteen, I grant you, but he's been around horses all his life, and he's the best stable boy since—"

"You?" Mac asked, his eyes saddening.

Tiffany pushed aside the unpleasant memories. When she had been a stable boy to her father, Mac had been with the horses on the racing circuit, but he had learned of her duties through Ellery. "Maybe," she acknowledged. "Now, go on, get out of here."

Mac took his cue and left Tiffany to watch over the new mother and filly. The little bay foal scampered around her mother on legs that had grown stronger with the passing of the night. "You're going to make it, aren't you?" Tiffany asked, before glancing at the foaling record and noting that everything had been recorded perfectly. The time that the mare's water broke, when the foal was born, when it stood, and when it first suckled were duly noted along with the foal's sex and color. Everything looked normal.

Tiffany looked at the impish bay horse and let out a long sigh. "Let her live," she prayed in a soft whisper that seemed to echo through the rafters in the high ceiling.

She was just straightening up the sitting-up room when she heard the door to the foaling shed creak open.

"Tiffany?" Dustin called softly.

"In here." She peeked around the corner and was surprised to find Dustin dressed in a business suit. "What's going on?" she asked, pointing a moving finger at his neatly pressed clothes.

"I'm going back to Florida."

"Today?" She stepped back into the corridor to meet him. His face was set in hard determination, and a small frown pulled at the corners of his mouth.

"Have to."

Tiffany held her palms up in the air. "Wait a minute! You just got here yesterday."

Dustin's gold eyes held hers. "Do you want me to stay?" he asked, his voice much too familiar in the well-lit building. The only other sound was the whisper of hay being moved by the horses' feet.

"Yes . . . no . . ." She shook her head in bewilderment. "If you want to. What's the rush?"

He looked genuinely disappointed and refused to smile. "I only came back to make sure that you were all right," he admitted, his frown deepening. "And from the looks of it, you're fine." His eyes slid down her slim form. She was clad only in worn jeans and a pink pullover, but with her hair wound over her head and the sparkle back in her intense blue eyes, she appeared both elegant and dignified, a no-nonsense lady who had her act together.

"Did you expect to find me in a crumpled heap— falling apart at the seams?"

Dustin shook his head but didn't smile at her attempt to lighten the mood. "I guess not. But it happened once before," he reminded her.

"That was different. Ellery was killed." She watched the smooth skin over Dustin's even features but saw no trace of any emotion that would betray his inner thoughts. Dustin acted as if he believed his brother dead.

"Right," he agreed.

"As well as Devil's Gambit."

Dustin looked up sharply, and in that split second Tiffany knew that he was lying to her. For the past four years, Dustin had been lying through his even white teeth. Without considering the consequences of her actions, she turned toward the stall and forced herself to appear calm, though her heart was pounding irregularly in her chest. It was time to find out how much of Zane's story was fact and how much was fiction, and she had to do it now, before Dustin left.

"I was thinking," she remarked, sliding a furtive glance in Dustin's direction.

"About?"

"Well, I still don't want to use Moon Shadow as a stud. Not until I understand what happened to those four foals, and I hear from the other owners."

Dustin nodded. Tiffany saw the movement from the corner of her eye. She propped her elbows on the rail and continued to watch the filly.

"So I was hoping to send some of our mares to other stallions, if it's not too late to nominate them."

"Sounds good to me." Dustin checked his watch and shifted from one foot to the other.

"You have any ideas on whom I should call?" she asked, her throat dry with dread.

"What?"

She shrugged. "Well, you're always high on one horse or the other. You know, a few years ago you thought we should breed Felicity to King's Ransom."

Dustin stiffened. The movement was slight, nearly imperceptible, but Tiffany caught it. "He's a good sire. Proof enough of that on the European tracks recently."

"Do you still think it's a good idea to send Felicity to him?"

"An impossible one, I'd say. King's Ransom's got to be booked solid."

Tiffany lifted one shoulder. "I just thought that maybe you knew the owner—could pull a few strings."

Dustin's eyes narrowed in suspicion. He came over to the stall and stood next to her. "You want favors? That's not like you, Tiff. You're the one who always plays by the rules."

"This is an unusual case—"

Dustin's arms reached for her, drew her close. "What

is it with you?" he whispered against her hair. "What's going on here?" His finger traced the line of her jaw before lingering on the pout of her lips.

Her mind racing fast, Tiffany slid out of the circle of his arms and clasped her arms behind her back. She cocked her head upward to meet his gaze. "I just feel pushed against a wall sometimes," she said, knowing she was treading on thin ice with the turn in the conversation. She forced her hands into the pockets of her jeans and hoped to God that she wasn't betraying her inner feelings.

"And how would breeding one of our horses to King's Ransom change that?"

"It wouldn't, I suppose. There are plenty of good studs, here in the States." Lord, she hoped that she was a better actress than she had ever given herself credit for. "But we need a winner—a real winner."

"We've got Journey's End," he volunteered, intrigued with the change in her. His brother's widow was a mystifying creature; wild one minute, sedate the next. Intelligent, proud and sexy as hell. Dustin decided then and there that he would gladly give half his fortune for the chance to tame her fiery spirit.

"I know," Tiffany replied. "But what we really need is another horse like Devil's Gambit."

Dustin paled slightly, his hands dropped to his sides, but for the most part, he managed to keep his composure intact. "He's gone, Tiff. So is Ellery. You've got to face it. You're never going to have another horse just like Devil's Gambit, and you've got to forget this unreasonable loyalty to a dead man."

He captured her arm with his fingers and tugged her gently to him. "You need to live again, Tiffany. Without the ghosts of the past surrounding you. Ellery is gone. . . .

Think about letting another man into your life." He paused dramatically, and his gilded eyes darkened with passion.

Tiffany wanted to recoil from him and shout that another man was already in her life, that she had committed her heart to a man she barely knew, and she was dying inside without him. Instead, she pulled away before the embrace became more heated.

"Think about me," he suggested, his eyes raking over her in lusty appraisal.

"I . . . I have too much on my mind to think about starting new relationships," she said, knowing the excuse was as feeble as it sounded. If she wasn't careful, Dustin would see through her act. "The foals—" she angled her head in the direction of the newborn filly "—Journey's End's career . . . a lot of things."

Dustin tugged at his stiff collar, but his golden eyes never left her face. "You said you felt pushed against the wall."

"I do." She lifted her shoulders in a nonchalant gesture and gambled with what she hoped was her trump card. "Someone's offered to buy me out."

Dustin froze. "What?"

It was too late to back down now. "A man was here last week."

"What man?"

"An Irishman. Zane Sheridan."

Dustin looked as if he would sink right through the floor. All of his well-practiced composure seemed to slide through the concrete.

"Ever heard of him?"

"Yeah. I know him." Dustin shook his head. "What does he want with this farm? He already breeds horses in Europe."

"Maybe he wants to break into the American market,"

Tiffany suggested, her fingers tightening over the railing of the stall. God, she was a terrible liar.

Dustin began to pace the length of the short corridor. "Maybe," he said as if he didn't believe a word of it. His mouth tightened and he ran a hand over his brow to catch the droplets of cold sweat that had begun to bead on his forehead. "I suppose he told you all sorts of wild stories."

"Like?" Tiffany coaxed.

"Like—hell, I don't know." He held up a hand in exasperation and looked up at the cross beams of the shed. "I may as well be honest with you, Tiff."

Here it comes. Dustin is about to confess, Tiffany thought, suddenly cold with dread.

"There wasn't much love lost between Sheridan and Ellery," Dustin announced. His topaz eyes softened, as if he wished he could save her some of the pain he was about to inflict. For the first time Tiffany realized that Dustin did, in his own way, truly love her. "They were involved in a poker game—for high stakes. Sheridan lost. I don't think the man likes to lose, and he took it none too well, let me tell you. He even went so far as to claim that Ellery had been cheating. God, I was there. I don't know how Ellery could have cheated. From where I sat, Ellery won fair and square."

"How—how much money was involved?"

"Somewhere around two hundred thousand dollars, I think. Supposedly it wiped Sheridan out. But apparently he's back on his feet again."

Tiffany's mouth was dry with tension. "You haven't seen him since?"

"No, but I know he breeds horses in Ireland. I've seen a few of them race. He's got a two-year-old filly who's ripping up the tracks."

"The filly sired by King's Ransom?"

Dustin cast her a worried glance and nodded curtly. "I wouldn't trust that man, Tiffany. He's got a reputation in Europe for being ruthless." Dustin began stalking back and forth in front of the stall. "I don't understand why he wants to buy you out. What did you say to his offer?"

"That I wasn't interested, and if I ever did want to sell out my part of the operation, you had first option."

Some of the tension in his shoulders dissipated. "Good." He raked his fingers through his hair. "Did he say anything else?"

"Not much," Tiffany lied with a twinge of regret. "But I think he'll be back with a concrete offer."

"Great," Dustin muttered, his gold eyes impaling her. "Whatever you do, Tiff, don't sell out to that bastard."

"Are you still interested in owning all the farm?" she asked. Several years before, Dustin had offered to buy her out, but she had steadfastly refused.

"Of course I am. I just never thought you'd want to sell."

"I'm not sure that I do."

"Then you will give me first option?"

"When the time comes. . . ."

Dustin appeared relieved, but there was something else that he was hiding from her; she could read it in the shadows of his eyes.

"Dustin." She touched his sleeve lightly. "Is there something you're not telling me?"

Dustin walked away from her and pushed his hands into the back pockets of his slacks. His shoulders slumped in defeat. "Well, maybe I shouldn't be telling you this," he grumbled, condemning himself. "It's all water under the bridge now."

Tiffany's heart nearly stopped. Was Dustin going to admit that Devil's Gambit was alive and siring foals as part of an incredible charade that would rock the Thoroughbred racing world on two continents? She felt almost physically ill with dread.

"Ellery was involved with a woman back then."

"Oh, God," she whispered, rocked to the very core of her soul as she began to understand what Dustin was saying. She felt cold all over; her heart was heavy in her chest. "A woman that Zane was in love with?" she guessed, praying that she had misunderstood her brother-in-law.

Dustin's brows quirked at Tiffany's familiar use of Sheridan's name. He let out an angry oath. "More than that, I'm afraid. She was Zane Sheridan's *wife, Stasia*."

Tiffany sucked in her breath and her throat began to ache painfully. Truth and fiction began to entangle in her confused thoughts. What was Dustin saying? "Wait a minute . . ." Dustin was giving her too much information and it made her head swim. She had thought he was going to confess about Devil's Gambit, but instead he had brought up Zane's ex-wife . . . and *Ellery*. Dear God, was that why Zane had come to the farm, his gray eyes filled with revenge? Had he pretended interest in her only to throw her off guard? "Nancy Emerson said something about Zane's wife running out on him, but not with Ellery. The man's name was—"

"Ethan Rivers."

Tiffany swallowed against the dread flowing in her blood. "No." She had to deny what Dustin was suggesting and her shoulders slumped.

"Tiffany, listen!"

She shook her head and fought against hot tears. "Are you trying to tell me that Ellery used an alias?" She clamped her fingers over the top rail of the stall for support.

"Sometimes."

Pained blue eyes delved into Dustin's murky gaze.

"But why?" Alexander's Lady sensed the tension and snorted.

Dustin waved off Tiffany's question as if it were insignificant. "Sometimes it was just easier . . . if people didn't know we, Ellery and I, were brothers."

"I don't understand." *And I don't think I want to. It would be easier not to think that Ellery used me in the past and that Zane is using me still. . . .*

"You don't have to," Dustin said harshly and then softened a little when he saw her stricken face. "Tiffany, it really doesn't matter, not now. When Ellery and I were first getting started, we had to do a lot of . . . maneuvering to get established. Sometimes, when we were in Europe trying to sell some of our stock, it was just easier for Ellery to pose as a rival bidder to drive up the price of one of our own horses. Once in a while it backfired and no one bought the horse in question, but other times, well, we came out of it a few dollars richer. We didn't really hurt anyone by it."

Tiffany's eyes grew round with horror. "Oh, no?" she rasped as anger replaced despair. She leaned against a post for support, but her blue eyes blazed with rage. "You can justify it any way you want, even give it such fancy terms as 'maneuvering to get established,' Dustin, but I think what you and Ellery did was manipulate people and the system to pad your wallet." Tiffany felt sick inside, empty. "That's illegal—"

"Probably not," Dustin denied. "Immoral, maybe, and probably unethical—"

"And crooked." She saw the fury spark in his eyes and she forced control on her own anger. "Oh, Dustin. Why didn't Ellery tell me?" she asked in a broken whisper. Her knees threatened to give way. She had been married to Ellery, loved him in her own way, and he had betrayed her trust.

"Hey, don't get down on Ellery," Dustin said as if

reading her thoughts. "This all happened before he knew you, and he did a hell of a lot for you and your bum of a father. Where would you have been if Ellery hadn't supported you, paid your way through college, and then married you?"

"I don't know," she admitted. "But the lies—"

He touched her chin and lifted it, forcing her to look into his eyes. He felt her tremble with rage. "Look, it's over and done with," Dustin said, his eyes searching hers. "Ellery's dead. . . ." He lowered his head and would have kissed her if it hadn't been for the question she had to ask.

"Is he, Dustin?" she demanded, pulling away from him and wrapping her arms protectively over her breasts.

Dustin was visibly stunned. "What kind of a question is that?"

"A legitimate worry, wouldn't you say?"

"Tiffany, listen to what you're saying!"

"How do I know that he isn't alive and using that alias . . . Ethan Rivers . . . or another one for that matter, in Europe somewhere?" Her hands were shaking at her sides. "For all I know, he could be living in France or England or Ireland, racing horses, married to someone else." She was rambling and she knew it, and she had to get hold of herself before she tipped her hand and gave her act away.

"I was there, Tiffany, at the accident. I saw Ellery. . . ." His face went ashen and in that single moment of honesty, Tiffany believed her brother-in-law. "As hard as it is for you to accept, Ellery's gone."

Tiffany managed to square her shoulders, but tears pooled in her eyes before trickling down her face in a broken silvery path. "I didn't really doubt it," she admitted, brushing the unwanted tears aside. "But you've just told me some things that are a little hard to accept."

Dustin glanced at his watch again and cursed. "Damn! I've got to go if I'm going to catch that plane." He looked at her longingly once again, silently offering himself.

Tiffany shook her head and lifted it with renewed determination. Her eyes, when they met Dustin's direct gaze, were cold.

"If you need me—"

"No. Journey's End needs you," she said. "The Florida Derby is next week."

"You could come down," he suggested without much hope.

"Not until I make sure that this little one—" Tiffany cocked her head in the direction of the inquisitive filly "—and her brothers and sisters are okay."

With a reluctant sigh, he turned away. "I'll call," Dustin promised, wondering why the hell he cared. He had lots of women who would do anything he wanted, so why was he hung up on his brother's wife?

"Good."

With only a moment's indecision, Dustin walked crisply out of the foaling shed, and Tiffany slumped against the wall in relief. *Ellery* was Ethan Rivers? *Ellery* had run off with Zane's wife, Stasia? The woman who had been Ellery's mistress when Tiffany was in college?

Tiffany's head was throbbing with unanswered questions. "Oh, Zane," she whispered brokenly. "What are you involved in?"

She was still going over the conversation with Dustin in her mind when Vance Geddes arrived to check the mare and foal. His brow knitted with worry as he started the examination, but the furrows slowly eased as he studied the frisky filly.

"It looks like she's going to make it," he said, relief audible in his voice. "By the time Charlatan was this old, there were already signs of distress."

"Thank God," Tiffany murmured, her mind only half on the conversation. Where was Zane? Why did he want the farm? Why hadn't he explained about Stasia and Ellery?

"Tiffany?" Vance asked for the second time.

"Oh, what?"

Vance shook his head and offered a small smile. "I said it looks as if we can take her out in a few days. I think you've got yourself a racehorse here."

"Wonderful." Tiffany eyed the little filly fondly. "Now we really do have a reason to celebrate."

"Pardon?"

"I was hoping that you could join the rest of us for lunch . . . brunch—" she lifted her shoulders "—whatever you want to call it."

"I'd be glad to. Just let me get cleaned up."

"I'll meet you at the house," she said, leaving the foaling shed and instructing the stable boy to look after the mare and filly. She headed toward the house and didn't notice the warm spring sunshine, the gentle breeze lifting the branches of the fir trees near the drive or the crocuses sprouting purple, gold, and white near the back porch.

All of her thoughts were centered on Zane and what, if anything, he wanted from her.

By the time Tiffany got back to the house, Louise was working furiously. The smell of honey-glazed ham, homemade apple muffins, black coffee, and steamed vegetables filled the room. Louise was humming as she carefully arranged a rainbow of fresh fruit in a crystal bowl.

"It smells great in here," Tiffany said as she walked into the kitchen and tried to shake off the feeling of impending dread that had settled on her shoulders during her discussion with Dustin. "What can I do to help?"

Louise smiled. "Nothing. All the work's about done. Just go change your clothes. We're eating on the sun porch."

"Ummm. Fancy."

"It's a celebration, isn't it?"

"That it is. Let me set the table—"

"Already done."

"You are efficient, aren't you?"

"I don't get much of a chance to show off anymore. It feels good," Louise admitted, holding up the clear bowl of fruit for Tiffany's inspection. The cut crystal sparkled in the late morning light.

"Beautiful," she murmured, and the housekeeper beamed. "If you're sure there's nothing I can do . . ."

"Scat! Will ya?" Louise instructed with a severe frown that broke down completely as she laughed.

Tiffany chuckled. "All right. I'll be down in about twenty minutes."

She walked toward the stairs and remembered the times she and Ellery had entertained. It had been often and grand. Louise had always enjoyed "putting out a spread" as she had called it. Ellery had insisted that entertaining potential buyers was all part of the business, and he had been at his best when dressed in a black tuxedo and contrasting burgundy cummerbund while balancing a glass of champagne between his long, well-manicured fingers.

It seemed like aeons ago. And all that time, while Tiffany was married to Ellery, he was probably leading a double life as a stranger named Ethan Rivers, and having an affair with Zane Sheridan's ex-wife, Stasia.

Tiffany's heart twisted painfully and she balled small fists in frustration. How could she have been so blind?

It would be easy to blame it on youth or naivete, but the truth of the matter was that she had been so anxious to love someone and have him love her in return, she had closed her eyes to the possibility that her husband had been anything but what she had wanted to see.

Stop punishing yourself, she warned, as she slipped out of her clothes, rewound her hair onto her head and stepped into the shower. *It's over and done!*

Or was it? Was Dustin telling the truth when he said that Ellery was dead, or was it just part of a complex cover-up to hide the fact that Devil's Gambit was alive and that another horse and *another man* died in the fire? Oh, dear God, would Ellery have been involved in anything so vile as murder? The thought turned her blood to ice water and she had to steady herself against the wet tiles. A cold wave of nausea flooded over her, and Tiffany felt for a minute as if she were going to vomit.

"Oh, God," she cried softly, forcing herself to stand.

No matter what else, she couldn't—wouldn't—believe that Ellery would take part in the death of another human being.

She turned off the shower and wrapped herself in a bath sheet without really thinking about what she was doing. With trembling fingers, while her head was still pounding with the cold truth of the past, she dressed in a bright dress of indigo polished silk, and pinned her hair in a tousled chignon. After touching up her makeup and forcing her morbid thoughts to a dark corner of her mind where she could examine them later, she started down the stairs. As she did, the doorbell chimed loudly.

"I'll get it," she called to Louise and hurried down

the remaining three steps to the foyer and walked to the door, her heels echoing sharply against the imported tile.

Squaring her shoulders, she opened the door, expecting to find Mac's wife, Emma McDougal. Instead, her eyes met the silvery gaze of the only man who had ever touched her soul.

"Zane," Tiffany whispered, and felt the need to lean against the door for support. It had been more than a week since she had seen him, and in that time so many truths had been uncovered.

Now, as she looked at the man she loved, Tiffany felt as if she were staring into the eyes of a total stranger.

Chapter Ten

Zane leaned against one of the white columns supporting the roof of the porch and stared at Tiffany. His hands were thrust into the pockets of his jeans, and his slumped posture was meant to be casual, but his shoulder muscles were tight, so tense they ached.

God, she was beautiful, more beautiful than he remembered. Dressed in shimmering blue silk, with her golden brown hair pinned loosely to her crown, Tiffany looked almost regal. A single strand of gold encircled her throat, and thin layers of silk brushed against her knees.

After what seemed like a lifetime, Zane finally spoke. "Are you going out?" he asked, his gray eyes delving into hers. One look at Ellery Rhodes's widow had destroyed all of Zane's earlier promises to himself. After the meeting with Griffith just three days ago, he had silently vowed that he would stay away from Ellery Rhodes's widow. Now, as he gazed into her intriguing blue eyes, he knew that keeping away from her would be impossible. Despite all the excuses he'd made to himself to the contrary, seeing Tiffany again was the single reason he had returned to Rhodes Breeding Farm.

Tiffany, recovering from the shock of seeing him again, managed to square her shoulders and proudly hold his gaze. Though her heartbeat had quickened at the sight of him, she forced herself to remember Dustin's condemning words. *Sheridan's got a reputation for being ruthless. . . . Ellery was involved with Zane Sheridan's wife.*

"No," she finally replied, "I'm not going out. . . . We're having a special lunch, sort of a celebration."

Zane detected new doubts in her exotic blue eyes, doubts that hadn't clouded her gaze when he had last seen her. The small hairs on the back of his neck prickled in warning. Something was wrong here, and he intended to find out what it was. Silently he cursed himself for staying away so long. In the course of the past week, someone had destroyed all the trust Tiffany had previously felt for him. It didn't take long to figure out who was to blame, and his fists balled at the thought of Dustin Rhodes.

Zane straightened and walked closer to her. "Tiffany, what's wrong?" he asked, gently placing his fingers on her shoulders and pulling her close.

"Don't," she whispered, knowing that her battle was already lost. She wanted to melt into him. Just seeing him again had been enough to make her heartbeat race in anticipation. Maybe Dustin had been wrong about Zane, maybe he had lied.

She leaned heavily on Zane, letting his strong arms wrap around her. Her face was pressed to his chest, and she could feel the warmth of his breath on her hair, hear the even rhythm of his pounding heart.

Don't fall under his spell again, a small voice inside her cautioned. *Remember what Dustin said about Ellery and Zane's wife. He's probably here just to get information about Stasia. He's been using you all along.*

"Tiffany?" Zane urged, his voice low, husky. She closed her eyes and let his earthy scent fill her nostrils. It felt so right to have his arms around her. Without examining her motives, she clung to him as if she expected him to vanish as quickly as he had appeared.

"I . . . I didn't think you were coming back," she whispered, ignoring the doubts filling her mind. He was here, now, with her. Nothing else mattered.

"I said I would."

"But it's been—"

"Too long." The corded arms tightened around her, and his warm hands splayed against the small of her back, pressing her body to his and heating her skin through the thin material of her dress. "I should have called," he admitted, feeling his body beginning to respond to the soft, yielding contour of hers, "but I've been in and out of airports for the better part of a week."

She lifted her head and studied the weariness in his face. Wherever he'd been, the trip had taken its toll on him. The brackets near the corners of his mouth had deepened, and there was a general look of fatigue in his eyes. His clothes, a pair of jeans and a plaid shirt, were clean but slightly rumpled, and his chin was just beginning to darken from the day's growth of beard.

"Have you been out of the country?" she asked.

"Part of the time."

Because of Devil's Gambit, or your wife?

Tiffany knew that she should pull away from him, now, before she was lost to him forever. She shouldn't let him into her house or her life. Not again. Too many events in his past were entangled with Ellery's life and left unexplained. There were too many questions that demanded answers. . . .

For a passing moment she considered confronting him with what she had learned from Dustin, just to gauge his reaction, but she couldn't. The sight of his drawn face, windblown black hair and slightly wrinkled clothing did strange things to her heart. Despite all of

Dustin's accusations, despite the lies, she still loved this rugged man from Ireland with every fiber of her soul.

"Come inside," she invited, managing, despite her doubts, the trace of a smile. "Louise is making a special brunch."

"Why?" Zane's dark brows cocked expressively. He was getting mixed signals from Tiffany; one moment she seemed to have a wonderful secret she wanted to share with him, and her indigo eyes sparkled; the next second her smile would fade and her lips would compress into a determined line of defiance.

"Alexander's Lady had a filly—a healthy filly," Tiffany said, pushing her dark thoughts aside.

Zane relaxed a little, and he gently touched her cheek. She had to concentrate to keep her mind on the conversation. "I assume from your expression that she had been bred to Moon Shadow."

"Yes." Tiffany attempted to extract herself from his embrace, to put some mind-clearing distance between his body and hers, but his strong arms refused to release her.

"When was the filly born?"

"Just last night."

"Isn't the celebration a little premature?" he asked softly, remembering the other colt, the one that had lived a day or so before collapsing from heart failure and dying.

"Maybe, but I doubt it. Vance thinks the filly will live," Tiffany said with conviction. She recognized the unspoken question in Zane's eyes and knew that he was thinking about Charlatan's short life. "Vance wasn't so sure last night," she admitted, "but this morning the filly's been scampering around her stall like a champion. Even Vance has taken her off the critical list."

Zane hazarded a charming half-smile that touched

Tiffany's heart. "That is good news." He kissed her lightly on the forehead, and Tiffany's heart seemed to miss a beat. *How could she react this way, love this man, when he had lied to her?*

"And there's more," she managed to say. "Hal Reece called and told me that his mare, Mile High, gave birth to twin colts—healthy colts, about three days ago. He's even been able to insure them."

Zane's grin spread slowly over his rugged features. He squeezed her for a minute and laughed. God, when was the last time he'd laughed? It had to have been years ago. . . . It was so easy with Tiffany, so natural. "You're right, you should celebrate."

Tiffany's eyes warmed. "Louise would love it if you joined us."

"Us?"

"Mac and his wife Emma, Vance, Louise and myself." She read the hesitation in his gaze and realized that he felt like an outsider. Her elegant features sobered. "It's not a private party, Zane," she said softly with a seductive smile, "and you're very much a part of it. After all, you were here the night Ebony Wine delivered. Besides, Louise would skin me alive if she knew you were here and wouldn't have brunch with us after all the work she's gone to."

"Then how can I refuse?"

"You can't."

She pulled away from him, but his fingers caught her wrist. "Tiffany?"

"What?"

When she turned to face him, he tugged on her arm again and pulled her close against his body. "Just one more thing."

"Which is?" she asked breathlessly.

In answer, he lowered his head and his lips brushed

seductively over hers. His breath was warm and inviting, his silvery eyes dark with sudden passion. "I missed you," he whispered against her mouth, then his lips claimed hers in a kiss that was as savage as it was gentle. The warmth of his lips coupled with the feel of his slightly beard-roughened face made her warm with desire.

Tiffany moaned and leaned against him, letting her body feel the hard texture of his. His tongue gently parted her lips and flickered erotically against hers. Heat began to coil within her before he pulled his head away and gazed at her through stormy gray eyes.

"God, I missed you," he repeated, shaking his head as if in wonder at the conflicting emotions warring within his soul.

Tiffany had to clear her throat. "Come on. Louise will have my head if her meal gets cold." Still holding his hand, she led him toward the back of the house and tried to forget that Zane had once been married to Ellery's mistress.

"I haven't eaten like this since the last time I was here," Zane remarked to Louise, who colored slightly under the compliment. Everyone was seated at the oval table in the sun room, which was really an extension of the back porch. The corner of the porch nearest the kitchen had been glassed in, affording a view of the broodmare barn and the pasture surrounding the foaling shed. Green plants, suspended from the ceiling in wicker baskets or sitting on the floor in large brass pots, surrounded the oak table, and a slow-moving paddle fan circulated the warm air.

"We should do this more often," Tiffany decided as she finished her meal and took a sip of the champagne.

"Used to be," Mac mused while buttering a hot

muffin, "that we'd have parties all the time. But that was a long time ago, when Ellery was still alive."

Tiffany felt her back stiffen slightly at the mention of Ellery's name. When she looked away from Mac she found Zane's gray eyes boring into hers. An uncomfortable silence followed.

"Hasn't been any reason to celebrate until now," Louise said, as much to diffuse the tension settling in the room as to make conversation. Her worried eyes moved from Tiffany to Zane and back again.

"What about Journey's End's career?" Vance volunteered, while declining champagne. He shook his head at Mac, who was tipping a bottle over his glass. "I've got two more farms to visit today." When Mac poured the remainder of the champagne into his own glass, Vance continued with his line of thinking. "If you ask me, Journey's End is reason enough to celebrate."

"Maybe we'd better wait on that," Tiffany thought aloud. "Let's see how he does in the Florida Derby."

"That race shouldn't be too much of a problem if Prescott handles him right," Mac said.

"What then?" Zane asked the trainer.

"Up to Kentucky for the Lexington Stakes."

"And then the Kentucky Derby?"

"That's the game plan," Mac said, finishing his drink and placing his napkin on the table. He rubbed one thumb over his forefinger nervously before extending his lower lip and shrugging. "I just hope Prescott can pull it off."

"He's a good trainer," Emma McDougal stated. She was a petite woman of sixty with beautiful gray hair and a warm smile. She patted her husband affectionately on the knee in an effort to smooth what she saw as Mac's ruffled feathers. She knew that as much as he might argue the point, Mac missed the excitement of the racetrack.

"When he keeps his mind on his horses," Mac grumbled.

"Don't you think he will?" Zane asked.

Mac's faded eyes narrowed thoughtfully. "He'd better," he said with a frown. "We've come too close to the Derby before to let this one slip through our fingers."

Tiffany pushed her plate aside. "Delicious," she said to Louise before turning her attention back to the trainer. "Would you like to work with Journey's End in Lexington? You could help Bob Prescott get him ready."

"Oh, there's no doubt I'd like to, Missy," Mac replied, ignoring the reproachful look from his wife. "But it wouldn't do a lick of good. Journey's End, he's used to Prescott. We can't be throwin' him any loops, not now. Me going to Kentucky would probably do more harm than good."

"So the die is cast?" Tiffany asked, feeling a cold premonition of doom as she looked through the windows and noticed the thick bank of clouds rolling over the mountains from the west.

"Aye, Missy. That it is . . . that it is."

Tiffany spent the rest of the afternoon with Zane, and for the first time in more than a week she began to relax. She had planned to drive into town in the afternoon but decided that she'd rather spend the time on the farm.

In the early evening, she took Zane into the foaling shed and proudly displayed Shadow's Survivor. Within the confines of the large stall, the inquisitive filly cavorted beneath the warm heat lamps.

"Vance says she'd be able to go outside in a couple of days," Tiffany said.

"I'll bet you're relieved." Zane's eyes moved from the mare and foal to Tiffany.

"I'll be more relieved when I hear from the rest of the owners," she responded as she led Zane out of the foaling shed. "Until I know that no more foals will die, I can't really relax."

Dusk was just beginning to settle on the hills surrounding the farm. Lavender shadows lengthened as the hazy sun settled behind the ridge of sloping mountains to the west. Clouds began to fill the darkened sky. "This is my favorite time of day," she admitted, watching as the stable boys rounded up the horses for the evening. The soft nickering of mares to their foals was interspersed with the distant whistle of a lonely stallion. Tiffany chuckled. "That's Moon Shadow," she explained. "He always objects to being locked up for the night."

"Do you blame him?" Zane asked.

"Oh, no. That's what makes him a winner, I suppose."

"His defiance?"

She frowned into the gathering darkness and linked her arm through his. A cool breeze pushed her dress against her legs as they walked. "I prefer to think of it as his fire, his lack of docility. He's always had to have his way, even as a foal. He was the boss, had to be in the lead."

"The heart of a champion."

Tiffany pursed her lips thoughtfully and her elegant brows drew together. "That's why I hate what's been happening to him—all this conjecture that there's something wrong with him."

"Have you found an answer to what happened to the dead foals?"

After expelling a ragged sigh, Tiffany shook her head. "Nothing so far. Vance has gone to independent laboratories, asked for help from the Jockey Club and the racing commission, and still can't get any answers."

"Not even enough information to clear Moon Shadow's name?"

"No." She placed a restraining hand on her hair as the wind began to loosen her chignon. "The new foals—the healthy ones—should prove that the problem isn't genetic."

"Unless another one dies."

She shuddered inside at the thought.

Zane noticed the pain in her eyes and placed a comforting arm over her shoulders. "You really love it here, don't you?"

"What?"

He rotated the palm of his free hand and moved his arm in a sweeping gesture meant to include the cluster of buildings near the center of the farm, the sweeping green pastures enclosed by painted white fences, the horses grazing in the field and the gentle green hills guarding the valley. "All of it."

She couldn't deny the attachment she felt for this farm. It was the only home she'd known. She felt as much a part of it as if it had been in her family for generations. It was, and would always be, the only thing she could call her heritage. "Yes," she answered. "I love it. I love the horses, the land, the excitement, the boredom, *everything.*"

"And is that what I felt when I came back here this morning?"

"What do you mean?"

"When I arrived here, you looked at me as if I were a thief trying to steal it all away from you."

"Did I?"

He didn't answer, but she saw the determination in the angle of his jaw. He wouldn't let up until he found out what was bothering her. She had no recourse but to lie or to confront him with what she'd learned from Dustin.

The day with Zane had been so wonderful, and she knew that it was about to end. "It had nothing to do with selling the farm to you, Zane. You, or anyone else, can't force me to sell."

The arm around her tightened. She felt the unleashed tension coiling his body. "Then what?"

"While you were gone, a few things happened," she admitted. They had been walking down a wide, well-worn path, past the old barn and through a thicket of maple trees surrounding a small pond. The water in the small lake had taken on an inky hue, reflecting the turbulent purple of the sky.

"What things?"

"Dustin came home."

All of the muscles in Zane's body tightened. The thought of Dustin Rhodes, here, alone with Tiffany, made his stomach knot with dread. It was insane to feel this . . . jealousy. Dustin owned part of the farm; he could come and go as he pleased. Zane's jaw hardened, and his back teeth ground together in frustration.

"You weren't expecting him?"

"No."

"Then why did he return?"

"He said it was because of all the bad press surrounding Moon Shadow. He wanted to make sure that I was all right."

"He could have called."

"I suppose," she admitted, taking a seat on a boulder near the pond. "But I think he wanted to see me face to face."

"Why?" Zane demanded, his eyes glittering in the dark night.

"Dustin helped me pick up the pieces when Ellery was killed," she whispered. "I was pretty shook up."

"Because you loved your husband so much?" he asked, reaching for a flat stone and thrusting it toward the water. He watched as it skipped across the pond creating ever-widening ripples on the water's smooth surface.

"Because my whole world was turned upside down." The wind picked up and clouds shadowed the moon.

"And if he walked back into your life right now?" Zane asked, bracing himself against the truth.

"It would be upside down all over again."

"And who would you lean on?"

Tiffany breathed deeply. "I hope that I'm strong enough to stand by myself—no matter what happens," she said softly.

The air was thick with the promise of rain, and the clouds covering the moon became more dense. High above, the branches of the fir trees danced with the naked maples.

Zane turned to face her and his broad shoulders slumped in resignation. Gray eyes drove into hers. "You know that I'm falling in love with you, don't you?"

Tiffany's heart nearly stopped. *If only I could believe you, Zane. If only you hadn't lied to me. If only I could tell what was true and what was false.*

She wrapped her arms around her knees and shook her head. "I don't think love can enter into our relationship," she said, staring at the dark water and refusing to face him.

"It's nothing I wanted," he admitted and pushed his hands into his back pockets. "But it happened."

"Zane—" her protest was cut short when he strode purposely over to the rock and scooped her into his arms. "Please don't . . ." she breathed, but it was the cry of a woman lost. When his lips crushed against hers, she responded willingly, eagerly to him, mindless of the wind billowing her dress or the heavy scent of rain in the air.

He gently laid her on the grass near a stand of firs, and his fingers caught in the golden strands of her hair. Slowly he withdrew the pins and twined his fingers in the silken braid as he pulled it loose. The golden hair fell to her shoulders, framing her face in tangled honey-brown curls.

"I've wanted to make love to you from the first moment I saw you," he whispered. His body was levered over hers, and his silvery eyes caught the reflection of the shadowy moon. She trembled when his hands lingered on her exposed throat to gently stroke the sensitive skin near her shoulders.

"That's not the same as loving someone," she replied, her voice breathless as his hand slowly, enticingly, slid down the silky fabric of her dress and softly caressed her breast.

A spasm of desire shot through her. "Oh, my God," she whispered while he looked at her, touching her with only one hand. Her breathing became rapid and shallow as slowly he caressed the silk-encased peak, rubbing the sheer fabric against her. Tiffany began to ache for the feel of his hands against her skin.

The fingers slid lower, down her thigh, to the hem of her dress. She felt the warm impression of his fingertips as they stroked her leg through her sheer stocking.

I shouldn't be doing this, she thought wildly. *I don't even really understand what he wants of me. . . .*

"Tell me you want me to make love to you," he rasped against her hair. His tongue traced the gentle shell of her ear, and his breath fanned seductively against her skin.

"Oh, Zane . . . I . . ." Her blood was pounding in her temples. She trembled with desire.

"Tell me!"

"Oh, God, yes." She closed her eyes against the truth and felt the hot tears moisten her lashes. *I don't want to love you,* she thought for a fleeting moment. *Dear Lord, I don't want to love you.* He lowered his head and kissed her eyelids, first one and then the other, tasting the salt of her tears and knowing that he couldn't deny himself any longer.

"I love you, Tiffany," he whispered, while his fingers strayed to the pearl buttons holding the bodice of her dress together, and his lips touched her neck, moving over the smooth skin and the rope of gold. His tongue pressed against the flickering pulse in the hollow of her throat.

"No." *If only she could trust him.*

"I've loved every minute I've spent with you. . . ."

Each solitary button was slowly unbound, and the shimmery blue fabric of her dress parted in the night. Her straining breasts, covered only by a lacy, cream-colored camisole and the golden curtain of her hair, pressed upward. The dark points seductively invited him to conquer her, and Zane felt hot desire swelling uncomfortably in his loins at the dark impressions on the silky fabric.

He groaned at the sight of her. He slowly lowered his head to taste one of the ripe buds encased in silk. His tongue toyed with the favored nipple until Tiffany's heart was pounding so loudly it seemed to echo in the darkness. His hands caressed her, fired her blood, promised that their joining would be one of souls as well as flesh.

Somewhere in the distance, over the sound of Zane's labored breathing, she heard the sound of lapping water and the cry of a night bird, but everything she felt was because of Zane. Liquid fire ignited from deep within her and swirled upward through her pulsing veins.

His warm tongue moistened the lace and left it wet, to dry in the chill breeze. She shuddered, more from the want of him than the cold. When his hands lifted the dress over her head, she didn't protest.

Tenderly at first, and then more wildly, he stroked her breasts until she writhed beneath him, trying to get closer to the source of her exquisite torment. He removed the camisole slowly and then let his lips and teeth toy with one sweet, aching breast. Tiffany moaned throatily, from somewhere deep in her soul.

His tongue moistened the dark nipple until it hardened beautifully, and then he began to suckle ravenously, all the while touching the other breast softly, making it ready. Just when Tiffany thought she could stand no more of the sweet torment, he turned to the neglected breast and he feasted again.

"Oh, Zane," Tiffany cried, her fever for his love making demands upon her. She was empty, void, and only he could make her whole again.

His hands continued to stroke her while he slowly removed the remaining scanty pieces of her clothing. She felt her lace panties slide over her hips. Warm fingers traced the ridge of her spine and lingered at the swell of her hips.

He touched all of her, making her ready, while she slowly undressed him and ran her fingers hungrily over his naked chest. His muscles rippled beneath her touch, and she was in awe at the power her touch commanded.

He kicked off his jeans almost angrily and was only satisfied when he was finally lying atop her; hard male muscles pressed heatedly against their softer feminine counterparts.

The need in him was evident; his eyes were dark with desire, his breathing labored, his heartbeat thudding, savaging against her flattened breasts. A thin sheen of sweat glistened over his supple muscles. His lips pressed hungrily, eagerly over hers.

"Let me love you, sweet lady," he coaxed, rubbing against her seductively, setting her skin aflame with his touch.

Her blood pulsed wildly in her veins. All thoughts of denial had fled long ago. The ache within her, burning with the need for fulfillment, throbbed with the want of him.

"Please," she whispered, closing her eyes against the glorious torment of his fingers kneading her buttocks.

Her fingers stroked him, and he cried out her name. He could withhold himself no longer.

With only a fleeting thought that this woman was the widow of Ellery Rhodes, he gently parted her legs and delved into the warmth of the woman he loved. His body joined with hers and he became one with the wife of the man he had vowed to destroy. He whispered her name, over and over again, as if his secret incantation could purge her from his soul.

He watched in fascination as she threw back her head and exposed the white column of her throat. Her fingernails dug into the muscles of his back before she shuddered in complete surrender. His explosion within her sent a series of shock waves through his body until he collapsed over her.

"I love you, Tiffany," he whispered, his breathing as raspy as the furious wind. He twined his fingers in her hair and let his head fall to the inviting hollow between her breasts. *Oh, but to die with this beautiful woman.*

Tiffany's entire body began to relax. The warmth

within her seemed to spread into the night. Zane touched her chin with one long finger and kissed her lips.

Lying naked in the dark grass, with only the sounds of the night and the gentle whisper of Zane's breath, she felt whole. Large drops of rain began to fall from the black sky, but Tiffany didn't notice. She was only aware of Zane and his incredible touch. His fingers traced the curve of her cheek. "I meant it, you know," he whispered, smiling down at her.

"What?"

"That I love you."

Tiffany released a tormented sigh and pulled herself into a sitting position. "You don't have to say—"

His fingers wrapped possessively around her wrist and his eyes bored into hers. "I only say what I mean."

"Do you, Zane?" she asked, her face contorted in pain as the doubts of the morning and her conversation with Dustin invaded her mind. God, how desperately she wanted to believe him.

"What is it, Tiffany?" he asked, suddenly releasing her. "Ever since I arrived, I've gotten the feeling that something isn't right. What happened?"

Tiffany decided there was no better time for the truth than now. Before she became more hopelessly in love with him, she had to settle the past. She reached for her dress, but Zane restrained her. "I want answers, Tiffany."

"Not nearly as badly as I do." She pulled away from him and grabbed her clothes. As she quickly dressed, she began to talk. "I told Dustin that you had been here and expressed interest in buying the farm." The rain began in earnest, running down her face and neck in cold rivulets.

Zane's expression grew grim. "He wasn't too pleased about it, I'd guess."

"That's putting it mildly. He nearly fell through the floor."

"And what did he suggest?"

"That I shouldn't even consider selling to you. In fact, he seemed to think that I shouldn't have anything to do with you."

"He's afraid, Tiffany."

She began working on the buttons of her dress while Zane slipped on his jeans. "That's what I thought, too. At one point I was certain that Dustin was going to confess about switching horses and admit that Devil's Gambit is alive."

Zane was reaching for his shirt but stopped. "Did he?"

"No."

He slipped his arms through the sleeves but didn't bother with the buttons. His shirttails fluttered in the wind. "Then what, Tiffany? Just what the hell did he tell you that upset you so?"

Tiffany wrapped her arms around her breasts and stared at Zane. The wind caught her hair and lifted it off her face which was glistening with raindrops. "Dustin said that not only did you lose most of your money to Ellery in an honest poker game—"

"Honest my ass!"

"—but that Ellery also ran off with your wife."

Zane gritted his teeth together and rose. "Damn!" he spit out as he stood and stared at the pond, legs spread apart, hands planted on his hips.

Tiffany's heart ached as she watched him. Deny it, Zane, she thought. *Tell me Dustin lied . . . anything . . . tell me again that you love me.*

"He told you only part of the story," Zane said. He walked over to the boulder and propped one foot on it as he stared across the small lake. "It's true, Stasia ran off with Ellery, and at the time I felt like killing them both."

He still loves her, Tiffany realized, and fresh tears slid down her cheek to mingle with the drops of rain.

"So did you come here looking for her?" she asked, her voice thick and raw.

"No."

"Then why?"

"I can't lie to you, Tiffany."

"You already have."

"No—"

"I asked you if you were married," she whispered.

"And I'm not."

"You just conveniently forgot that you had been?" She looked up at the cloudy sky. "You never even mentioned her."

"She's not something I like to think about," he confessed.

"But your feelings were strong enough to bring you here. You can't expect me to believe that you're not looking for her."

He walked over to the grassy knoll on which she was sitting, knelt down and placed his fingers over her shoulders. She quivered betrayingly at his familiar touch. "I knew she wouldn't be here, but yes, I need to find her."

Tiffany closed her eyes against the truth. "Why?"

"Because she's the only one who can clear up what happened to Devil's Gambit . . . and Ellery."

"Ellery is dead," Tiffany murmured, hugging her knees to her and setting her chin on them.

"How do you know?"

"I asked Dustin."

"He wouldn't tell you the truth—"

"Dustin cares about me, Zane. He admitted some pretty horrible things, such as conning other owners at the yearling sales in Europe. He said that Ellery would pose as another person, someone named Ethan Rivers."

"Did he explain about Devil's Gambit?"

"No."

"But?" he coaxed.

"From his reaction, I'd have to guess that your assumption about Devil's Gambit is correct. He wouldn't admit that Devil's Gambit was alive, but it was fairly obvious when I mentioned King's Ransom and Devil's Gambit in the same breath that something wasn't right."

"You should be more careful around him," Zane warned. "He's dangerous, and he has a lot to lose if he's uncovered."

"I'm not sure that he's the man in charge."

"What do you mean?"

"I don't know, just a feeling I got that there was someone else pulling his strings."

"I don't know who it would be."

"Neither do I."

"That's why I have to find Stasia," Zane said. "She might be able to help us."

"I doubt it."

Zane lifted his head and his sharp eyes bored into Tiffany. "You knew her?" he guessed incredulously.

Tiffany nodded, remembering Stasia's long, dark hair, even features and seductive dark eyes. Stasia's sultry beauty was enough to capture any man, including Zane. "She was here on the farm with Ellery when I was in college. Later, once I had returned, my father died and Ellery asked me to marry him."

"What happened to Stasia?"

"I don't know. Ellery wouldn't talk about it. The day after he asked me to marry him, she moved out. I never saw her again, but I'm sure that she despises me."

"Probably," he said with a snort. "Stasia knows how to carry a grudge." He saw the unasked questions in Tiffany's wide eyes and began to explain about a time in his life he would rather have forgotten.

"When I met Stasia, she was barely eighteen. She was beautiful and anxious to get out of a bad home situation. I thought at the time that I was in love with her, and we got married. I was just starting then, trying to set up a successful farm of my own. Fortunately, I had a few decent breaks. I was lucky and after a few years, I . . . we, Stasia and I, owned a small farm about thirty miles from Dublin. It was a beautiful place," he said, smiling slightly at the fond memories, "thick green grass, stone fences twined with bracken, the rolling Irish countryside . . . a perfect place for breeding Thoroughbreds. That's when I started breeding successfully. And how I met Ethan Rivers."

"Ellery," Tiffany whispered.

Zane's smile had left his face and his rugged features pulled into a dark scowl. "One and the same. It happened about six years ago. Ethan was looking for some yearlings and came out to the farm. Later that night we began drinking and playing poker with another man from America who was supposedly interested in some of my horses."

"Dustin," Tiffany guessed, not daring to breathe.

"Right again. Anyway, on that night, Dustin folded early, claimed the stakes were too high for him. But I kept on drinking and playing, urged on by my lovely wife."

"Oh, no—"

"That's right. Stasia was already involved with Ethan Rivers, and when I lost it cost me two hundred thousand dollars. I had to sell the farm to pay Rivers off."

"But if you thought the game was crooked—"

"I didn't. Not then. Only much later, when I went back to that pub and got to talking to one of the regulars, I learned that the old man, who was named O'Brien, had watched the game and thought it might be rigged. A few days later, he'd overheard Dustin and his brother talking—about the game and Stasia."

"Why didn't he talk to you sooner?" she asked. "There must have been plenty of time before you sold the farm."

"O'Brien was caught eavesdropping by Ellery. Ellery was furious that he might be found out, and he threatened the old man with his life. O'Brien didn't doubt for a minute that Ellery would make good his threats to kill both him and his wife. By the time his conscience got the better of him and he found me, I'd managed to sell the farm."

"Who would buy it so quickly?"

Zane's jaw became rigid and his eyes turned deadly. "A corporation."

Tiffany finally understood, and her throat went dry with dread. "Emerald Enterprises."

"That's right. The farm I used to own now belongs to Dustin and Ellery, if he's still alive."

"Oh, God, Zane," she murmured, covering her face with her hands. *Had she been so young and foolish that she had never seen Ellery for what he really was?* She lifted her eyes and felt her hands curl into fists of frustration. "I don't understand. Knowing how you must feel about him, why would Dustin allow you to breed any of your mares to King's Ransom?"

"First of all, I didn't know that Emerald Enterprises was Dustin Rhodes. The original sale of the farm was handled through a broker, and neither Dustin's name nor Ellery's ever appeared on any of the documents. As for Dustin, either he's just gotten cocky and doesn't think he'll be discovered, or maybe he thinks I've buried the hatchet. After all, I have been able to put myself back on my feet. It took several years, mind you, but I was able to start again. I didn't lose everything when I sold the farm, and I managed to keep two good mares and a stallion."

"And from those three horses, you started again?"

"Yes. Fortunately I'd already established myself as a breeder. The three good horses and my reputation gave me a decent start."

"And . . . and your wife?"

"She left me immediately. I suspected that she'd followed Ethan—who I later found out was Ellery—to America. When Stasia filed for divorce, I didn't fight her.

"I spent the next several years working to reestablish myself."

"And you never forgot about taking your revenge on Ellery," Tiffany whispered as thunder rumbled in the distant hills.

"No. That's the reason I came here. When I heard that Ellery had married, I assumed that it was to Stasia." Zane walked back to the lake and stared across the black water, watching as the raindrops beat a staccato rhythm on the clear surface. "Of course later I learned that he had married a woman by the name of Tiffany Chappel."

"And you wondered what had become of your ex-wife." Tiffany felt a sudden chill as she finally understood Zane's motives. He had come looking for Stasia. . . .

"Yeah, I wondered, but I found that I really didn't give a damn." He shrugged his broad shoulders. "The next thing I heard about Ellery Rhodes was that he, along with his famous horse, had been killed. My fever for revenge had cooled, and I decided to put the past behind me."

"Until you found the horse you think is Devil's Gambit."

"The horse I *know* is Devil's Gambit."

Zane hazarded a glance at the threatening sky before looking back at Tiffany and noticing that she was shivering.

"Come on," he suggested softly. "We'd better get inside before we're both soaked to the skin."

Tiffany refused to be deterred when she was so close to the truth. Her emotions were as raw as the wind blowing over the mountains. Everything Zane was suggesting was too far-fetched, and yet parts of his story were true. Even Dustin had backed him up. She ran shaky fingers through her hair and watched his silhouetted form as he advanced on her and stared down at her with bold gray eyes.

"When I figured out the scam that Ellery and his brother had pulled, I knew he had to be stopped. Using one stud in place of another, and falsifying the death of Devil's Gambit is a scandal of international proportions."

"Then you think that Ellery is still alive?" she murmured, feeling lost and alone.

"That, I'm not sure of."

"Dear God," she whispered, sagging against him. Had she just made love to a man while still married to another? Guilt and fear darkened her heart. "I don't think he's alive," she murmured.

"Because Dustin says so?" he asked cynically.

"Yes. And because I don't believe that Dustin or Ellery would have let another man die in that trailer." The image of the truck carrying Devil's Gambit, as well as Ellery, charred and twisted beyond recognition, filled her mind and she shuddered.

Zane placed comforting arms over her shoulders and kissed her rain-sodden hair before urging her forward, toward the path that led to the house. "You have to face the fact that your husband might still be alive," he whispered.

"I . . . I don't—"

"Shh!" Zane whispered, cutting off her thought. He cocked his head to one side and listened.

"What?" Tiffany heard the faint sound rumbling in the distance, barely audible over the rising wind. With a sickening feeling, she recognized the noise. "Oh, no!" The sound became louder and more clear. Thundering hooves pounded the wet earth, charging through the pastures with lightning speed. "One of the horses is loose," she said, turning toward the direction of the sound and trying to break free of Zane's arms.

"Wait." Zane restrained her just as the black horse broke through the trees and bolted toward the lake. He raced to the edge of the pond with his ebony tail hoisted and his long legs stretching with boundless energy.

"Moon Shadow," Tiffany whispered, her heart pounding with dread as she watched the magnificent creature rear and whirl on his hind legs when he reached the water's edge.

Tiffany started toward him, all her thoughts centered on the horse and how he could injure himself by slipping on the wet grass. Zane's fingers tightened over her arm. "I'll go after the horse, you call the police."

"The police?" Tiffany's mind was racing with the stallion.

"If he gets out and onto the road, it could get dangerous. Not only for him, but for motorists as well."

"Oh, God. I don't think he can get out," she said, trying to convince herself. Shielding her eyes against the rain, she squinted into the darkness, searching the black night, trying to recall the boundaries of the farm. The horse splashed in the water and started off at a dead run to the opposite side of the pond.

"What's on the other side of the lake?" Zane pointed in the direction in which Moon Shadow disappeared.

"Nothing . . . some trees, it's all fenced."

"No gate?" He started to follow the stallion, his long legs accelerating with each of his strides.

"Yes, but it should be closed."

"Good. With any luck, I'll be able to catch him." Zane chased after the horse while Tiffany turned toward the buildings near the house.

Her heart was pounding as she ran through the open field, stumbling twice when her heels caught in the mud. Once, when she fell, she heard her dress rip, but didn't bother to see how bad the damage was. All her thoughts centered on Moon Shadow. *Who had let him out? Was it carelessness on the part of the stable boy or . . . what?* At the sinister turn of her thoughts, she raced more quickly. *No one would let the prized stallion out on purpose!*

Once she made it to the stallion barn, her heart hammering, her lungs burning for air; she noticed that the door to Moon Shadow's stall was swinging outward. It caught in the wind and banged loudly against the building. Other stallions within the building stamped nervously and snorted at the strange sounds.

Tiffany hurried inside and with numb fingers, flipped on the lights, flooding the building with illumination. The horses moved restlessly in their stalls.

As quickly as her trembling fingers could punch out the number, she called Mac. Rain peppered the roof of the barn as she counted the rings . . . three, four, five . . . "Come on," she urged. Finally the trainer answered.

"'Lo," Mac called into the phone.

"Moon Shadow's out," Tiffany explained breathlessly to the trainer. "His stall was unlatched and he bolted."

Mac swore loudly. "Where is he?"

"I don't know," she replied, trying to remain calm. Her chest was heaving, her words broken, her heart thudding with fear. "He took off past the old barn and the pond."

"God in heaven," Mac whispered. "We've been workin' on that fence on the other edge of the lake."

Tiffany swallowed hard against the dread creeping up her throat. "Is it down?" she whispered, her fingers clenched around the receiver.

"I don't think so. . . ." He didn't sound too sure.

"What about the gate?"

"It should be closed."

"But you're not certain?"

Mac swore roundly and then sighed. "I'll be right over. Is anyone else around?"

"Just Zane. Everyone went home for the night."

"I'll call John and a few of the other stable hands that live close. We'll be at the house in ten minutes."

"I'll meet you there."

She hung up and then dialed the number of the local police. Within minutes she was explaining her situation to the officer on the other end of the line.

When she had finished with the phone call, Tiffany hurried outside and listened to the sounds of the night. The rain was beginning to sheet and run on the pavement. It gurgled in the gutters and downspouts. In the distance, faint to her ears, she heard the sound of running hoofbeats . . . on asphalt.

"Oh God," she swore in desperation. *Moon Shadow was on the road!*

Tiffany began running down the long driveway toward the county road that bordered the farm. She heard the truck before she saw it, the loud engine reverberating through the night.

"No," she cried, spurred even faster. Her legs were numb, her lungs burning. Headlights flashed between the trees bordering the farm, and the roar of the truck's engine filled the night.

She heard the squeal of locked brakes, and the sound of the truck's dull horn as it slid out of control on the wet pavement. "Moon Shadow!" Tiffany shrieked over the deafening noise.

A stallion squealed, the truck tore through the trees, crashing against the solid wood until finally there was nothing but silence and the sound of the pouring rain.

"Oh, God, no," Tiffany whispered as she raced to the end of the drive. Tears blurred her vision and her voice seemed distant when she screamed. *"Zane . . ."*

Chapter Eleven

Tiffany raced down the slick pavement of the county road, mindless of the rain running down her back. The smell of burning rubber filled the night and the truck's headlights angled awkwardly up through the broken branches of the giant oaks, like a pair of macabre searchlights, announcing the place of the accident.

As she approached, all she could hear was her own ragged breath and running footsteps. "Zane, dear God, where are you?" she screamed, listening for a sound, any sound indicating there was life in the wreckage. Her mind filled with a dozen bloody scenarios involving Zane and Moon Shadow, but she pushed her horrible thoughts aside and dashed toward the jackknifed truck.

"Goddam it, man, what the hell was that horse doing loose?" a gravelly voice demanded. The truck driver was crawling out of the cab and swearing profusely. Rain poured down upon him, and the broken branches of the trees snapped as he stepped onto the road.

Zane must be alive! Who else would be absorbing the angry trucker's wrath?

Tiffany made it to the wrecked truck. Her heart was thudding wildly in her chest, and she had to gasp for air. The truck was lying on its side, the cab at an awkward angle. It looked like some great downed beast with a broken neck. In her mind's eye Tiffany saw another truck, the rig that had taken Ellery and Devil's Gambit from Florida to Kentucky, the one that had rolled over and burst into flame, killing both horse and driver. Her stomach turned over at the painful memory.

From inside the cab the sound of a CB's static pierced the darkness and brought her thoughts crashing to the present.

"Zane?" she cried, looking into the darkness, searching for any sign of the man and the horse.

"Hey, lady! Over here!" The large truck driver commanded her attention by calling out in his gravelly voice. "What're you doin' out here? Jesus, God, you're soaked to the skin!"

"Zane . . . My horse—"

"That black son of a bitch? He's your goddamn horse?" His agitated swearing continued. "Christ, woman, can't you see what that horse of yours did? He ran right up the road here—" the trucker pointed a burly arm toward the bend in the road "—like some demon. Scared the hell out of me, let me tell you."

"He got out. . . . I'm sorry. . . ." She looked around frantically, dread still taking a stranglehold of her throat. "Where is he . . . ?

Where is Zane?"

"Who the hell is Zane? The horse?"

"No!"

"Tiffany," Zane shouted from somewhere in the thick stand of oak and fir trees near the road. Tiffany's head snapped in the direction of the familiar sound, her heart nearly skipped a beat and relief washed over her in soothing rivulets.

Without another glance at the truck driver, who was busy clearing debris from the road and placing warning flares near his truck, Tiffany hurried toward the familiar welcome of Zane's voice.

Then she saw him. Wet, bedraggled, mud-streaked and walking toward her. He was leading a lathered Moon Shadow, who skittered and danced at all the commotion he had inadvertently caused. "Oh, God, Zane," she cried, "you're alive."

Without further thought, she ran to him and threw her arms around his neck. "I thought . . . Oh, God, I heard the horse and the truck. I was sure that . . ." Tears began running freely down her face, and she sobbed brokenly, clinging to him.

"Shh." He wrapped one strong arm around her and kissed her forehead, smearing mud on her face. "I'm all right, and I think Moon Shadow will be, too. But you'd better have the vet look at him. He's limping a little."

"What happened?" she asked, refusing to let go of the man she loved, letting her body feel his, confirming that he was here, alive and unhurt. Rain glistened in his ebony hair, sweat trickled down his jutted chin and a scarlet streak of dried blood cut across his hollowed cheek. Still he was the most ruggedly handsome man she had ever known.

"The fence was down. I followed Moon Shadow through it and called to him, but he wouldn't listen."

"Of course," Tiffany replied, patting the horse's sweaty neck fondly. "He never does."

"He just took off down the road. Bolted as if he were jumping out of the starting gate. I heard the truck coming and tried to stop him by cutting across a field. That's when I got this." He pointed to the ugly slash on his face. "When I realized I didn't have a prayer of catching him in time, I called to the horse and yelled at the truck driver, waving my arms, hoping to catch his eye. Even though I was farther down the road, I thought the driver might see my shirt before the black horse.

Anyway, Moon Shadow jumped over the ditch and ran into the trees just as the truck hit the brakes."

"Hey, you think I could get some help over here?" the furious trucker shouted.

Zane went to help the driver just as Mac's old Dodge rumbled down the road. After parking the pickup some distance from the mangled truck and trailer, Mac scrambled out of the Dodge. "Holy Mother of God," he whispered as he eyed the wrecked truck. He expelled a long whistle and grabbed the lead rope from the front seat of his pickup. "What the devil happened?"

Then he saw Moon Shadow. Knowing that Zane and the trucker were doing everything that could be done with the truck, Mac walked over to Tiffany and snapped a lead rope onto Moon Shadow's wet halter. "Well, Missy," he said, eyeing the wrecked truck. "It looks as if you've had yourself quite a night." His eyes narrowed as he surveyed the anxious stallion.

"One I wouldn't want to repeat," she admitted. "Zane says Moon Shadow's walking with a misstep," she said. "Left hind leg."

"Let's take a look at him." Mack talked to the horse while he ran his fingers down his back and along each leg. "Yep, it's a little tender," Mac decided. "But I don't think anything's broken, probably bruised himself, maybe a pulled tendon. I'll take him back to the barn, cool him down and check for any other injuries." He tugged on the rope, and Moon Shadow tossed his great black head. "I always said *you* should have been the one named Devil's something or other," Mac grumbled affectionately to the nervous stallion.

The sound of a siren pierced the night and increased in volume. Bright, flashing lights announced the arrival of the state police. A young officer parked his car, leaving the lights flashing in warning, and walked stiffly toward the crumpled truck. "What happened here?" he demanded.

"One of the horses got out," Zane replied, tossing a broken branch off the road.

"And I damned near hit him," the trucker added with a shake of his head. "Just lucky that I didn't."

The officer's suspicious eyes moved from Zane to Tiffany. "Are you the lady who called?"

"Yes."

"*Before* the accident?"

"That's right. I was afraid something like this might happen."

The officer studied the wreckage and whistled. "Where's the horse?"

"Over here." Mac led Moon Shadow to the officer. The black stallion shied away from the flashing lights of the police car, and reared on his back legs. The lead rope tightened in Mac's hands, but he began to talk to the horse and gently led him away from the crowd.

"Blends in with the night," Officer Sparks remarked, watching the nervous black stallion shy away from the crumpled vehicle. The policeman turned his hard eyes back on Tiffany. "How'd he get out?"

"Someone left the stall door unlatched, and he found a hole in a fence we're repairing."

"Wait a minute, let's start at the beginning." He walked back to his car, reached for a note pad on the dash and began writing quickly.

"Why don't we do this inside," Zane suggested, "where it's warmer and drier?"

The young officer pursed his lips together and nodded. "Fine. Just let me take a few measurements and report what happened on the radio. Then we'll call a tow company and see if we can get this rig moved."

Three hours later the ordeal was nearly over. After two cups of coffee and what seemed to be a thousand questions, the police officer was satisfied that he could accurately report what had happened. The trucker had taken the name of Tiffany's insurance company and had left with the tow truck driver, who had driven up with a truck similar in size to the wrecked rig. Moon Shadow was back in his stall and Mac had attended to his injury, which turned out to be a strained tendon. With Zane's help, Mac had applied a pressure bandage and called Vance, who had promised to stop by in the morning and examine the horse.

"You're sure Moon Shadow's all right?" Tiffany asked the trainer. She was just coming back into the kitchen. After the police officer and the trucker had left, she had gone upstairs, showered and changed into her bathrobe. Her hair was still wet, but at least she was clean and warm.

"He'll be fine," Mac assured her. He was sitting at the table and finishing his last cup of coffee.

"Where's Zane?"

Mac scowled at the mention of the Irishman. "He went to clean up. Same as you." He looked as if he were about to say something and changed his mind. "He knows horses, that one."

"Who? Zane?"

"Aye."

"I think he's worked with them all his life." Tiffany poured herself a cup of the strong coffee and took a sip as she leaned against the counter. "Mac, is something bothering you?" Tiffany asked, her brows drawing together in concern. "Is Moon Shadow all right?"

Mac was quick to put her fears to rest. "Oh, I imagine he'll have a few stiff muscles tomorrow, and it won't hurt to have Vance take a look at him. But I think he'll be fine."

"Great," Tiffany said with a relieved sigh.

Just then, Zane strode into the kitchen, wearing only

a clean pair of jeans and a T-shirt that stretched across his chest and didn't hide the ripple of his muscles as he moved. He had washed his face and the scratch there was only minor.

"Another cup?" Tiffany asked, handing Zane a mug filled with the steaming brew.

"Thanks."

Mac rotated his mug between both of his hands and stared into the murky liquid. He pressed his thin lips together and then lifted his head, eyeing both Tiffany and Zane.

"Now, Missy," he said, "who do ya suppose let Moon Shadow out?"

Tiffany was surprised by the question. She lifted her shoulders slightly. "I don't know. I think it was probably just an oversight by one of the stable hands."

"Do ya, now?"

"Why? You think someone let him out on purpose?" Tiffany's smile faded and a deep weariness stole over her. So much had happened in one day and she was bone tired.

Mac reached for his hat and placed the slightly damp fedora on his head. "I checked the stallion barn myself earlier. Moon Shadow was locked in his stall."

Tiffany dropped her head into her hand. "I don't want to think about this," she whispered quietly, "not now."

"I think you have to, Missy," Mac said. "Someone deliberately let the stallion out."

"Buy why?"

"That one I can't answer." His gaze moved to Zane. "You wouldn't know anything about it, would you?"

Zane's gray eyes turned to steel. "Of course not."

"Just askin'," Mac explained. "You were here when it happened." He rubbed his hand over his chin. "And the way I understand it, you had a grudge against Ellery Rhodes."

"That was a long time ago," Zane replied.

"Aye. And now you're here. Pokin' around hopin' to buy the place." He shot a warning glance to Tiffany.

"Mac," she said, horrified that he would consider Zane a suspect. "Zane caught Moon Shadow tonight. If it hadn't been for him, the horse might be dead."

Mac rubbed the tired muscles in the back of his neck and frowned. "I know you're a fine horse breeder," he said to Zane. "You have the reputation to back you up, but sometimes, when revenge or a woman's involved, well . . . a man's head can get all turned around."

"I would never do anything to jeopardize a horse," Zane stated calmly. "And I care too much for Tiffany to do anything that might harm her." His voice was low and deadly. His indignant eyes impaled the old trainer.

Mac managed to crack a smile. "All right, Sheridan. I believe you. Now, can you tell me what you think is going on around here? It seems to me that someone is trying to sabotage the operation. Who would do that? Maybe a man interested in buying a farm and gathering a little revenge to boot?" With his final remark, Mac pushed his chair away from the table. The legs scraped against the wooden floor. After straightening his tired muscles, he turned toward the back porch. He paused at the door, his hand poised on the knob, and glanced over his shoulder at Tiffany. "And just for the record I'll be sleeping in the stallion barn tonight. Wouldn't want to have another 'accident,' would we?"

"You don't have to—"

"I'm sleeping in the barn, Missy," Mac insisted. "That's all right with you, isn't it?"

"Of course, but really, there's no need. . . ."

Mac tugged on the brim of the fedora over his eyes

before stepping outside. Tiffany heard his footsteps fade as he walked down the back steps.

"Mac's grasping at straws," Tiffany said, feeling the need to explain and apologize to Zane. She lifted her palms and managed a frail smile. "He . . . he's just trying to find an explanation."

"And I'm the logical choice."

"Everyone else has been with the farm for years, and, well, Mac's a little suspicious when it comes to strangers."

Zane set his empty cup on the counter and rammed his hands into his pockets. His eyes narrowed, and his lower jaw jutted forward. "And what do you think, Tiffany?"

She lifted trusting eyes to his. "I *know* you didn't let Moon Shadow out."

"So who did?"

"God, I don't know. I'm not really sure I want to. I'm just so damned tired . . ." She felt her shoulders slump and forced her back to stiffen. "If I had to guess I'd say that it was probably just some kids who broke into the place and thought they'd get their kicks by letting the horse out."

"Not just any horse," he reminded her. "Moon Shadow."

"He's been getting a lot of attention lately."

"How would the kids know where to find Moon Shadow?"

"His picture's been in the paper."

"And at night, to an untrained eye, Moon Shadow looks like any other black horse."

"But—"

"What about your security system?" Zane demanded. "You said yourself that the fence was down."

"Wouldn't that dog of yours bark his head off if a

stranger started poking around the place?" he demanded, daring her to ignore the logic of his thinking.

"I . . . I guess so."

"You see," he surmised, "there are too many unanswered questions. I don't blame Mac for thinking I was involved." He raked his fingers through his hair and let out an exasperated sigh.

"He's just worried . . . about me."

"So am I." Zane's arms circled her waist and he leaned his forehead against hers. "Someone's trying to ruin you and I think I know who."

Tiffany squeezed her eyes shut and shook her head, denying his suggestion before he had a chance to speak. "Dustin," she thought aloud, "you think he's behind all this?"

"No question about it."

"But he's in Florida—"

"Is he?"

Tiffany hesitated. She hadn't actually seen Dustin get on a plane. "Journey's End races the day after tomorrow."

"And Dustin was here this morning." His strong, protective arms drew her close. "If you do have a saboteur, sweet lady, I'm willing to bet on your brother-in-law."

"Just because one horse got out—"

"And four foals died."

"No!" Tiffany tried to jerk away but couldn't. His powerful arms flexed and imprisoned her to him.

"And the story was leaked to the press."

"It wasn't leaked—we never tried to hide what was happening with the foals." She sprang instantly to Dustin's defense. No matter what else had happened, Dustin was the man who had helped her when Ellery had died. "Dustin himself was concerned about the story in the papers. That's why he came back."

"So he claimed."

"You're just trying to find someone, anyone, to blame all this on!"

"No, Tiffany, no," he whispered, his breath fanning her damp hair. "I'm trying to make you understand the only logical explanation. If you think Dustin's so innocent, what about Devil's Gambit and King's Ransom?"

"I . . . I can't explain that."

"What about the fact that Ellery may still be alive?"

"But he's not—"

"We're not sure about that," Zane said slowly, making no attempt to release her. She sagged wearily against him. "But we both know that Dustin posed as a rival bidder, interested in Ethan Rivers's horses, when in fact Ethan was Ellery and Dustin was his brother. Dustin admitted to bidding on his own horses, just to drive the prices up."

Tiffany's throat went dry. "But I just can't believe that Dustin would try and ruin our operation. It doesn't make any sense. He owns part of the farm."

Zane's voice was firm. "Has it ever occurred to you that Dustin might want to own it all? Hasn't he already offered to buy you out?"

"Only because he thought it was too much for me," she whispered, but the seeds of distrust had been planted, and she hated the new feelings of doubt that were growing in her mind. Three weeks ago she would have trusted Dustin with her life. Now, because of Zane's accusations, she was beginning to doubt the only person she could call family. She shuddered, and Zane gathered her still closer, pressing her face against his chest.

"I'm not saying that Dustin doesn't care for you," he said, gently stroking her hair.

"Just that he's using me."

"He's the kind of man who would do just about anything to get what he wants."

She shook her head and stared out the window. Raindrops ran down the paned glass. "Funny, that's just what he said about you."

Gently Zane lifted her chin with his finger, silently forcing her to look into his eyes. "I've done a few things in my life that I'm not proud of," he admitted. "But I've never cheated or lied to anyone."

"Except me?" Tears began to scald her eyes.

"I didn't lie about Stasia."

"You omitted the facts, Zane. In order to deceive me. Call it what you will. In my book, it's lying."

A small muscle worked in the corner of his jaw, and he had to fight the urge to shake her, make her see what was so blindingly clear to him. He couldn't. He'd wounded her enough as it was. Tiffany seemed to stare right through him. "I've never wanted anyone the way I want you, Tiffany," he whispered. "I wouldn't do anything that would ever make you doubt me."

Her throat tightened painfully, and she squeezed her eyes against the hot tears forming behind her eyelids. "I want to trust you, Zane. God, I want to trust you," she admitted. "It's just that you've come here when everything seems to be falling apart . . ."

"And you blame me?"

"No!"

"Then look at me, damn it!" he insisted. Her eyes opened and caught in his silvery stare. "I love you, Tiffany Rhodes, and I'll do everything in my power to prove it."

She held up a protesting palm before he could say anything else. She felt so open and raw. Though he was saying the words she longed to hear, she couldn't believe him.

He took her trembling hand and covered it with his. "You're going to listen to me, lady," he swore. "Ever since I met you that first morning when Rod Crawford was here, you've doubted me. I can't say that I blame you because I came here with the express purpose of taking your farm from you . . . by any means possible."

Her eyes widened at his admission.

"But all that changed," he conceded, "when I met you and began to fall in love with you."

"I . . . I wish I could believe you," Tiffany whispered. "More than *anything* I want to believe you." Her voice was raspy and thick with emotion. She felt as if her heart were bursting, and she knew that she was admitting far more than she should.

His fingers tightened over her shoulders. *"Believe."*

"Oh, Zane . . ."

"Tiffany, please. Listen. I want you to marry me."

The words settled in the kitchen and echoed in Tiffany's mind. Her knees gave way and she fell against him. "I want you to be my wife, bear my children, stand at my side. . . ." He kissed the top of her head. "I want you to be with me forever."

She felt the tears stream down her face, and she wondered if they were from joy or sadness. "I can't," she choked. "I can't until I know for certain that Ellery is dead."

Zane's back stiffened. "I thought you were convinced."

"I am." Her voice trembled. "But what if there's a chance that he's *alive?"*

His arms wrapped around her in desperation, and he buried his head into the hollow of her shoulder. "I'll find out," he swore, one fist clenching in determination. "Once and for all, I'll find out just what happened to your husband."

"And if he's alive?" she whispered.

"He'll wish he were dead for the hell he's put you through."

She shook her head and pushed herself out of his possessive embrace. "No, Zane. If Ellery's alive, he's still my husband."

"A husband who used and betrayed you." Anger stormed in his eyes, and his muscles tensed at the thought of Ellery Rhodes claiming Tiffany as his wife after all these years. *The man couldn't possibly be alive!*

"But my husband nonetheless."

"You're still in love with him," he charged.

"No," she admitted, closing her eyes against the traitorous truth. "The only man I've ever loved is you."

Zane relaxed a bit and gently kissed her eyelids. "Trust me, Tiffany. Trust me to take care of you, no matter what happens in the future." He reached for her and savagely pressed her body to his, lowering his head and letting his lips capture hers.

Willingly, her arms encircled his neck, and she let her body fit against his. The warmth of him seemed to seep through her clothes and generate a new heat in her blood.

When his tongue rimmed her lips, she shuddered. "I love you, Zane," she murmured as her breath mingled and caught with his. "And I want to be with you."

He leaned over and placed an arm under the crook of her knees before lifting her off the floor and carrying her out of the kitchen. She let her head rest against his shoulder and wondered at the sanity of loving such a passionate man. Zane's emotions, whether love or hate, ran deep.

Carefully he mounted the stairs and carried her to her bedroom. Rain slid down the windows and the room was illuminated only by the shadowy light from the security lamps near the barns. "I never wanted to fall in love with you," he admitted as he stood her near the bed and his fingers found the knot to the belt of her robe. Slowly the ties loosened, and he pushed the robe over her shoulders to expose the satiny texture of her skin.

She was naked except for a silky pair of panties. Zane kissed her lips, the hollow of her throat, the dark stiffening tips of each gorgeous breast as he lowered himself to his knees.

She wanted to fall to the floor with him, but his hands held her upright as slowly he removed the one scanty piece of cloth keeping her from him. His fingers lingered on her skin and rubbed her calves and thighs as he kissed her abdomen, moistening the soft skin with his tongue. His eyes closed, and Tiffany felt his eyelashes brush her navel. Tingling sensations climbed upward through her body, heating her blood as it raced through her veins.

The heat within her began to turn liquid as his tongue circled her navel. Tiffany's knees felt weak, and if it hadn't been for the strong arms supporting her, she would have slid to the floor and entwined herself with him.

Zane's hands reached upward and touched the pointed tip of one swollen breast. It hardened expectantly against the soft pressure of his fingers and Tiffany closed her eyes against the urge to lie with him. Zane groaned against her abdomen, and his hot breath warmed her skin.

"Zane," she pleaded, the sound coming from deep in her throat as her fingers caught in his black hair. "Love me."

"I do, sweet lady," he murmured against her skin, his warm hands pressing against the small of her back, pushing her closer to him.

As if in slow motion, he forced her backward, and she fell onto the bed. Her hair splayed against the comforter in tangled disarray. Her cheeks were flushed, as were her proud breasts with their alluring dark peaks.

As she watched him, Zane quickly removed and discarded his clothes. When completely naked, he came to her. Lying beside her elegant nude body, he caught his fingers in the silken tresses of her hair and rolled atop her. Corded male muscles strained against hers as he captured one blossoming nipple in his mouth. His tongue slid enticingly over the soft mound, and she cradled his head against her, moaning in contentment as he suckled. Her breasts, swollen with desire, ached for his soothing touch, yearned for the tenderness of his lips and tongue.

"Tiffany, I love you," he vowed as his hands roved over her skin, exploring the exquisite feel of her. His lips murmured words of love against her ear, forcing the heat within her to expand until she could stand the torment no longer.

"Please," she whispered into his ear, her fingers running over the smooth skin of his upper arms and back, feeling the ripple of solid muscles as he positioned himself above her. "Now!"

The ache in his loins throbbed for release, and he took her eagerly, becoming one with her in the heated splendor of his love. His lovemaking was violent, explosive, as he claimed her for his own and purged from her body forever any thoughts of the one man who had betrayed them both.

Tiffany soared to the heavens, her soul melding with Zane's as the clouds of passion burst open and showered her in hot bursts of satiation. She shuddered against his hard male frame; her love for him was complete and infinite. Trliany knew that no matter what the future held, she would never stop loving him.

"I love you," she heard him vow again and again. Listening to the wonderful sound, she smiled and curled her body close to his to fall into a deep, exhausted sleep.

It was barely dawn when Tiffany awakened. She reached for Zane, but he was gone. The bed sheets were cold. Thoughts of the night before began swimming in her sleepy mind; then she heard him walk back into the room.

"Zane?" she murmured, groggily trying to focus her eyes.

He came to the bed and sat on the edge near her. "I didn't mean to wake you."

He was completely dressed, as if he were leaving. "What's going on?" she asked, glancing at the clock. It was only five-thirty. Even Mac didn't start work until after six.

"I have to go."

"Where?"

"Back to San Francisco."

She looked into his eyes and saw the sadness lingering in the gray depths. "Why?" she asked, forcing herself into a sitting position. She tugged at the comforter to cover her naked breasts and then leaned forward so that her face was near his. Something was wrong. She could feel it. In the course of a few short hours, Zane's feelings toward her had changed. Her heart, filled with love of the last few hours, twisted painfully.

"I have things I have to do," he said. "You'll just have to trust me."

"Does this have anything to do with Dustin?" she asked, shivering from the cold morning air.

"I don't know." He placed a warm hand on her shoulder. "Just trust me, okay?"

She nodded and forced a frail smile. "You'll be back?"

He laughed and broke the tension in the room. "As soon as I can. If I'm not back in a couple of days, I'll call."

"Promises, promises," she quipped, trying to sound lighthearted. He was leaving. Her heart seemed to wither inside her. "I left the phone number of my hotel on the note pad in the kitchen. If you get lonely—"

"I already am." Lovingly she touched the red scratch on his face. "My hero," she whispered with a seductive smile.

"Hardly."

She curled her hand around his neck and pulled his face next to hers.

"Look, lady, if you don't cut this out, I'll never get out of here," he growled, but a pleased grin stole over his angular features to charmingly display the hint of straight white teeth against his dark skin.

"That's the idea."

Zane let out an exasperated sigh. "Oh, Tiffany, what am I going to do with you?"

"I don't know," she murmured against his ear as her fingers began working at the buttons of his shirt. "Use your imagination."

An hour later he was gone, and Tiffany felt more alone than she ever had in her life. She was more alone than she had been on the morning her mother had abandoned her, for then she had still had Edward, and when her father had died, she had married Ellery.

When Ellery was suddenly killed, Tiffany had relied on Dustin.

Now, as she cinched the belt of her robe more tightly around her waist and stared out the window at the rain-washed countryside, Tiffany was completely alone. She had no one to rely upon but herself. She shivered more from dread than from the morning air, and she watched as Zane's car roared to life and disappeared through the trees.

Chapter Twelve

After Zane had gone, Tiffany found it impossible to return to bed. Instead she dressed and walked outside, stopping only to scratch Wolverine behind the ears. The dog responded by wagging his tail enthusiastically.

"Some hero you are," Tiffany reprimanded fondly. "Where were you last night when I needed you?"

She refilled Wolverine's bowls and walked to the stallion barn. The rain had become no more than a drizzle, but the ground was still wet. and when she ventured off the pavement. her boots sank into the soaked earth.

Mac was already up and checking on Moon Shadow's injury.

"So how is he?" Tiffany asked, patting the black stallion's neck and forcing a smile at the grizzled old trainer. Mac had slept in his clothes and it was obvious from the way he was walking that his arthritis was bothering him.

"Moon Shadow?" He pointed a thumb in the direction of the horse's head. "He's fine."

"And you?"

"Getting too old for all this excitement."

"Why don't you take a day off?" Tiffany asked. "You deserve it."

"Not now, Missy," he said, shaking his head. "What would I do while the missus knits and watches those

soap operas? Nope. I'm better off here. 'Sides, I want to
see what Vance has to say after he looks this old boy
over." Mac gently slapped Moon Shadow's rump, and
the stallion snorted and tossed his head in the air.

"I thought I'd check on Shadow's Survivor next,"
Tiffany said.

"Good idea."

Mac walked with her and Wolverine trotted along
behind. The rain had stopped and the clouds were beginning to break apart, promising a warm spring day.
Tiffany realized for the first time that the flowering trees
were beginning to bloom. Pink and white blossoms
colored the leafless trees with the promise of spring.

"Say, Missy," Mac said as they approached the foaling shed.

"Yes?"

"I noticed that Sheridan's car is gone."

"He left early this morning."

"Because of what I said last night?"

"No." Tiffany shook her head and smiled sadly.

"I was out of line."

"You were concerned. We all were . . . are." She ran
her fingers through her hair and squared her shoulders.
"Something's got to give, doesn't it? We can't go on this
way much longer."

Mac frowned and reached for the handle of the door.
"You're right—it's time our luck changed, for the
better."

They walked inside the foaling shed and heard the
soft nickering of Alexander's Lady. A tiny nose attempted to push through the rails of the stall. "Here's
our good news," Tiffany said with a smile as she tried
to reach out and touch the skittish filly. "Maybe I
should change her name to that. How does Good News
strike you?"

"Better'n Shadow's Survivor or whatever the hell you came up with before," the old man chuckled.

"I don't know. . . ."

"She's your horse, Missy. You name her whatever you like." Mac grinned at the sprightly little filly. "Just wait, little one," he said to the inquisitive young horse. "As soon as we get the okay from the vet, you'll get your first look at the world."

The rest of the day was filled with more good news. Two owners called to say that their mares had delivered healthy foals sired by Moon Shadow, and Vance Geddes checked Moon Shadow's leg injury and gave the stallion a clean bill of health.

"As soon as that tendon heals, he'll be good as new," Vance predicted after examining the stallion.

"He sure knows how to get into trouble," Tiffany complained with a fond look at the horse in question.

"Maybe it's not the horse," Vance suggested.

"What do you mean?"

"Seems to me, he had a little help getting out of the stall last night."

"I suppose."

"Got any ideas who unlatched his stall door?" Vance asked, placing all his veterinary supplies back in his case and walking out of the stallion barn.

"No. I thought it might be vandals, but Zane seems to think it was an inside job, so to speak."

"Somebody with a grudge?"

Tiffany lifted her shoulders. "I couldn't guess who."

"You got any trouble with employees?"

"Not that I know of."

"Haven't fired anyone, a stable boy . . . or maybe

done business with someone else, made a competitor angry?"

"No." She sighed wearily and spotted Louise's car rumbling down the long drive. "I've thought and thought about it. I'm sure I've made a few enemies, but no one that would want to hurt me or my horses. . . . At least I don't think so."

Vance put his bag into the truck and grimaced. He turned his kindly bespectacled eyes on Tiffany. "Just be careful, okay? Anyone who would let Moon Shadow out would do just about anything to get what he wants."

"If only I knew what that was," she said anxiously. "Any news on the foals' deaths?"

"Not yet," Vance said, sliding into his pickup, "but I've got a couple of new ideas. They're long shots . . . probably end up in dead ends, but maybe . . ."

"Keep me posted."

"Will do." Vance had just pushed his key into the lock and was about to start the engine, but Louise shouted at him. "Hey, wait!" the housekeeper called as she bustled up to Vance's truck. She was waving a newspaper in the air. "Look, here, on page one." She proudly handed Tiffany the sports section from the *Times*. In the lower left-hand corner was a picture of Journey's End along with the article written by Nancy Emerson.

Tiffany's eyes skimmed the columns of fine print and her face broke into a smile. Then, slowly, she reread Nancy's report, which did bring up the subject of the dead colts but also concentrated on Moon Shadow's career as well as his two strongest progeny, Devil's Gambit and Journey's End. The article ended on an upbeat note, suggesting that Moon Shadow's victories on the racetrack and as a proved sire overshadowed the unfortunate deaths of the four foals.

"Wonderful," Tiffany said, feeling a little relief. "At least we got a chance for rebuttal."

"Now," Vance stated, "if we can just come up with the reason those foals died."

"You think you're on to something?"

"I'm not sure," Vance replied. "I'll let you know in a couple of days. Like I said—it could be another dead end."

"Let's hope not," Tiffany prayed fervently.

"Come on, you two," Louise reprimanded. "Things are turning around, just you wait and see."

"I don't know about that," Tiffany replied.

"Why? What happened?"

"Moon Shadow got out last night. It looks as if someone did it deliberately."

"What!" Louise was more than shocked.

As the two women walked toward the back porch, Tiffany explained the events of the evening before and Louise clucked her tongue in disbelief.

"But who would do such a thing?" Louise wondered once they were in the kitchen.

"That's the mystery."

"You got any ideas?"

"No . . . but Zane seems to."

Louise's eyes sparkled. "That one, he'll figure it out. Just you wait and see."

When the telephone rang, Tiffany expected the caller to be Zane, but she was disappointed.

"Hello, Tiff?" Dustin asked through the fuzzy long-distance connection.

"Dustin? Where are you?"

"In Florida and, well, brace yourself for some bad news."

Tiffany slumped against the pantry, the receiver pressed against her ear. Her fingers curled over the handle until her knuckles showed white. "What happened?" she asked, dread steadily mounting up her spine.

"It's Journey's End," Dustin said.

Tiffany's heart pounded erratically, and she felt as if her whole world were falling apart, piece by piece. "What about him?"

"He was injured. Just yesterday, while working out. From everything we can tell, he's got a bone chip in his knee."

"Oh, God," Tiffany said, letting out her breath in a long sigh. When would it end? She ran shaking fingers through her hair and wished that Zane were with her now.

"It looks bad, Tiff. I think his career is over—"

"Before it really began."

"We can retire him to stud."

"I guess that's about the only thing we can do," she reluctantly agreed, her shoulders slumping. "Other than the knee, how is he?"

"The vet says he'll be okay, but we'd better not count on him racing anymore. It wouldn't hurt to have Vance look at him when he gets home."

"How is Bob Prescott taking the news?"

There was a long silence on the other end of the line. "That's a little bit of a sore point, Tiff. I think Prescott ran him knowing that something was wrong."

"No!"

"I can't prove it."

Tiffany felt sick inside. "Let me talk to him," Tiffany demanded, rage thundering through her blood. The last thing she would stand for was anyone on her staff mistreating a horse.

"Too late."

"What?"

"I fired him."

"On suspicion?" Tiffany was incredulous.

"He's been involved in a couple of shady things," Dustin said. "I just didn't want to take any more chances."

"But who will replace him?"

"I'm talking to a couple of guys now. Big-name trainers . . . I'll call you after I meet with them."

"I don't know—"

"Look, I've got to go. I'll make all the arrangements to send Journey's End home."

"Wait. Before you hang up."

"What?" Dustin demanded impatiently.

"Last night someone let Moon Shadow out of his stall."

There was silence on the other end of the line. "What do you mean 'someone let him out'?" Dustin asked, his voice cold.

Tiffany gave a brief account of the events of the evening and Dustin's voice shook with rage. "Zane Sheridan was there again? What does he want this time? Don't tell me he's still pressuring you into selling to him."

"No, Dustin, he's not," Tiffany replied.

"Then why the hell is he hanging around?"

"Maybe he enjoys my company—"

"I'll bet. If you ask me, he's the culprit who let Moon Shadow out. He's probably trying to make it tough on you so you'll sell him the farm." Dustin swore descriptively.

"I don't think so."

"That's the problem, isn't it—sometimes you just don't think. Period."

With his final words, Dustin slammed down the phone, and Tiffany knew in her heart that everything Zane had said about her brother-in-law was true. A deep sadness stole over her, and she spent the rest of the day locked in the den, going over the books, hoping to block out the bitter truth about Dustin and what he had done.

Dustin would be back on the farm with Journey's End by the end of the week. When he arrived, Tiffany planned to confront him with the truth.

Four days later, she still hadn't heard from Zane. Things had settled into the usual routine on the farm, and she had spent her time working with Mac and the yearlings.

The fence had been repaired, and there had been no other disturbances on the farm. Moon Shadow was healing well, and Mac had prepared a neighboring stall in the stallion barn for Journey's End. "A shame about that one," the old trainer had remarked when he learned about the accident. "Sometimes fate seems to deal out all the bad cards at once."

Later that night, Tiffany was seated in the den going over the books. The house was dark except for the single desk lamp and the shifting flames of the fire burning noisily against dry oak. Tiffany felt cold and alone. The portrait of Devil's Gambit seemed to stare down from its position over the mantel and mock her. Where was Zane? Why hadn't he called?

She tried to force her attention back to the books and the red ink that was beginning to flow in the pages of the general ledger. The farm was losing money. Without Moon Shadow's stud fees or any income from Journey's End's racing career, Tiffany had little alternative but to sell several of the best yearlings.

The rap on the French doors surprised her, but she knew in an instant that it had to be Zane. She saw his haggard face through the glass, she opened the doors with trembling fingers and flung herself into his arms.

He stepped in with a rush of cold air that chilled the room and fanned the glowing embers of the fire and billowed the sheer draperies. "Thank God you're here," she whispered against his neck before lifting her head and studying the intensity of his gaze.

The look on his face was murderous. Dark shadows circled his gray eyes, and a weariness stole over his features making the angular planes seem more rugged and foreboding. He looked as if he hadn't slept in weeks.

"Zane?" she whispered as his dark eyes devoured her.

"It's just about over," he said as he closed the door and walked over to the fire to warm himself.

"What is?"

"Everything you've been going through." He reached for her and drew her close to him. "I wish I could make it easier for you—"

"Easier?"

"Shh." He brushed his lips over hers, and his hands locked behind her back, gently urging her body forward until her supple curves pressed against him and he groaned, as if in despair. She felt her body respond to his and heard the uneven beat of her own heart when he kissed her hungrily and his tongue touched hers. Her fingers lingered at his neck, and she felt the coiled tension within him, saw the strain on his face.

"What happened?" she asked, when at last he drew his head back.

"It's a long story."

"I've got the rest of my life to listen," she murmured.

Zane managed a wan smile. "Oh, lady, I've been waiting for four days to hear you say just those words," he whispered, his arms tightening around her. "God, I've missed you." He kissed the curve of her neck, his lips lingering near her earlobe, before he gently released her.

"So tell me."

He rammed his fingers through his black, windblown hair and poured them each a drink. "I found Stasia," he admitted roughly, Tiffany's heart nearly missed a beat. "It wasn't all that easy, and if she'd had her way, I never would have located her."

He walked over to Tiffany and handed her a snifter of brandy, before taking a long swallow of the warm liquor and sitting on the hearth, hoping that the golden flames would warm his back.

"How did you find her?"

"A private investigator by the name of Walt Griffith." His gray eyes searched hers. "I had him do some checking on you, too—"

"What!"

He smiled devilishly and his eyes twinkled. "I didn't figure you'd like it any more than Stasia did. But it was necessary. To find Ellery."

Tiffany nearly dropped her drink. Her hands began to shake as she lifted the glass to her lips.

"I'm getting ahead of myself," Zane said. "Walt found Stasia living with some artist-type in Carmel. When I approached her she was shocked, but managed to fall right back into character—she agreed to tell her side of the Ellery Rhodes story for a substantial fee."

"You paid her?" Tiffany was outraged.

Zane's eyes rested on her flushed face and he smiled. "Believe me, it was worth it."

Tiffany wasn't so sure. "What did you find out?"

"About the accident that supposedly killed Devil's Gambit."

Tiffany's heart was pounding so loudly it seemed to echo against the cherrywood walls. "Wait a minute," she insisted as the cold truth swept over her in a tidal wave of awareness. "What you're saying is that—"

"Stasia was Ellery's mistress. Even when he was married to you, he was having an affair with my ex-wife. Seems that they were hooked on the excitement of carrying on when there was the danger of being discovered."

"I . . ." Tiffany was about to say that she didn't want to believe it, but she knew it was the truth. She'd come to the same conclusion herself once she had talked to Dustin. The affair explained so much about Ellery that she had never understood.

"So Ellery?" she asked breathlessly.

"Was killed in the accident," Zane assured her.

"I . . . never wished him dead," Tiffany whispered, walking across the room and sitting next to Zane on the hearth.

"I know. You just had to know the truth." Zane looked into her eyes and smiled. "It's going to be all right, you know."

"God, I hope so."

"We'll be together."

Tiffany's eyes filled with tears of happiness. "Then you're right—everything will work out."

"Stasia admitted that the horses were switched," he said, continuing with his story. "Ellery had thought that the insurance forms had already been processed—"

"The ones that were waiting for his signature?"

"Yes. No one but Ellery, Dustin and Bob Prescott knew that Devil's Gambit had pulled a ligament after his last race."

"Not even Mac?"

"No."

"When?"

"While exercising a few days after his last race. It looked as if Devil's Gambit, the favored horse, wouldn't be able to race in any of the Triple Crown races. If Ellery could make it look as if Devil's Gambit had died in an accident, when in fact it was really another, considerably less valuable horse who was killed, he could breed Devil's Gambit under an alias in another country, collect stud fees and get the insurance money to boot. It was better odds than just putting him out for stud before he'd really proved himself."

"Oh, God," Tiffany said with a long sigh. Nervously she ran her fingers through her hair.

"It wasn't a foolproof plan by any means and it was extremely risky. But Ellery enjoyed taking risks—remember the stunts he and Dustin would pull in Europe when he posed as Ethan Rivers?"

Tiffany nodded, her stomach turning over convulsively. What kind of a man had she married? How had she been so blind?

"There was always the chance that Devil's Gambit would be recognized because of the Jockey Club identification number tattooed on the inside of his lip. And of course there was the remote possibility of something going wrong with Ellery's plans."

Tiffany had broken out in a cold sweat. She wrapped her arms around herself as she relived the horrible night when she was told that Ellery and Devil's Gambit were killed.

"Everything backfired when Ellery was trapped in the truck and killed along with the switched horse, which, by the way, Bob Prescott supplied. It seems that the trainer was involved in the scam with Ellery and Dustin."

"And all this time I've let him work with our horses . . . God, how could I have been so stupid?"

"There's no shame in trusting your husband, Tiffany," Zane said softly and kissed the top of her head before smiling. "In fact, your next one will insist upon it."

She felt his warm arm slide around her waist. "And Dustin—what about him?" she asked.

"He decided to gamble and carry out Ellery's plan."

"With Bob Prescott?"

"Right. Stasia claims he was absolutely furious that the insurance forms hadn't been signed, and that you, not he, as the new forms indicated, would get the settlement." Zane shrugged and finished his drink in one swallow. "But by that time it was too late."

"So what are we going to do?"

His arm tightened possessively around her, and his fingers toyed with the lapels of her robe. "For now, go to bed. Tomorrow we'll deal with Dustin."

"How?"

"I have it on good authority that he'll be here with Journey's End. Come on." He pulled her gently to her feet and walked her to the stairs. "I haven't slept in days—" he slid an appreciative glance down her body "—and somehow I get the feeling that I'll have trouble again tonight."

They mounted the stairs entwined in an embrace. Once in her bedroom, he let his hand slip inside her bathrobe and felt the shimmery fabric of her nightgown. "I've been waiting for so long to be with you again," he whispered into her ear as he untied the belt of the robe, pushed it gently over her shoulders and let it drop unheeded to the floor.

True to Zane's prediction, Dustin arrived around nine. He marched into the kitchen and stopped abruptly. The last person he had expected to see was Zane Sheridan. Dustin's composure slipped slightly and his broad shoulders stiffened. His jeans and shirt were rumpled from the long, cross-country drive, and three days' growth of beard darkened his chin. In contrast, Zane was clean-shaven and dressed in fresh corduroy pants and a crisp shirt. His hair was neatly combed, and the satisfied smile on his face made Dustin's hair stand on end.

The differences in the two men were striking.

Dustin cast a worried glance in Tiffany's direction before placing his Stetson on a hook near the door.

"'Morning, Dustin," Zane drawled. He was leaning against the counter sipping coffee while Tiffany made breakfast.

Dustin managed a thin smile. "What're you doing here?"

"Visiting." Zane took another long drink.

The meaning of Zane's words settled like lead on Dustin's shoulders. "Oh, no, Tiffany," he said. "You're not getting involved with this bastard, are you?" He hooked a thumb in Zane's direction.

Zane just smiled wickedly, but Tiffany stiffened. "I don't see that it's any of your business, Dustin. Is Journey's End in the stallion barn?"

"Yes."

"With Mac?"

"He was there and that veterinarian, Geddes."

"Good."

Dustin became uneasy. "What's going on?"

Zane propped a booted foot on a chair near the table. "That's what we'd like to know." Zane's gray eyes glittered ominously, and Dustin was reminded of a great cat about to spring on unsuspecting quarry. His throat went dry.

"Tiffany?" Dustin asked.

She turned to face her brother-in-law and he saw the disappointment in her eyes. *She knows. She knows everything!* Dustin's palms began to sweat, and he tugged at the collar of his shirt.

"I think you need to answer a few questions, Dustin. Did you let Moon Shadow out the other night?" she charged.

Dustin's gold eyes narrowed treacherously, but he refused to fall into any of Sheridan's traps. "Of course not. I . . . I was in Florida."

"It's over, Rhodes," Zane cut in. "I checked the flights. You were booked on a red-eye."

"No—I mean, I had business in town. . . ."

Tiffany's shoulders slumped, but she forced her gaze to bore into Dustin's. "Zane says that Devil's Gambit is alive in Ireland, that he's siring foals while King's Ransom is taking all the credit." Dustin whitened. "Is it true?" Tiffany demanded, her entire body shaking with rage and disappointment.

"I don't know anything about—"

"Knock it off," Zane warned, straightening to his full height. "You're the primary owner of Emerald Enterprises, which happens to own a farm where King's Ransom stands. I saw Devil's Gambit and I've got the pictures to prove it." His face grew deadly. "And if that isn't enough proof to lock you up for the rest of your life, Stasia is willing to talk, for the right price."

"None of this is happening." Dustin turned his gold eyes on her. "Tiff, you can't believe all this. Sheridan's just out for revenge, like I told you. . . . Oh, my God," he said as he recognized the truth. "You're in love with the bastard, aren't you? What's he promised to do, marry you?" He saw the silent confirmation in her eyes. "Damn it, Tiffany, don't be a fool. Of course he proposed to you. He'd do anything to steal this farm from you."

"The only time I was a fool, Dustin," Tiffany stated, her voice trembling with rage, "was when I trusted you."

"I helped you—when your world was falling to pieces, I helped you, damn it."

"And you lied. About Devil's Gambit and about Moon Shadow." Her eyes blazed a furious shade of blue. "You let me think that Moon Shadow was the cause of the dead foals and you leaked the story to Rod Crawford."

"What are you saying?" Dustin demanded.

"That the jig is up. Vance Geddes has discovered that the only unhealthy foals sired by Moon Shadow were all conceived during one week—a week you were on the farm," Zane said, barely able to control his temper. "He hasn't discovered what you injected the mares with yet, but it's only a matter of time before he knows just what happened."

"That doesn't mean—"

"Give it up, Rhodes!"

Dustin turned furious eyes on Tiffany. "You've got it all figured out, haven't you? You and your lover! Well, I'm not going to bother to explain myself. It looks as if I'm going to need an attorney—"

"I'd say so," Zane stated. "The police are on their way. They've already rounded up Bob Prescott, and I'm willing to bet that he sold you out."

Dustin visibly paled. He lunged for Tiffany; his only chance of escape was to take Tiffany hostage.

Zane anticipated the move and as Dustin grabbed for Tiffany, Zane landed a right cross to Dustin's cheek that set him on his heels.

"Don't even think about it," Zane warned as Dustin attempted to get up. In the distance, the sounds of a police siren became audible. "I'd be thinking very seriously about an attorney myself, if I were you," he said.

When the police arrived, they read Dustin his rights and took him in for questioning. As he left he was still rubbing his jaw and glaring angrily at Zane.

"I've waited a long time for that," Zane admitted. He stepped onto the back porch and watched while the police cars raced out the drive with Dustin in custody.

"I just can't believe it's over," Tiffany murmured, her eyes looking over the rolling hills that she'd grown to love. "And to think that Dustin was behind it all. . . ."

Zane tilted her chin upward and looked into her worried eyes. "Like you said, it's over." He kissed her tenderly on the eyelids and tasted the salt of her tears, before leading her back to the den. "I came here intending to ruin you," he admitted roughly. "I wanted to buy this farm no matter what the cost." He took out the legal documents that John Morris had prepared. After showing her the contract of sale, he tossed it into the fireplace, and the coals from the previous night burst into flame against the crisp, white paper. "It was all so damned pointless," he said. "All I want is for you to be my wife."

"And I will be," she vowed.

"Even if it means living part of your life in Ireland? We have to bring Devil's Gambit home, you know."

"It doesn't really matter where," she said. "As long as I'm with you."

Zane folded her into the protection of his arms. "I'm not a patient man," he said.

"Don't I know."

"And I'm not about to wait."

"For what?"

"To get married. The sooner the better."

"Anything you want," she said, her blue eyes lingering on his handsome face.

"Anything?" With a wicked smile, he urged her slowly

to the floor with the weight of his body. "You may live to regret those words."

"Never," Tiffany whispered as Zane's lips covered hers and she entwined her arms around the neck of the man she loved.

* * * * *

END

Please turn the page for an exciting sneak peek of
Lisa Jackson's next thriller

OUR LITTLE SECRET

coming soon wherever print and ebooks are sold!

Piper Island, Oregon

I didn't think it would end this way.

It's not what I planned.

But here I am, lugging the dead-weight of a body into the cold sea.

It's heavier than I'd imagined as I haul it into the icy surf.

I've left footprints on the sand, but they will disappear when the tide turns. Hopefully before anyone sees them.

I shift the awkward weight as the frigid water splashes over my ankles, the surf roaring in my ears. I suck in my breath, trudge on, and note how thick the fog is on this stretch of beach. A perfect cover.

Come on, come on, I tell myself as I drag the wretched corpse farther into the ocean, icy spray on my face, salt touching my lips, the sand beneath my feet moving outward in a rush, my feet sinking as the tide is going out, taking with it sand, debris, and hopefully, this damned corpse.

I struggle, my body numbing as I'm hip deep. Finally I feel the shelf beneath me give way to deeper waters, the drop-off lurking deep beneath the surface.

Good.

I stop.

Let go.

On cue, the tide surges, snatching the body away from me, pulling the rolling corpse out to sea to disappear into the wide, dark Pacific.

Yesss! Finally!

The sooner it's gone, the better.

I stand on the ledge, bracing myself against the strength of the ocean.

A final wave approaches, curling with white foam, rushing to the land, the body bobbing closer for a second, close enough that I can see its eyes and for a second they seem to stare at me, straight into my soul.

No!

Don't be ridiculous.

Dead is dead.

I stare back.

Oh, shit, did it blink?

Open its mouth?

No, no, no!

Horrified, I take a step back as it's carried away. "Go!" I yell. "Get the hell away from me!" For a second it's lost again in the undulating water.

Then the sea turns again, the icy water receding swiftly, dragging the corpse close enough that I think I hear it speak-hiss my name over the thunder of the ocean. But that's crazy, right?

In a second, it's swept out to sea again, farther this time, the torso sinking into a froth of wild foam to be dragged to the open waters and disappear into the fog forever.

I lose sight of it.

Thank God.

I let out the breath I didn't realize I'd been holding and feel a bit of elation, a little buzz. It's over.

After all these years.

I breathe deeply, the briny air filling my lungs, my cramped muscle relaxing. I need to get back. Quickly I glance back at the barely visible shoreline, the smudge of lights winking through the mist. Still, I linger, numb to my waist as I brace against the pull of the ocean and stare once more toward the west where the water melds into the fog.

Squinting, trying to peer through the curtain and slowly let out my breath. The body has finally vanished.

That part of my life—of our lives—is finally and thankfully over.

I close my eyes for a second. Wipe my face with the back of my nearly-numb and send up a quick prayer. As I open my eyes again, I start to turn, but stop. There, not thirty feet away, I catch sight of the body riding on the swiftly moving surface. I tell myself not to worry.

This was bound to happen.

It takes a while for—

A hand shoots upward.

What!

No!

My heart clutches.

Alive?

"No." I shake my head. Disbelieving. Blinking against the salty spray. "No . . . no, no, no!" It can't be! But my heart is thundering, pounding against my rib cage.

Desperately I try to focus, to dislodge my worst fears as the surf thunders, crashing against the rocky outcrop to the north. I stare in disbelief and tell myself that it's all in my head, that I've conjured up my worst fear. I mean, I've done it before so many times that it could be just a horrid figment of my imagination, of my guilt—

"Oh, fuck!"

And there it is again.

I can hardly breathe, the tide dragging at my buckling legs, the sand shifting beneath my feet. Bracing myself, horrified, I focus hard as a massive wave rolls. Above it, before it crests, a hand rises, arm stretching from the swells, stark and white, fingers twitching.

Beckoning.

Daring me.

"God *damn* it!" I start to follow, then think better than to step off that sandy shelf. Instead, I whirl and plow through the icy water to the shore. Most of the feeling has draining away from my legs as I slosh ever faster toward the strand, the tide splaying against my ankles as I reach the beach where, beside the still-visible drag marks, I find a long piece of driftwood, just about the length of a baseball bat. Snatching it up, hefting it, checking its weight, I feel my fingers clench more tightly around the sodden wood.

Perfect!

Without thinking twice, my jaw set, I turn again, and with a new determination, I march steadfastly into the frigid surf. The wind slaps me in the face, the salt spray sticks to my skin as my eyes narrow on the faint ghost of a hand still visible in the dark roiling water.

I can do this.

I *must* do this.

And so I will.

Chapter One

"Come on, buddy! Can't you drive faster than ten?" Brooke muttered, glancing at her speedometer before glaring at the rear end of the huge car in front of her. She was late and getting nowhere fast as she tried to negotiate her way through the clogged streets of Seattle.

She took a glimpse at her watch, felt the drip of nervous sweat collecting on her spine. She wasn't going to make it. Her daughter's school would be out in less than ten minutes and she was, at this rate, fifteen minutes—maybe twenty—out.

"Damn it all to hell." Nerves strung tight, fingers holding the steering wheel in a death grip, she managed to cut around the old Pontiac with its even older driver, then avoided the downtown area with its steep hills and skyscrapers knifing into the sky. Instead, she skimmed the western edge of the city, closer to the waterfront, her mind racing even if the cars and trucks and vans around her were not. Frustrated, aware of time ticking by, she glanced to the west at the sun sinking low in the horizon to the west, golden rays visible behind the craggy Olympic Mountains on the far side of Puget Sound. "Come on, come on," she muttered, her frustration

matched by most of the other drivers as two lanes
funneled into one as they inched around three workmen
in orange vests surrounding a manhole where barricades
filled one full lane. She checked the dashboard digital
clock. Already late.

"Great."

But Marilee would wait for her.

Unfortunately Brooke was known for being chroni-
cally late, a character flaw that she vowed each new
year to correct which, of course, was crazy and never
lasted more than two weeks.

Now, minutes ticked by, making her ever later, her
fingers beginning to sweat on the steering wheel.

She'd stayed too long. Again.

And now she was late.

And now she had to pump up her alibi. Keep her lies
going for just a little longer. God, she was a fool.

Why couldn't she just end it? Like-now. Call Gideon
or send him a text from her burner phone? Even the
thought that she had one of those cheap cell phones
caused a bloom of heat to rush up her neck. She never,
never should have gotten involved with him.

"What's done is done," she reminded herself as his
image came easily to mind. She couldn't seem to forget
their recent lovemaking, his hard body in a tangle of
sheets in the small bed of the cabin in his sailboat, nor
his silhouette as he stood in the tiny bathroom, his muscles cast in relief with light from a small porthole.

"Stop it!"

She hit the button to lower the window, feeling the
warmth of Indian summer invade the interior, hearing
the hum of traffic while smelling just the hint of salt
tinging air already heavy with exhaust from a diesel
truck chugging up the hill the next lane over.

ASAP.

She had already solidified her alibi, proof in the

half-drunk iced latte that she'd grabbed on the fly at a drive-through Starbuck's, and the dry cleaning that she'd picked up earlier hung over the back seat near her gym bag half full of sweat-soaked clothes.

It wouldn't explain all of the hours—especially if anyone checked the cameras at the gym, but, for now, it would have to do and it was the last time.

She checked the GPS to see if she could find a route where traffic wasn't blocked and swore under her breath as she missed a light for the third time due to road construction. Nervously she glanced at the clock again and tapped her fingers on steering wheel in the snarl of vehicles as workers with shovels laid down a patch of pavement, steam rising, the scent of the hot asphalt permeating the air already tainted with exhaust from yet another idling truck.

She was officially late.

Marilee's school was now officially over for the day. Great.

Come on, come on! Move it!

She texted Marilee that she was on her way, just as the flagger turned her sign from STOP to SLOW, and the driver of a yellow Porsche had the nerve to cut in front of her. The top of the sports car was down—a baseball cap turned backward on the driver's head—and she caught a glimpse of mirrored sunglasses as the guy swung his head to look at her as he'd sped into the gap.

"Jerkwad," she muttered, slowing even further.

She took another swallow of her watery drink, the ice long melted. Her cell phone buzzed.

Not the burner, but the one she had registered to her name. She glanced at the screen. No caller ID.

Don't bother picking up. It's probably a telemarketer.

But she did. "Hello?" she said as the light turned green. The Porsche shot forward.

A hesitation. Then a click, like the clucking of a tongue.

"He's not who he says he is," a flat voice whispered. Raspy. Almost indistinct.

"What? Who is this? What are you—?"

But she knew who the caller was referring to.

Gideon.

Who else?

Someone knew about them?

Someone who had her unregistered phone number?

Her head buzzed, her pulse jumped. What the hell?

"Be careful . . ."

Visit our website at
KensingtonBooks.com
to sign up for our newsletters, read
more from your favorite authors, see
books by series, view reading group
guides, and more!

BOOK CLUB
BETWEEN THE CHAPTERS

Become a Part of Our
Between the Chapters Book Club
Community and Join the Conversation

Betweenthechapters.net

Submit your book review for a chance to win exclusive
Between the Chapters swag you can't get anywhere else!
https://www.kensingtonbooks.com/pages/review/